KILLING FOR THE COMPANY

Chris Ryan

WINDSOR
PARAGON

First published 2011
by Coronet
This Large Print edition published 2012
by AudioGO Ltd
by arrangement with
Hodder & Stoughton Ltd

Hardcover   ISBN: 978 1 445 81533 6
Softcover   ISBN: 978 1 445 81534 3

British Library Cataloguing in Publication Data available

Printed and bound in Great Britain by
MPG Books Group Limited

ACKNOWLEDGEMENTS

To my agent Barbara Levy, publisher Mark Booth, Charlotte Haycock, Eleni Fostiropoulos and the rest of the team at Coronet.

I believe that God wants everybody to be free. That's what I believe. And that's one part of my foreign policy.
George W. Bush, 13 October 2004

To the end there shall be war.
The Book of Daniel, 9:26

PART ONE

Northern Serbia, December 1998

ONE

17.00 hrs.

Chet Freeman didn't know which smelled worse: himself or the bar he was sitting in.

They'd taken up position by a table next to the toilets. From a surveillance point of view it was perfect: they could see every part of the bar, and there was a direct line to the exit in case of a clusterfuck. From a comfort point of view it was the pits, not least because of the reek of piss and stale cigarette smoke. Chet had been in some rough joints in his time, but this place made the Lamb and Flag in Hereford look like the fucking Ritz.

At least it was warm. The snow had been falling for about an hour and was already a couple of inches thick on the ground. But warmth was the only thing this bar had going for it. A broken fruit machine in one corner. A picture of Milosevic on the nicotine-stained wall alongside it. Three strip lights on the ceiling, of which the middle one buzzed and flickered on and off. Other than that, a short bar with a grossly fat barman and only two optics fixed to the wall behind it—slivovitz and vodka—and ten plastic-topped tables screwed to the ground, each with a red Coca-Cola ashtray overflowing with butts. This was a place for drinking and smoking, nothing more. True, there was an old TV fixed to the concrete wall behind the bar itself. It was on loud enough to hear, but of the twenty-three men—no women—pulling on bottles of warm beer, no one even glanced at it.

Chet looked at his watch. 17.03. Give it another

3

three hours and he'd put money on most of these guys being dead drunk. Or, in one case, just dead.

He scratched at his leg. An insect, probably drawn by his stinking clothes, had bitten him just above the knee. He could feel the bulge of the bite even through the coarse material of his trousers. He scratched it hard and took a small sip from his bottle of Zajecarsko, the local beer.

'Jesus, buddy, if I didn't know you better, I'd have said you actually just drank some of that piss.'

Chet's mate Luke Mercer had a shaved head, slightly crooked teeth and a south London accent. He spoke quietly and his voice was almost drowned out by the noise of Boyzone wailing from the TV. They didn't want anybody to hear they were talking English.

Luke looked as rough as Chet. Three days' stubble, and another three days' dirt beneath it. A black donkey jacket flecked with cement. Worker's shoes, dirty and heavy. Luke so closely resembled a labourer that no one would give him a second look, not here where everybody was dressed in the same way. Their fellow drinkers might be surprised to learn, though, that the donkey jacket concealed a shoulder holster packing a Sig 9mm pistol and a mike for covert comms fitted under the lapel. The tiny pink radio earpieces each man had in one ear were invisible to anyone who wasn't looking for them. They were linked to radio transmitters in the pockets of their tough, battered trousers. This would keep them in contact with the other two members of the unit, Sean Richards—a grizzled old-timer with flecks of grey in his beard, who was as much a fixture of B Squadron as the squadron hangar back in Hereford—and Marty Blakemore,

4

fresh to the Regiment from 3 Para and keen to make a good impression on his first major op.

Sean and Marty were parked in a nondescript white Skoda saloon outside the bar on the opposite side of the street. The boot of the car was filled with heavier weaponry: suppressed M16s, Maglite torch attachments with IR filters, med packs. All four of them knew that this could be a long night, and they needed to be properly equipped.

Chet's three years in the Regiment had taught him that his chosen career would sometimes mean carrying out operations you didn't much like and just getting on with the job. Operations that you wouldn't have thought existed before you walked into the compounds of Hereford HQ. Operations that you wouldn't talk to anybody about, unless they were badged too. So sometimes, he thought to himself as he sat there, it was good to know you were out to nail a bona fide scumbag. Someone you wouldn't think twice about sending to meet their maker—though fuck knows what kind of maker would come up with a piece of work like Stevan Ivanovic. As scumbags went, he was solid gold.

Chet knew Ivanovic's CV well. Four days previously at their forward operating base—a cordoned-off area of a busy UN military installation on the Bosnian border—the ops officer Andy Dell had given Chet's four-man unit the low-down as he handed round the photograph of a balding, jowly individual with flared nostrils and a sour look.

Andy Dell had the stuck-up tones of a Sandhurst officer, but as Ruperts went he was all right. 'This is your man,' he had announced. 'Born 1957, made Chief of Police in Bosanski Samac, north-eastern Bosnia and Herzegovina, April 1992. Lasted eight

5

months in the job, during which time twelve men—all Bosnian Muslims—died in his custody: seven from beatings, five from causes unknown. Six Bosnian males have independently testified that he forced them to perform sex acts on each other just to humiliate them.'

'Sex acts?' Chet had interrupted.

'Blow jobs, since you ask. Three women have accused him of rape. One of them was fifteen years old; another ended up face down in the river after she spoke out.'

'And we get to slot this cunt, right?' Luke had asked.

'Do me a favour, Luke, and shut the fuck up till I've finished.' Luke, who had been brought up by his dad on a council estate in Lewisham, always had something to say, and it didn't always endear him to the Ruperts. 'Ivanovic is on the run. He left his post as Chief of Police in '93, after which he was a leading figure in the ethnic cleansing of Bosnian Muslims. Our boys tried to get their hands on him during the siege of Sarajevo. Too slippery. He's been underground since the end of the Bosnian war. Only he's just stuck his head above the parapet. The Firm have definite intel on his location, and the war-crimes tribunal at the Hague want him in the dock for persecution on political, racial and religious grounds.'

It all made sense. Chet had been around long enough to know that it wasn't just the ragheads who could be religious nuts. When it came to ethnic cleansing, some of those Serbs were pure Domestos.

Turning their attention to a map of the region, Dell had pointed at the FOB, situated just west of

6

the Serb border. 'You're to insert into Serbia by vehicle in the guise of UN peacekeepers. They're a common sight, so you shouldn't attract too much attention. Our intel suggests that Ivanovic is hiding out in Prizkovo, a one-horse town twenty miles south of Belgrade. We have the imagery for you to study. When you get to the area you'll need to ditch the UN gear. That part of Serbia is a nationalist hotbed. The peacekeepers know that the best way to preserve the peace is to keep away.'

'Good job we're not there to keep the peace, then,' Luke had murmured.

The ops officer had ignored him. 'We have reports that Ivanovic is surrounded by at least four heavies,' he continued. 'They're dispensable, but Ivanovic needs to be alive. You've been given temporary powers of arrest. These probably won't stand up in an international court of law, and Ivanovic will most likely know that. He's not going to come quietly.'

Quiet. Noisy. It made no difference to Chet. He was just looking forward to getting his hands on this bastard. And it wouldn't be long now.

He picked up a dinar from the sticky table and flicked it in the air.

'Tails,' said Luke. He looked like he wanted a response, but he wasn't going to get one from Chet, who just scowled and continued to flip the coin.

Flick, catch.

Flick, catch.

'You going to do that all night, buddy?' Luke asked. ''Cos I don't mind telling you, it's getting on my wick.'

Flick, catch. Flick, catch.

The TV behind the bar was grainy and flickered

every few seconds. To Chet's relief, the music came to an end and an image caught his attention. The British Prime Minister, Alistair Stratton, his boyish face earnest and open, his suit well cut and his red tie perfectly neat, was sitting in an anodyne studio being interviewed by some bird Chet recognised but couldn't name. What the fuck Stratton was doing on Serbian TV, Chet didn't know. Certainly the punters in the bar paid as little attention to him as they had to Boyzone.

'Always the fucking way,' Luke drawled. 'You come on holiday to get away from it all . . .'

Chet glanced back up at the screen. 'Stratton's all right,' he said.

'Stratton,' Luke replied, 'is a politician. Therefore Stratton is a wanker. End of.'

Chet shrugged. He wasn't going to argue. But he had enough friends in the regular green army to know that in the year since Stratton had come to power, things for them had improved. Better kit, better conditions. It was no secret in the military that the government was gearing up to move into Kosovo if Milosevic carried on giving the Albanians the Stalin treatment, but really Chet knew very little about the politics. That wasn't his business. All he knew was that anyone who supplied his mates with the gear and the weapons they needed to do their jobs was OK by him. As Luke would say: end of.

Still, it was odd to come across Stratton's voice in this back end of nowhere, miles from home and translated into impenetrable Serbian by the subtitles at the bottom of the screen. The PM's earnest tones reached Chet's ears.

'The trouble with talking about faith is that frankly people think you're a nutter . . .' Stratton

8

smiled a boyish smile. 'But yes, my faith is extremely important to me. You know, in this job, you're asked to make some pretty tough decisions, and I'd like to think that my faith always puts me on the right path . . .'

Chet heard Luke snort. Did Stratton know that at that moment a four-man SAS unit was preparing to make an illegal arrest on foreign soil, and most likely take out a number of foreign nationals as they did so? If so, had he consulted the big guy upstairs about the rights and wrongs of it? Chet didn't much care either way. The only things he had faith in were his Sig and the PPK strapped to his left ankle. The disco gun, they called it back home, but there'd be no dancing tonight.

Chet's attention wandered from the blaring TV and he started to scan the other drinkers. They were hard-looking men. Flinty-eyed and rough-faced, their hands big and their skin chapped. One of them stood up from the bar and lurched towards the toilet. He noticed Chet and Luke sitting there. Newcomers. He stopped to give them a look that told them how unwelcome they were.

The look Chet and Luke returned was cool. Unruffled. Perhaps the Serbian decided it wasn't worth his while kicking it off with these two. Perhaps he'd never intended that in the first place. He found his way into the foul-smelling toilets, leaving the two SAS men to continue scanning the remainder of the clientele.

One of them was their key to Ivanovic. And if everything went according to plan, they'd soon know which one.

9

*   *   *

17.32 hrs.

Stratton had been replaced by some incomprehensible game show. Chet and Luke's beers were still full. It wouldn't be long before someone clocked that they weren't really drinking. Their contact was now seventeen minutes late. It was beginning to look like he'd bailed out, which would mean the last few days had been for nothing.

A voice in the earpiece. Sean, outside in the Skoda. 'OK, fellas. The preacher's arrived. About fucking time too—it's Baltic out here, so make him feel comfortable. He looks about twelve.'

'The preacher'. Prearranged code for the tout they were awaiting.

Ten seconds later the door opened. The icy air from outside disturbed the warm fug of the bar, and a young man walked in. Only three men clocked his arrival: the fat bartender and Chet and Luke. Unlike almost everyone else in the room, he was clean-shaven. He wore jeans, a thick lumberjack shirt, a hat that covered his ears and was tied under his chin, and a black rucksack over his shoulder. The rucksack was the sign by which the unit were to recognise him, but it made the kid look more like a student than a worker. Everything had a dusting of snow over it.

As the door closed behind him, he looked round nervously, like a teenager not sure if his girlfriend had stood him up.

Chet looked towards the frosted glass at the front of the bar. He could just make out two silhouettes, one on either side of the door. He knew what that meant: Sean and Marty, having clocked

10

the kid, had moved from the Skoda and were now standing guard outside, ready to burst in if anything kicked off.

The kid's glance fell on Chet and Luke, and he nodded slightly.

'Fuck's sake.' Chet cursed quietly and looked away. He could sense Luke doing the same. This dickhead might be here to help them, but as touts went he was clearly wet behind the ears, and if he stood there gawping at them much longer, he was going to screw the whole operation.

Chet slid the dinar off the table once more.

Flick, catch.

Flick, catch.

The tout was looking around now. His eyes narrowed, as if he had seen something—or someone—he'd been looking for. He slipped the rucksack off his shoulder, carrying it by his side, and approached the bar. The tout chose his place carefully, selecting a stool next to one of the regular drinkers.

That was the sign. The kid was too scared to meet with the unit. Too scared to point out their man in an overt way. So the spooks had got to work on him. It was local knowledge that Ivanovic was in the area. Nobody knew where, but they did know that one of his guys drank in this bar during his time off. The kid was to come in here at a given time and take a seat next to the target. If they wanted to find Ivanovic, all they had to do was follow Ivanovic's man.

Chet stopped flipping his coin and took another pretend pull on his beer as he scoped out the tout's new drinking buddy. He could only see the guy's back. He was broad-shouldered and had thick black

11

hair, slightly greying. He sat hunched forward, his elbows on the bar. When the tout sat next to him, he made no attempt at conversation.

The younger man pointed at one of the optics and ordered a slivovitz, which the fat bartender plonked in front of him. Then he settled down to drink it. Just another loser passing the time.

       *   *   *

17.46 hrs.

Ivanovic's man stood up.

As he turned away from the bar, Chet could see he was unsteady on his feet. His face looked like it had been carved out of rock, with an immense flat nose—well reddened from booze—hooded eyes and deep frown lines on his forehead. He scowled at nobody in particular and walked uncertainly towards the street door. Chet pressed the button on the transmitter in his pocket. 'Eyes on Target 1,' he murmured. 'He's leaving now.'

'Roger that,' came Sean's voice in his ear.

Chet and Luke waited until their man was outside before scraping back their chairs and moving towards the exit. Chet could sense the tout watching them over his shoulder, but he gave no sign of recognition. That was for the kid's safety.

They stepped out into the cold night air. It had been dark for no more than half an hour, but already it must have been two below. Chet gave himself a moment to take everything in. The street was lined with Communist-era concrete buildings— 'Makes Peckham look like Belgrave fucking Square,' Luke had noted when they first arrived— and while the falling snow softened everything a little, Priskovo was still as bleak as the bar they'd just walked out of. The road itself wasn't busy. A half-empty blue and white bus trundled past, then a couple of vans with tarpaulin over the back. A few locals hurried past on the pavement, huddled against the snow and concentrating on nothing other than getting home. Certainly they paid no attention to Chet or Luke.

Ivanovic's man had turned left out of the bar. He'd gone about twenty metres and was weaving his drunken way towards a white Ford Transit with a dent in the back. Sean and Marty had crossed the road and returned to the Skoda—just two more faceless figures in the snow—and were opening the doors to climb back in. Chet and Luke had another Skoda, but theirs was brown. They got in and Chet switched on the engine. The wipers cleared the snow from the windscreen to reveal Ivanovic's man getting into the Transit. Seconds later he moved off. Chet followed, and in his rear-view mirror could see the white Skoda pull out as well.

The Transit drove quickly, swerving slightly as it went. Luke shook his head. 'Dumber than a box of rocks . . .'

Chet didn't answer. The snow was hurtling against the windscreen and the road was treacherous. He kept his eye firmly on the target and drove on.

*　　　*　　　*

17.51 hrs.

The thin young man whose black rucksack was now lying at the foot of his bar stool was called Anton. He had been cold when he walked into

13

the bar. Now the blood in his veins was running hot. The heat of excitement. It had gone well. He had earned his 50,000 dinars. Now all he wanted to do was get out of this horrible place and back to his small apartment, where his girlfriend was waiting for him. He would buy her flowers. And if he bought her flowers, perhaps she would give him something in return.

The slivovitz made his eyes water and his throat burn. But he supposed he'd better finish it. He caught the barman's eyes and nodded—a friendly gesture that wasn't returned. Anton shrugged, then watched as the guy wiped the bar with a frayed, grey rag and picked up the bottle that Ivanovic's man had left.

A confused look crossed the barman's face. He held up the bottle, and Anton immediately saw what was puzzling him. The bottle was full.

The heat in Anton's veins turned to ice. He dismounted from the bar stool, grabbed his rucksack, then ran to the door and out into the street.

They were waiting for him there.

Two men, each twice as broad as Anton, and twice as strong. They grabbed him, one man to each of his thin arms.

'*Pogmati!*' he yelled in Serbian. 'Help me!'

But none of the passers-by was going to do that.

The two men pulled Anton along the pavement for about thirty metres, then turned into an alleyway. It was dark here, and the snow was drifting against the wall on one side. The tips of Anton's feet left two lines in the powder as the men dragged him along the alley and out into a courtyard surrounded by the high walls of deserted

14

buildings. Breeze-blocks were piled in one corner and an old cement mixer stood nearby, but it was clear from the virgin snow that nobody had been here recently.

Again Anton shouted for help. But there was no one to hear, and his voice just echoed off the walls.

The first blow was not the hardest, but it was the one that shocked him most: a sudden and brutal knee to the groin that bent him double with pain. From that moment on, Anton was unable to distinguish between the two men. One of them struck him on the side of his head with a wooden cosh. As Anton collapsed to the ground, the other man started kicking him in the stomach and the face. Thirty seconds later blood was oozing from his nose and spewing from his mouth. His teeth were smeared crimson and he was vaguely aware of the way the blood first stained, then melted the snow around him.

He tried to shout again, but the wind had been knocked from his lungs and he couldn't so much as croak. He didn't see the knife—smooth on one side, jagged and cruel on the other—until its point was pressed against his neck.

For the first time, one of the men spoke. His voice was heavy and rasping. *'Sisadzijo!* Cocksucker! That pretty little bint of yours waiting back in your flat. My friends are fucking her right now. When we've finished with you, we'll go join them. Let her know what it's like to feel real men inside her.'

Anton forced himself to speak. *'Molim te . . .* Please . . . please leave her alone. I'll tell you everything . . .' They laughed. It wasn't a nice sound.

15

'Tell us everything?' the man with the knife said. 'Don't be stupid. We *know* everything. You think your little game in the bar was a secret?' Another boot to the stomach. 'We're not torturing you, *sisadzijo*. We're killing you.'

Anton shook his head just as he felt a warm sensation spread across his trousers. The men laughed again. 'Pissed himself. What a joke.'

Anton closed his eyes and started to pray, murmuring words he hadn't uttered since he was a reluctant child taken to the Orthodox church his mother attended. *'Our father in heaven, hallowed be your name . . .'*

When he opened his eyes again, he wondered for a moment if his prayer had been answered. The man was no longer pressing the knife against his neck, but was standing, looking down at him.

Pushing himself up into a sitting position, Anton looked, through his blood-bleary eyes, towards the two men. The knife man still had the blade in his hand; but his accomplice had something else. It was a thin loop of plastic, about fifty centimetres long, the ends fastened with a small notch. Only when the man holding it started to approach him did Anton work out what it was: a cable tie.

A fresh wave of dread crashed over him. He had heard of these people and what they did with this simple, everyday item. If he didn't get away now, he never would. He scrabbled around, but a final kick in the chest was enough for the man with the knife to floor him again; seconds later the other one was forcing the loop of plastic over his head.

Anton's hands went to his neck, as though he was strangling himself. In truth he was protecting it. The knife man was having none of it: with a flick

16

of his wrist he slashed the back of Anton's hand so deeply that he felt the blade hit bone. The pain was searing, and the blood smeared all over the back of his hands and down his shirt. So much blood. But he kept a hold of his neck because to let go would be suicide.

The knife man dropped the bloodied blade in the snow. Then he grabbed Anton's hands and pulled them down to his side.

'*Ne* . . . No . . . I'm begging you . . .' Anton's desperate plea was cut short by the sudden tightening of the cable tie around his neck—a sharp yank that forced the plastic to squeeze his skin and severely restrict the flow of air into his lungs.

The two men stood back to watch as Anton desperately tried to loosen the cable tie. To get his fingers in between the plastic and the skin. It was impossible.

His lungs started to burn as his body silently screamed for air. He fell to his knees again, his panic matched only by the agony of his breathlessness. The knife was still there on the ground, no more than two metres away. Anton reached for it with his damaged, bleeding hand.

If he could just cut through . . .

But as he stretched for the knife, one of the men was there, stamping on the back of his hand with such force that Anton would have screamed like an animal if he'd only had the breath.

He collapsed.

Everything was spinning now. Confused. He saw the snow falling in slow motion. He saw the blood pumping from his hands. He saw the two men standing over him, the bright light of cruelty in their eyes.

17

And there was a moment, before Anton passed into unconsciousness and then death, when the pain disappeared and the lack of oxygen in his blood left him with only a sleepy, doped-up feeling.

The two men didn't wait to check that he was dead. They knew the cable tie would do its work, and anyway they still had to get their rocks off with Anton's girlfriend.

*　　　*　　　*

18.00 hrs.

The little town soon melted away into deserted outskirts, then came empty countryside. After following the Transit for ten minutes, Chet pulled over and allowed the white Skoda to overtake. Ivanovic's man was probably too drunk to clock a tail, but they still had to follow SOPs. Once Sean and Marty were trailing the van, Chet caught up with them and followed at a distance.

Luke was studying a small map of the area, following their route carefully by the light of a thin, red-filtered torch. On his lap was a bulky GPS unit, blinking their position at him.

The snow fell harder, making the going slow, and the number of other cars was reducing. The white Skoda had been leading for about five minutes when Chet's earpiece burst into life. It was Sean. 'No one else on the roads. We should kill the lights.'

'Roger that.' Chet pulled up and turned off the headlamps; up ahead he could see the white Skoda had done the same. Beyond that, only just visible through the blizzard, were the red rear lights of the Transit. Chet reached behind the driver's seat and

18

located his night-vision headset, which he put on and engaged. The world became bathed in green light, and the tail lights of the Transit were perfectly bright. So long as they had line of sight, they could follow a couple of klicks behind and Ivanovic's man would be none the wiser.

They drove in silence, Luke keeping any wisecracks to himself. After another five minutes, Luke—who was still consulting the map—spoke into the comms. 'This road ends at the edge of a large lake,' he said so that both Chet and the others could hear. 'Unless our man fancies a swim, that's where we'll be stopping. There's no other roads off this one.'

'How far to the water's edge?' Sean asked.

'Two klicks, buddy. No more.'

'We'll stop a klick away and approach on foot,' Chet said. 'Our man might be pissed up, but that doesn't mean his friends are. Any closer than that and they'll be able to hear our vehicles even if they can't see them.'

Silence over the radio meant everyone agreed.

Five minutes later they pulled up in a rough lay-by—more like a ditch—where tractors could pass, though there would be no tractors at this time and in this weather.

Chet turned to Luke and asked, 'You got a fix?'

Luke took a moment to double-check their position, on both the map and the GPS unit. He nodded. 'I'll call it in.'

The secure comms system that allowed them to communicate with base back over the border was installed in the glove compartment. Luke spoke into the bulky handset. 'Zero, this is Delta Three Tango. Over.'

19

A moment of silence, then the comms crackled. 'Delta Three Tango, this is Zero.'

'Advancing now on the Alpha. Stand by to record our position.'

'Standing by, Delta Three Tango.'

Luke checked the GPS unit, before reading out their grid reference slowly and clearly. He waited for it to be repeated over the comms before disconnecting and climbing out of the car.

Sean, who had been driving and also had his NV goggles fitted, opened up the boot of the white Skoda to reveal the men's gear. They took off their donkey jackets and ops waistcoats, fitted their body armour and replaced the waistcoats. Each man put on a helmet, cut away around the ears.

'UN badges?' Marty asked. He meant the armbands, powder blue with large white writing. By rights, if they were about to make an arrest under the auspices of the UN, they should be wearing them.

'Fuck that,' Sean growled. 'We'll be spotted with that shit on.' The voice of experience and he was right. The white lettering would be a beacon in the darkness.

Each man removed his M16, fully loaded and with Maglites attached; Luke and Marty also mounted their NV on their helmets.

Chet took a kite sight from the boot and used it to scope out the environment: the surrounding countryside was flat and sparse, no less bleak and industrial than the town they'd just left. In the distance he could make out the red lights of the Transit, still ploughing through the snow. Beyond that, perhaps there was another, more distant light; in this visibility it was hard to be sure.

'I hope our lad in the bar wasn't bullshitting us,' Luke said as he slung his assault rifle across his chest. 'I fucking hate the snow. If we get down to the water and find Mr White Van Man's just been looking for somewhere quiet to take a leak, I'm heading straight back up there to shove his rucksack up his arse.' No one replied. 'Come back Brecon Beacons,' he grumbled to himself. 'All is forgiven . . .' He cocked his rifle and set it to the lock position.

The unit headed up the road single file, in the tracks left by the Transit so their footprints didn't show up, each man five metres from the next. The blanket of snow deadened all sound—even their footsteps—and the air was filled with the frosty clouds of their breath.

* * *

18.32 hrs.

As unit leader Chet was second in line. He held up one hand. Everyone stopped—including Luke, who was at the front as lead scout but checked the men behind him every twenty seconds. Chet looked through the kite sight to scope out what lay ahead. As he recced the place in his mind, he spoke out loud so that the others could tell what he'd seen.

'The Transit's come to a halt approximately 100 metres away, directly to the north,' he said, his voice barely louder than the settling snow. 'No other vehicles, no sign of enemy targets. A small copse of trees on its west side, a large building on its east. More trees eastwards of that. Looks like some kind of deserted farmhouse. I can see one, two, three outhouses, but there may be more. Two rooms on the western side of the house have lights on; everything else I can see is in darkness. Luke, I think I can see your lake just beyond the house, but it's difficult to make out.'

He lowered the sight to see Sean examining the ground in front of them, snow gathering on his beard. 'One set of vehicle tracks, freshly laid. That's the Transit. Snow could have covered any others, but I can't see any indentation. I'd say fuck all else has come up here in the past four or five hours.'

'Footprints?' Chet asked.

'Yeah. A deer. Maybe a wild boar. No sign of humans.'

Chet nodded and turned to Luke and Marty. Their faces were intent. Alert. 'When we get down there, two groups. Sean, Marty, head to the east side of the house and secure any exits there. If Ivanovic knows we're coming for him, he'll most likely try to escape that way. You grab him if he does.'

'It'll be a pleasure,' said Sean.

'Luke, we'll take the front. Identify the main power supply and kill the lights. Then house clearance room by room. I want any guards dead before they have the chance to shout out. We'll flush the fucker out that way.'

Luke nodded.

Each man performed a final check on his weapons, engaged his NV and turned to Chet, waiting for the word.

'OK,' he breathed. 'Let's move.'

TWO

18.49 hrs.

The road to the lake went gently downhill, but in the snow it still took ten minutes to travel it. They were fifty metres from the house when Sean and Marty veered off to the east so they could get round to the back.

Chet and Luke continued to follow the line of the Transit's tracks. When they reached the van—parked about fifteen metres from the front entrance of the house, its exhaust still warm from its journey—Chet spoke.

'Cover the door,' he said. 'I'll find the power.'

Luke nodded, then settled down on one knee in the firing position while Chet silently approached towards the house.

Now he was closer, he could make more sense of the structure. It was an old place, timber-clad. The paint—he couldn't tell what colour it was in the dark—was peeling and the window frames rotten. Of the two lights that were on, one was on the ground floor and the other on the first. Chet kept away from those parts of the snowy ground where the windows cast light.

There was no electricity pylon leading to the house, which meant there must be some other power source. As Chet crept round to the northern side, his ears began to tell him what it was: the low hum of a petrol generator. He found it in a small outbuilding. The warmth of the generator had melted the snow for a metre around the building; inside, the air was filled with the greasy stench of fuel. It took Chet only a few seconds to locate the pump, with a plastic isolating valve at one end. He turned this. The engine spluttered, and the buzz of the generator died away immediately, to be replaced by total silence.

He made his way back to Luke, who hadn't moved from the firing position, his rifle aimed firmly at the front door of the house. 'Anything?' Chet whispered.

Luke shook his head.

They gave it a minute. A minute for raised voices or someone inside to walk out and check the genny. A minute for them to walk into a flying bullet from Luke's suppressed M16.

No one came.

Why was no one coming?

Chet spoke into the radio. 'Sean, Marty?'

'Roger that,' Sean's voice filled his earpiece.

'Any movement your side?'

'Negative.'

Chet and Luke looked at each other. 'If Ivanovic and his numpties are just hiding out here, they probably don't know how the house works,' Luke suggested.

Again Chet peered towards the house, then spoke into his radio. 'We're moving in.'

* * *

Chet's voice rang clearly in Sean's earpiece. Situated near the eastern wing of the house, Sean was about twenty metres from the back door, just behind a metre-high wall that marked the end of a back yard. His right knee was pressed firmly into the snow, the butt of his rifle was tight into his shoulder and the weapon was trained on the exit. Marty was in the

24

same position, another ten metres along the wall. Fifteen metres behind them both was a line of tall spruce trees, heavy with snow. Both men had their NV goggles engaged, and the IR-filtered Maglites on their weapons lit up the area in a ghostly green haze, for them but for no one else. Not that there *was* anyone else. The whole place was as silent as a graveyard.

Something nagged at Sean. It was so quiet here. He knew these fuckers were in hiding, but still . . .

He spoke into his mike. 'Go careful, fellas.'

'Roger that, buddy,' Luke's voice came over the radio.

Sean suppressed a shiver. Chet and Luke were good, but the anxiety still gnawed at him. This op should be like shooting fish in a barrel. Marty looked over at Sean briefly before returning his gaze to the house. He couldn't see the younger soldier's eyes but he could sense that the kid was anxious too.

Sean thought back through the events of the past hour. He had seen Ivanovic's man staggering out of the bar. From the white Skoda he had watched the guy weave along the pavement, pissed as a parrot. Once in the Transit van, he'd pulled carelessly out into the traffic and sped off.

Sped off.

Sean remembered the few times he'd been drunk behind the wheel, back when he was a teenager in Salisbury. He'd never driven quickly. A drunk man drives slowly, he thought. He doesn't want to get caught . . .

And once they'd dumped their vehicles and approached the location on foot, the Transit van's tracks had been perfectly straight. It was not the

25

haphazard route of a drunk man. Not like a drunk man at all . . .

An icy chill clenched Sean's stomach. *It was a set-up. They had to abort. Now.* He moved his hand down to his pocket, ready to activate the comms and hiss the warning into his mike.

He never got the chance.

He heard it at the same time as he saw it: a distant thud from behind, like someone knocking once on a wooden door. And the moment of impact, as a round slammed with fatal precision into the back of Marty's neck, just below the helmet. There was a small explosion of gore, not only at the entry point but also at the exit wound at the front of the throat, and Marty's body slumped dead.

Sean spun round. The Maglite lit up the area between him and the spruces behind, and he scanned the line of trees, desperately trying to make out the shooter. As the IR torch moved from left to right, it illuminated a face in the darkness. Sean only saw it for a fraction of a second, but he knew it well enough: the hooded eyes, the huge flat nose. The man from the bar. Only now he had a rifle, and it was pointing straight at Sean.

The SAS man's movements were lightning fast as he swung his M16 back to where he'd seen the image, ready to take him out the moment he got the fucker in his sights.

That moment never came.

The second bullet entered just below Sean's forehead with the same accuracy as the first, mincing the upper half of his face. He fell to the ground.

He'd had no chance to warn Chet and Luke that

they were walking into an ambush.

*   *   *

The front door was open. Chet and Luke slipped quietly into the house.

It was as silent inside as out. They found themselves in a hallway about six metres long, with an old wooden floor, a door on either side and one at the far end. Chet pointed at the left-hand door first. Luke covered him while he tried the handle. Locked. The same went for the right-hand door. They crept towards the far door.

Chet opened it and Luke entered, scanning the place with the IR beam from his Maglite.

It was a big room. Seven or eight metres square. It smelt of neglect and there was no furniture— Luke sensed that the house had long since been abandoned—but at the far end there were two open staircases, one leading up to the first floor, the other leading into the basement. In that far wall, under the upper staircase, was a further door. Chet pointed at the door to indicate to Luke that they would clear the adjoining room before investigating the rest of the house, then stepped towards it.

Movement.

Luke swung round to his left but at first saw nothing. A couple of seconds later, though, his sight fell on a fat rat, close against the left-hand wall and looking up at them with eyes that glowed in the NV. Luke cursed silently to himself, then continued towards the door.

The adjoining room was bigger than the one with the stairs. On the left-hand wall was a large fireplace, and as Chet and Luke stepped further into the room, they saw a child's cot standing against the far wall and a hobby horse to its right.

But no people.

Nothing.

'FRAG!'

Chet's voice shattered the silence. Luke saw an object, the size of a spray paint can, falling towards him.

Two metres away.

One.

It all happened so quickly. Seconds later Luke felt the full force of Chet's bulky body smash into him, knocking him towards the edge of the room and forcing him off balance. As he fell to one side, he saw his mate try to kick the fragmentation grenade back out of the door, towards whoever had thrown it at them. It exploded just at the moment his boot touched the canister.

The explosion echoed round the room, and Luke's reflex action was to hit the ground and clasp his hands at the back of his neck to stop the falling shrapnel from embedding itself in his flesh. He felt something shower on to his helmet, but by some miracle none of the shrapnel pierced his body.

He also heard Chet's scream. It sounded all the louder since they had spent the last forty-five minutes in near silence.

Luke pushed himself to his knees and instinctively let a couple of rounds from his rifle fly towards the open door. Then he turned his attention to Chet.

No casualty simulation exercise could ever have prepared Luke for the state of his friend. Chet's right leg had taken the brunt of the detonation. The grenade had burned the material of his trouser leg away, but that was not all. Flesh had been blasted away from the leg in chunks, and through the grainy haze of his NV, Luke could see splinters of bone and torn flesh. Chet's body armour had absorbed the force of some of the blast, but the fragments had peppered his face—the skin was punctured, mangled and bleeding.

He was writhing in agony, flailing like a landed fish, and was crying out so loudly that he was already hoarse.

Luke fired another two rounds through the open door, then screamed into his radio: *'I need backup. Now!'*

No response.

'Sean, Marty?'

Nothing.

'Shit!'

Either the comms were down, or the rest of his unit were.

Voices outside. Several men, shouting instructions at each other in Serbian. They were mobilising themselves. They were coming.

Chet needed morphine, and he needed it now. Luke had two shots, safely in their plastic casing, attached to a cord round his neck. He grabbed one of them, then slammed it through his mate's clothing and into the top of his left thigh. He could feel the needle piercing the skin, and for a moment he wondered whether he should go for a second shot. Chet was fucked, but at least the drugs would make him more comfortable until . . . Until what?

Luke was just reaching for the second jab when the first round flew over his head and splintered the hobby horse behind him. He felt the rush of displaced air and threw himself down on the

29

ground. Suddenly the enemy were there. In the darkness and confusion, it was difficult to tell how many. Three, maybe four, and armed—Luke thought he caught sight of an MP5 Kurz. They were shouting at him, a harsh, guttural sound. Luke made to spray a burst of rounds into them, but a heavy boot hit his rifle and knocked it from his hands. The Serbians started to pile in. They kicked Luke in the face and groin; the NV goggles cracked and were then ripped off him. One of the men grabbed the rifle. Two others seized him by the arms and hauled him to his feet. Luke felt one of them cut his ops waistcoat away from his body, before he was pushed, roughly and at gunpoint, towards the door.

'*Get down the stairs!*'

The instruction came in harshly accented English, and Luke felt a gun barrel in the back of his neck. Chet's screaming had stopped. Bad sign.

Luke twisted his head to see what was going on behind him, but that just earned him another push. '*Get down the fucking stairs or I kill you now . . .*'

Luke stumbled in the darkness. In the adjoining room he bore left towards the lower staircase. At the top he looked towards his captors, but they were just shapes in the darkness. Shapes with MP5s, and Luke didn't doubt for a moment that they were willing to use them. What he didn't understand was why they hadn't killed him yet.

Another bad sign.

One more push and Luke stumbled down the stairs. He tried to work out his options. His rifle was gone, and so was his waistcoat. The only weapon he had was the disco gun strapped to his ankle. The Serbians hadn't found that yet, but if he went for it now, chances were they'd nail him before he even stood up again. He was just going to have to bide his time.

He reached the bottom of the stairs. *'Keep going!'* the voice behind him ordered. He found himself in a damp-smelling cellar room. Candles were burning—perhaps half a dozen of them—but they weren't bright enough to light up the walls, so Luke couldn't tell how big this place was.

But what he could tell was that somebody was waiting for him.

Even in the dim candlelight, Luke recognised the man from the photo the ops officer had shown them back at base. The almost-bald head, a few strands combed from one side to the other. The flared nostrils. The sour look. Stevan Ivanovic stared at Luke with something approaching satisfaction.

Suddenly there was silence again. Shadows from the candles danced on Ivanovic's face.

'Get on the ground,' he whispered as one of his men threw something on the floor. For a moment Luke thought it was just his waistcoat, but then he realised it was Chet's gear. They'd removed it all. He didn't even want to think what they'd done to his mate.

His mind turned somersaults as he let his head fall to his chest.

Let the fucker think he's the big man, he thought. Let him think I'm beaten. He refused to admit to himself that he probably was.

It was only as Luke lowered himself down to his knees that he noticed what Ivanovic had in his hands. A loop of thin plastic. The former police chief was running it through his fingers. Caressing

31

it, almost.

'You British,' Ivanovic said, his voice very soft. 'You think you can interfere in *everybody's* affairs. You think you still boss the whole world, like you used to.'

Luke kept silent. His head hung. Here, in the kneeling position, his hand was nearer his PPK, but he knew he had to choose his moment carefully.

Ivanovic smiled. It was a cold, humourless expression. 'That . . . that *pantomime* in the bar. It was very clumsy. The young man is dead now. And his girlfriend.' Another smile. 'Well, almost. Oh, and your two friends.' He nodded, his eyes suddenly bright. '*Mrtav*. Dead.'

Ivanovic turned his back on Luke and appeared to address the empty rear portion of the room. 'I am lucky to have such loyal men. But you know, really it seems not fair that they should have *all* the fun.'

To Luke's right stood two men with MP5s pointed directly at him. They handled their weapons like pros. Beyond them he counted three others. He tried to identify the guy from the bar, but he couldn't. That meant he was still out there somewhere.

One of him, six of them—and that was just down here. Not good odds.

Ivanovic turned to face him again. Luke noticed his hands trembling, as if in excitement. As he took a step nearer, Luke saw he held a cable tie— exactly what he himself had stashed in his waistcoat for use as Plasticuffs. He knew what these Eastern European fucks did with them. The skin round his neck tingled.

Ivanovic said something that made his men

32

laugh. Luke closed his eyes. The moment he went for his PPK, the guards would shoot. But if he didn't, Ivanovic would throttle him. Maybe he should let that happen. Once the cable tie was on, Ivanovic and his guys would be off their guard. He could nail them and then hunt for a knife, but he wouldn't have much more than a minute to find one . . .

'I can give you information . . .' he said hoarsely. It was bullshit, but it might buy him some time.

Ivanovic appeared to find this very funny. 'Information? I knew already you were coming. What information could *you* . . . ?'

His gloating was cut short.

Gunshot, coming from the staircase. And then a thump.

The men with MP5s turned to see what it was, and in their moment of distraction, Luke moved.

He rolled away from Ivanovic and, as he did do, pulled the PPK from his ankle holster. By the time the two armed guards knew what he was doing, Luke had discharged two rounds, one into the first guy's neck, the other into his mate's head. As the men crumpled, spattering Luke's face with blood, he had a direct line of fire to the other three. They were scrabbling for their guns, but they didn't scrabble fast enough: Luke had all three down in less than two seconds, and it was as they dropped to the ground that he saw what the disturbance was.

Something had fallen down the stairs. Some*one* to be precise. He was now lying face down at the foot of the steps, the back of his head blown away. He might have lost half his brains, but it was unmistakably the man they'd followed back from the bar.

Luke had hesitated too long. Ivanovic was launching himself at him, the plastic loop gripped tight. Luke pushed himself to his feet just as the Serb came within range. With all the force he could summon, he brought the edge of his hand up against the underside of Ivanovic's nose. There was a definite crack, and Luke felt his hand was wet. Ivanovic roared in pain, but the blow didn't floor him. With blood gushing down his chin, he came at Luke again.

Luke's orders had been to take him alive. But that didn't mean he couldn't hurt the bastard.

He discharged two rounds from the PPK: one into each of Ivanovic's shins. From two metres, the 9mm rounds would all but destroy each bone. Certainly the guy would never walk again. For a moment, the Serb's roaring stopped. But only for a moment. As he fell backwards, his damaged legs no longer able to support the weight of his body, his shrieks echoed off the concrete walls.

But Luke was barely paying attention to that. Because, in the few seconds after Ivanovic's man had come crashing down the stairs, he had become aware of something else.

A figure was standing at the top of the steps.

Luke pointed his PPK in that direction. 'Chet?' he called out. Surely he wasn't on his feet. But who else would have nailed Ivanovic's man?

No reply from the top of the stairs. Blood and sweat dripped down Luke's face.

'*Fucking hell, Chet*,' he shouted over the noise of Ivanovic's screaming. '*If that's you, say so.*'

The sound that followed was not a voice. It was the noise of a body falling. The figure at the top of the stairs toppled. It hit the steps face downwards, then tumbled heavily into the basement.

It was Chet all right. The side of his face was mashed. His leg was a mess. How the hell he'd even got to his feet with the injuries he'd sustained, Luke couldn't guess. He was like some fucked-up Lazarus, his chest moving, but only just. Even Ivanovic stared at the monstrous sight of Chet's damaged body with a look of horror, his screaming now subsided into a series of desperate gasps and groans.

But Luke didn't care about the Serb and his injuries. Or about the bodies all around them. All he cared about was his Regiment mate, collapsed and close to death, on the ground.

THREE

For a moment, everything was silent.

Luke looked around. Six corpses; two gravely injured men. Pools of blood everywhere, and a strange cocktail of smells: the dampness of the basement, the cordite of the gunshots, a faint smell of shit from where one of the men had taken a round in the guts.

He tried to get his head straight. Chet was his priority now. Ivanovic wasn't going anywhere. If he died of his wounds, so be it. The Ruperts and the spooks would see red, but they weren't on the ground, making the decisions. Luke could only look after one of these two casualties.

But the first thing was to secure Ivanovic. He dragged him towards one of his dead and bloodied men, then pulled some cable ties from his ops waistcoat, cuffed Ivanovic's wrists behind his back and tied each of his ankles to the corresponding leg of the corpse, before moving any remaining weapons well out of his grasp.

'If I see you trying to move, I'll kill you,' he told him.

Had he understood? Luke didn't know: the guy just lay there groaning, sweating and shaking.

He turned his attention to his mate. Chet was totally still. Luke put two fingers to his jugular. There was the slowest, the faintest of pulses. If Chet had any chance of making it, he needed a casevac. Luke's priority now was to stabilise him and get on the radio back to base. He didn't want to leave him, but he had no choice. The unit's med pack was back with the vehicles. So was the secure comms unit. Luke needed both.

He'd never run so fast. The snow was falling heavier than ever. Visibility, ten metres max. He stumbled and fell three times, but just got up and carried on running.

Snow had drifted against the vehicles. Breathlessly, Luke dug it away from the brown Skoda, scrambled into the front seat and grabbed the radio.

'*Zero, this Delta Three Tango. We have two men down and one injured. I need a casevac.*'

A pause.

'*Zero, this is Delta Three Tango. I need a goddamn casevac.*'

More silence. And then:

'*Delta Three Tango, this is Zero. Is the target acquired? Repeat, is the target acquired?*'

Luke felt like crushing the handset in his fist. '*Fuck the target! I've got a man dying. Get a chopper here—now!'*

He threw the handset down and hurried from the car towards the white one. Twenty seconds later he had the med pack in his hands and was sprinting back towards the house. Quicker to run than try to dig out the car.

He burst back into the house and down into the basement. Neither man had moved. He checked Chet's vital signs again. Weaker. Luke split open the med pack and pulled out a saline drip and intravenous cannula. He ripped open the material of Chet's left sleeve and slid the cannula into a vein. He needed to raise the level of the saline pouch above Chet's arm, so he pulled two of the corpses towards him, lay one on top of the other, and rested the transparent pouch on top of that.

Luke checked his vital signs again.

Shit. He's stopped breathing.

He knelt to one side of Chet's body, put the heel of his right hand on his ribcage and laid his left hand over it. He pressed down sharply on the ribcage so that it sank five centimetres, then let it rise again without taking his hands away. He performed another twenty-nine chest compressions before placing his mouth on Chet's and administering two rescue breaths. Blood from his mate's face smeared his lips.

Thirty chest compressions, two rescue breaths.

Luke repeated the CPR routine that had been drilled into him countless times. Once he'd done five sequences, he checked Chet's vitals for a third time.

He was breathing.

Luke turned his attention to Chet's leg. Jesus, what a mess. Amazingly, the bleeding wasn't

37

too bad, but he grabbed a bandage anyway from the med pack and quickly applied a makeshift tourniquet to the top of his thigh, tying it as tight as possible to constrict the blood flow. He started to wind a second bandage around the damaged leg. Chet groaned when the material touched the wound. Clearly it hurt like hell, but that wasn't such a bad thing. At least it meant he was sentient.

Luke was panting heavily by now. He tried to clear his mind, to think through his medical training and work out if there was anything else he could do. There was nothing. Monitor his vital signs, perform CPR if necessary and wait. He pictured the map of Serbia in his mind and tried to estimate the distance between here and the FOB. A hundred miles perhaps. In normal conditions a QRF chopper should be able to cover that distance in forty-five minutes. But in this kind of snow, it was impossible to say.

He relived the moment Chet had kicked the grenade away. The wounded man lying here on the ground had saved his life that night, no question, and the chances were high that he'd pay for it with his own. Luke felt a surge of anger at the Serbian bastard lying in the cellar with him. It was all he could do to stop himself from slotting him now.

Chet muttered something. It was gibberish. 'Hold on, buddy,' Luke said through gritted teeth. 'We're going to get you out of here soon.'

Luke didn't know how long it was before he heard the noise. It crept up on him gradually: the faint but steady beating of rotor blades. He ran up the steps and outside.

Two Pumas were coming in to land. They appeared to wobble in the air as they tried to set down, their lights glowing through the white-out of snow that surrounded them as they touched down. Luke knew that it was no picnic for the RAF pilots, flying a heli in this kind of weather. If it wasn't life and death, they wouldn't have ventured out at all.

The moment after the first Puma touched down, seven men jumped out, all carrying bright torches. They wore DPMs and hard hats and Luke instantly recognised the maroon flash of 1 Para on the arms of six of them. The seventh man had no hard hat and a regular uniform: Chris Andersen, OC B Squadron, and a man who had just gone up several notches in Luke's estimation for making the journey out here.

'*Follow me!*' Luke roared at the Para QRF over the noise of the helicopters, and he sprinted back into the house.

There were two medics among the Paras. One look at Chet and their faces turned grim. But they were in charge now, and Luke knew to leave them to it.

The OC walked down the stairs. 'Ivanovic?' he asked.

Luke pointed at the Serb lying on the floor. 'All yours, boss,' he said. And then: 'Sean and Marty are dead.'

A dark look crossed Andersen's face, and Luke could tell he was feeling equally murderous. They had their orders, though. Ivanovic was to stay alive. The Hague wanted their trophy conviction, no matter what had happened here tonight.

Minutes later Luke was back outside in the snow. He watched Chet being stretchered into one of the waiting Pumas, then stood with a frown as the Paras carried the two bodies up into the chopper.

Ivanovic came next, held under the arms by a couple of Paras who made no attempt to spare him any of the agony caused by dragging his splintered shins across the ground. Amid his shouts of pain, he took a second to cast a hateful look at Luke, who returned it. The bastard didn't know how lucky he was Luke hadn't given him one behind the ear.

And then Andersen was there again. 'Let's go,' he ordered, and the two of them boarded the Puma that was carrying Chet and their fallen comrades.

As the heli lifted up into the air, Luke crouched down by Chet's stretcher, steadying himself by gripping the webbing that covered the inside of the aircraft. His mate's face was covered with an oxygen mask and he had a new drip in each arm. A blood pressure and pulse monitor beeped next to him. His face looked as white as death.

Luke stared at the man who'd saved his life.

Suddenly Chet's eyes flickered open.

'Fuck me, buddy,' Luke burst out. 'What does it take to put you down?'

'Don't ... bullshit ... me ...' Chet could barely get the words out, and Luke struggled to hear them over the roar of the chopper. 'Am I going to make it?'

Luke looked him up and down. He saw the damaged leg and the tubes sticking out of his body. He saw the medics, their faces severe.

He fixed his expression in what he hoped looked like reassurance.

'Course you are, mate,' he said, as he felt the Puma struggling against the elements. 'Course you are. That's a promise.'

He turned away so that Chet couldn't see his face any more.

40

Luke Mercer wasn't a religious man, but as the Puma struggled through the blizzard and the dark night of Eastern Europe, he found himself muttering a silent prayer—to God and all the fucking angels on high—that this was a promise he'd be able to keep.

PART TWO

January 2003, two months before the coalition invasion of Iraq.

FOUR

London.

'It's six o'clock on Monday, 7 January. This is the news.'

In a small ground-floor flat just off Seven Sisters Road, a man stared at his reflection in the mirror while the radio babbled in the background.

'UN weapons inspectors have reported that there is no indication that Iraq is in possession of weapons of mass destruction. The chief weapons inspector Hans Blix, however, has stated that, while Iraq has cooperated on a practical level, it has not demonstrated a genuine acceptance of the need to disarm unilaterally. This follows claims by the United States that Saddam Hussein has ordered the death of any scientist who speaks to the inspectors in private, and it is expected that . . .'

The man switched off the radio and went back to staring in the mirror. It wasn't a pretty sight. His right eye was hooded, the result of an old injury. Just below his left eye there was a two-inch scar, bright pink and crooked. When he smiled the scar made his face look more damaged. Not that he smiled much these days. Today—his birthday, as it happened—he was more than usually aware of how fucked up he looked. He scowled and glanced around the tiny bathroom. Thirty-four years old, and this piece-of-shit flat in one of the scummiest bits of London was all he had to show for his life so far.

Chet Freeman looked down to see the prosthetic limb strapped to the stump of his right leg. It always hurt—especially when he put pressure on it, which he did every time he stood up. The remnants of his shattered knee bone were forever breaking down; his skin was often bleeding and sore. When people saw an amputee, they only ever saw the prosthetic limb, never the damaged flesh that sat in it. The limb itself was hi-tech and well cushioned, but the flesh was human and it ached 24/7.

Yet in a weird way his prosthesis reminded him how lucky he was. For Chet, life was divided into 'before Serbia' and 'after Serbia'. When things started to get him down, he just reminded himself that the 'after Serbia' bit could easily never have happened.

He had no memory of the blast. No memory of the evacuation or amputation. One minute he was in a room with Luke, a kid's cot and a hobby horse; the next he was back in the UK at Selly Oak Hospital, his home for a year. He lost count of the times the doctors sliced wafers of skin from his back to graft over his wounds, all the while telling him that by rights he should be dead. Then he'd been moved into rehab at Headley Court.

At Headley they taught him to walk again—a long, slow process. Nothing like a stint in that place to make you count your blessings, though. Chet's amputation was below the knee. That at least gave him the movement of the knee joint. In rehab he met several double above-the-knee amputees, and even one basket case—a quadruple amputee whose life seemed to Chet to be barely worth living, though the guy seemed remarkably positive given his circumstances.

The Regiment had offered Chet a desk job back in Hereford, but he wasn't the desk-job type and quit the military. His pay-off had been just enough to buy this tiny flat, and there was a small army pension; but it was barely enough to live on, and anyway he needed something to get him out of bed in the morning. To sit and brood would have been the death of him.

By the time he was dressed, Chet just looked like a regular guy. Some of the amputees he knew didn't mind their prosthetic limbs being on show. Not him. He liked to cover up his leg—not out of shame, but because he didn't want people treating him differently. His trousers successfully hid the limb. A specially made shoe hid the foot. There were the scars on his face, sure, but that was no different to any of the ex-army winos who staggered up and down Seven Sisters Road. At least he looked better than them. Just.

He limped into the kitchen just as the phone rang. Chet let the answering machine on the work surface click in. *'This is me. Leave a message.'*

'Chet, mate, it's Doug . . .' Doug Hodgson, a leg amputee like himself thanks to an anti-personnel landmine in Kosovo. They'd gone through rehab together. He was a good lad, but his prosthesis wasn't his only war wound. The poor guy was riddled with PTSD. He hid it well, but Chet knew it filled his nights with dreams and woke him early every morning. Hence the six a.m. call. 'Happy birthday, yeah? So if you haven't got plans to get your chin buttered tonight, how about meeting up for a few jars? Call me, right?'

Chet frowned. Doug had this image of Chet as a ladies' man, but with one leg and a scarred face he was hardly catch of the day. A glance at the state of the kitchen showed that the place lacked a woman's

47

touch: peeling yellow wallpaper, a filthy hob, the only decoration a Blutacked poster of the London skyline that had come with the flat but Chet had never bothered to change.

The remnants of last night's booze were still visible in the kitchen: half a bottle of Bell's, a couple of empty tins of Asda's strongest lager. The first thing the occupational therapists had told him at Headley Court had been to lay off the sauce, but they weren't the ones who had to put up with the discomfort, or the embarrassment, or the frustration. Still, he didn't like to be reminded the morning after of how much he'd knocked back, so he pressed the empty cans into the already overflowing bin and stowed the whisky bottle in a cupboard, before taking a loaf of bread from its packet and hacking off a hunk with the only sharp knife in the kitchen. As he ate the dry bread, he picked up a piece of paper from the side, stained with a ring from the bottom of a coffee mug.

It was a letter, written on expensive vellum paper and emblazoned with an elaborate letterhead: an ornate G, printed in gold foil, with the words 'The Grosvenor Group' in copperplate underneath it. They sent Chet one of these notes every time he did a bit of work for them, short and businesslike, the wording always the same:

Dear Mr Freeman
Please take this letter as confirmation that we will expect you at 7.30 a.m. at 132 Whitehall on 7 January 2003. As usual, the details of this engagement are subject to the non-disclosure agreement in force between ourselves.

48

Chet looked at the clock on the greasy oven. 06.28. Time to get going. Today might be his birthday, but a job was a job, and he needed it. He grabbed his rucksack full of gear and left the house.

It felt bitterly cold as he stepped outside. His old black Mondeo—automatic transmission so he could drive it with one foot—was parked outside, a dent in one side, three key scrapes along the other. Back in the Hereford days he'd gone everywhere on a Yamaha R1. Those days were gone and so was the motorbike.

Leaves swirled in the wind, but the sky was crisp and blue. He could have driven, or waited for a bus to take him to the tube station, but Chet was stubborn. His leg hurt as he walked as briskly as he could along the road, but he was damned if he was going to live his life any differently because of that. At Headley Court they'd suggested he got himself a wheelchair for occasional use. He would rather die.

Jobs for amputees that didn't involve sitting behind a desk were hard to come by. The usual bodyguarding gigs that most Regiment personnel fell into on leaving the army weren't open to Chet, but he still had certain skills that people and organisations were willing to pay for. The Grosvenor Group was one of them. They were a big American firm manned by brash men in expensive suits. They clearly made a great deal of money in ways Chet didn't really understand, and with money came paranoia. Almost weekly the company called Chet in to sweep offices where they were holding meetings. Different locations every time, but always the same request: check for bugs, check for surveillance. What the hell went on in these meetings, Chet had no idea.

49

The tube was busy and sweaty. Chet was glad to emerge at Piccadilly Circus, just another face in the crowd as he made his way down to Whitehall, stopping about thirty metres before he reached the familiar MoD offices.

Number 132 was a tall building with wide stone steps and a tinted-glass revolving door. Inside was all marble and mirrors. Chet entered and headed straight for the security desk in the middle of the cavernous atrium. A friendly-looking, Brylcreemed man, in his sixties and wearing a grey suit, smiled up at him.

'Good morning, sir. Can I help?'

Chet nodded. 'I'm expected.'

'Your name, please, sir?'

'Chet Freeman.'

The man consulted his computer. 'Sixth floor, sir. I will need to check your bag before you go up.'

Chet shook his head and a brief look of alarm crossed the man's face. 'It's security regulations, sir. I'm sure you'll . . .'

'Call up,' Chet interrupted him. 'They'll clear it with you.' He turned and wandered away from the desk.

A minute later the security guard gestured him back. 'Please go up, sir. Everything's fine. You'll just need to sign in.'

Chet nodded again, waited while the security guard issued him with a plastic ID card to clip on his shirt, then headed for the lift.

He got out at the sixth floor to see a wide, open-planned office on his left, all carpet tiles, pot plants and water coolers. There were perhaps twenty people working there, mostly female. The air was filled with the sound of phones ringing softly; each call was answered immediately.

The person who emerged from the huddle of desks to greet him was male, early twenties, with dishevelled hair. He looked at Chet like he was looking at dog shit. 'Have you been here before?' he asked, his voice dripping with public school.

'Where are the rooms, pal?' Chet asked curtly.

'Up here, on the right. They've set two aside for us, next to each other. We'll choose which one to use at the last min . . .'

'Thanks. I know the drill. So who is it today?' The kid shrugged just as they stopped beside a grey door.

'This it?' asked Chet.

The kid nodded.

'Why don't you run along then?' Chet winked at him. 'You must be very busy.'

The kid got the message and left him to it.

Chet entered the room. It was entirely unremarkable. A beech-coloured meeting table with twenty or so chairs around it took up most of the space. There was a whiteboard at one end with an overhead projector, and three large tinted windows looking out over Whitehall and from which, if you looked up, you could just see the roofs of the buildings opposite.

He got to work. From his rucksack he pulled a set of screwdrivers, a torch, two bulky Nokia mobile phones and a radio-frequency bug detector. He started with the plug sockets—unscrewing each one, directing the torch into the cavity and searching for bugs or any sign of tampering—before climbing awkwardly on to the board table and investigating the light fittings.

Once he was satisfied that the sockets and lights

were clean, he started calibrating the RF detector. He laid it on the table and turned the dial fully on. The detector started beeping rapidly, so Chet gradually turned the dial down until it stopped. He picked up one of the mobiles and used it to call the other. The radio signal from the phones caused the detector to start beeping again.

Holding the phones, he stepped back three metres, towards the windows. The rate of the detector's beeping decreased, but not by enough. He adjusted the dial, then stepped back again. This time the beeping was right. He disconnected the phones and the detector went silent. Now he could start to sweep.

He ran the detector along the blinds above the windows and carefully checked the OHP. He swept under the table and chairs and examined each of the carpet tiles for signs of tampering, before carefully sweeping all the walls and the ceiling. It took half an hour before he was satisfied that everything was clear, at which point he packed up his gear, left the room and, now that he'd swept it, tacked a red cordon over the door so nobody could enter. Then he moved to the adjoining office— which was identical in every way—and started to repeat the operation.

Chet was just unscrewing the first socket when the door opened. He looked over his shoulder to see a woman. A couple of years younger than Chet, which would put her in her early thirties. And cute. Definitely cute. She was carrying a small vacuum cleaner and wore a blue and white checked uniform that identified her as one of the office's cleaning ladies, but a lot easier on the eye than most. She had long red hair, pale, clear skin, green eyes. Her nose turned up attractively at the end and there was a tiny silver stud through the left nostril.

She looked surprised to see him. 'Oh . . . Excuse me . . . I thought . . .'

Chet stood up and gave her one of his rare smiles. 'Sorry, love,' he said, then noticed a flicker of annoyance on her face. He took a couple of steps towards her and read the name on her plastic name tag. Suze McArthur. 'Sorry, *Suze*. No cleaning in here today.' He caught the faintest whiff of a perfume he recognised from an ex-girlfriend, but that had been a long time ago.

Suze looked flustered. 'I'll go next door . . .'

''Fraid not. Out of bounds.'

'But I have to clean . . .'

'Looks like you might have the morning off.' Chet hesitated. 'Tell you what—I'll be free in a couple of hours. I'll buy you coffee . . .'

The girl backed away. She scurried back up the corridor, taking her vacuum cleaner with her and casting just a single glance over her shoulder as she went. She almost appeared frightened.

Jesus, Chet thought. I didn't think I looked *that* bad.

He went back to sweeping the room. Twenty minutes later he was done. After cordoning off the room, just as he had the first, he stood watch in the corridor outside.

He'd only been standing there a few minutes when he heard a commotion by the lift, which he could just see from his position. A group of five people had arrived. Three of them were muscle—he could tell just by the way they held themselves. The fourth man was entirely bald, his face and scalp tanned and shiny, his suit a bright blue that

53

suggested he was foreign—French or Italian, perhaps. As he drew nearer, Chet could see that he held across his chest a leather wallet file with the ornate G emblem of the Grosvenor Group. He was speaking loudly, with an American accent, to the fifth man.

And Chet recognised *him*.

'What the hell . . . ?' he muttered to himself.

The Prime Minister wore a well-cut suit and his trademark red tie was impeccably tied. Alistair Stratton almost had the bearing of a film star, out of place in this workaday office environment, and was listening attentively to the bald man as they walked, his brow creased in earnest concentration. Stratton glanced at Chet as he approached, and clocked his scarred face, before quickly recovering and turning his attention back to the bald man. There was something about being in his presence that impressed Chet, despite himself.

They stopped outside the first cordoned-off door. 'Who's in charge of security here?' the bald man asked abruptly. He clearly hadn't noticed Chet standing there. 'I *said*, who's in charge of . . . ?'

His eyes fell on Chet.

'You?'

Chet nodded.

'Which room?' He snapped his fingers. 'Come on, we don't have all day.'

'Take your pick. They're both clean.'

The American looked at the two doors, shrugged, chose the closest, then stretched out one arm to indicate that the Prime Minister should enter.

Stratton, however, waited for a moment. 'Ex-military?' he asked Chet.

Chet wasn't surprised the PM could tell. He knew he had the bearing. He nodded.

The PM held out his hand for Chet to shake. His skin was cold and dry, his grip firm. 'Thank you,' he smiled. 'I, er . . . I don't believe people say that enough.'

The bald man looked a little surprised that Stratton had taken the time to stop, but he quickly followed his lead. He slapped Chet's upper arm in a comradely way. And if he noticed that Chet was unimpressed, he didn't show it.

'Shall we, Prime Minister?'

Stratton nodded and followed the American inside, closing the grey door firmly behind him.

The muscle immediately took up position: one outside the room, one where the corridor entered the open-plan area and the third by the lift. None of them even acknowledged Chet's presence. He shrugged. If they wanted to stonewall him, fine. He needed to stick around till the meeting closed, so he took himself off into the empty room to wait.

Chet sat on the edge of the large meeting table, facing towards the windows looking out over Whitehall. It felt good to take the weight off his leg. He pulled a fifty-pence coin from his pocket and started flicking and catching it as he tried to make sense of what he'd just seen. Chet made a habit of not asking too many questions about these meetings the Grosvenor Group wanted to keep so secret. It suited him just to do the job and get paid. He couldn't help wondering, though, what Stratton was doing here and what conversation was being held in the adjacent room.

He walking over to the window, absent-mindedly tapping on the tinted glass as he looked down on to Whitehall. It was full of buses, taxis and pedestrians, silent from this height. Number 10 was just up the road. The Houses of Parliament too. Stratton had any number of places he could conduct meetings. Why here? Unless he didn't want this meeting to be common knowledge . . .

He flicked the coin again and caught it.

He remembered a conversation he'd had years ago, sitting in a Serbian bar. Luke Mercer was speaking quietly so as not to be overheard. '*Stratton is a politician. Therefore Stratton is a wanker. End of.*' Chet had seen Luke three weeks ago as he was preparing to go away on ops. He'd asked where, but Luke had given him an apologetic look. 'Sorry, buddy. You know the deal.'

Yeah, Chet knew the deal. With the Americans and the Iraqis squaring up to each other, and the Brits showing every sign of wanting to come along for the ride, Chet could make an educated guess about what Luke was up to. But a guess was all it could be. He was out of the Regiment and out of the loop. Get used to it, buddy.

It was as these thoughts circulated in his head that something caught his eye. A flash of sunlight reflecting off something on the opposite roof.

Movement.

Chet squinted, trying to make out what was up there. Partly hidden behind a railing was a figure. He grabbed his bag, pulled out a pair of binoculars and quickly focused them. The blurred figure grew sharp.

A woman. Long red hair. Cute nose. Stud on the left. Some kind of machine in front of her.

'Cleaning lady, yeah right,' Chet muttered.

And as he said it, he was already hurrying

towards the door.

FIVE

Chet moved as quickly as his leg would allow him—out of the door and past Stratton's security people.

'Hey—where you going?' the guy outside the meeting room shouted.

Chet ignored him and walked on.

His mind turned over. What had he just seen? The woman on the roof opposite was in no position to make an assassination attempt: the angle was ridiculous. And whatever the apparatus was that she had set up in front of her, it hadn't looked to him like a sniper rifle. She was up to something else.

The lift took an age to get to the ground floor, and the moment the doors opened he half ran, half limped out of the building. The PM's black limo was parked outside, with two more security men standing next to it. As Chet ran past, one of them put a sleeve to his mouth and started talking; Chet ignored them and hurried across the road towards the building opposite. He didn't enter. The reception area was crowded, with thirty or forty office workers milling around and a security check-in. There was no way he'd talk his way through that. The same went for the girl. There had to be another access.

He looked back across the road. Stratton's security hadn't left their positions, but they were watching him and updating someone on the radio. Fine. He could explain his actions later. Right now he needed to get up to the roof. He hurried round to the side of the building, where a thin passageway separated it from the next one. It led to a much smaller side street running parallel to Whitehall, and as he turned left he found the rear of the building had a fire-escape door with an external metal staircase leading up to the roof.

He was fit enough to climb the five storeys to the top of the building in less than a minute, but his leg hurt like hell all the way. As he stepped out on to the roof, he felt the wind blowing strongly. It brought with it the honking and roaring of the traffic below. The top of the London Eye rose in the distance.

He saw her immediately. Suze, or whatever her name really was, had her back to him and was slightly bent over, with her hands over her ears.

The howling of the wind was so strong that Chet didn't bother with stealth. He strode straight towards the young woman. When he was about a metre behind her, he saw that she was crouched over what appeared at first glance to be some kind of photographic equipment on a tripod. Chet quickly twigged what it actually was, though: a long-range laser listening device. All you had to do was point the viewfinder in the direction of a window. The device would pick up the vibrations on that window caused by people speaking inside, then convert them back into sound. Linked to it was a little black cassette machine that was recording whatever the listening device picked up.

Chet had used something similar once himself, during a short tour in Northern Ireland just before he was dispatched to the Balkans. On that occasion he'd been treated to the sound of a PIRA bomb-maker in flagrante with some slapper he'd picked up in a pub a few hours previously. He was still getting stuck in when they burst into the flat.

Back then, the laser listening device had been supplied by 14 Intelligence Company, surveillance experts with all the latest equipment at their disposal. Where the hell this girl had acquired such a piece of kit was anyone's guess. Maybe he'd just ask her.

Chet tapped her on the shoulder. She jumped and spun round. She was wearing headphones connected to the apparatus, and her eyes were slightly wild.

'OK, sweetheart,' he said. 'Let's go.'

Her eyes darted from Chet, to the apparatus, to the office on the other side of the road—through the window of which Stratton and the American couldn't be seen because of the tinted glass. She seemed unable to speak. 'Oh, God . . .' she breathed.

'I'm not going to hurt you,' Chet said calmly, holding his hands palm outwards to try to calm her down. He found his eye drawn to the curve of her neck. The smooth, unblemished skin.

'*No . . .*' Suddenly there were tears in her eyes. 'Please. *Please!*'

'Just come with me and we'll sort this out.' She seemed terrified, so he tried to sound as reasonable as possible.

'*Please . . .*' Her tear-filled voice was hoarse now. 'They'll kill me if they find out. I swear, they'll kill me . . .'

She was desperate. That much was obvious. Desperate or nuts. Why was it always the cute ones that ended up being loonies? Chet could tell

59

by the way she glanced over his shoulder that she was preparing to bolt; when she did, he was ready for her. He grabbed her by the top of one arm before she could even get past him. She started to writhe violently, but her slim build was no match for his strength. He kept a firm grip on her until her struggling had subsided into short, panicked breaths.

'Listen to me carefully,' he told her. 'Nobody's trying to kill anybody. You just need to come with me . . .' But the girl was shaking her head again. She glanced down at the meeting room, then looked as if she'd made a sudden, reckless decision.

She removed the earpiece she was wearing and handed it to Chet. 'Listen,' she urged him. 'Listen to what they're saying . . .'

Chet shook his head. He wasn't interested. If he brought her in, the Grosvenor Group would think the sun shone out of his arse. The gig would be his for life. He made to grab her again.

The girl shrank back. 'If you don't listen,' she said, 'you'll have to carry me kicking and screaming out of this building, I swear. They'll think you're . . . *raping* me or something . . .'

Chet stared at her. She was totally wired, and looked as if she might just do what she threatened.

'For fuck's sake,' he said. He grabbed the earpiece and put it in his ear, half wondering if he'd be humouring her like this if she wasn't a looker.

At first all he could hear was an indistinct and horrible cacophony—interference from the wind and the traffic down below—all of which was clearly affecting the vibrations of the window glass. He winced as he got an earful of static, which slowly morphed into something that sounded like several men talking underwater.

'I can't hear a thing,' Chet said.

'Keep listening.'

More static. More noise.

Then there was a word. Just a single word out of the meaningless burble.

'*Baghdad.*'

Chet strained to hear more, but the distortion had returned. It dissipated a few seconds later, however, and he was able to make out a second word.

'*Military.*'

Hold the fucking front page, Chet thought. So Stratton was discussing military action in Iraq. The guy probably didn't talk about much else these days. The girl was looking at him with wide, expectant eyes. Chet made to pull the earpiece away, but she grabbed his hand. '*Listen! You have to listen!*'

Chet winced again as a burst of static exploded in his ear. But this time it was immediately followed by a few seconds of clarity.

He heard the bald American, the guy from the Grosvenor Group. He sounded lazy and confident. '*Trust me, Prime Minister Stratton. This war is good to go . . .*'

A couple of seconds of distortion, then the voice became clear again.

'*. . . the Americans are all on board . . . The question is, how are* you *going to get it through . . . ?*'

The voices disintegrated once more into noise.

Chet removed the earpiece. 'Very interesting,' he said. 'Now pack your bags. You're coming with me.'

The fear returned to the girl's face. 'No . . . You haven't heard what I've heard . . . You can't have . . .'

61

'That's enough.' He grabbed her by the arm again.

'I'll tell them we're working together,' she gabbled. 'When we spoke outside the meeting rooms, they'll have that on CCTV.' She looked at the listening device. 'I'll say you helped me get this . . .'

Chet felt himself getting angry. She had a fucking screw loose. But his employers were paranoid—that was what kept him in a job. It wouldn't take much for them to start having second thoughts about him. *Fuck it.*

It only took one swipe of his arm for Chet to knock the girl's listening equipment on to the hard concrete of the roof. It smashed as it fell, and she looked terrified. She got down on all fours and scrambled to eject a cassette from the recorder. 'You're *fucking* crazy,' Chet hissed, and he pulled her away from the edge of the roof back towards the fire-escape stairs. She wriggled and writhed, her face a picture of dread, but there was no way she was going to get free from Chet's grip. He pushed her on to the staircase first, then bore down on her so the only thing she could do was descend. As she went, she started begging again. 'Please . . . you don't understand . . . you've got to let me go . . .' And when it was clear this wouldn't work, she started up with the threats again. Chet just kept forcing her down.

He knew, when they hit ground level, that she'd try to run, and he was ready for that. He grabbed her arm once more and for a moment they stared at each other, he with dislike, she with fear.

Fuck it, thought Chet. Let her go. If she started putting ideas about him into people's heads, he could kiss the Grosvenor Group job goodbye. He pointed to his left, the direction from which he'd come. 'Stratton's people are going to be looking for me,' he said. 'Go that way.'

He released his grip and the girl jumped backwards like a frightened animal. 'Thank you,' she said softly. Chet didn't reply. He watched her hurry away, then turned right and headed back round the corner of the building into Whitehall.

Straight away he clocked Stratton's muscle—two of them standing on the pavement, thick necked and slightly out of breath. They were looking around over the heads of the passers-by, searching for something. When they saw Chet, they bore down on him like a couple of fire and forget missiles.

'All right, fellas?' he murmured once they were standing on either side of him. Sweat trickled down the nape of his neck. 'Fag break, is it?'

'You,' said one of the men, and he poked his finger in Chet's direction. 'With us.'

Chet looked from one to the other. He considered trying to sweet-talk them, but if ever a couple of goons looked impervious to charm, they were it. He forced himself to smile at them, but they didn't once lose that dead-eyed look as they led Chet across the busy road and into the building he had been contracted to sweep.

The ride in the lift up to the sixth floor was a silent and uncomfortable one. Chet's mind turned cartwheels. Had Stratton's guys followed him when he left the building? Did they know what had happened on the roof? How the hell should he play this?

They exited the lift and strode towards the

meeting rooms, all eyes from the offices on them. From the corner of his vision, Chet could see the kid who had first greeted him, now watching intently. The third bodyguard was still standing outside the room Stratton and the bald man were using. As they approached, he knocked gently on the door.

Almost immediately the bald American stepped outside. 'What the *hell*,' he whispered when he saw Chet, 'is going on?'

Chet started to formulate a response, but he didn't get a chance to speak.

'We *saw* you up there,' the bald man said. 'Who was it? What were you doing?'

'I thought there was a security breach,' he replied firmly. 'I went to investigate.'

'And?'

He almost told them—about Suze McArthur and the listening device. But something stopped him. He didn't know what. The tension the man was displaying, perhaps. The palpable anxiety oozing from him.

'It was nothing. A student peace protester putting up a banner. I sent her packing.'

Silence.

Suddenly the door opened and Stratton appeared. He said nothing, but his face was pale.

'We should leave, Prime Minister,' the bald man said.

Stratton nodded, then strode back down the corridor, followed by the bald man and the bodyguards. Chet stood there and watched the PM's entourage head towards the lift. As the doors opened, Stratton looked back over his shoulder. He narrowed his eyes, then faced the front again and

64

hurried into the lift.

Chet's heart was thumping. He could feel the blood in his jugular. He walked into the other room, where his rucksack was still on the table. He gathered it up quickly and looked out of the window as the girl's voice echoed in his head. *You haven't heard what I've heard . . .*

But Chet had heard enough. That fragment of conversation he'd heard suggested that the PM was being pressured by the Americans to go to war. But everyone knew war was coming anyway. Certainly Chet could read the signs. Was there anything more to it than that? Probably not. Suze McArthur was just a kid with a head full of ideals. There were a million anti-war campaigners like her the length and breadth of the country. They didn't understand the real world. They didn't understand that sometimes war was the price you had to pay for peace.

He realised as he made his way back down the corridor towards the lift that the price for the morning's events could well be his job. And all thanks to that stupid girl. The bald guy from the Grosvenor Group was clearly annoyed, and it was nothing to him that the chances of Chet finding another job like this were practically zero.

'Happy fucking birthday,' he muttered as he limped out of the room. It was time to go find himself a drink.

SIX

Somewhere near the Jordan–Iraq border.

A car drove through the dusk. A red Toyota, automatic transmission. Its chassis showed signs of wear—a large dent along the side, a broken brake light and rust patches all along the undercarriage. But despite being beaten up, it was lovingly decorated. A picture of Saddam Hussein, the disciple of Muhammad, was propped on the dashboard and surrounded by little fairy lights; multicoloured garlands were pinned along the top of the windscreen. Arabic pop music played softly on the radio.

The driver had a short beard. Normally his hair was brown, but he'd dyed it black and applied enough fake tan to darken his skin a few shades. He wore a traditional Arabic *dishdash*, which fitted loosely enough for his shoulder holster and ops waistcoat to be invisible. It was stained and crumpled, saturated with the previous wearer's sweat and stinking on account of it. The driver had gone to great pains to make sure he looked like the lowest of the low. The poor were looked down upon where they were headed. They were anonymous. Invisible, almost. That could be a distinct advantage.

The figure in the passenger seat wore a burka: a plain, black outer garment and a long face veil with a small grille for the eyes. At this moment the passenger was staring ahead, along the straight, featureless road with desert on either side. Then he spoke, his voice several octaves lower than the average burka-wearer, and with a Derry accent. 'If you think I'm wearing this shit once we get in-country . . .'

Luke Mercer winked at him. 'Finn, relax. You look fucking gorgeous. We bump into any ragheads, you'll be fighting them off with a shitty stick.'

'Fuck you, Luke.'

'Worst comes to the worst, you might have to. You know, for the sake of appearances and all . . .'

Finn muttered something under his burka that Luke didn't quite catch. He suspected that it wasn't entirely complimentary. Finn had been sulking ever since he'd lost the toss to decide who'd be Abdul and who'd be Aisha on their little sortie into enemy territory. Still, Finn was four years younger than Luke and definitely the junior party in their little unit. From what Luke knew about him he'd moved out of the Province to the outskirts of Farnham before he was a teenager and his only ambition in life had been to join the British Army. Nice enough fella, but a bit of a trigger-happy reputation. He was new to the Regiment, though—just six months in. It wouldn't take long for him to settle down, but as far as Luke was concerned, the coin had landed the right way up.

They were driving along the main road leading east towards the border with Iraq, which by Luke's estimation was about twenty klicks away. For a main thoroughfare it was pretty empty. Not surprising, really. Given the way the Yanks and the British were flexing their muscles, Iraq wasn't exactly a top tourist destination at the moment.

'They still got us?' Finn changed the subject.

Luke looked in the rear-view mirror. The road might be empty, but one vehicle was staying close:

67

a white pick-up, manned by four other members of their squadron.

'Rear-echelon motherfuckers,' Luke said.

Luke and Finn wouldn't be risking the official border crossing. Too dangerous. The car and its occupants might look authentic to the casual observer; they might have forged entry documents; but it wouldn't take much to find the gear stashed in the back: two Colt M4A1s—compact, efficient weapons with sight and torch fitted—a Minimi light machine gun, an anti-tank rocket and the chunky black boxes and red wires of their comms gear. There were NV goggles, two boxes of grenades—fragmentation and white phosphorus—and several small blocks of C4 explosive. All in all, not a cargo they really wanted to start explaining to Iraqi border officials.

They drove in silence for a couple of minutes, before approaching a side road that veered off in a southerly direction. Luke slowed down while Finn took a GPS unit from the glove box. 'This is it,' he said.

To call it a road was overstating things. It was a neglected, stony, bumpy track. Luke took it slowly. The car wasn't up to much, and the last thing they needed was to stop to make running repairs. It had a lot more work to do yet.

They followed the track for ten klicks before going static. The pick-up pulled up a few metres behind them. It was fully dark now, and Luke killed the lights while Finn pulled off his headdress to reveal a mop of black hair, high cheekbones, a black beard and a fake tan just like Luke's. Good-looking and he knew it. They climbed out of the car.

The moon was low and bright, with clouds drifting occasionally past. It lit up the surrounding desert. Luke looked back the way they'd come. He could just make out the headlamps of the occasional vehicle on the main road. At right angles to that road was the Iraqi border. It looked to the two soldiers like a dome of light in the dark desert sky, and beyond it Luke could see more lights in the desert: Iraqi border-control vehicles, no doubt, patrolling the frontier. Get picked up by one of them and they'd be enjoying Saddam's hospitality before they knew it—assuming they survived the initial arrest.

This was still Jordanian territory, though. They needed to find somewhere to cross into Iraq.

The driver of the pick-up joined them. Nigel Foster—Fozzie—was a tall man with a nose that had been broken in two places and a balding head. He was wearing civvies—ripped jeans and an AC/DC T-shirt—and he grinned at Finn. 'What's a nice girl like you doing in a place like this?'

Finn ignored him and removed a kite sight from the boot of the Toyota. The unit had studied the imagery and the intelligence long enough to know that the border was marked by a berm—a low ridge of earth constructed to stop vehicles crossing—as well as, in places, a barbed-wire fence. But they also knew that there were places where the border could be breached. Black-marketeers smuggled their goods into Iraq at these locations. Every border was porous, if you knew where to look.

The night air was still, but suddenly an unsettling noise reached their ears, like a baby screeching. Luke knew that wild dogs roamed the area in packs, lean and hungry. Impossible to tell how close they were—sound travels in strange ways in the desert. But Luke had the distinct impression that they were looking for dinner.

Which wasn't a bad idea. Fozzie returned to the pick-up. Luke got back into the Toyota and got some food down him—a foil pouch of sausage and beans, cold and stodgy—while Finn scanned the border with the kite sight. Every twenty minutes they swapped. The temperature dropped and a chill wind started to whip around the car.

'Nothing,' Finn said after an hour. 'Looks like Abu Dune Coon might be spending another night with the goats before we get to him. Hope he likes the smell of shit.' He handed the kite sight to Luke. 'I hate the fucking desert.'

Luke shrugged. 'There's worse places than this.' He started scanning the border again, running through their objectives in his mind. Abu Famir was an Iraqi academic who had been educated in the West and was an outspoken anti-Baathist. Given Saddam's penchant for disappearing anyone who disagreed with him, Abu Famir had done well to survive this long. Plenty of men with similar politics had ended up rotting away in Abu Ghraib prison or at the bottom of a mass grave.

It was clear the Americans were closing in on Saddam. Nothing to do with his human rights abuses, of course. He'd been happily torturing and killing people even back in the day when the Yanks considered him an ally. No, the politicians had reasons of their own for an invasion. If and when Saddam was deposed, they'd need a new government in place—a government they'd be able to control.

Which was where Abu Famir came in.

War was only weeks away. That was an open secret. The UN weapons inspectors currently combing the country for WMDs weren't looking for evidence; they were looking for excuses—excuses for a war that was going to happen anyway. Half the Regiment was already behind enemy lines, scouting, gathering intelligence, paving the way for an invasion. Luke's unit had a more specific objective: locate Abu Famir, currently in hiding in the Al-Anbar region of western Iraq, and smuggle him back across the Jordanian border. When Saddam and his psychotic sons had gone the way of the dodo, the invaders could bring in Abu Famir and men like him to construct a new administration. The Regiment's target was the man the coalition had earmarked as the new prime minister of Iraq once the regime had been changed.

That was the theory. But first they had to find him.

Local intelligence reports suggested that Abu Famir was hiding out in the village of a Bedouin tribe about 100 miles from the border. The Bedouin were nomadic, herding cattle, sheep and goats, as they had done for hundreds of years. It was accepted even by the Iraqi government that they could wander across the borders into Jordan and Syria. In another time that would have been a good way to smuggle Abu Famir out of the country, but not now. The Iraqi government knew war was around the corner. They'd upped their border controls and even the Bedouin were no longer allowed to cross.

So if they wanted to get Abu Famir back into Jordan, someone had to go and get him. That was where the Regiment came in. Luke and Finn were to infiltrate the border and snatch Abu Famir; Fozzie and the boys in the pick-up were to stay on the Jordanian side, ready to be called in if anything went wrong. And the chances of that happening were higher than normal. They weren't the only people who wanted Abu Famir. It was impossible to say who they might run into.

'I've got something.'

Luke spoke quietly. Through his kite sight he'd located exactly what they'd been looking for. Two vehicles, headlamps switched off to avoid detection, cutting across country, eastwards towards the border. He zoomed in and focused on them. Two klicks away. Here was their passport into Iraq.

He turned to Finn. 'Let's move.'

The light of the moon was bright enough for Luke and Fozzie to operate without headlamps. If the vehicles they'd seen *were* smugglers, they'd get spooked if they clocked a tail. So Luke kept his distance, while Finn maintained eye contact with the vehicles through the kite sight.

'They're slowing down,' he said after they'd been trundling along for half an hour. 'Reckon they're crossing?'

'Could be, buddy,' Luke said. 'Could be.'

They went static again and watched. The vehicles were still, but there was movement around them. 'That's the border,' Luke said. 'Got to be.' Finn climbed out of the car with a Silva compass, already set to adjust for the magnetic variation of the area. He stepped a few paces away so the metal of the vehicle wouldn't affect the needle and quickly took a bearing so that they would be able to locate the crossing point—the smugglers, after all, were unlikely to hang around once they'd penetrated the

72

border.

'Bearing 272 mils,' he mumbled to Luke when he was back at the car, before pulling out his GPS unit and taking a precise fix of their location. Once he knew their lat and long, he opened up his map on the bonnet of the Toyota. The border was clearly marked in red and it was only a moment's work to locate their current position and draw the bearing from it. Where the bearing hit the border, that was their crossing point. He punched the coordinates into his GPS as a separate waypoint before folding the map, giving a quick thumbs up to the guys in the pick-up and getting back into the Toyota.

'Got it?' Luke asked.

'Got it.'

Two minutes later they watched as the vehicles in the distance headed north.

Luke took the Toyota offroad and, following Finn's direction, struggled over the stony desert. Fifteen minutes later they approached the border.

The berm that marked the boundary between Jordan and Iraq was about two metres high, but here there was a small indentation, just wide enough for a vehicle to pass through. On the other side of the berm, however, was a ditch about a metre deep, and beyond that a barbed-wire fence. While it was possible to drive through the berm, it wasn't immediately obvious how the smugglers had crossed the ditch or got through the barbed wire.

As Luke got out to investigate with three of the guys from the pick-up, the cold desert wind blew sand into their eyes. It took them no time to locate two long planks of wood abandoned in the trench. These they used to bridge the gap, then examined the barbed-wire fence. Someone had cut and unfurled it, before closing it back up again so it didn't attract attention. Luke curled the cut wire back and returned to the car. Fozzie had left the pick-up, and now all six Regiment men were standing round the Toyota.

'You'll radio check with base, let them know we've crossed over?' Luke asked.

Fozzie nodded. 'Take care, fellas,' he said. He grinned. 'Hope it's not a one-way ticket.'

'Next time there's an opportunity for one of us to get his bollocks shot off by a raghead,' Luke retorted, 'the job's yours.'

'Deal,' said Fozzie. 'We'll RV in twenty-four hours.'

Luke and Finn got back into the car, and a moment later they were trundling over the planks and through the breach in the fence. In the mirror Luke saw the guys returning everything to normal. He looked at the clock on the Toyota. 22.18. They'd gone from safety to danger in a matter of seconds.

'Welcome to Disneyland,' he muttered, and started driving.

* * *

It was two minutes past midnight when they joined the arterial road that ran west back to the border and east through the desert and eventually to Baghdad. Luke and Finn wouldn't be travelling that far. According to their intel, the Bedouin village they were heading for was approximately eighty miles east of this location. Not far in ordinary circumstances; but behind what were effectively enemy lines, it was a very long way. The road wasn't busy, but occasional vehicles passed in either direction.

They drove in silence. As they passed a large Arabic road sign, Finn turned the radio up slightly and the wailing of an Arabic singer filled the air. 'Voice of a fucking angel,' Luke muttered. Finn said nothing.

They'd been driving for no more than an hour when Luke saw lights up ahead. 'Checkpoint,' he said tersely. It wasn't a surprise. They knew there was one permanent checkpoint between the border and the place where they were intending to turn off into the desert. This was it. 'Hope you've got the lingo, mate,' said Finn.

Luke's Arabic was good, but it wasn't perfect. Not for the first time in the past six years he found himself wishing that his partner on this op was an old friend.

'Guy I know called Chet Freeman,' he murmured. 'We could use him here.'

'The pegleg who caught a frag out in Serbia?'

Luke kept his eyes firmly on the road ahead. 'You call him that again,' he said bluntly, 'I'll waste you here and now. Roadblock or no fucking roadblock.'

Yeah, Chet was a good man in a tight spot. At least he had been once. His days of adventure were at an end. But with a bit of luck, Luke's own language skills would be sufficient to get them across this roadblock.

Finn switched off the radio, removed his Sig from its holster strap, slipped the headdress on again and tucked the weapon into the folds of the burka. Luke pulled over on to the stony ground beside the highway. He removed his own handgun and placed it beside him in the door, before keeping his eyes fixed on the rear-view mirror.

They stayed like that for five minutes, until Luke saw three sets of headlamps approaching from behind. It was better to hit the checkpoint as part of a convoy rather than on their own, as it meant they had less chance of being stopped. A reasonable strategy, but reasonable strategies sometimes have a way of going pear-shaped. As the third vehicle passed—a pick-up not unlike the one the guys were in back at the border—he pulled out into the road and drove towards the checkpoint.

Two hundred metres to go.

A hundred metres. Luke saw another vehicle approaching from behind and gaining on them quickly.

Fifty.

As the vehicle twenty metres ahead started to slow down, Luke did the same. Only now could he make out the details of the checkpoint up ahead. There was a concrete bunker on the side of the road, presumably there to protect the soldiers manning the checkpoint from the sun. The rest of it looked makeshift: two barriers, one for each side of the road; a light-armoured military truck parked up on one side, its headlamps lighting up the road; and—Luke counted them—seven Iraqi soldiers in shabby olive-drab uniforms and black berets. Three of them stood in a group beside the truck, smoking cigarettes, their breath billowing around them in the cold night air; the remaining four were in pairs, each pair manning a barrier.

The vehicle ahead crawled almost to a halt. As it did so, one of the guards raised the barrier and waved it through with a bored expression. He was young, probably just a teenager. Luke checked his mirror. The vehicle that had been approaching them from behind was now only about ten metres away and coming to a halt. Its headlamps dazzled him, but even so he could just make out the shape of a military truck.

Not good. 'We've got company.'

Finn looked over his shoulder. 'Personnel carrier.' His muffled voice was curt. 'But there's a fucking top-gunner . . .'

Luke accelerated slightly to follow the car ahead through the checkpoint while the barrier was still open.

No such luck. The barrier lowered and the soldier raised a palm to stop him.

Finn was looking in the side mirror at the vehicle behind them. 'Republican Guard,' he said, his voice tense. Luke felt his blood pounding in his veins. This was the *last* thing they needed. The Republican Guard with their red berets were the elite of the Iraqi Army. Better trained and better equipped than the shitkicking squaddies who were probably manning the checkpoint as part of their national service. Ordinary citizens referred to the Republican Guard as *zanabeer*—wasps— on account of the way they swarmed around the country. If things went noisy now, the SAS men would have a truckload of the fuckers—maybe twenty of them—swarming around the Toyota, and that was a scrap Luke didn't fancy. He checked his own mirror. Sure enough, he could see the driver of the truck leaning out of his window, his red beret fully on display. Luke sensed Finn gripping his pistol. 'Looks like we might be calling Fozzie in earlier than we thought,' Finn said, his lips hardly

77

moving.

Luke couldn't answer. A second young soldier had approached the driver's side, so he wound down the window. There was no greeting. The soldier shone a torch into the car while his colleague walked round to the back.

'*Salam*,' Luke muttered as the light fell on his face.

The soldier gave him a sharp look. Had he noticed a chink in Luke's accent? The cold night air bit his skin, but Luke still felt sweat soaking his back as he glanced in the rear-view mirror. The figure of the first guard was silhouetted against the lights of the Republican Guard truck.

He was right by the boot of the Toyota.

If he opened it, they'd have no choice: Luke moved his arm down to his side, inches from his gun.

There was a shout, and both soldiers looked round. The Republican Guard driver from behind was yelling something at them. Luke couldn't tell what he was saying, but he understood the tone of voice as this higher-ranking soldier bellowed orders at the two Iraqi squaddies like they were a piece of shit on his shoe. Fear crossed their faces as they hurried back to the barrier and started to raise it, all thoughts of Luke and his dodgy accent apparently gone.

Luke didn't fuck about. He sped through the barrier the moment it was high enough to pass. As he reached the other side he saw that the military truck was flashing its lights at him. Moments later it overtook and stormed down the road ahead.

Finn let out an explosive breath. 'Thought I was going to have to waste a round on that fucker,' he

78

said, his voice muffled behind the burka, as they continued to drive into the darkness.

'Would have been a shame to get your glad rags all bloody.' Luke checked his mirror. Nobody from the checkpoint was following. And up ahead, the truck was out of sight.

The road was poor—potholed and broken down by the countless heavy military vehicles that had passed along it over the previous two decades. At 01.00 they passed some buildings by the side of the road—a filling station and a mosque next to each other, where several cars had stopped. Luke and Finn had no need of prayer or fuel—there were canisters of petrol in the boot, along with their more specialised gear—so they just pressed on.

At 02.12 they came to a fork in the road. Luke bore left, then doubled back, heading north-west up towards the Syrian border. Guided by Finn's GPS, he soon took a right-hand turn off the main road and into the desert. He drove on for some ten kilometres before Finn quietly spoke.

'Let's go static,' he said. 'The village is about two klicks up ahead.'

Luke came to a halt and killed the lights. 02.58. Three hours till sunrise. They'd be entering the village at dawn. Lift Abu Famir and then swastika it back to Jordan.

But until then they'd just have to wait.

SEVEN

Chet had lost count of the number of pints of cold Stella he'd chucked down his neck that afternoon. He'd headed straight for a basement pub just off Leicester Square where the barmaid looked like a bulldog licking piss off a thistle. He celebrated his birthday surrounded first by the office workers in for a liquid lunch, then by tourists taking the weight off their feet after a day's sightseeing, and finally by the office workers again, boisterous and increasingly arseholed now work was over.

But Chet had barely noticed any of them. As he sank the beers, he couldn't stop thinking about the events of that morning. There had been rumblings over the past few days about an anti-war march through London. If it went ahead, Suze McArthur was exactly the kind of leftie who'd be up at the front waving some wanky banner for the TV crews. Chet was the kind of person who'd be at home. The last people asked their opinion about a war, he knew, were those who'd been in one. And if the girl was surprised that the decision to move into Iraq had already been taken, she was more naive than most. 'This war is good to go,' the American had said. Well, of course it was. When the hell did people think decisions like that were taken—the day before troops moved in?

No, it wasn't Suze with her wild eyes and embroidered nose who kept coming to the front of Chet's mind. It was Stratton. What was so important that he had to come to meet an American businessman, rather than the Yank going to him? Why was he talking to the Grosvenor Group in some anonymous office and not in Number 10? And what did the Grosvenor Group have to do with it anyway?

Fuck it, Chet thought as he signalled to the bulldog for another pint of Stella. Not his business. As long as he kept pulling the pay cheques, the suits could discuss whatever the hell they wanted. Trouble was, after today's bollocking he didn't know how long the pay cheques would carry on coming.

At 22.30 he'd gathered up his rucksack of gear and staggered to the tube. Time to get his head down.

As he left Seven Sisters station, the cold was sobering. He walked as briskly as he could down the main road and into his little side street of terraced houses and maisonettes. The street lamps bathed the pavement in a yellow glow, but only a handful of houses had lights on in any windows. The booze and the darkness meant that he fumbled slightly as he unlocked his own front door. Once he was in, he slammed the door behind him and made his way in the darkness along the narrow hallway and towards the kitchen.

As he stood in the doorway of the kitchen he saw a red light flashing. The answer machine on the work surface, indicating a single message was waiting for him. His rucksack still slung over his back, Chet stomped into the kitchen and, still in darkness, pressed the play button.

He half expected it to be his amputee friend Doug, berating him. It wasn't. A voice—female, posh and brisk—filled the kitchen. 'Good afternoon, Mr Freeman. This is Angela Glover,

81

Grosvenor Group human resources. I've been instructed to inform you that your services are no longer required by the gr . . .'

Angela Glover, whoever the hell she was, didn't get to finish her message, because Chet had pulled the wires from the back of the answer machine and hurled it to the floor. The cheap plastic shattered against the floor, and Chet made to stamp on it with his good heel. 'Fucking *bitch* . . .'

'You should learn to calm your temper.'

Whoever had entered Chet's kitchen behind him had done so in absolute silence. Chet felt the unmistakable sensation of cold metal against the back of his head.

He froze.

'I'll explain what's going to happen.' The intruder was female, her voice quiet and throaty, with an accent Chet couldn't quite place—not American, exactly, but as though she'd learned English from a Yank.

'You're going to tell me the name of the woman you spoke to outside the meeting room today. If you do that, you might live to see morning.'

'And if I don't?'

'Do you really need me to answer that?'

No, he thought. Not really . . .

Chet's eyes were getting used to the dark, but he knew that in the absence of light his peripheral vision was the strongest. He used that now. To his left, within reach, was the half-eaten loaf of bread from that morning, with the kitchen knife lying to its side.

'I didn't speak to anyone,' he said.

Get her talking, he figured. Then, when I make my move, she'll be distracted.

82

No reply. Just the continued pressure of a weapon against the back of his skull.

'Feel like telling me how you got into my flat?'

'I feel like killing you. I'm going to count to five. If I don't have a name by the end of it, that's what I'll do. One.'

He could grab the knife with his left hand. It wouldn't take much to overpower this woman, whoever she was.

'Two.'

His fingers twitched.

'Thr . . .'

Chet yanked his head to the left just as he grabbed the knife and spun round. He didn't fuck around with threats: he just sliced the blade into the back of the intruder's gun hand. She cursed as the weapon fell to the floor, but used her good hand to swipe a blow at Chet.

It wasn't just the force behind that blow that surprised him; it was the training too. The side of the intruder's hand dug sharply into Chet's neck, startling him momentarily and giving her the opportunity to raise her right leg and kick him hard in the stomach. Chet stumbled back, the wind knocked from him and his balance shaky. He saw the woman a metre in front of him, bending down to pick up the gun that she'd dropped, and he knew that he only had moments. This woman was a pro, no doubt about it, and she wasn't going to give him a second chance.

He barged towards her, using all the strength in his good leg and the advantage of his greater bulk to knock her out of the way. She clattered against his rickety oven, and as she did so, he listened for the sound of the gun being knocked out of her hand again. He didn't hear it, but she hissed something in a language Chet didn't recognise: *'Harah!'*

And then there was a gunshot.

The weapon was suppressed, so the sound it made was just a dull thud. Chet saw a spark as the round left the barrel and he felt it whizz just inches from his hip before it thumped into the wall.

She could fire another round in seconds. Chet had to get out of there.

He didn't give her time to re-aim, but burst out of the kitchen and hurtled back along the hallway, all traces of his previous inebriation a memory. When he got to the front door, he could hear the woman coming out of the kitchen. He could almost sense her raising the weapon again.

As he stepped over the threshold and pulled the door closed behind him, a second round splintered the wood from the inside. Chet limped down the pathway and round to the far side of his dented Mondeo, where he ducked out of sight.

He froze, his heart pumping furiously, and he listened carefully.

At first there was nothing. Then, after about ten seconds, footsteps. The shooter had turned left out of his house and was heading off down the street fast. Chet pulled the keys from his pocket, unlocked the driver's door and entered. He threw the rucksack of gear on to the passenger seat, turned the key in the ignition and the engine jumped into life. The tyres screeched as he pulled out into the road and sped away. Chet glanced in the rear-view mirror as he accelerated. He could just see her, standing on the pavement, lit up by a street lamp, looking in his direction: black clothes, wavy black hair down below her shoulders, full lips, a beautiful, angry face.

And as Chet turned left out of his road, his mind was ablaze with questions. Who was she? How did she get into his flat? And why the *hell* had she just tried to kill him?

EIGHT

05.00 hrs.

Just under an hour till dawn. Luke and Finn could see the Bedouin village up ahead.

They'd approached slowly, keeping the engine noise to a minimum. In the distance they had seen the lights of what they assumed to be Iraqi border patrol vehicles. If they were discovered by one of these, things could get messy. But the desert was big and they were small. Nobody saw them.

Now they had left the car and were approaching on foot. They were on a dusty track that bore tyre marks but also animal footprints. On either side the terrain was dotted with boulders and low brush. Five minutes after they left the Toyota they passed a rusting car chassis. God knows how long it had been there. Years, probably.

Finn had changed out of his burka and into grubby gear much like Luke's. They had both used the cover of darkness to double-check the gear packed away in their ops waistcoats that were hidden under their *dishdashes*: magazines for their pistols, grenades, Plasticuffs. Their disco guns were fitted to their ankles, but their main weapons were closer at hand. They had each looped a piece of bungee cord in a figure of eight around the butt of their carbine, then threaded this around their arms so the weapon itself was hanging underneath their armpits—well disguised by the *dishdash* but accessible in a split second. With luck, they'd be in and out, but they didn't know what was waiting for them up ahead, so they had to be prepared. And that meant packing some heavy shit.

Within ten minutes of leaving the car, they could see the outskirts of the village. They checked it out through the kite sight. It was a poor place—a seemingly random agglomeration of about twenty breeze-block houses, each a single storey high and with a shallow-sloping corrugated-iron roof. About 200 metres from the outermost of the houses was the shell of an older dwelling. The blockwork had crumbled, there was no roof and an old acacia tree, heavy under its own weight, had grown through one of the walls. Luke pointed at it. 'We'll set up an OP there,' he said.

Finn nodded and together they headed for the derelict house. They were ten metres away when there was a sudden movement. Both men instinctively went for their weapons, only to see a beady-eyed goat scramble to its feet and put a few metres between itself and them. The bell round its neck gave a repeated dull clunk as it moved, and its breath steamed as it watched them make their way into the OP. The ground was covered with rubbish—old tins, rusting jerrycans and sturdy branches from the acacia tree. A gap in one wall where a window used to be formed a perfect place from which they could observe the village, and Finn took up position here. He pulled an A4 photograph and a pencil-thin red-filtered torch from under his robe. It was a satellite image of the tiny village.

Each house was easily identifiable—there were twenty-two in total, and they were mostly set in a rough circle around a central courtyard—and one of them had been circled in black marker. This, if their intelligence was correct, was where they would find Abu Famir.

The two Regiment men examined the image together. Within seconds they had identified their OP, which was on the southern edge of the village, just east of the track leading into it. Their target location was on the north-eastern edge of the village, backed by an area of low brush and with a solitary tree growing about ten metres behind. Finn handed the photo to Luke, before bending down with his kite sight and scanning the darkness.

'I've got eyes on,' he said after a minute. He stood back so that Luke could have a look.

It took Luke about thirty seconds to take everything in. The central courtyard was about forty metres wide and littered here and there with large objects that were difficult to make out from this distance. The shell of another abandoned car? A collection of disused oil drums? Wandering around these objects were a number of animals—more goats, Luke assumed. The tree that they had noted on the satellite image was easy to make out; just beyond it Luke could see the target house. It was no different to any of the others: just a poor, blockwork dwelling with no windows and an iron roof.

Luke stepped back from the kite sight. 'We wait till first light,' he said. 'Then we move in.'

Finn nodded, and went back to surveying the village through the kite sight.

Within less than twenty minutes the cold, grey

light of dawn was starting to push back the inky night sky. Luke and Finn were ready. This was the best time to lift their target. It was dark enough to give them a bit of cover if they needed it, early enough for nobody to be about, and sufficiently late that any noise they made wouldn't cause alarm. As they'd been waiting, a couple more goats had wandered up to the OP. That could be to their advantage. Luke selected a thin, sturdy acacia branch, about a metre long. If he could use that to guide a few goats into the village, they would look like Bedouin wanderers.

They stepped out from the OP. Three goats had congregated about ten metres away. Luke approached slowly, making a clicking sound in the corner of his mouth. One of the goats bolted, its bell jangling noisily as it disappeared into the night; but the remaining two lingered. The musty smell of the beasts and their shit reached Luke's nose; when he tapped one of them firmly on its haunch, it made a shuddering sound. Another tap and both animals started wandering in the direction of the village.

A thick silence surrounded them—a silence in which the clanking of the goats' bells and their own footsteps sounded deafening. Luke brandished his acacia branch firmly, but he also kept his left arm loosely by his side, ready to access his carbine. But at the moment there was nobody around. The goats in the central courtyard gazed at them curiously as the two SAS men stood at the edge of the settlement and looked in. The object Luke had seen through the kite sight was indeed the deserted chassis of an old car; and as they ventured further in, he could feel some residual warmth from the oil drums. Clearly someone had lit a fire in them the previous night.

Thirty metres to the target. Luke tapped one of the goats, and the men walked side by side past the oil drums and towards the building where they hoped to find Abu Famir.

From the corner of his eye, Luke sensed movement.

Somebody had appeared from one of the houses at their ten o'clock, no more than twenty metres away. Luke looked closely at the figure. It was a boy, no more than twelve years old, though his face already bore the ravages of a hard life. His body did too. The bottom half of his left leg was missing and he was able to stand only with the aid of a sturdy stick nestled under his left armpit. He wore a heavy cloth robe and a brightly coloured hat, and in his right hand he was carrying a metal bucket. He stared at the two strangers with wide eyes full of mistrust.

'You clocked the kid?' Luke murmured.

'Roger that,' replied Finn.

As he spoke, there was more movement. The door of the target house—distance, twenty-five metres—was opening.

Then—*fuck!* Four figures emerged from the house. They were all wearing plain Arabic dress, though one was a lot older than the others. He had a short white beard and little round glasses, and Luke immediately recognised him from pictures he'd seen: Abu Famir. The man's eyes darted around.

As they exited the building, the younger men surrounded the Iraqi academic. They were not quite so dark of skin, and they each carried an MP5 Kurz. They made no attempt to hide their weapons and held them like they knew how to use them. Abu Famir had good reason to seem on edge: it looked like Saddam's men had already caught up with him.

Luke and Finn stopped dead in their tracks. Abu Famir's entourage did the same.

The two groups of men stared at each other, nothing but three old oil drums and two goats between them.

And then there was a shout.

It came from the lame boy. He had dropped his bucket and was pointing furiously at Luke and Finn. His words were a little garbled, but Luke had enough Arabic to work out what he was saying.

'They have stolen the goats!'

Abu Famir's guards quickly looked at each other, as if deciding what to do; but the two goats had already made their decision. Clearly startled by the boy's shouts, they turned and bolted. One of them collided with Finn, who was momentarily knocked back. His *dishdash* twisted, revealing the bottom couple of inches of his carbine's barrel.

One of the men shouted. He had seen the weapon, and was raising his.

'Get down!' Luke yelled, and both men hit the ground just soon enough to avoid a burst from the MP5 thundering into them. It hit the oil drums in the middle of the courtyard, causing a harsh, metallic sound to ring out across the air, and puncturing entry and exit holes in the metal. By now, though, the SAS men had accessed their own weapons. And that was bad news for the ragheads.

The guy who'd just fired his MP5 was the first to get it: two rounds, one from Finn, one from Luke, both full in the face. His features seemed to explode, and he was thrown back violently against

90

the front wall of the house, his blood soiling Abu Famir's grey robe as he fell. The boy was stumbling back into his house, but Luke's attention was already on their target's remaining companions. One of them—the taller of the two—was taking aim at Finn; the other was just behind Abu Famir.

The taller man fired a burst in Finn's direction, just as one of the goats bolted between them. The animal's squealing was cut short as rounds from the MP5 hacked into its flesh, ripping a seam along its side and spewing its entrails. Finn wasn't hit, but Luke knew his mate wouldn't get a second chance. He fired, and delivered another headshot to this trigger-happy Arab, who spun down into the dust.

The man behind Abu Famir was short and stocky, with rumpled dark hair and sharp dark eyes. He raised his weapon to fire over the academic's shoulder, but as he did so Abu Famir—his face full of fright and his glasses skewiff on his face—began to run.

'Get him!' Finn roared at Luke as he fired at the remaining companion, catching him not in his face, but at the top of his left shoulder. The guy went down like a sack of shit, and the two SAS men scrambled to their feet. Luke headed right, following Abu Famir the way he had run—fast for an old man—round the back of the house; Finn went in the opposite direction.

The back of the house was like a junkyard: rolls of barbed wire lay beside old tyres and metal troughs. There was a vehicle parked here—a modern black 4 x 4. They found the old Iraqi pinned against the far side of the vehicle, his eyes wild and his body shaking. He had the expression of a man who was sure he was about to die. He shook

91

his head as he saw Finn and Luke advancing on him; and although he had opened his mouth to say something, no words came.

Finn grabbed Abu Famir by the collar of his robe while Luke checked the vehicle. The key was hanging in the ignition. *'Get him in!'* he barked.

Finn opened up the back seat and bundled Abu Famir inside, then took a seat next to him, rolled down the window and propped his weapon through the opening while Luke took the driver's seat and started the engine. As he put his foot down, Abu Famir started jabbering in Arabic. 'Shut the fuck up!' said Luke as the vehicle started to move.

But the Iraqi wouldn't quieten down. 'British?' he asked anxiously in English.

'Bullseye,' Luke growled as the car accelerated round the corner of the house.

'Where are you taking me?'

'Jordan. All expenses paid.'

'Jordan? But . . .'

He didn't finish what he was saying. As Luke drove into the main courtyard, he checked over his shoulder. The two corpses hadn't moved, of course, but the stocky third man—the one Finn had caught in his shoulder—was up on his knees, one hand pressed against his badly bleeding wound.

'Down him!' Luke shouted at Finn.

'NO!' Abu Famir's voice was strangely high-pitched, and as Finn prepared to take the shot, the Iraqi threw his thin body against him. Finn fired, but the shot went awry and by the time he had pushed Abu Famir away, the vehicle was halfway across the courtyard: the angles were wrong and Finn's face was stormy.

'You must go back for him,' Abu Famir shouted.

92

'You've got a fucking death wish, mate,' Luke said as he continued to burn the 4 x 4 across the courtyard.

'They weren't here to kill me. They are my brothers—Jordanians—here to *help* me. We were preparing to leave together and you killed them . . .'

Luke hit the brakes. 'What are you talking about?'

Abu Famir's frightened eyes darted from one man to the other. 'They were here to help me.' He twisted round to look out of the rear window. 'But he . . . he is *not* Jordanian. He is Iraqi . . . my colleague, in hiding with me. You cannot leave him there to die . . .'

'Fucking try me,' Finn muttered. He turned to Luke. 'Let's get the hell out of here,' he said.

But something stopped Luke from hitting the gas. Their orders were clear: get Abu Famir out of Iraq. Nothing more, nothing less. Even so, sometimes on the ground you had to adapt.

Abu Famir started up again. 'If Saddam goes, my friend will be an important man. Yes, a *very* important man . . . my deputy . . . he must be saved . . .'

'Finn,' Luke instructed. 'Shut him up.'

His mate held his weapon against Abu Famir's body. 'You heard him,' he said. And then: 'Jesus, Luke—what are you *doing*?'

Luke had gone into reverse and was now speeding back towards the house. He didn't answer his friend, but when he was ten metres from where the wounded man was lying, he hit the brakes and the 4 x 4 screeched to a halt. He jumped out and ran round to where the guy was lying, keenly aware that seven or eight Bedouin men had come out of their homes and were looking towards the site of the firefight, though they kept their distance.

It was immediately obvious that the guy was in a mess. The blood from his wound had almost fully saturated the robe he was wearing; his face was pale, his lips slightly blue; his right hand was pressed against his left shoulder where the bullet had entered, and blood was oozing between his fingers.

Luke got out of the vehicle and strode towards him. The man, trembling violently, whispered, '*Harah, harah, harah*...' Then he reached for his MP5, which was lying on the ground about three metres from where he had fallen, but Luke got there first, grabbed the weapon and stood over him.

The man's eyes widened and he stopped muttering. He stared at the weapon in Luke's hand. '*Lo*...' he whispered. '*Lo*...'

Luke bent over, grabbed the injured man just under his good shoulder and pulled him roughly to his feet. He gasped in pain and it took all Luke's strength to keep him upright. He yanked him towards the 4 x 4 and bundled him into the passenger seat, ignoring his hollers of pain. In the process the man's blood smeared Luke's own robe.

The Bedouin men watched impotently as this scene unfolded in front of them. Maybe they were used to such horrors; maybe they were just scared to get involved. Either way, Luke floored it out of the place, acutely aware that Finn didn't agree with what he'd just done. Tough shit. He was calling the shots and he'd made his decision.

Within a couple of minutes they had reached the Toyota and come to a halt. As the two SAS men climbed out of the 4 x 4, Finn yelled, 'For fuck's sake, look at him. He's going to compromise us.'

Luke opened the boot of the Toyota, took out a med pack and handed it to Finn. 'Let's get them into our vehicle. You can treat him on the go.'

'Treat him? You're fucking losing it, Luke. Let's just nail the bastard now and get out of here.'

Luke ignored him. 'We're going to get right away from the village, then get on the radio to base, tell them what's happening. If the order comes through to extract him too, that's what we'll do. If not, we waste him. Now stop fucking arguing and let's move.'

He walked round to the other side of the 4 x 4, opened the door and dragged the wounded man back towards the Toyota.

NINE

Two and a half thousand miles away, in a poky top-floor studio flat just off Edgware Road in London, Suze McArthur was half asleep on the sofa.

The sofa was covered with an embroidered ethnic throw that Suze had bought on a shopping trip with friends to Camden Market. The friends had long since deserted her for jobs and husbands and kids, no longer content with the world of student marches and protests. Suze would be thirty in just two months. The throw had adorned the sofas in the various bedsits she'd rented ever since college, her job as a midwife never allowing her to afford anything bigger.

In front of the sofa was a small wooden chest

that doubled as a table, on which a patchouli joss stick had almost burned down to the end. Next to the joss stick was a Dictaphone loaded with a C90 cassette. There was only one picture on the wall—a slightly crumpled old *X-Files* poster showing Mulder and Scully, arms folded and back to back, looking down into the room. A TV was on in the corner and on top of the set there was a photograph: a picture of Suze with her arm around a much older lady sitting in a wheelchair, a pink hyacinth blooming in the background. The floor was covered with newspaper cuttings, and in one corner a lava lamp shone dimly.

Dramatic music from the TV, and Suze came to. Her last memory was of watching *100 Worst Serial Killers*, some crap American rubbish. She looked at her watch. Half past eleven. The big-haired female presenter was standing outside a forbidding Victorian building. Slowly Suze tuned in to what she was saying.

'It is here, in Broadmoor psychiatric hospital in Berkshire, England, that the man known as the Yorkshire Ripper lives, and it is here that he will most probably die.'

A familiar orange-backed picture of a black-haired man appeared on the screen.

'In 1981 Stuart Sutcliffe was convicted of the murder of thirteen women. The Ripper claimed during his trial that a voice in his head had instructed him to kill prostitutes, and that this was the voice of God. The Yorkshire Ripper is not the only serial killer to have made such claims. A significant number have made similar assertions that God . . .'

Suze fumbled for the remote control and turned the TV off. She shivered. Some things were better not watched alone and in the dark. That included tales of serial killers and religious nuts. She remembered something she'd read a long time ago: the world is divided into good people and bad people. Good people will do good things, bad people will do bad things. But for good people to do bad things takes religion.

Good people. Bad people. Sometimes, she thought to herself, it was difficult to tell the difference.

She got down on her knees and starting collecting the clippings. A jumble of headlines that she'd read a hundred times before filled her mind. 'PROFITS SOAR . . . AEROSPACE INDUSTRY ON UPWARD TRAJECTORY . . . MANAGEMENT BUYOUT BOOSTS STOCKS'. When she had them in a pile, she placed them all back in the box file where they lived, and on the spine of which she had written two words in clear black marker pen: 'GROSVENOR GROUP'. She carried it to the other side of the room, where she slotted it into its place on a rickety Ikea bookshelf, next to an identical box file with a single word written on the side: 'STRATTON'.

Her pretty face curled into an expression of dislike.

She went over to look out of the room's one small window. From here she could see the street below—Wimbourne Terrace—and, above the opposite roofs, the A40 flyover, with plenty of cars travelling in either direction even at this time of night. She turned and looked back into the room, and her eyes fell on the Dictaphone.

Maybe she should take the tape to the press. Make it all public. But did she trust them? And would they believe her anyway, even with the

97

evidence?

Suze shook her head. The truth was, she didn't trust anybody. She had gone to such lengths to acquire the contents of that tape on the table—it made her feel sick, the memory of the danger in which she'd put herself—and now she wasn't only afraid of its contents, she was afraid to do anything with it!

You're fucking crazy. The words of the man with the limp who had caught her on the rooftop earlier that day rang in her head. She winced as she thought of the things she'd threatened him with. Shameful things.

Maybe he was right.

Maybe she *was* crazy.

Maybe these bastards had dragged her down with them.

Perhaps she should throw the tape away? Burn it. Forget she'd ever heard its contents and just get on with her life. Get herself a husband and some kids, like all her friends had. Like her mum had tried to persuade her to do for so many years, until her mind had started to wander.

But she knew she wasn't going to do that. She knew what she'd heard. And even if she didn't yet know the full story, she knew she had to do something to stop it.

Suze put the Dictaphone on the bookshelf alongside her research files, then found herself a blanket and snuggled up on the sofa again. She needed a clear head, and for a clear head she needed sleep.

Whether sleep would come, with all these thoughts spinning around in her mind, was a different matter entirely.

*   *   *

Chet drove.

His mind was racing. What the *fuck* had happened? Who was the intruder? Who had tried to kill him?

You're going to tell me the name of the woman you spoke to outside the meeting room today. If you do that, you might live to see morning.

Suze McArthur. That pale-faced redhead with a stud in her nose and the smell of incense in her clothes had someone running scared. But who? And why?

He remembered what he'd overheard on the rooftop. *Trust me, Prime Minister Stratton. This war is good to go . . . the Americans are all on board. The question is, how are* you *going to get it through . . . ?*

Was that enough to persuade someone to make an attempt on his life? No way. Chet knew the decision to take out an individual like that was never made lightly—especially if the hit had to be carried out on home turf. Too many things could go wrong. Killing someone was easy; covering it up was more difficult. The conspiracy theorists loved the idea that the intelligence agencies would think nothing of assassinating suspected terrorists or troublesome members of the royal family, but that was bullshit.

And in any case, the woman in his flat had *not* been British. As he drove, Chet desperately tried to place her accent. *'Harah!'* she had said. Chet was a first-class Regiment linguist, and he thought the word seemed familiar, but he couldn't quite place it.

99

It was just past midnight when he turned off Euston Road to drive down Gower Street and into the West End. He parked his car in the NCP on Wardour Street, hid his rucksack underneath the passenger seat and limped through the maze of red neon, pubs and sex shops. A woman, comfortably in her forties and with too much make-up on, called to him from a doorway. 'Looking for a bit of business, love?'

He put his head down.

'Beggars can't be choosers, darling!' The woman's voice had turned angry when she realised she was being ignored.

Chet carried on towards Trafalgar Square, and from there to Whitehall. He walked down the opposite side to number 132 and stood for a moment observing the entrance. He didn't really know what he was looking for—maybe an unmarked van parked suspiciously nearby; individuals carrying out surveillance in the street. He knew the signs to look for and right now he saw none of them, so he crossed the road and made his way into the building.

The big, marble-floored atrium was entirely empty, with the exception of a solitary security guard on reception—different to the guy Chet had spoken to that morning. He had black skin and dreadlocks and was reading a copy of the *Sun*. He glanced up when Chet was a couple of metres from the reception.

Chet smiled at him. 'Graveyard shift, mate?'

The guard put down his newspaper and Chet noticed that he'd been examining page 3. 'You said it, brother,' he sighed.

Chet looked around, then leaned in a bit

closer. 'I wondered if you could help me out with something.'

'Ain't no one here this time of night,' the guard replied. 'Except me, of course.' He prodded the newspaper. 'And Delightful Debs from Dagenham.' He laughed, and Chet joined in.

'Not looking for someone here. I'm looking for someone who *was* here,' said Chet. 'A chick.'

A broad grin crossed the guard's face.

'I did a little security job here this morning. The name's Chet Freeman. Check your computer if you like.'

The guard shrugged and tapped at the keyboard of his terminal. 'Yeah,' he said after a moment. 'I got you.'

'So I got talking to this girl. Said her name was Suze. Cleaning lady. Redhead. Kind of . . .' Chet made a gesture with his hands to indicate a shapely figure. 'Should have got her number there and then, I guess . . .'

A troubled look came on to the guard's face. 'Ah, I don't know, man. I'm not supposed to give that kind of information out. You know, home addresses and shit.'

'Hey, course not. I understand. I was just thinking, you know, maybe a phone number . . . if you had it . . .'

He winked at the guard, who gave an amused shake of the head and replied, 'I don't know, brother. She must have been pretty cute for you to come chasing after her at this time of night.'

'Yeah. Or maybe I'm just desperate.'

The guard laughed, then once more tapped on his keyboard. 'Suze McArthur?' he asked.

'That's my girl.'

101

'She's a temp. Only worked here yesterday.' The guard scrawled a number on a yellow Post-It note and handed it to Chet. 'Hope you get yourself some pussy, brother.'

Chet grinned. 'You and me both, my friend.'

He turned and walked out of the building, the square of paper clasped firmly in his right hand.

It took him half an hour to get back to his car. It would have taken him less, but he went a roundabout way, down quiet side streets where he could look back and check he wasn't being followed. By the time he'd got back to his vehicle, his leg was killing him—sharp, stabbing pains shooting from the stump up into the thigh, and a nagging soreness where flesh met prosthesis. It was a relief to sit behind the wheel. He drove out of the West End, pulling over on Tottenham Court Road to check he wasn't being trailed, before heading to Aldenham Street in the maze between Camden and Euston Station. There were modern housing blocks on either side, but the street was deserted at this time of night and he parked in the gloom below a broken street lamp. He recovered his rucksack and removed one of the bulky mobile phones that he'd used to debug the offices earlier.

Seconds later he was dialling Suze's number.

It rang six times.

Seven.

He was about to hang up when a voice came on the line. It was sleepy.

'Hello?'

'Suze McArthur?'

'What . . . who is this?' The girl sounded suspicious. Frightened.

'Your friend from the roof.'

102

A pause.

'How did you get my number?' Her voice cracked slightly.

'How did *you* get your hands on a laser listening device?'

Silence.

'I let you escape today,' he said finally. 'You owe me. I want to know what you thought you were listening . . .'

'I'm hanging up.' Suze's voice was wavering as she interrupted him.

'Don't you fucking dare.'

'I'm hanging up . . .' She sounded like a scared kid standing up to a bully. 'I'm hanging up *now*.'

A click on the line, then silence.

'Fuck's sake,' Chet muttered. He dialled the number again, but this time it rang out.

He chucked the phone on to the passenger seat, leaned back against the headrest and closed his eyes. He was dead beat. The beer, the scuffle at the flat, walking too far with his bad leg—it was all taking its toll. He ought to rest, but rest wasn't on the menu. He'd be insane to go back home, but he needed somewhere to lie low. Where he couldn't be found. Somewhere to get his head in order. With someone he could trust.

But as far as Chet was concerned, trustworthy people were as rare as a nun in a bikini. If Luke Mercer was in the country, Chet would already be on the way to Hereford. But he wasn't, and in the absence of his old SAS mucker, there was only one other person he would even think of approaching. He picked up his phone and called a number that he knew by heart.

It rang for several seconds before a voice

answered. 'Who the hell . . . ?'

'Doug, it's me. Chet.'

A heavy sigh. 'Jesus, Chet. What time is it?'

'I don't know—about 01.00? Listen, mate, I need a favour.'

'Chet, this a wind-up? You been on the beers?'

'No. Yes, but . . . look, can you meet me?'

A pause.

'Now?'

'Now. It's important.'

'Mate, I can't. I'm out of town. Trains are done for the day. You never called—I went to the girlfriend's place.'

Chet vaguely remembered Doug saying that his latest squeeze lived somewhere south of town. Mitcham Junction, was it?

'Plus,' Doug continued, 'it's one o'clock in the fucking morning.'

Chet cursed silently, his brain still racing.

'Can you RV first thing?'

'I guess . . .'

'Clapham Junction. Platform 15—one five—06.30.'

'Fine. Look, Chet, what the hell's this all about?'

I wish I knew, Chet thought to himself.

'06.30,' he repeated. 'Don't be late.'

He hung up before Doug could reply.

Chet threw the phone down again and caught himself checking the rear-view mirror. Checking for what? He didn't know, but he knew his heart was racing and his mouth was dry.

Fear? Damn right. But that didn't mean he was going to succumb to it. He kept his gaze on the mirror, and prepared to sit it out till morning.

Suze McArthur stared at her phone like it was a snake. She was shaking. How had that guy tracked her down? Who was he working for?

A chill sickness welled up in her stomach. She found herself shivering, and felt as though all the strength had left her limbs. She pulled her blanket more tightly around her, but that did no good.

A noise in the corridor outside.

Suze heard herself gasp.

It was nothing, she told herself. She remembered being a child, terrified by strange sounds after her lights had been turned out. Her doctor father, when he was not away, would come in and smooth down her hair. 'There's no one here, princess,' he'd whisper. 'Just Mummy and Daddy, and we won't let anything scare you. All you can hear is our old house creaking. That's what happens at night.'

But there was nobody here to smooth her hair down now. Her father was dead, killed by a landmine in Angola when he was out there tending to sick children. Her mother couldn't look after herself, let alone Suze.

Another noise. 'It's just the old house creaking,' she whispered to herself.

The front door was locked. The windows too.

So why didn't she feel safe?

It crossed her mind that she could go downstairs. Sometimes she picked up groceries for Vern and Dorothy, the sweet old couple who lived underneath her. She'd become friends with them. They were always on her case, telling her she should be settling down with a nice young man. A week ago they'd gone off on a cruise of the Norwegian fjords, and had left their key with Suze, just in case. But something prevented her even from moving, let alone venturing down the staircase in the middle of the night.

I should get out of here, she thought. Go somewhere else for a few days. Get my head straight.

That's what she'd do. First thing in the morning. Pack a bag. Get out of London.

But morning seemed a long way off. She glanced over her shoulder at the front door. She *had* locked it, hadn't she?

Another chill ran through her. She felt too scared to get up and check.

*   *   *

03.26 hrs.

Chet awoke suddenly.

It took him a few seconds to remember why he was sitting behind the wheel of his car in this dark side street, and he cursed himself for having dropped off. He was frozen. Somewhere in the distance he could hear a police siren. But this street was quiet.

Almost.

He squinted in the gloom. Through the windscreen he could see a figure up ahead. Twenty metres away, max, and walking towards him.

Instinctively, Chet felt his fingers creeping towards the ignition key. The figure was moving quickly. At fifteen metres, he could make out that it was a woman. Slim. He couldn't see her face, not in the darkness.

The angry features of the intruder in his flat

flashed through his mind.

Ten metres. Chet started the engine and put the lights on full beam. The figure stopped, throwing her hands up to her face, alarmed by the sudden glare. When her hands moved away, Chet saw that her skin was elderly and wrinkled, her hair grey and her clothes old. She cast a fearful look in Chet's direction, then turned heel and hurried off.

Just an old woman wandering the streets at night. Chet turned off the engine and the lights, aware of a damp patch of sweat against his back despite the coldness of the air. He cursed his paranoia. Of *course* nobody knew where he was.

He checked his watch. 03.28. Three hours till he RV'd with Doug. It couldn't come soon enough.

* * *

06.23 hrs.

Early, but the main roads of London were already crammed with traffic. The bus drivers were beeping their horns in frustration at each other as their headlamps glowed in the semi-darkness.

Commuters were already hurrying into Clapham Junction in their suits and overcoats, beating the crowds as they gripped their briefcases and free sheets and paper cups from Starbucks with plastic lids. Their breath steamed in the cold morning air, and nobody seemed in any way interested in anyone else around them.

Certainly nobody gave Chet a second glance as he queued up to buy a ticket from the machine. He decided to use cash rather than his card—too easy to trace.

Ticket in hand, he walked along the covered

walkway from which a number of flights of wide stairs led down to the platforms. The sound of trains arriving and departing was everywhere. Station announcements echoed over the Tannoy. Chet checked his watch. 06.29. Platform 15 was at the other end of the walkway. He limped towards it as commuters hurried past.

He was at the top of the steps leading down to Platform 15 when he heard the sound of a train coming into the station, its wheels making the familiar, rhythmic sound over the tracks, blotting out the sound of a station announcement; and he was just hauling himself down the steps when he heard a man scream.

Chet stopped. He could hear the train braking quickly, then there was shouting. He limped quickly to the top of the stairs, where he saw an already crowded platform. There was a commotion at the end of the platform from which the train had arrived and it sent a sick feeling through Chet's body. 'Get out of my way,' he roared as he barged past a couple of commuters. 'Move!'

The train had stopped now. Chet turned left, towards the front end. The other travellers were giving each other anxious looks, as if they didn't know quite what to do; a few made angry remarks as Chet stormed through them.

He was alongside the front carriage when he heard a second scream. A woman. Hysterical. 'Oh my God! Oh my *God!*'

Chet continued to push his way through.

'Someone *help* him,' the woman sobbed.

He reached the edge of the platform and pulled the sobbing woman out of the way. There was a streak of blood on the front of the train, and

108

through the windscreen glass he could see the driver with a horrified look on his face.

Chet stared down at the track. It was impossible to make out the features on the mangled body that lay there. The side of the face that was visible was just an oozing welt of gore. One arm was pinned behind the figure's back in a gruesomely unnatural position, the shoulder joint and the elbow obviously snapped and splintered; the other arm was simply crushed.

But Chet didn't need to see the face. All he needed to see was the prosthetic leg, almost identical to his own. It was still vaguely attached to Doug's knee, but pointing out at a ninety-degree angle, and split about halfway down.

Dread and anger seeped through Chet's bones in equal measure. He staggered back from the edge of the platform to allow two Transport Police officers to take his place. 'Ladies and gentlemen, *please* step back from the platform,' one said loudly. 'Please step back—the emergency services need to come through.'

Chet hardly heard them. He pressed his back against a rail map on the platform wall as the chaos unfolded, trying to suppress the sickness, trying to think clearly.

Was his friend dead by coincidence? Like hell he was.

But with the possible exception of Doug's girlfriend, nobody knew they were meeting. Nobody knew they were there.

Suddenly Chet felt his blood turn cold. He pulled his mobile phone out of his pocket and stared at it.

Somebody must have been listening in to their conversation.

He cursed himself for being so stupid, then quickly fumbled with the handset's rear panel and removed the battery and SIM card so that the phone couldn't be tracked. He stuffed the SIM card into his wallet; the phone he could dump when he found a bin.

Quickly he replayed in his head what he and his friend had said on the phone. Would any eavesdropper have known that Doug was an amputee too? Chet didn't think so. And there was only one conclusion to draw from that . . .

'*Jesus, mate*,' he whispered to himself. '*They were after me, not you. I'm so fucking sorry.*'

Then his skin prickled as another realisation hit him.

He'd made more than one call using this phone the night before.

A face rose in his mind. Red hair. A small silver stud in her pretty, turned-up nose.

Suze McArthur.

Chet stuffed the dismembered phone in his pocket and started to push his way hurriedly back along the platform. He had no idea where the young woman lived. He had no idea what she knew. But he had to get to her now. And fast.

Before someone else did.

TEN

Chet had a name. He had a phone number. Ten minutes later, after a call from a public phone box to an old army mate of his who had access to the Police National Computer, he had an address committed to memory.

Flat 6, 124 Wimbourne Terrace, W2. He consulted his mental map of the capital. Suze McArthur, whoever she was, lived on the other side of London. It would take him the best part of an hour to get there, and an hour could easily be too long. He called her number: maybe he could persuade her to get the hell out of her flat. But the phone rang out. Was that good or bad? Chet didn't know. He slammed the receiver down and limped back to his car. His only option was to struggle through the rush-hour traffic.

It was getting lighter now, but the sky was cloudy and grey. He kept seeing the intruder—her cold face—and Doug's mangled and broken body. He kept hearing the American voice he'd overheard the day before. *Trust me, Prime Minister Stratton. This war is good to go . . . the Americans are all on board. The question is, how are you going to get it through . . . ?*

There was something more to it than that. There *had* to be. What *else* had they been saying in that meeting? What was so important that somebody had tried to kill him, and succeeded in taking the life of his friend? There was only one person who might know the answer to that, and Chet had to get to her soonest.

He lost count of the number of cars he cut up, or of red lights that he ran, or of angry shouts from drivers as he forced his way across London. Even with all that, it was still just shy of 07.45 when he pulled into the top of Wimbourne Terrace, a narrow street of mansion-block flats round the back of Edgware Road tube station.

It was a residential road. No shops or cafés, but still a fair number of people walking along either side. Chet drove slowly down the road, looking out for number 124. It would be on the right, and . . .

He took a sharp breath.

Number 124 looked like all the other blocks with its black and white chequerboard pathway leading up to an ornate red-painted door with two frosted-glass panels. But on the other side of the road, sitting in a white VW Golf, was a woman he recognised. Dark, wavy hair. A beautiful face. The last time he'd seen her was in the rear-view mirror of his own car, as she stood outside his flat, pistol in hand.

Chet lowered his head as he passed. Had the intruder clocked him? He fucking hoped not.

At the far end of Wimbourne Terrace, some twenty metres away, he pulled into the kerb. He realised he was breathing deeply, trying to keep his mind and body steady. Was she alone? Were there others conducting surveillance on Suze McArthur's flat? What was her strategy—to wait until the girl left, then follow her? Or was an accomplice already inside?

Whatever was happening, Chet couldn't just walk up to the door and ring the bell. The woman in the Golf was, to Chet's certain knowledge, armed; he wasn't. She was able-bodied; Chet was far from it.

112

He considered moving round to the back of the block to see if there was another entrance, but there was no way he was going to take his eyes off the woman. He needed a distraction. Something quick.

There was a public phone in a Perspex booth a few metres from the car. Leaving the car on a double yellow—there was no other choice—he hurried over to the booth. He looked around, checking for CCTV. Nothing jumped out, not that that meant much. Whether he was on camera or not, he had to act quickly.

He could still see the Golf as he picked up the receiver and dialled 999.

A female voice answered after two rings. 'Which service do you require?'

'Police,' Chet replied.

'Please hold the line.'

A pause, then a new voice. 'Go ahead, caller. You're through to the police.'

Chet affected a note of panic. 'I . . . I think I've seen someone with a gun.'

'Where did you see this?'

'Wimbourne Terrace, W2. It's a woman. I saw her getting into a white VW Golf.'

'Do you have the registration number, caller?'

'No . . . it's about halfway up the street.'

'Where are you now?'

'Just up the road. I thought I should call . . .'

'Please tell me what number you're calling from.'

Chet recited the number displayed in the phone booth.

'Stay away from the area, caller. A patrol car will be . . .'

But Chet had already hung up.

113

He knew the police would be there quickly. Any sniff of gun crime and they were all over it like the clap. Would it be quick enough? He'd have to wait and see. Chet walked back towards where the white Golf was parked. He stopped about twenty metres away from it, on the same side as number 124. From here he could see the entrance to Suze's building, and also the vehicle. If the intruder made a move, he could intervene. But otherwise he was going to wait.

A minute passed.

Two.

It was faint at first, almost indistinguishable from the general hubbub of London, and the roar of traffic on the flyover. But gradually it got louder: the sound of sirens, two of them, maybe three, it was difficult to tell. Chet had to time it right. Too early and he'd announce his presence to the intruder. Too late and the police would be here, stopping him from gaining access to the flat.

He waited until he could see the first car, its blue light flashing, scream round the corner into Wimbourne Terrace before he moved. He covered the distance to Suze's flat as quickly as he could, keeping his head down so the intruder wouldn't recognise him until it was too late. But, stepping on to the chequerboard path, he couldn't help looking over his shoulder.

The driver's door of the Golf was open. A figure was getting out.

He rang the bottom bell as the sound of the sirens got louder.

Five seconds passed before there was an answer. It felt like five years. 'Hello.'

'Police,' Chet replied, knowing the occupant

114

would be able to hear the sirens. 'Open the front door and stay in your flat.'

The woman from the Golf had crossed the road.

'*Open the door, now!*' Chet barked.

A buzzing sound and the latch clicked. He pushed the door open and slipped inside. As he turned to close it behind him, he saw her: the woman's eyes were flashing angrily and she was striding towards the door, no more than five metres away. Chet pushed the door closed, hearing the latch click just as she reached the threshold. Through the frosted glass he saw her silhouette, with the blue lights of the police car flashing behind her.

Chet didn't linger. He moved along the short hallway, past the door of the ground-floor flat and up the thinly carpeted stairs. By the time he'd climbed three flights, his leg was in agony, but he kept going. Less than a minute later he was standing outside the door to the top flat. Flat 6. He hammered on the door: three heavy thumps, followed by another three when there was no answer. But he could hear movement inside. 'Suze,' he shouted. 'Open the door. You're in danger and you need to let me in.'

No reply.

Chet spoke quickly. Urgently. 'Listen to me. One man's already dead because of yesterday. One of us will be next unless you open this door now.'

At first there was nothing. But then, just when Chet thought he was going to have to break his way in, the door opened just an inch. Warily he nudged it open wider with his foot.

The tiny flat was in darkness. Chet saw a sofa, coffee table, TV, bookshelves, and a window with the curtains closed. The place reeked of incense and panic. At the other side of the studio, by the TV, stood Suze. She looked like she hadn't slept; her eyes were red and mistrustful; and she was holding a kitchen knife.

Chet stepped inside and closed the door. 'We need to get out of here,' he said. 'Now.'

Suze shook her head and raised the knife a little higher. 'I'm not going anywhere with you,' she whispered.

He gave her a steady glare, then moved over to the window and opened the curtains. He could see the flyover, solid with rush-hour traffic. Below, and immediately outside, were three police cars, with four officers surrounding the white Golf. Standing about thirty metres away, as though she was just a bystander, was Chet's wannabe assassin. She'd clearly slipped the attention of the Old Bill. He pointed in her direction. 'See that woman?' he said. 'She tried to kill me last night and she was parked outside your flat when I arrived.'

Suze stared down on the street. Chet could sense her trembling.

'Believe me,' he said quietly. 'If it was me that wanted to kill you, you'd be dead by now. I don't know who this woman is, but she's armed, she has access to information and she's a professional assassin. We have to get away from her, and we have to do it right now. Is there any way out of here, other than the front door? A fire exit? Can you get on to the roof?'

'No . . . I don't think so . . . no, I'm sure.' She looked like all her worst nightmares were coming true.

Chet tried to keep a clear head. 'Do you know

116

anyone else in this block? Do you have friends here? People you can trust?'

It took Suze a moment to reply, as though the question hadn't quite sunk in. 'An old couple,' she said finally. 'Flat 5. Vern and Dorothy. Not friends, exactly, but . . . but . . . they're not there anyway . . .'

'Are you positive?'

'They've gone away . . . on a cruise . . . I've got their keys . . .'

'Give them to me. Now.' Chet looked out of the window again as Suze put the knife down on the windowsill and rummaged in her colourful patchwork handbag. The police had created a cordon around the white Golf; the woman was still loitering thirty metres down the street, leaning against a tree and watching.

'You've got thirty seconds to get ready,' Chet told Suze as she handed him a set of keys.

'Thirty seconds . . . I can't . . . I . . .' Chet grabbed her by the arm and pulled her towards the door. She started to struggle. 'Wait,' she said. 'The tape.' She broke free and scrambled towards the bookshelf where a Dictaphone was lying at an angle. When she came back with the tape, he gripped her arm again and dragged her out of the flat and down the stairs.

By the time they reached the door to the flat below, Suze was crying, but she'd stopped fighting so much. Chet unlocked the door and pushed her inside before quietly closing it behind him. Flat 5 was bigger than Suze's attic studio. They were in a long hallway, lined with oil paintings and even a small alabaster statue on a pedestal of a cherub peeing. Suze's sobbing was noisy. 'Get away from the door,' Chet whispered. 'Stay away from all the

117

windows, don't switch on any lights and don't make a fucking noise.'

Suze stared at him. She was breathing in short, frightened gasps.

'*Get away from the door!*'

She staggered back along the hallway, and collapsed on the thick carpet.

Chet grabbed the figurine. It was small enough to grip in one hand, heavy enough to do some proper damage to someone's skull. He stayed by the entrance. There was a spyhole in the door, through which he could see the landing outside. He kept his eyes on the exterior of the flat, gripping the statue in his right hand. 'Shut up,' he said. When it was clear the girl couldn't stop crying, he tried to block out the sound so that he could concentrate on any noise that came from the stairwell.

Two minutes passed. There was a brief commotion—voices talking excitedly—that sounded like it came from the floor below, though it was difficult to be sure. It was followed by the banging of the door, and then silence.

'What's happening?' Suze asked.

'Shut up.'

'Who *are* you?'

'*Sshh!*'

Someone was coming. He found himself holding his breath.

It was fleeting—the black-clad figure of the woman slipping past like a ghost before heading up to the top floor—but it was enough. Enough for Chet to see the determination on her face and the weapon in her fist.

Chet turned to Suze. She'd recovered a little, but she still looked shit-scared. He tried to sound reassuring, but it was difficult, given what he had to say. 'She's going into your flat,' he whispered, 'and she's got a gun. We have less than a minute before she realises you're not there. We've got to go now, and we've got to go quietly. OK?'

She looked up at him and nodded. Chet helped her to her feet, and pulled her gently towards the door.

'Ready?'

'Ready.'

He opened up as quietly as possible, and they stepped out into the landing and towards the stairs. Chet nodded at Suze to go first, and followed close behind as she descended. He was still grasping the cherub. Not much use against a nine-millimetre, but it was all there was. Every four or five steps he looked back over his shoulder, but he saw nothing. The further they got towards the ground floor, the faster and more panicked Suze's steps became, until it was difficult for Chet to keep up. By the time they were both on the ground floor, she was sobbing again.

'You're doing fine,' Chet said, out of breath, as he opened the street door. 'Keep going.'

They stepped outside. There were still two policemen by the cordoned-off Golf, but they were talking so casually it was clear they'd found no weapons and didn't consider the situation serious. Chet kept hold of Suze's arm and guided her across the street.

'Where are we going?' she asked.

'My car.'

'Where then?'

'I don't know.'

'Why are you limping like that?'

119

Chet sniffed. 'Don't worry about it. I'll explain later.'

Suddenly he stopped. He didn't know why. Just a feeling. An uneasy one. He turned around and looked back towards Suze's block. He could clearly see the top-floor window, the one he'd looked out of just minutes previously.

There was a face at the window, looking out on to the street. It might have been indistinguishable at this distance, but somehow Chet knew, with absolute certainty, that the face was watching them leave.

'What is it?'

'Nothing. Keep going.' He continued to walk. And as he walked, his mind turned over. Whoever this woman was that they'd just escaped from, she was skilled and she had resources.

She was dangerous. And she wasn't the type to give up.

A good thing, then, that neither was he.

Chet's face was grim as he led Suze to his car and opened the door for her before looking up again at the window in the distance. He could still see the woman there, and that meant she had clocked his car. Nothing he could do about that now, though. He climbed in and drove off.

*   *   *

The woman standing at the window watched her two targets disappear. Her face was expressionless.

She turned away. Things had not gone well at all. She had killed the wrong man at the station that morning. That was a bad error, and as they had drummed into her during her training, one mistake

120

invariably leads to another. A kitchen knife lay on the windowsill. Her fingers sought it out, almost of their own accord, and she gripped the handle. With a sudden burst of rage, she raised the knife in the air and drove the point down so heavily into the sill that the wood split. *'Ben zonah!'*

Her eyes flashed and it needed every ounce of self-control to stop the anger from once more bursting out of her. She took a couple of deep breaths and ran her hands through her hair.

Think, Maya, she told herself. You have to think.

She closed her eyes. She forced herself to become calm.

When she was a little girl, her parents had told her the story of Hansel and Gretel and how they were able to retrace their way through the forest because they had dropped little bits of bread behind them. It frequently struck her that most people dropped bits of bread behind them, even if they didn't know they were doing it. If you wanted to find the person, all you had to do was follow the crumbs.

She looked around the flat. It was a tiny place— smaller even than her safe house in Tel Aviv—but that didn't mean it held no secrets. She continued to breathe deeply so as to calm her temper, and started to search.

It took her seconds to spot the two box files marked 'Stratton' and 'Grosvenor Group'. The image of the British Prime Minister rose in her mind, but she gave their contents only the most cursory of glances. That wasn't the kind of thing she was after.

A photo on the TV showed a young woman and a disabled old lady. So different, yet somehow

121

similar. Now *that* was a different matter. She ripped off the back of the frame, pocketed the print and continued her search.

She returned to the shelf where she had found the two files, but concentrated instead on the shelves below. There were a few books here, neatly lined up; a small mahogany box with some loose change inside; and on the bottom shelf what looked like a square briefcase with a lockable clasp. She pressed the clasp and it clicked open. Inside the briefcase were approximately ten green foolscap wallet folders, alphabetically arranged with neat, hand-written labels.

Banking. Insurance. Rent.

She ignored all these, and instead focused on a folder labelled 'Mum'.

To find the person, all you had to do was follow the crumbs.

Smiling now, she opened up the folder and started to read.

*   *   *

'How much money do you have?'

They were heading up Edgware Road.

'None,' Suze snapped, like a moody kid. 'You made me leave the flat without getting anything, remember?'

Chet grunted. If she was after an apology for saving her life, she'd have a long wait.

'Who the hell are you anyway?' she demanded. Chet didn't answer. He pulled out his wallet from the inside pocket of his jacket and threw it on to her lap.

'How much is in there? Count it.'

Suze gave him a harsh look, but started to rummage through the wallet. 'A hundred and sixty,' she said finally.

Chet glanced at the fuel-level indicator. Half full. That was thirty quid gone before they'd even started. Not good.

'We can't use any credit cards,' he said, more to himself than to his passenger.

Suze looked confused. 'Why?'

Why? It was a good question, and now that they'd got safely away from her flat, it was one that was occupying every moment of Chet's thoughts. The intruder had tracked the girl through the call he'd made to her. That wasn't straightforward. It took time. Resources. Who was equipped to track phone calls at such speed? Five? The Firm? If so, they'd need to go through GCHQ, and that meant someone high up had given the order. That wasn't a very comfortable thought. Someone wanted to find them. *Really* wanted to find them. Tracking their phone calls was just one way of doing that. Following a trail of credit-card payments was another. And there were more. Chet was going to have to make sure he was ahead of the game.

Suze was biting her fingernails. 'Where are we going?'

'Out of London.'

'That doesn't really narrow it down.'

'I don't know yet, all right? Just shut up and let me think.'

Suze looked like she was going to respond, but she thought better of it. Instead she sat in silence, looking out of the window, still gnawing at her thumbnail.

Chet made for the M1. The road was clear, but

he kept a steady speed—to get pulled over now would be a really bad idea—and it was twenty minutes or so before they hit the junction with the M25. He took the clockwise carriageway and drove steadily round to just before the Dartford Tunnel, where he pulled off for petrol at Thurrock services. The service station was crowded and they had to queue for a pump. Only when they drew alongside one did Chet speak.

'Keep the doors locked.'

'Why? No one knows we're here.'

'Keep them locked.'

Chet filled up and went in to pay. He bought a stash of chocolate bars, bananas and high-energy drinks, before stepping back out on to the concourse.

He clocked it immediately: a police car parked up just by the air and water machine. Two uniformed officers next to it, one talking into a radio mike fixed to his lapel, both of them looking at—and now walking towards—the black Mondeo.

Chet put his head down, and continued walking to the car. He was coming towards it at a different angle to the police, and was slightly closer. But he didn't want to speed up yet, because that would alert them to his presence.

Ten metres to go. He tried to catch Suze's eye, but she was staring vacantly into space and clearly hadn't noticed either Chet or the officers.

Five metres.

Chet could hear the crackle of the police radio. He pressed his key to unlock the doors, and the lights flashed twice.

'Excuse me, sir. *Sir!*'

Chet opened the door and climbed in. He was

turning the key even before the door was shut. The two officers were right in front of him, one of them holding up his hand, palm outwards, while the other was hurrying round to Chet's side.

'Oh my God,' Suze wailed.

Chet said nothing. He centrally locked the doors, then put his foot on the accelerator and drove slowly towards the policeman blocking his way. At first it looked like the cop was going to stand his ground, but he jumped to one side when he realised Chet wasn't going to stop. The second policeman managed to rap his knuckles on the driver's window, but Chet had the space to accelerate now, and that's what he did, ignoring the alarmed looks from the other customers at the petrol station.

The Mondeo's tyres squealed as he raced towards the exit. In his mirrors he saw the two police officers running back towards their car.

'What's . . . what's happening?' Suze stammered. 'How did they know where we were?'

Chet swung round the perimeter road of the service station and back on to the northbound M25, pushing the car through its revs until it was touching ninety.

'Number-plate recognition,' he murmured, his jaw clenched with determination. 'Police cameras at all the main motorway junctions. They use them to track stolen vehicles. Gets fed through to the Police National Computer.'

'Bastards!'

He checked his mirrors. No sign of the police tailing him yet. 'Someone's instructed them to bring us in.'

'But . . . but if you *knew* all this, why did you . . . ?'

'I want them to think we're heading east out of London, OK?' Chet explained himself more to keep her quiet than anything else. 'At least that was the idea.'

'Well, the idea's not working . . .'

'Thanks. Next time I need someone to state the fucking obvious, I'll know where to come.'

'We need another car,' Suze continued as if he hadn't said anything. 'We could hire one, maybe . . .'

Chet shook his head. 'Too easy to trace.'

'So what are we going to *do*?'

Chet checked his mirror. No sign of the patrol car. He took the exit on to the A13. He knew he was on the money—that to beg, borrow or steal another vehicle would be a beacon to anyone trying to locate them. But they *could* do the next best thing . . .

As he drove along the A13, he looked left and right. He knew what he was searching for. It wouldn't be too long before he found one.

Ten minutes later he saw it: a retail park just off the main road, with all the usual shops and a monstrous concrete car park, six or seven storeys high. A minute later he was pulling a ticket from the automated entry gate and slowly crawling along the parking bays of the ground floor.

'What are we doing?' Suze asked.

'Looking for something.'

'What?'

But Chet didn't answer. He was too busy concentrating on the other cars in the multi-storey. Nothing on the ground floor, so he climbed the ramp to the first. Still nothing. He cursed under his breath and headed higher.

They were four floors up before he found what he was looking for: another Ford Mondeo, black. Two years newer than his, but it would do. He selected a parking spot in a corner of the car park, boxed in by a bulky Range Rover, then rummaged in his rucksack and pulled out the screwdriver from his debugging kit. Seconds later he was bending down in front of the car, prising off the plastic screw covers of his number plate and removing it. In under a minute he had both plates off.

'Get out of the car,' he told Suze.

'Why?'

'Just get out and come with me.'

Suze looked wary as she followed him across the deserted car park towards the other black Mondeo. 'You see anyone coming, distract them,' he said under his breath. 'I'm going to switch the plates.'

'How?'

'You're a clever girl. You'll think of something.'

'I can't . . . I mean, I . . .'

One look from Chet, though, and she fell silent.

They approached the car together. Chet crouched down and removed the front number plate quickly enough, but he was just preparing to swap it for his when the banging of a door echoed around the car park.

He gave Suze a sudden, urgent look.

'Right . . .' she said. 'OK.' She dug the remains of her fingernails into her palms and started walking towards the stairwell. 'Um . . . excuse me . . . *excuse me* . . . could you tell me where the nearest . . . ?'

Chet blotted out the sound and concentrated on the plates. A couple of minutes later they were swapped, and he was striding back to his own car, with Suze trotting along behind him. Elsewhere they heard an engine start and a vehicle move away. Then silence again. Chet fixed the new plates to his vehicle, and moments later they were driving out of the car park.

'This'll buy us a bit of time,' he said. 'Until the owner of the other car realises what's happened. Or the police catch up with them.' He paused. 'Or anyone else does. But we still have to be careful.'

'Careful how?'

'We stay off the motorways until we get where we're headed. The cameras tend to be on the main arteries. It'll keep us under the radar. Hopefully.'

Suze stared at him. 'And where *are* we headed?' She stared some more, then clutched her red hair in her hands. 'Christ, you haven't even told me your *name* . . . and how do you . . . how do you *know* all this stuff?'

He glanced at her as he drove. She looked exhausted. Terrified. He didn't blame her. He felt the same. The only difference was that Suze was physically shaking. Chet wasn't.

'You did well back there,' he said, and he meant it.

Suze didn't reply.

'My name's Chet Freeman,' he said quietly. 'I know all this stuff because it's my job to. At least, it used to be. We're going somewhere out of the way that I know pretty well. And when we get there, you and me are going to have a little talk. You're going to tell me everything you know, and you're not going to leave out a single fucking thing. Right?'

Suze looked straight ahead and returned her thumbnail to her teeth.

It took her a moment to reply, and when she did, her voice was quiet. Not meek-quiet, but determined-quiet.

'Right,' she said.

ELEVEN

'Zero, this is Tango 17.'

The red Toyota had its boot up and Luke and
Finn were sheltering behind it. That way they
wouldn't stick out on the horizon as the sun rose
to the east, and they could operate the patrol radio
stashed in the back with the rest of their kit. Their
hostages were still in the car, Abu Famir in the
front and the second man, now unconscious, in the
back.

A couple of miles to the south was the main
road that ran from the Jordanian border all the
way to Baghdad. Everywhere else was desert.
When they'd stopped it had been light enough
for them to see the traffic on the road with the
naked eye. Busier than last night. Plenty of small
cars, indistinguishable at this distance from their
own, but plenty of military vehicles too. Luke
couldn't tell from up here if they were moving men,
munitions or other supplies. But he could tell there
were enough of them for that road to be a very
dangerous place for two members of the British
Army and two dissident Iraqi hostages, one of them
with blood pissing from a gun wound.

The radio crackled, and then was silent.

'Zero, this is Tango 17.'

A pause.

'Tango 17, this is Zero. Send.'

'We have the target, but we got into contact. Two

129

men down, one wounded. We have the casualty in tow. Target claims he's a fellow dissident. Request further instructions.'

'*Tango 17, wait out, figures 5.*'

The line went quiet. Luke looked around. A desert falcon was circling up above. Apart from that, no movement in the immediate vicinity.

After five minutes that felt like a lot longer, the radio came to life again.

'*Tango 17, this is Zero. Proceed to RV with both captives.*'

Luke glanced at Finn. He was shaking his head.

'Zero, we're in a bad spot here. We need medical assistance. Request pick-up.'

A brief pause, then: '*Tango 17, pick-up cancelled. No heli assets.*'

He heard Finn cursing under his breath. 'What about Fozzie and the others?'

A pause.

'*Back-up unit compromised. Enemy aircraft in border area airspace. Return via vehicle or foot. Repeat, return via vehicle or foot.*'

Luke nodded grimly. 'Roger that, Zero.' He replaced the handset of the patrol radio.

'Fuck's sake.' Finn looked towards the main road. 'I'm telling you, with that guy in the car it's fucking suicide down there. We should just nail him now, say he died of his wounds.'

For a moment Luke didn't reply. He walked round and glanced into the vehicle. The wounded man was pale and sweating, despite Finn's on-the-hoof medical attention. He had a large swab bandaged to his wound, but it was already saturated with blood. He needed serious attention and this wasn't the place to go looking for it. Maybe Finn

130

was right. Maybe they should just ditch him.

'You given him a shot?' Luke asked.

'Not the kind I'd like to.'

'Have you given him a shot?'

'Of course I've given him a fucking shot. But he needs more than morphine.'

Luke continued to weigh things up. He didn't like the sound of the situation at the border. With Fozzie and the others compromised, getting over into Jordan was going to be tough. Maybe they should ditch the car and head across the desert on foot. But it was 100 miles to the border, and that was a big ask even for the two Regiment men. For an old boy like Abu Famir it was an impossibility. And as for the wounded man . . .

In any case, they had their orders. Luke looked over at Finn. 'We need to get him into the burka,' he said. If nothing else it would cover up the guy's wounds.

'We need to waste the fucker.'

Luke gave Finn a dangerous look before opening up the front passenger door to talk to Abu Famir.

'What's his name?' he demanded.

The Iraqi academic avoided his gaze.

'What's his fucking name?'

'He needs a doctor,' Abu Famir mumbled. It was clear he was avoiding the question.

'Fuck's sake,' Luke sighed, before opening the rear door and moving his attention to the casualty. Their companion stank of sweat and was shaking. 'Hey, buddy,' Luke said—speaking English because he didn't know what else to speak. 'How you doing?'

The wounded man opened his eyes, but there didn't seem to be much understanding behind

131

them.

'You got a name, buddy?'

When the man answered, it was in a hoarse almost-whisper. 'Amit,' he said.

That didn't sound like an Iraqi name to Luke. He glanced in Abu Famir's direction, then turned back to the wounded man.

'OK, Amit, you need to stand up by the car so we can put something over you. Stop anyone paying us too much atten . . .'

'Where's Abu Famir?' Amit asked. His accent had a strange tinge to it. 'I need to get Abu Famir out . . .' A moment of breathlessness. 'I need to get him out of . . .'

'Abu Famir's here. We're taking care of it.' Luke felt a moment of respect for Amit, if that was really his name. 'Now come on, buddy. I'm going to help you out . . .'

Luke could do nothing other than place two strong hands under Amit's armpits to lug him from the vehicle. The wounded man gasped in pain, but he didn't resist and moments later he was leaning against the car, his body crooked but his face a little more alert than it had been—even though the dressing of his wound was like a sodden sponge.

'Your friend wants to kill me?' he whispered.

Luke gave him a long look. 'You want to give him a reason not to?'

Amit closed his eyes. 'What do I need to wear?' he whispered.

All of a sudden Finn pulled his Sig from under his robe and held the barrel of the gun hard against the man's forehead. 'Answer the fucking question,' he instructed. But as soon as Finn had spoken, Luke knocked his gun away from Amit, and the two

132

Regiment men found themselves staring each other down.

'Leave it,' Luke said. 'That's an order.'

'This is insane,' Finn spat. 'We hit a roadblock and it goes noisy, half the Republican Guard are going to be on our tail. It's daylight. They'll be able to see us from fucking Syria.'

Luke looked back at Amit. The guy was leaning, exhausted, against the car.

'We'll find a lying-up point,' Luke decided. 'Wait till nightfall and work out what to do. Let's get him covered up.'

With obvious reluctance Finn fished the burka and headdress out of the boot. Amit didn't really seem to register what they were doing as the two SAS men struggled to get the robe over him and the headdress on, before Luke helped him into the back of the car again. By the time Amit was sitting down, his head lolling at a slight angle and his face obscured behind the veil of the headdress, it was impossible to tell if he was awake or asleep. Hell, it was impossible to tell if he was even still alive.

Luke put the bonnet down, got back into the car and turned to Abu Famir, who was still in the front passenger seat. The Iraqi had calmed down and was looking defiantly at Luke over the top of his little round spectacles.

'I will have great influence in the new Iraq,' he announced with great self-importance. 'I will see to it that you are well rewarded . . .'

'Fuck your rewards,' Luke replied. 'Who is he?'

'My deputy,' Abu Famir stated flatly. 'And I will not see him killed.'

Luke glanced at Finn. You might not get a fucking choice, he thought to himself as he started

133

the engine. Abu Famir was still talking. 'I know your Prime Minister Stratton well. We have spoken on the telephone. He has great respect for my judgement . . .'

They set off again. They'd been travelling for five minutes when Luke became aware of a sound from the back seat. He looked over his shoulder. Amit was moving—shaking his head—and muttering to himself. 'What's he saying?' he asked Finn.

'Fuck knows. Delirious.'

'He must see a doctor,' Abu Famir declared.

'Thanks. I'll phone for a fucking appointment.'

A couple of minutes later Luke hit the brakes. Something had caught his attention. He and Finn got out of the car. The terrain to the right was rough and undulating, and 500 metres away there was an outcrop of bare rock, about the size of a small house. A thin wadi ran towards it, alongside which was a rough dirt track that fed off the road on which they were travelling about thirty metres forward of their position.

Luke took the wheel again. They trundled slowly towards the track, turned right along the wadi and made their way to the rocks. The closer they drew, the higher the rocks loomed. He stopped ten metres from them.

'Let's recce,' he said to Finn. The two soldiers grabbed their carbines and started walking round the rocks. The sides were smooth and weathered; to start with, they looked like they offered little in the way of protection, but on the far edge, out of sight of the car, they found a crevice about three metres wide and ten high. It was dark inside—from the opening Luke and Finn could only see a couple of metres in.

134

'Cover me,' Luke said.

Finn nodded, and aimed his rifle into the crevice while Luke stepped in.

It smelt musty. The temperature was a couple of degrees lower than outside, but it was dry and the ground was flat. As his eyes grew used to the gloom, he saw that the crevice was about twenty metres deep and—crucially—unoccupied. No doubt the desert dwellers of this area knew of it, but as somewhere to lie up for the day it would do. He walked outside and nodded to Finn. 'We can get the motor in,' he said. 'Let's do it.'

Finn didn't look happy, and he started to reason with Luke. 'Look, mate, don't tell me you can't see there's something strange going on here. We can still ditch him. He could still die of his wounds. Abu Famir doesn't have to realise, nor do the Ruperts back at base.'

Luke looked back across the bleak expanse of the desert. It looked totally empty, but he knew that danger could appear almost from nowhere: desert patrols, Republican Guard troops investigating the shoot-out back at the village, even innocent Bedouin wanderers stumbling across them. Their situation was dangerous, no doubt about it. Sometimes, though, you just had to go with your gut. This was one of those times, and Luke wasn't going to waste Amit until he knew exactly who he was.

'We lie up here till dark, then we go,' he told Finn in a tone of voice that offered no argument, and the two of them hurried back round to the other side of the rocky outcrop to collect their car and their strange pair of passengers.

Chet and Suze headed west, then north. It was slow
going. When Chet first pulled over, Suze looked
alarmed. 'What's wrong? What are you doing?'

'Checking for tails.'

He repeated this every twenty minutes.
Occasionally he would do a U-turn, retrace his
steps and take another route. A good tail, he knew,
would drive past him when he pulled over, reduce
their speed and then wait for Chet to catch up.
He needed to try to scupper any tricks like that. It
wasn't foolproof, but it was the best he could do.
Suze only asked him what he was doing once. After
that they sat in awkward silence.

They stayed off the main roads, driving south of
Oxford then north up towards Birmingham before
bearing west towards the Welsh border. When
he saw the first sign for Hereford, Chet had to
fight the urge to follow it. He had friends there, of
course. If he made a couple of phone calls, there'd
be a welcoming committee for him at Credenhill.
But a welcoming committee wasn't what he wanted.
Chet was going dark—for how long, he didn't know.

*   *   *

The weather started to change around 15.00 hrs.
Big black clouds billowed in from the west and the
windscreen started to become spotted with rain.

'A storm's coming,' Chet murmured. Suze didn't
respond.

As they crossed the border, thunder boomed
across the sky and the rain fell more heavily. Ten
minutes later it was a torrent. Every time there

136

was a crack of thunder, Suze jumped in her seat. She was like a timid animal, ready to bolt but not knowing which way to go. Chet had no words of comfort for her. His mind was on other things. With the windscreen wipers going full pelt and everyone's headlamps on, it had become more difficult for him to keep an eye on anyone following. Not good—but at least it was equally difficult for anyone trying to tail them.

The light was beginning to fail when he headed south, passing through several grim mid-Wales towns, their streets deserted because of the insistent rain. And it was almost dark when his headlamps lit up a signpost that read: 'BRECON BEACONS NATIONAL PARK'.

'Nearly there,' he told Suze, like he was talking to a child at the end of a long journey.

Chet knew the geography of the Beacons better than he knew anywhere. He'd lost count of the number of nights he'd spent there, freezing his nuts off in the months approaching SAS selection, and many times subsequently on exercises. Every peak and valley was familiar to him; every road and every stream. When people are on the run, they return to places they know well. Chet's pursuer might be expecting him to go back to his little flat off Seven Sisters Road; but in fact the rugged landscape of south-east Wales felt more like home than any shitty little corner of north London ever could.

The quieter and more winding the roads became, the more relaxed Chet felt. There were no cars now. Nobody following. No risk of vehicle identification cameras or unexpected police patrol cars. Just the Beacons, the heavy rain and a few hardy, bedraggled sheep. When he saw their

137

final destination—the lights of a single, solitary farmstead a couple of hundred metres away, he felt more relieved than at any moment since he'd awoken on his birthday. And that seemed like weeks ago.

'Where are we?'

It was the first thing Suze had said for a couple of hours. Her voice was cracked and quiet.

'A B&B. We should be able to get a room here for the night. Stay under the radar.'

A pause.

'We'll tell the owners we're married.'

Suze frowned. 'What? Why?'

'Because nobody remembers boring married couples. And because I want you in the same room as me, where I can see you. And where we can talk.'

Suze swallowed hard. 'Right,' she said, and they drove in silence up towards the farmhouse.

The rain was still heavy, and although it was only a short run from the car to the front door, they were half-soaked by the time they got there. They sheltered in a shallow porch where an old sign said 'VACANCIES', and they had to ring the bell twice before anyone answered. The door was opened by an elderly lady—seventy-five, perhaps older—with wispy grey hair, half-moon glasses and hearing aids on both ears. She peered at them suspiciously, as though guests were the last thing she expected at this bed and breakfast, while a floppy-eared cocker spaniel sniffed around her feet.

'Yes?'

'We need a room.' Chet's voice was abrupt.

'A room?' The old woman had a faint Welsh accent. She looked up at Chet's scarred face with a distinct lack of enthusiasm.

Chet was about to reply, when Suze butted in. 'We've travelled a very long way,' she said, in much more friendly tones. 'Might you have somewhere for us?'

The old lady's face softened slightly now that Suze was talking to her. 'Ah well, you'd better come in,' she said. She took a few paces back, and the two of them walked into the house. 'You can leave your rucksack in the porch,' she told Chet. 'We don't want it dripping all over the floor now, do we?'

'It's dry,' Chet told her. It was also heavy on account of the alabaster figurine he'd stashed in there.

Stepping into the farmhouse was like stepping into another century. Heavy oak beams traversed the low ceiling of what appeared to be a large reception-room-cum-kitchen, and a fire smouldered in a blackened inglenook. There was a very old gas oven along one wall, tired-looking floral worktops on either side, and a large butler's sink, cracked and stained yellow. Heavy flagstones covered the floor and the whole place smelt of woodsmoke.

The spaniel started investigating Suze, sniffing round her feet and nuzzling her ankles with its nose. She bent down to scratch its ears and this seemed to please the old lady, who directed her conversation only at Suze. 'She likes you,' she said, in the slightly too loud tones of the almost-deaf.

Suze smiled and stood up again. 'She's beautiful.'

'How many nights, dear?'

Suze glanced at Chet, who covertly held up a single finger.

'Just one,' she replied, and the old lady took a leather-bound guestbook from the heavy mahogany sideboard.

'I'll be needing your names.'

'Carter,' Chet said quickly. 'Mr and Mrs Carter.'

The old lady ignored him. 'I'm sorry, dear,' she said to Suze. 'I'm a little hard of hearing . . .'

Suze smiled and helped write the name in the guestbook. Moments later they were being led across the flagstone floor, into an adjoining hallway and up a wide, winding, stone staircase that led to the first floor. The old lady climbed it with difficulty. 'I can't be doing with stairs at my age,' she complained. 'I only come up here for guests.'

The landing had threadbare rugs and creaking floorboards. They passed one room on the right-hand side of the landing before the old lady showed them into a second room. Suze took one look at it and, still in buttering-up mode, said, 'It's perfect. We'll . . .'

But Chet interrupted her. 'No,' he said. 'Not this one.'

'Why ever not?' asked the old lady.

He glanced up to the ceiling where there was a removable panel, presumably leading to an attic. 'What else have you got?'

The old lady looked offended, but she led them back along the landing towards the first door they'd passed. This room was much more basic than the other. Frayed curtains, a lumpy, iron-framed double bed. Next to the bed was an occasional table with a beige, functional telephone on it. The adjoining bathroom had mildewed grout between the tiles and an avocado-coloured suite stained white with limescale.

Chet checked the window. The frame was thin and rotten, but it was locked and it looked out on

140

to the front where he'd parked. There was no attic hatch.

'This will do,' he said.

'I can't give you anything to eat, you know,' the old woman announced. It sounded like an accusation. 'And there's nowhere nearby.'

'Please, don't worry,' Suze told her. She clearly had a way with the oldies. 'We're glad for the room. You're very kind to . . .'

'Is there a key?' Chet interrupted.

'I beg your pardon?'

'A key?'

The old woman looked at him as if he'd made a lewd suggestion. 'Oh no . . . no, there's no key.'

She shook her head and left the couple, muttering to herself and leaving the door ajar. Chet closed the door, then stood with his back against it. He gave Suze a piercing look—one that she couldn't withstand for long. She sat on the edge of the bed and put her head in her hands.

'Are you sure we're safe here?'

He walked over, grabbed a high-backed chair that was against the wall and lodged it under the door handle. 'As safe as we can be. But if that woman who's chasing us is the person I think she is, we won't stay safe for long.'

'Who *do* you think she is?'

But Chet didn't answer.

She looked up at him again. 'Thank you,' she said. 'For helping me.'

Chet shrugged. Suddenly his leg was very sore, and as he stepped into the room his limp was more pronounced than usual.

'Your leg?'

He frowned. Then, after a moment, he pulled

141

his trouser leg up a few inches to reveal the sturdy black shin of his artificial leg. Suze's eyes widened but, he noticed, she didn't look appalled. 'I didn't realise . . .' she said. 'How did it happen?'

'I had a little disagreement with a man called Ivanovic. It was some time ago.'

'That looks like more than a disagreement.'

'He wanted to kill me. I didn't want him to.'

'Were you in the military?' Suze asked.

'You could say that.'

A pause.

'Does it . . . does it *hurt*?'

Chet didn't want to discuss his disability. There were more urgent topics. 'Tell me, why were you eavesdropping on that meeting?'

Suze bit her lip and looked as though she was gathering her thoughts. 'It's the Grosvenor Group,' she said at last.

'What do you mean?'

'Don't you know who they are?'

Chet walked over to the window and looked out. The rain was still sheeting. It hammered against the window. 'Not really,' he said. 'Dickheads in suits?'

'You work for them?'

'I'm a freelance security consultant. They pay me to debug rooms, that's all. It's not like I'm sitting round the board table.'

'Of course not. You're not the kind of person they want.' She took a few deep breaths and looked around nervously. 'They can't find us here, can they?'

Chet shook his head. 'I don't think so.'

Suze closed her eyes briefly and carried on talking—slowly and in fragments, as though she was unsure of herself. 'The Grosvenor Group . . .

142

it's an American ... a multinational ... a kind of ...' A look of frustration crossed her face as she searched for the right word. '... A *conglomeration* of venture capitalists. They invest money in other, smaller companies ... sometimes they buy them out totally ...' She gave an apologetic little smile. 'I don't really understand how all that stuff works.'

Nor did Chet. As far as he could tell, the Grosvenor Group was a bunch of money men. In his book, that meant arseholes.

Another crash of thunder, and the rain gave a renewed burst against the windowpanes. Suze stood up and started pacing the room. Suddenly her green eyes were flashing. 'The Grosvenor Group mostly puts its money into military enterprises— arms companies, aerospace, that kind of thing.' She stopped pacing. 'Basically, they invest in people killing other people.'

Yeah, Chet thought. Welcome to the world.

'The Grosvenor Group makes a lot of money,' Suze continued. 'I mean, like, a *lot* of money. Billions. You don't make that kind of cash without influence. Their board is like a ... a *Who's Who* of Western politics. Former American senators, people with influence in Washington and Whitehall, politicians who might one day return to office. They've even got former US presidents advising them.'

Chet shook his head. 'So some politicians are involved in the arms trade. That doesn't explain why somebody's trying to kill us.'

Suddenly she turned. 'For God's sake,' she snapped. 'Don't you *see*? If the US and the UK go to war in Iraq, it'll be like all the Grosvenor Group's Christmases have come at once. Arms

143

concessions, reconstruction deals.'

'People have always made money out of war, Suze.'

She stared at him contemptuously. 'And for some people, it's all they care about. My father was killed by a landmine in Angola. He was out there immunising kids. *You* might think it's OK to sell shit like that. *I* don't. Where's that bloody tape?'

Chet walked over to his rucksack and rummaged around. He pulled out the Dictaphone and handed it to Suze, who sat back down on the edge of the bed and started fiddling with the controls.

For a while there was no sound in the room other than the rain against the window and the rewinding of the cassette. When Suze pressed play, all Chet heard was the crackly static that had filled his ears when he'd listened in with the headphones the day before, which morphed every ten or fifteen seconds into the sound of distorted, indistinguishable voices. He looked at Suze. She was hunched over the machine, her face intent.

They'd been listening for a couple of minutes when, all of a sudden, the static and distortion evolved into something recognisable.

'. . . *it's extremely important that any funds payable now or in the future cannot be traced.*'

'*Prime Minister, that's a given. We're very good at it . . .*'

'*How do you propose to . . . ?*'

The voices disappeared for a few seconds, replaced with a high-pitched whine of feedback. When that faded, the American was speaking again.

'. . . *worldwide network of business associates. If we ask them, they'll offer you consultancy fees, speaking arrangements—all highly lucrative, Prime Minister.*

144

Highly *lucrative. And untraceable to the Grosvenor Group. Hell, you won't even need to rely on your memoirs for a pension. You could give the advance to charity. You'll be raking it in from all . . .'*

Static.

Distortion.

Chet stared at the machine as the implications of what he'd just heard sunk in.

It continued to play for another minute, before he heard words that were more familiar to him.

'*Trust me, Prime Minister Stratton. This war is good to go . . . the Americans are all on board. The question is, how are you going to get it through . . . ?'*

More static.

Suze stopped the tape and looked up at him.

Chet had a sick sensation in his stomach. At the same time he felt as though a fog had been lifted. 'The Grosvenor Group are *paying* Stratton to take us to war? Paying him *personally*?'

Suze stared hopelessly at him.

Chet thought about his Regiment mates—behind enemy lines, if his guess was right; he thought of the regular green army troops, preparing to move on Baghdad. How many of them would make it home?

'Who else knows about this?'

'Nobody. Only us.'

'Aren't you part of some protest group—activists?'

Suze shook her head almost apologetically.

'Where did you get the laser listening device?' he asked. The question had been nagging him for a while.

'The Internet. There's a guy who . . .' She gave him a hopeless look. 'I spent everything I had . . .' It seemed like she was telling the truth.

Chet tried to clear his head. So many things suddenly made sense: Stratton's meeting on the QT, away from Downing Street; the relentless assassin, tracking down first him, then Suze. The order had clearly gone out to eliminate them, and that order would stand for as long as they stayed alive.

Unless . . .

'It's extremely important that any funds payable now or in the future cannot be traced . . .'

Chet was trained to make the best use of the materials at his disposal, and right now that tape was their best weapon. Their *only* weapon. A scant resource, and they had to use it wisely.

'What are we going to do?' Suze asked.

Chet looked around the room. Hiding out here was OK for a bit, but it wasn't a long-term solution.

'We make it public,' he said.

Suze blinked at him. 'Won't that . . . ?'

'As soon as this is in all the papers, Stratton and the Grosvenor Group will have bigger fish to fry.'

'Are you sure?'

Chet gave her a direct look. 'No. Not really. But we haven't got a choice. They *will* find us, Suze. Eventually. Somehow. They *will* find us.'

She swallowed hard. 'All right,' she said, her voice timid.

'Until then, we stay dark. We don't contact anyone. We avoid populated areas where we might get picked up on CCTV. We don't use mobile phones, bank cards or passports. And you stay close to me, you understand?'

Suze nodded, and Chet limped over to the window again. The storm was raging, the rain hammering against the window and the night was

146

black. That was something, at least.

'I'm scared,' Suze said.

'Good,' Chet replied. 'Stay scared. That way you don't mess up.'

He turned to look at her and saw that fear was written clearly on her face. He didn't blame her, because he felt it too.

*   *   *

The sound of the rain was joined by the sound of the shower in the en-suite bathroom. Chet paced, waiting for Suze to finish. Even though she was only in the adjoining room, he felt edgy not having her in his line of sight.

The shower stopped and the door opened. Suze appeared. Her red hair was clean and scraped back off her face, some of it sticking to the nape of her neck. She wore a towel wrapped around her torso that revealed her slim arms and her slight, sloping shoulders; and she was carrying a little bundle of her clothes in front of her. Her lips were slightly parted. She looked beautiful, but fragile. Like she could break at any minute. Suddenly she was no longer the crazy girl on the roof or the frightened target of a ruthless assassin. She was a young woman—vulnerable, certainly, but attractive and looking at Chet with an expression he understood.

'I feel better now I'm clean,' she said. There was a slight tremor in her voice, and Chet could tell she was trying to sound conversational.

'I can wait in there if you want to get changed,' he offered.

Suze didn't answer. Instead she put her clothes in an untidy pile on the floor, then took a tentative

147

step towards him. Another step, and when she was close enough she rested her head against his chest.

They stood there like that for a moment. Awkwardly. Chet could hear her nervous breathing, and feel the beat of her pulse against him. He wrapped an arm around her shoulders, and then another. Suze felt tiny in his embrace. Her damp hair soaked through his shirt, and its fragrance filled his senses. It smelt good.

A boom of thunder. Suze was startled. 'When will this bloody storm finish?' she whispered. As if, in the grand scheme of things, a storm was important.

She looked up towards Chet and he felt her breath against his face. Her body was warm.

'You should get some sleep,' he said. 'Take the bed. I'll . . .'

'I'm sorry about the things I said to you,' she interrupted him.

'No . . .'

He didn't finish, because suddenly—as if she might lose the courage if she didn't act immediately—Suze had brushed her lips against his. Chet frowned. It had been a long time since anybody had given him that kind of attention; since anybody had seen past the scars on his face or his awkward gait.

Suze stepped backwards. There was no smile on her face; just a kind of nervousness, as if she couldn't quite believe what she had just done. Especially here. Especially now.

'I need to wash,' Chet told her. His words were stilted.

Suze glanced at the floor. 'Right . . .' she said. 'OK . . .' She watched him as he limped self-

148

consciously past her and into the bathroom.

It was still steamy in there from her shower. Chet had to wipe the condensation from the mirror, and he only had a few seconds to look at his tired, scarred face before it misted over again. He unbuttoned his shirt and splashed cold water over his face and torso, hoping it would clear his mind as well as his skin. It didn't. The words on the tape replayed themselves in his head, and the smell of Suze's freshly washed hair lingered in his senses. She was scared. Vulnerable. That much was obvious. She was relying on him to protect her. Chet was no psychologist, but it wasn't too hard to work out that her advances just now were a symptom of that.

Images rose in his mind. The intruder in his room, her face full of steely purpose. Doug, his friend, dead, broken and spattered in his own gore on the railway track. Despite all his setbacks, the guy had been so full of life. And now . . .

Chet winced at the memory.

The wind howled outside once more, and a fresh wave of rain battered the window. For a moment Chet forgot about shadowy intruders and corrupt politicians. It was bleak outside and they were alone. Why shouldn't they take comfort in each other's company? Seize the day—that's what soldiers always did. He wiped the mirror again. A battered face looked back out at him. Chet grabbed a towel and dried his face and upper body, before slinging it round his neck, taking a deep breath and opening the door into the bedroom.

'What the *hell* are you doing?' he barked the moment he saw Suze.

She was sitting on the edge of the mattress,

her towel still wrapped around her, and she was fumbling with the beige telephone on the side table, slamming it back down on its cradle.

'I was just . . .'

'Christ, Suze, do you think this is some sort of game? They want to *kill* us.'

She stared at him, looking like she might cry.

'I said we don't contact *anyone*. Do you know how easy it is to trace a fucking phone call? Who were you calling? I said, *who were you calling?*'

'I . . . it was . . . oh God . . . it was just the Met Office. I wanted to know how long this storm was going to last.'

Chet stared at her, then closed his eyes and drew a deep breath. 'Just don't . . . use . . . the phone, all right?'

When he opened his eyes, she was standing by the side of the bed. 'I'm really . . . I'm really sorry. I didn't think it was . . .' His voice trailed off and she chewed at her lower lip.

Suze took a tentative step towards him, and then another. Before Chet knew it, she was in his arms again, trembling slightly as she pressed her damp hair against his chest. They stayed like that for a minute before she stepped backwards again.

One pace.

Two.

She inclined her head slightly, then let the towel fall. It dropped heavily to the floor to reveal her slim, delicately curved body, her pale skin and her small breasts.

Chet glanced over to the door. It was still wedged shut with the chair. He turned to look at Suze. She was lying on the bed, and finally managed to give him a nervous smile.

'Look after me,' she whispered.

Chet hesitated for a moment, but then, without another word, he went to her.

*   *   *

As the rain fell in the Brecon Beacons, it also fell on the southern outskirts of London. It kept most visitors away from the Greenacres Retirement Home, a recently, and cheaply, built establishment next to the main road through Morden. In truth it hardly took freak weather conditions to discourage visitors to this place. The corridors were starkly lit and smelt of disinfectant and hospital food. There were no stairs, but lifts and ramps to enable wheelchairs to move around the buildings. The day room was decorated with floral curtains and dark carpet tiles. Channel Four News was playing on the TV, even though there was nobody there to watch it; at this time of the evening all the clients of Greenacres were encouraged to be in their rooms. It was easier for the poorly paid, often temporary, often Eastern European staff that way.

In Room 213, on the second floor overlooking the main road, an old lady sat in her wheelchair. It was dim in here—only a low-voltage bulb in a bedside lamp lit the room, but she preferred it that way. Her eyesight was deteriorating, and she found that bright lights almost blinded her.

Her right foot and ankle were swollen and wrapped in a bandage to protect the sores on her skin. She had decided a long time ago that it was easier to stay in the wheelchair all day than haul herself in and out of the armchair that was, with the exception of her single bed and a glossy pine

151

dressing table, the only piece of furniture in her sparse room. A pink hyacinth—her favourite flower—was blooming on the windowsill behind her. Its fragrance went some way to disguising the institutional smell of the place, but the old lady wasn't thinking about that. She was holding the telephone against her ear, and she was clearly flustered and confused.

'I . . . I don't understand dear,' she stammered. Her voice was as frail as the thin hands that held the receiver.

The old lady frowned as she listened to the voice at the other end.

'But . . . but . . . where *are* you? What do you mean, you can't visit me? I don't understand. Hello? *Hello?*'

She looked at the phone. And then, with frightened and perplexed eyes, she let it fall from her hands and squinted up to see the other woman in the room with her, half hidden in the shadows behind the door.

'Stay quiet, or I'll kill you.'

It was clear to the intruder that the old woman was confused, struggling to understand who she was and why she was here. It was perhaps the strangeness and uncertainty of her situation as much as the Beretta Model 70 semi-automatic aimed at her head that was now distressing the old lady.

'Your daughter?' the younger woman asked.

The old lady shook her head but she was too scared to keep the pretence up for long, and after a few seconds a pathetic little mewing came out of her lips, accompanied by a trembling of her whole body.

The woman put a mobile phone to her ear. She waited a moment before saying a single word. 'Traced?'

The reply was equally curt. A male voice that belonged to someone she had never met and never would. 'Traced.'

She put the phone back in her pocket and returned her attention to the old lady. She was still making fretful little noises. Still shaking. But she had the presence of mind to reach for the body of the phone—an attempt, the woman presumed, to call through to reception and alert them to the intruder in her room. It was a moment's work to pull the phone from her weak hands and place it out of reach on the dressing table. The mewing grew a little more desperate.

She needed to be killed, of course. That much was obvious. She had seen the intruder's face and knew what she was after. A gunshot was out of the question. Often the best you could do was mislead people about the cause of death. So it came quite naturally for her to look around the room in search of a more subtle instrument than the Beretta.

It didn't take her long.

The old lady's dressing table was neatly arranged. Two fading family photographs of a young girl and an older man, a hairbrush, a bottle of Nivea skin cream and a Tupperware box containing an array of medication. The woman looked through the box, discounting the vitamins and the cod liver oil and paying attention to the less benign drugs. The bottle she finally selected was made of brown glass and bore a printed pharmacist's label. Warfarin. One capsule to be taken once a day, it instructed, and—in stark, bold letters—'IN CASE OF OVERDOSE

153

SEEK IMMEDIATE MEDICAL ATTENTION'. She shook the bottle. It was almost full.

'I mustn't take those,' the old lady whispered. She sounded rather like a child repeating her parent's instructions. 'The nurse gives them to me. I mustn't take them myself . . . it's very important . . .' She nodded rapidly to emphasise her point.

The woman ignored her and, laying her Beretta on the dressing table way out of reach, spilled some of the little pink capsules into the palm of her hand. The old lady started shaking her head as she drew near, and the mewing started again, more panicked than before.

The first capsule was the most difficult to insert into the old lady's mouth. It meant pinching her papery, wrinkled cheeks with one hand—not too hard, so as to avoid bruising—and using the other to force it past her brittle teeth and on to the back of her tongue. Warm saliva collected around the woman's two fingers as she forced the old lady's head back, and inserted two more capsules in quick succession. There was a strangled, gargling sound from her throat, which grew more severe as the capsules were forced down. Now the old lady tried to beat her attacker with her fists, but she was much too weak to make any difference. Another three capsules were forced down her throat.

Then three more.

And another three.

The old lady was choking for breath now, holding her grey, veiny hands around her neck as the woman stood back and examined her handiwork. She didn't fully know what the short-term effects of a Warfarin overdose were, but that didn't matter. The capsules were only there in the unlikely event

154

of an autopsy. She stepped over to the bed, picked up the pillow and returned to the wheelchair.

Even through the fog of her confusion, the old lady knew what was about to happen. She looked up with bloodshot eyes and shook her head as forcefully as she could. 'Please,' she managed to gasp through her breathlessness. 'Please, no. My daughter . . .'

The woman put her lips just an inch from the old woman's ear. 'Your daughter will be joining you very soon,' she whispered. 'When I kill her, I will explain that her mother died squeaking like a cat.'

The old lady shook her head and a tear forced its way from her withered tear sacs into the corner of her eye. 'Suze is a good girl,' she whispered. 'A *good* girl. You mustn't hurt her . . .'

The woman sneered slightly at these words— the last, she knew, that the old lady would ever utter. She placed the pillow over her face—gently, because she knew that to press too hard could cause bruising around the nose and mouth—and then lightly pressed with her free hand against the back of her head, entwining her fingers in the thin, dry hair.

It was pathetically easy. The old lady's struggles were feeble; the way she flailed her arms and kicked her thin legs quite ineffectual; her mewing stopped and she was silent. The woman's eyes shone in the gloom as she went about her work. And because her victim was old and her lungs were tired, the process was quick. After forty-five seconds the flailing had eased off; after a minute and a half the body had slumped in the wheelchair. The woman removed the pillow and put two fingers to the jugular. Nothing. The old lady's face was still and grey. She replaced the pillow on the bed, then wheeled the chair in front of the dressing table, where she left the Warfarin bottle open just within reach of the fresh corpse.

A new smell hit her senses. Urine. That was no surprise. Now she was dead, the old lady's muscles were relaxing, and that included the bladder. Sometimes it happened sooner, sometimes later. In this case it had happened almost immediately, and now there was a dripping of liquid from the edge of the wheelchair on to the carpet. The woman was experienced enough to know that the bowels would probably follow, but by the time that occurred, she would be long gone.

It was calm in the room now. The rain continued to spatter against the window; the pink hyacinth remained the only splash of colour in this gloomy place. The woman allowed herself a bleak smile. The staff here would be used to occupants dying. When they found the old lady they would surely assume that she had come to the end of her natural life. If anyone did decide to investigate further, they would discover the overdose of Warfarin and assume that the confused old lady had had one bout of confusion too many.

She opened the door and walked out. The corridor was deserted, and she didn't encounter a single person until she was down in reception, where nobody paid her any attention anyway. Outside the home, she pulled out her phone and called a number.

'Mrs McArthur has quietly slipped from our embrace,' she said.

Then she waited as the voice at the other end read out an address.

TWELVE

For a soldier in the field, the sound a chopper makes is like the sound of Christmas bells. Nine times out of ten it means casevac or exfiltration. One time out of ten it means something more sinister. This was one of those times.

Luke knew from the rough, mechanical sound of the rotary blades it was a Russian MI-8, even before he saw it. 'Not one of ours,' he told Finn as they stood quietly by the mouth of the cave, their assault rifles strapped to their bodies. They weren't expecting an exfil, but if it had been a rescue helicopter it would be travelling low, fast and in a straight line towards them. This one sounded like it was circling above. Searching.

They stayed in the shadows as they looked out and up into the cloudy sky. Two minutes later the MI-8 appeared and circled above the desert just half a klick from their position, low enough for them to be able to see it.

'Reckon they're looking for us?' Finn's voice was dry.

'If Fozzie and the others are compromised, maybe it's just increased security?' Luke frowned. 'Put it this way: I don't think it's a jolly.' He checked his watch. Midday. Ample time for word of the firefight back in the village to have reached military headquarters in Baghdad and for them to have dispatched a heli. Did the authorities know that Abu Famir had been hiding out there and was now on the move? Maybe, maybe not. But Luke had to plan for the worst. He had to assume that the Iraqis were coming for them.

He looked over his shoulder into the gloom of the cave. Abu Famir was half kneeling, half lying by the Toyota, deep in prayer. The guy was a pain in the arse—weaselly, whingeing, never stopped talking. No wonder the British and Americans wanted him to be prime minister of the new Iraq: he had all the right qualities.

He turned back to Finn. 'We better hope that cloud cover stays put,' he said.

'Roger that,' Finn replied. 'We get a bright moon tonight and it'll be the shortest E and E in the history of the fucking Regiment.' He looked back over at Abu Famir. 'I'd like to put one in the back of that wanker's head and all,' he said.

At that moment the noise of the chopper altered. From their hidden vantage point, they saw it change direction and head straight towards the cave. The two men stepped back quickly, taking cover further inside, and Luke felt himself holding his breath as the helicopter hovered almost exactly above them. It stayed like that for a full minute, no more than thirty metres high and now so loud that it was impossible to talk. Then it curled away as quickly as it had arrived.

The two men exchanged a glance. It was clear they were both thinking the same thing: have they spotted us?

Another noise, but from inside this time: Amit crying out in pain. Finn made no attempt to hide his irritation, but before he could speak, Luke told him, 'Keep stag,' then stepped back into the cave.

They had driven the Toyota as deep inside as possible, opened all the side doors and turned the back seat into a makeshift hospital bed. Finn had suspended a drip bag from the roof and mainlined it into the back of Amit's hand, but things weren't looking good for their companion. He'd lost a lot of blood and they had only one morphine shot left. His bouts of delirium were now more frequent than his bouts of lucidity. All in all, the guy was fucked up.

Luke crouched down by his head. 'Amit, buddy,' he said quietly. 'How you doing?' His voice was accompanied by the gentle drone of Abu Famir's muttered praying.

Amit's eyes shot open. *'Maya?'* he whispered. *'Efoh at . . . Maya . . .'*

Whatever language he was speaking, it wasn't Arabic. Which meant Abu Famir was lying to them: their companion wasn't Iraqi. No fucking surprise there. But he wasn't Jordanian either.

'Hey, buddy. Nobody called Maya here.' He looked over at Abu Famir, who was still praying, then back at Amit. 'You want to tell me who you're working for?'

Amit took a few shallow breaths before he spoke again. 'Abu Famir,' he said. 'I need to . . . I need to get him out . . . It doesn't matter about me . . .'

Luke was about to reply when there was a noise from the mouth of the cave. A hiss. Finn was beckoning him over.

'I'll be back in a minute, buddy. You hold on, OK?'

He hurried silently over to where Finn was stationed, and he didn't need to speak to know what the problem was. There was a voice on the wind. A lone voice, singing.

Someone was nearby. Luke held his breath.

159

Through the mouth of the cave he could see, just coming into view from the right and about fifty metres away, a herd of perhaps fifteen goats. A single person was driving them—a Bedouin, from the look of him, wearing a white *dishdash* and red headdress. He was looking up at the chopper still circling in the sky about 200 metres away, but there was no doubt that the goats were wandering towards the cave.

'Shit,' Luke muttered.

He hurried back inside to find Abu Famir still praying. He nudged the Iraqi with his foot. 'Shut up,' he said.

'But I am . . .'

'Shut the fuck up. Someone's coming.'

Abu Famir scrambled to his feet.

'Get in the car,' Luke told him. 'Now.'

'No violence,' Abu Famir whispered. 'I will not . . .'

'Get in the fucking car!'

He returned to the front of the cave. Finn was in the shadows, one knee on the ground and his weapon in the firing position. The goatherd was driving his beasts directly into Finn's line of fire. He was only twenty metres away now, and from this distance Luke could make out that he was singing in accented English, and gradually the words became clearer. *'Walk like . . . an Eee-jyp-shuun . . . walk like . . . an Eee-jyp-shuun.'*

Luke loosened a knife in his ops waistcoat. 'If he sees us,' he said quietly, 'I'll jump him before he can shout out. If he runs, slot him.'

Finn kept his sights on the goatherd, while Luke took up position in the shadows on the other side of the cave's mouth, one knee on the ground and

160

weapon engaged.

The singing had stopped and now there was silence. After about a minute, however, another sound reached Luke's ears: a gentle clanking of the bells round the goats' necks. An occasional bleat. Then the musty, shitty stench of the animals as they wandered within ten metres of their position.

Luke felt his blood pumping in his veins. It was only a goatherd—no trouble for two fully equipped Regiment soldiers, but that wasn't the point. If they killed him, he might be missed—they were no more than five miles from the village, and that would mean more people searching the area; but if he saw them, they couldn't risk letting him go and warning other people of their presence.

The first goat—a scrawny thing with great, bulging eyes—came into view. It stopped just outside the cave and pawed at the dust while several other animals surrounded it.

The goatherd joined them.

Luke could see his face. He was in his early teens, the dark skin of his cheeks coated with bumfluff. He shouted something at the goats in a reedy voice, and made a clicking sound with his throat, but it seemed to have no effect. The goatherd shrugged, then removed a leather satchel from his shoulder and sat cross-legged on the ground. He rummaged in his satchel and pulled something out. Luke examined it through the sight of his assault rifle. It was an old cassette Walkman. The kid fitted the earphones to his head, pressed a button and continue to rummage in the satchel. This time he pulled out a rolled-up flatbread and started to eat.

The Regiment men stayed perfectly still. Luke

kept the youth's head firmly in his sights. Now and then a goat strayed into his line of fire, but that was OK, because he knew Finn had the kid covered too.

A groan from inside the cave. It was Amit, and the sound made Luke's skin prickle. One of the goats looked up, but the goatherd was lost in the music. Five minutes passed while he finished his meal, unaware of the danger he was in. He licked the fingers of his right hand, removed the Walkman and stood up again. He clicked ineffectually at his goats once more. Then he turned round to peer inside the cave.

Luke prepared to fire.

The goatherd sniffed.

He turned his back on the cave and looked out towards the desert. It was as if he was checking for something. Maybe Luke should nail him now, before he saw them and cried out . . .

The goatherd looked left and right. Apparently satisfied that he was alone, he crouched down on the ground and raised the hem of his *dishdash*.

That's right, buddy, Luke thought to himself. Have yourself a good shit and then fuck off out of here.

Luke was thankful for the stench of the animals, as it masked the waft of the kid's turd. Neither man moved as the goatherd wiped his arse with his left hand, then stood up and allowed the *dishdash* to fall back down to his ankles. He shouted at the goats again, urging them away from the cave's entrance, and started wandering off. The goats followed, but after only thirty seconds the goatherd turned and looked back towards the cave.

Had he seen them? Or was he just checking on the two goats that were straggling?

162

Two minutes later the kid was out of sight, the noise and stench of his beasts had disappeared and everything was silent.

Luke lowered his weapon and moved over to Finn. 'Remind me not to shake Abdul by the hand if we bump into him again.'

Finn ignored the comment. 'There could be more where he came from,' he said.

Luke nodded, then looked back into the cave. Should he tell Finn his suspicions about Amit? He decided not. His mate was bordering on insubordination as it was, and feeling mutinous. Give him a whisper of an excuse and he'd plug Amit on the spot. Luke didn't want that to happen until he knew *exactly* what he was dealing with.

He checked the time. 12.28. Five hours till sunset. When darkness came, they'd need to get on to the road and hope their luck held. And in the absence of luck, they'd have to use force.

He couldn't really decide if he was looking forward to nightfall, or dreading it.

*　　*　　*

21.32 hrs.

They were ready to go. The cave was pitch-dark, and Luke and Finn operated by means of NV. Each set had an infrared torch which lit up the cave for them but was invisible to Amit and Abu Famir, both in the back of the Toyota. The Iraqi's frightened eyes stared blindly in the darkness and glinted in the haze of the night vision, whereas Amit's were covered by the burka headdress that he was wearing again. A fresh saline drip was hanging from the plastic handle above the passenger door,

163

covered with a spare hanging *dishdash* by way of disguise.

Amit was shaking feverishly, his wound almost as bad as any Luke had ever seen. The flesh looked like liquidised liver, and the blood had started to congeal around it, crispy in places, thick and wobbly in others. As well as shaking, Amit was talking to himself. Through the burka it was difficult to make out what he was saying, and most of it was in a language Luke didn't understand anyway. But he caught the name 'Maya' more than once, and occasionally a confused reference to Abu Famir; otherwise Amit's words just sounded like slurred ramblings.

Luke recced outside. Since the goatherd had gone on his way, three choppers had flown over their position. Now the night sky was mercifully cloudy: no starlight, no moon. The temperature was already dropping and there was a slight wind, which once more brought with it the distant howling of the wild desert animals. If there were any patrol vehicles in the vicinity, Luke couldn't see them. He returned to the cave, where Finn was standing five metres from the car.

'Ready?' he asked quietly.

'Yeah.'

Luke paused. 'Look, mate,' he said. 'I know you don't agree with my decisions, but the one thing that's going to screw this up is if we're not singing from the same hymn sheet.'

Silence. And then Finn asked: 'What's the plan?'

'We've got eighty miles of main road to cover before we can turn off. I reckon we're looking at two hours. We only passed one static checkpoint on the way through, and that was about an hour

164

in, so we should reach it about 11.00. Fifty-fifty they'll just wave us through, but if not we'll have to use force then floor it to the border. Maybe swap vehicles if we can hijack another one. You still have the crossing we used marked as a waypoint on the GPS?'

'Of course.' Finn paused. 'We need a Plan B. If we have to get off the road and take Abu Famir across country by foot, we can't leave his bum chum to tell anyone what we're up to or where we're headed. We'll have to do him.'

'All right then. Agreed. Keep your weapon at the ready. Let's move.'

They climbed into the Toyota, where their carbines were stashed by the front seats, and Luke started the engine. It echoed around the cave as he carefully manoeuvred out into the desert night and back along the dirt track to the road.

They drove slowly by the light of their NV. They saw no one. After about twenty minutes on undulating ground, the main highway came into view again, vehicles passing at the rate of about one every thirty seconds. Luke pulled into the side of the road. They removed their NV and Luke double-checked his Sig, which now had a black silencer fitted to the barrel. As he manipulated the gun, he spoke to Abu Famir. 'If anyone stops us, I'll do the talking. Right?'

In his rear-view mirror he saw the Iraqi's spectacles glint in the darkness. 'No violence,' he said.

'No fucking talking,' Luke retorted.

They pulled out into the main road. Like the previous night, it wasn't very busy. About one vehicle in twenty was military, but there were sufficient civilian cars for the Toyota to be quite unremarkable.

Luke kept a steady speed. Sixty klicks an hour. Not too fast, not too slow. As he drove, his mind turned over. He remembered the three heli flypasts while they were in the cave. Was that just a coincidence—a standard military manoeuvre in this time of heightened security? Or were they looking for someone specific? Had word of the firefight in the village sixteen hours earlier reached the authorities? They had to assume it was known that somewhere out there was a vehicle with four occupants, one of them injured. They had to assume that the checkpoint guards had been alerted.

They'd been travelling along the main road in tense silence for some fifty minutes when Finn reached out and tuned in the car radio. Arabic music filled the car.

'Fuck's sake, Finn,' Luke snapped. 'Turn that shit off.' He reached out and switched it off himself, ignoring the look Finn gave him.

Amit groaned in the back. In the mirror Luke could see that his head had slumped and Abu Famir was looking at his burka-clad neighbour with a worried expression. 'How far until we . . . ?'

'Shut it.'

There were lights up ahead. The checkpoint. Vehicles in front of them were slowing down.

A blanket of silence fell over the car, ruffled only by the short, sharp breaths coming from beneath Amit's headdress. Luke felt for his handgun and sensed Finn doing the same. He looked ahead. On the other side of the road the barrier was down and a long line of vehicles—eight or nine in total, their headlamps dazzling in the darkness—were queuing behind it. The soldiers on duty surrounded around the frontrunner.

'I've got three men on the other side,' Finn reported. 'Could be more behind the oncoming headlights.'

Luke nodded and turned his attention to their side of the road. Here the barrier was pointing upwards, and because they weren't dazzled by the lights of the oncoming traffic, he was able to count the troops more precisely: four guards were manning their side of the road, but they were talking and laughing.

There were five cars between them and the checkpoint, spaced about twenty metres apart and all travelling at a respectful crawl. Directly ahead was a chunky old grey Mercedes, one of its brake lights not working. 'Put your fucking foot down,' Luke murmured. But none of the cars increased speed. If anything, they slowed down as they approached the checkpoint. It made sense: nobody wanted to attract any more attention to themselves than they needed to, even if they didn't have enough gear to start a small war stashed in the boot.

The Merc was just passing through the open barrier when Luke caught the eye of one of the guards. He looked a bit older than the others, and his expression was a little flintier. His AK was hanging diagonally across his body, but he had one hand firmly resting on the handle. He had set himself apart from his three colleagues and was paying more attention to the checkpoint.

Luke looked away, concentrating on the road and doing what he could to appear unassuming; but his peripheral vision was focused on the guard, who was moving towards the barrier. Luke felt his blood chill. 'Stand by,' he muttered to Finn.

His mate was already wielding his Sig.

'Burn it,' said Finn, his lips barely moving. 'Just get through . . .'

Luke accelerated slightly—not fast enough to make him look suspicious. All the while, his mind was calculating. What if the barrier went down before they reached it? Could he crash through? Probably not: the impact would take out their windscreen at the very least. They'd be blinded by glass fragments . . .

'Luke, if this goes noisy we'll have these fuckers on our tail from here to . . .'

'Thanks, buddy,' replied Luke. He trod down a bit more.

The guard was just making to close the checkpoint when they crossed. In the mirror, Luke saw the barrier slam down and the car behind them come to a halt. The guards swarmed, but now Luke was able to speed up, and the checkpoint soon vanished into the darkness.

Finn exhaled hard. 'Jesus. I thought it was all about to go Tora Bora for a minute back then.'

Luke allowed himself no such expression of relief. In the sky up ahead he could see lights. They were several klicks in the distance and they were circling.

'We're not out of the woods yet,' he murmured.

*　　　*　　　*

22.17 hrs. Distance to the border: thirty klicks.

There was a fit of coughing from the back of the

car that morphed into a strangled kind of sound. Amit slumped across the seat, falling on Abu Famir and yanking the drip down from its hanging place. Luke pulled over and opened up the bonnet as cover while Finn opened Amit's door and pulled him up to a sitting position. He removed the burka. The wounded man's face was deathly white; his eyes were rolling and an awful smell was coming off his body. Finn reattached the drip and slipped the headdress back on. Then he turned to Luke. 'Trauma. Massive blood loss. The guy hasn't got long.'

'If he dies, he dies,' Luke said flatly. 'We can dump the body.' He looked down the road. 'It can't be more than ten klicks till we turn off down towards the smugglers' route. Bit of luck, we'll be out of this shitty country by . . .'

He looked up, suddenly aware of a chopper approaching from a couple of klicks away. The two men exchanged a glance.

'Let's keep moving,' Finn said.

'Roger that.'

They took their seats again, and continued down the road.

*　　　*　　　*

22.31 hrs. Distance to the border: twenty-two klicks.

Finn had his GPS unit on his lap. 'Two klicks till we turn . . .'

He stopped.

'What the . . . ?' Luke groaned.

Two hundred metres ahead, he could see a line of red brake lights; thirty seconds later they too were part of the queue. Two light-armoured

169

military vehicles were parked up on either side of the road, and Luke counted seven armed Red Berets, three of them standing in the middle of the highway forming a temporary roadblock—newly established since the previous night—while the remaining four were searching each vehicle that passed. Not a cursory glance, either: all the occupants of each car were outside; the bonnets and the boots were raised. And as the Red Berets allowed each searched vehicle through the roadblock, only to repeat the operation on the next car, it became clear that they were stopping everyone.

'What . . . what are you going to . . . ?' Abu Famir's voice trailed off.

Luke and Finn didn't reply. They just glanced at each other, nodded once and subtly readied their pistols. Luke felt for his carbine.

Four cars to go before it was their turn to be searched.

Three.

From the back came a murmur. Abu Famir had closed his eyes and was muttering as if in prayer. Luke looked at the fuel gauge. Half a tank. Enough to get them across the border again? It would have to be, because once he put his foot on the accelerator, there'd be no time to stop.

Two cars ahead of them in the queue. Ten metres between them and the nearest guard.

The Regiment men didn't need to speak. They knew what they had to do. Luke pulled the hammer back on his suppressed Sig and checked the mirrors. Six cars were waiting behind them: all—so far as he could tell—civilian. Each man scrambled to get his M4 ready, poised down by his leg.

170

'No violence,' Abu Famir repeated, but even he sounded unconvinced, as though he knew there was only one way this was going.

One car.

The Merc's occupants—two elderly men—stood obediently by the vehicle while the Red Berets searched it. It took about two minutes, after which the guards nodded to the driver to get back into the car. They were walking towards the Toyota even before the car in front started moving.

Luke wound down his window. Finn did the same.

Strike hard, strike fast. It was the only way. If they drove through the roadblock without taking out the guards, they'd be showered from behind by a torrent of AK rounds and they wouldn't be out of range for 400 metres. Not an option.

Now the guards were alongside them, one on Luke's side, one on Finn's. They bent down at the same time to look into the car. And they never knew what hit them.

The suppressed Sigs made the dullest, deadest of sounds as Luke and Finn shot each guard once at point-blank range in the face. The rounds entered and exited in a split second, blood spattering the two gunmen as their victims' faces instantly dissolved into a mash. The guards crumpled to the ground. It happened so silently that the remaining Red Berets didn't even notice what was going on until Luke and Finn had stepped out of the car and raised their M4s. But by then it was too late.

The firefight was strangely quiet. Very few shouts from the enemy and none from the other drivers, who didn't exit their vehicles. Just the hum of car engines and the chugging of the M4s and

AKs. Finn fired bursts towards the opposite side of the road while Luke dealt with the two remaining guards on his side. They were standing about twelve metres from his position, readying their weapons at the sound of gunfire. It took him a couple of seconds to down them—single chest shots for each man—before he turned ninety degrees to add his fire to Finn's. By now Finn had dropped three men, but there were two more standing behind a civilian vehicle, distance twenty-five metres, their weapons resting on the top of the car and ready to fire.

'Go left!' Luke shouted.

A spark from one of the enemy rifles, and a round hit the side of the Toyota, just forward of Finn's door. Luke kept calm. He lined up his cross hairs with the head of the man who had fired and took the shot quickly. He knew as he squeezed the trigger that his aim was good, and he immediately switched his attention to the last guard. Finn had taken a shot but instead of hitting the final Red Beret, he'd shattered one of the windows of the car they were using as a shield. Another incoming round, inches above Luke's head. But then he fired, and as he did so he heard a crack from Finn's rifle at almost the same time. Impossible to say which of them had hit the last man, but one of them had.

Nobody left the vehicles behind them as Luke and Finn jumped back into the Toyota. Abu Famir's eyes were wide. 'No *violence* . . . I gave you my instructions!' Luke didn't answer. He floored the pedal and the car roared away.

'You cannot just kill men like that!' Abu Famir shouted. 'I will have you reported . . .'

Finn looked over the back of his seat and pointed his Sig directly at Abu Famir. 'If you don't shut up,

172

I'll do you too.'

For once the pomposity seemed knocked out of the old man.

They sped down the highway for a minute. Luke felt the sticky blood of the guards drying on the skin of his face, but he ignored it and kept one eye on the road, one on the mirror. Nothing chasing them yet. How long before the shooting back there was reported by one of the civilian onlookers? Impossible to say. Minutes, probably.

'Turning in 500 metres,' Finn said.

Luke nodded. Once they were off the road, they could get out the NV and drive to their covert border crossing. But when they were 100 metres from the turn-off, it became clear that it wasn't going to be so easy.

'Vehicles,' said Finn. 'They're offroad—looks like border control.' He was right. The desert off to the left—which had been all but empty the previous night—was now dotted with headlamps. To make matters worse, another chopper—or perhaps the same one—had turned up. It was hovering over their escape route, only this time it had a searchlight illuminating the road they needed to follow.

'They're looking for us,' said Luke.

'If we head down there, we're fucked . . .'

Finn was right. That route was closed to them. No doubt about it. They sped on past it.

'How far to the border?' Luke asked after a moment.

'Twenty klicks. If they don't see us heading that way, they're going to twig pretty soon that we're taking a different route . . . We should start thinking about Plan B.'

173

'Plan B?' Abu Famir piped up, his voice nervous. 'What is Plan B?'

Neither of the Regiment men answered, but Luke glanced in the rear-view mirror at the slumped, burka-clad figure of Amit.

Five minutes passed. Ten. Options and alternatives tumbled around in Luke's mind, but no other solution presented itself. They were heading straight for the Iraqi border. It would be well guarded, with God knows how many soldiers and how much military equipment. Certainly they were insufficiently equipped to break through.

They saw it from a couple of klicks. The road ran downhill to the border post, so they had the advantage of height. The checkpoint itself was illuminated in the darkness. There were two sections—the Iraqi and the Jordanian—separated, Luke estimated, by about 200 metres of open ground. Even if they could break through the Iraqi side—and given the large number of vehicles and lights and movement, that was hardly a straightforward prospect—it would be open season on them as they crossed that patch of no-man's-land. The Iraqis would have artillery covering it, especially now. Attempting to cross that border by vehicle was out of the question. Retreating to find their covert border crossing was also off the menu because the chopper and border-control vehicles had eyes on. They had only one option: to ditch the Toyota, travel by foot and try to find a weak point in the border fence. With border control on high alert, that was a dangerous call. They'd find it tough enough with Abu Famir in tow. There was certainly no room for any more stragglers. Especially wounded ones.

174

A kilometre from the border, Luke pulled over. There was no cover in the vicinity, and he was forced to ditch the car among the brush just four or five metres from the road. He looked at Finn, his face grim, and nodded.

'Get out!' he told Abu Famir.

'What is happening?'

'*Get out!*'

'I refuse to . . .'

Luke held his Sig up against the Iraqi's head.

'I'm not fucking around, old man. If you want to shoot the shit with Allah, stay where you are. Otherwise, get out of the car. Now.'

Abu Famir stared at the silenced Sig, his eyes bulging. His hand felt for the door lever and he quickly scrambled out of the car, slamming the door behind him. He went and stood about five metres away, close enough for Luke to keep an eye on, far enough away to be out of earshot.

There was a moment of silence. And then, from behind the veil of the burka, Amit spoke. 'You're going to . . . to kill me now?' His voice was thin and shaky. It was clearly a struggle for him to say even a single word.

'We have to go cross-country,' Luke said. 'You're too weak. You won't make it.'

Amit's body was trembling. 'Take this thing off my head,' he said.

Luke pointed his weapon at Amit and nodded at Finn to do as the man had asked. Even in the darkness of the car they could tell that Amit was on the way out. His eyes were glazed, his skin corpse-white. He appeared to be staring into the middle distance, every breath an effort, and for a moment Luke thought the delirium had returned.

175

He became horribly aware of the cars passing them, just five or six metres from their position. Each time one went past, the interior of the Toyota lit up, then faded into darkness. It would only take one of them to stop and see if they needed help, and then . . .

Amit spoke again.

'Abu Famir *has* to get out.'

'That's the plan, buddy,' said Luke.

'You're . . . you're British special forces, right?' Neither of them replied. It didn't seem to bother Amit. 'Can you do it? Can you get him across-country?'

'We can try.'

A passing car slowed down, but then sped up again.

'I'm going to die, aren't I? Of my wounds, I mean.'

A pause.

'You're in bad shape, buddy.' Luke glanced at Finn, then back at Amit. 'You want me to end it now? It'll be quick.'

Amit swallowed. His breath became a bit shorter, and he shook his head. 'It's my job to ensure Abu Famir is safe.'

'Who are you working for?' Luke demanded. 'You might as well tell us, mate. Seems we're both trying to do the same thing.'

Amit closed his eyes. 'For the Institute . . . Mossad. For Israel.'

Luke's mind began to click through the gears. Israel was top of Saddam's hit list. He'd demonstrated that before Desert Storm, when he'd started chucking scuds in the general direction of Tel Aviv.

176

'Saddam would bomb my people again if he could,' said Amit. 'It's my duty to ensure that the West invades . . .' He opened his eyes again. 'Perhaps you do not understand . . .'

It didn't matter if Luke understood or not. This was only going to end one way. 'You're not coming with us, buddy. I'm sorry . . .'

'For fuck's sake, Luke,' Finn cut in. 'We can't hang about.'

Luke nodded. What Finn hadn't said—what he hadn't *needed* to say—was that they couldn't leave Amit alive. It would be easy for the enemy to torture their plans out of him.

'Do it,' Finn said.

'Wait . . .' Amit's plea left him breathless. 'I can help you.'

'You're a bit past that, mate.'

'Listen to me. I can drive the car to the border. Cause a distraction.'

Luke and Finn exchanged a glance. 'Go on.'

'Do you have explosives?'

Luke nodded.

'What do you have?'

'C4. Frags. White phos.'

Amit nodded. His eyes flickered from one man to the other. And then, in his breathless, stilted way, he continued to speak.

*　　　*　　　*

Two minutes later Luke and Finn were standing five metres from the car, rifles slung round their necks and frowns on their foreheads. Four or five klicks to the east, they could see a chopper still circling, and on the highway one or two vehicles were still

177

passing every minute.

They spoke in low whispers. 'Do you trust him?' Finn asked.

'We haven't got much choice.' He looked towards the border. 'There's no way we'll get through there. We either slot Amit now, or we . . .'

Or we what? The checkpoint was a kilometre to the west. If he, Finn and Abu Famir headed in a north-westerly direction, they would have to cover about a klick and a half if they wanted to intersect the border a kilometre to the north of the checkpoint. That would take about fifteen minutes, but the choppers and border-control vehicles would have a high chance of finding them. They needed a distraction. Something to focus the attention of the enemy on a position where the SAS men and their Iraqi passenger wouldn't be. Something to give them a window of opportunity. And it was exactly that which Amit was offering.

'He's a good man,' Luke murmured. 'Don't know if I'd have the balls . . .'

'We need to make a decision now,' Finn said.

A pause.

Luke nodded. 'Let's do it.'

Abu Famir was standing by the car, waiting for them. 'What is happening? I *demand* to know what is happening.'

'Get ready to walk,' Luke told him. 'We're heading cross-country.'

'What about my deputy? He is too sick to . . .'

'You can drop the deputy bullshit now. He's come clean . . .'

Finn was opening up the boot. He started moving all the ammunition, explosives and grenades they had into the front passenger seat, while Luke bent down to speak to Amit. 'It's time,' he said.

Amit grabbed Luke's arm and turned his ghostly face to look at him. 'I have a sister,' he whispered. 'You must find her. You must tell her what I did, and that I did it for my country.'

'Course I will, buddy,' Luke lied.

'You *must*. Otherwise she will not understand.' Amit took a moment to catch his breath. 'Her name . . . her name is Maya Bloom.' His face became anguished. 'You *must* find her.'

Luke looked over his shoulder to see Finn standing just by him. He had two white-phosphorus grenades in his hands.

'Come on,' Luke said to Amit. 'Let's get you into the front.'

It wasn't easy. Amit's legs were too weak to carry him, and his knees buckled the moment he tried to stand. Another car slowed down and pulled up alongside them. The driver shouted something in Arabic.

'Tell them we're fine,' Luke instructed Abu Famir, who shouted out a response and the car drove away.

By the time Amit was in the driver's seat, he was coughing badly—a dreadful hacking, wheezing sound.

'Get Abu Famir away from the car,' Luke told Finn, taking the grenades from him and turning his attention back to Amit. The Israeli was slumped forward, his forearms flat against the steering wheel and his body shaking violently.

'Quickly,' he murmured. '*Quickly* . . .'

Luke turned the ignition key. He wound down the windows, then carefully removed the pin from one of the grenades, but kept the safety lever tightly squeezed.

'You sure you can grip it?' he asked. Amit nodded, and Luke curled the fingers of the dying man's left hand around it. If Amit lost his grip, Luke would only have a couple of seconds to get the hell away. He primed the second grenade, then carefully placed it in Amit's right hand.

'OK, buddy,' he said. 'You're good to go.'

'You will find Maya?'

'You got it.'

'In London.' His weak voice was hardly audible above the noise of the engine.

'I'll find her.'

'Then leave me.'

Luke didn't need telling twice. He stretched over Amit's body, put the vehicle's transmission into drive, then shut the door and sprinted away from the side of the road. He was at least thirty metres away when he turned to look back.

The Toyota had moved off. It was going very slowly, but it had joined the main carriageway and had started on the final kilometre before the border.

Abu Famir stared at the car. 'He did this of his own free will?' he asked.

'Hundred and ten per cent. A lot of people want you out of the country, my friend.' He watched the car until it disappeared.

'Think he'll make it?' Finn asked flatly.

Luke sniffed. 'Probably not,' he said. 'He's pretty fucked up. But even if he goes bang before he hits the checkpoint, it'll be a diversion.' He looked due north-west. It was dark, of course, but he'd seen the satellite imagery and he knew there was open ground here. 'I reckon we've got fifteen minutes.

180

Let's not hang around.'

'Roger that.'

The three men turned and started to walk across the desert.

* * *

Amit shook.

The pain was everything. It was no longer just the wound that hurt. Now it felt as if the pain had seeped into his blood and melted through his whole body. It was all-consuming. So intense that movement or even speech felt like obstacles he could never scale. He wanted it to be over. Finished. Gone.

But through the pain, one thing was clear to him. If he *must* die, let it be for a purpose. In a corner of his mind he saw a scene of devastation. It was an image that had haunted his dreams since he was a child: the aftermath of a Palestinian suicide bomb on the streets of Tel Aviv, his own parents the victims, torn—quite literally—limb from limb.

If he *must* die, let it be for a purpose. Not like them.

It took all his strength to clutch the safety levers of the grenades. He steered with his forearms, which had the full weight of his body behind them, but the car required little steering. The checkpoint was straight ahead. He could see it, even though his vision was blurred, but he was too confused to work out the distance. All he knew was that he had to make it, however far it was.

And he had to keep gripping the safety levers.

He couldn't allow the final remnants of strength to drain from his body too soon . . .

The rear lights of the cars that passed him drew long, red-neon lines through space. Amit felt as though a mist was gathering all around him. The closer it came, the less strength he had.

A car overtook, the driver beeping his horn at Amit's slowness. He barely noticed. His concentration was all used up.

How far to the border? *Harah*, how much further could he last?

Time passed. He had no conception of it.

He saw Maya in his mind. His sister. He saw her as a child, kneeling on the pavement by their mother, shrieks of indescribable grief reaching to the rooftops. And he saw her now. So ruthless. So angry. When she learned what he had done, she would be proud of him. That thought alone gave him a little extra strength. A little extra resolve.

The lights outside were brighter. More numerous. There were people. Uniforms. Men with guns. He removed his foot from the accelerator and pressed the brake a little too sharply. The Toyota juddered to a halt. Ahead of him there was a queue. Three vehicles, perhaps four.

He closed his eyes, panting, trembling. He had to wait until he was closer to the barrier, twenty metres ahead, where he could cause maximum damage. Through the open windows he heard noises. Vehicle engines. Voices shouting harshly to each other in Arabic. Bustle. People. The queue crept forwards. Slowly. So slowly . . .

There was only one car ahead of him now. His body was shaking even more violently. The strength was leaving his wrists. He mustered his determination and moved one arm down to rest on the ammo boxes on the passenger seat.

182

The lights were getting dimmer. He could barely breathe—just short, desperate gulps.

The car ahead had moved off. Amit advanced a final few metres towards the barrier.

Figures surrounded the Toyota, shadowy and indistinct. Amit had no idea how many there were. He was past counting. Past caring.

But he knew there were only seconds left.

'*Barukh atah Adonai, Elokaynu, Melekh ha-Olam,*' he prayed with the last remnants of his breath. '*Barukh atah Adonai, Elokaynu, Melekh ha-Olam . . .*'

It wasn't a conscious decision to let his grip on the detonation levers slip. His strength had come to the bottom of the tank.

Amit didn't hear the explosion of the grenades, or of the ammunition stash in the passenger seat. He didn't see the burning white fluorescence that filled the car and burst out of the open windows, or the way the hot phosphorus sprayed over the faces and uniforms of any border guards within twenty metres of the Toyota.

And he was dead before the car exploded, throwing shrapnel, rounds, fire and burning chemicals high into the air, and raining down on the border post and the soldiers who guarded it.

*   *   *

In the darkness of the desert, Luke, Finn and Abu Famir heard the explosion—a single boom, followed by a series of aftershocks. They turned in the direction of the border. It was a little less than a klick away, and they could see a distant glow—the remnants of the Toyota, of their weaponry and of

183

Amit.

Abu Famir shook his head in disbelief, visibly moved. 'Who was he?'

Luke wiped a trickle of sweat from his forehead. 'A decent guy,' he replied quietly.

A pause.

'In your world,' Abu Famir said, 'do decent guys always cause such destruction?'

From the opposite direction, they saw the lights of a chopper burning along the highway towards the border. The Iraqis' resources would now be concentrated on the location of Amit's makeshift suicide bomb. For a short while, at least. That would leave the three of them free to find a place to cross into Jordan on foot. Luke estimated that the border was now 800 metres north-west of their position. If they could reach the fence in the next ten minutes while the Iraqis were looking the other way, and with a bit of luck, they should be able to find a crossing point.

Luke turned his back on the explosion. He nodded at Finn, who nudged Abu Famir with the butt of his M4.

'Get moving, sunshine,' he said. 'We've got a border to cross.'

THIRTEEN

Chet woke up with a start.

It was a thunderclap that had roused him. He was lying on the bed, with Suze's naked body beside him, one slim arm over his chest. He checked his watch without waking her. 02.23 hrs. He cursed himself for having fallen asleep, but then what did he expect? He'd hardly had any shut-eye for nearly two days.

The room was dark and the rain hammered against the window. Suze murmured something in her sleep. He couldn't tell what it was, but she was clearly disturbed by her dreams. Her body jolted, like she'd received an electric shock, but she remained asleep.

He lay there, his mind churning. He heard the tape in his head. Stratton's voice, and the American's. The evidence that Britain's Prime Minister was being bribed to go to war.

He remembered the firm handshake the PM had given him thirty-six hours previously.

He saw Doug's broken body.

He saw the face of the woman who wanted to kill him. The wavy black hair. The black eyes.

It was a noise that brought him back to the here and now. It wasn't loud. Quieter than the thunder and almost masked by the torrent of the rain. He could easily have missed it. He got out of bed, dressed quickly and went to the window.

What he saw made him feel as if the blood had drained from his veins.

The rain was sheeting down, in thick waves

185

that limited his vision to about twenty metres. But twenty metres was all he needed to see that a vehicle was approaching. Its headlamps were off, but there was the faintest glow from the dashboard, which disappeared as the car came to a halt by the black Mondeo, fifteen metres from the farmhouse, and the driver turned off the engine.

He checked his watch again. 02.31 hrs. Who would be approaching this place at such a time? And driving in this weather without lights?

Only somebody who didn't want to be seen.

But how the hell . . . ?

Chet looked over to where Suze was still sleeping fitfully. He moved over to her side of the bed, put one hand on her shoulder, one over her mouth, and shook her. She woke up suddenly, looking round as if she didn't know where she was.

'I'm going to ask you this once,' said Chet, 'and honestly, Suze, you'd better tell me straight. *Who* did you call earlier?'

A pause. Suze looked at him with wide eyes, but she couldn't keep that gaze going for long. She lowered her head and Chet removed his hand from her mouth.

'My mum,' she whispered. 'I'm sorry . . . I just *had* to speak to her. She's in a home and she's expecting . . .'

Chet closed his eyes. He wanted to be angry, but there was no time for that.

'Listen to me carefully,' he said. 'Your mother's dead.'

She stared at him.

'You'll be dead too, if you don't do *exactly* what I say. Get dressed.' Suze didn't move, so Chet grabbed her by the arm and pulled her naked to the window. 'You see that vehicle? It arrived less than a minute ago.'

As he spoke, a light came on in the car as the door opened and a figure got out.

'Oh my God . . .' Suze whispered.

'Get dressed. Now.'

'Is it her?'

'Now!'

While Suze scrambled to get her clothes on, Chet rummaged around in his bag. Christ, what wouldn't he give for a nine-milly now? His fingers touched the cold surface of the alabaster cherub he'd stolen from Suze's neighbours. Hardly a weapon of mass destruction, but it was better than nothing. He moved to the doorway and switched on the light.

'What are you *doing?*' Suze cried, pulling her jumper on over her head. 'She'll know where we are.'

Chet shook his head. 'She'll *think* she knows where we are,' he said. He grabbed her by the arm again and pulled her out of the room. The landing was dark and it took a moment for his eyes to get used to it; but he didn't hesitate as he dragged her to the opposite end and quietly opened the door of the other bedroom they'd been shown. The lights were off in here, but Chet knew the layout was much the same as the room they'd just left: en-suite bathroom, double bed, window in the far wall. There was still the loft panel, but he calculated that the intruder would go straight for the room with the light on.

'Wait here,' he told Suze. 'Don't move.'

From downstairs came the sound of the dog barking. Once. Twice. Each bark seemed to go right through Suze. Chet made for the door, but she grabbed hold of him. *'Please* don't leave me . . .'

'I'll be right back. Keep the door closed and don't make a sound.'

'Chet . . . I . . .'

'Don't make a sound.'

He left the room and made his way along the landing again. At the top of the stairs, he stopped and listened.

And listened.

Nothing. Just the sound of the rain battering the house, and a howl of the wind.

And his heart, pumping heavily behind his ribs.

He made his way down the stairs, slowly and very quietly. Something creaked—a beam, perhaps, on the other side of the house. At the foot of the stairs he stopped to listen again; the whole place sounded dead.

It was darker than the barrel of a gun down here. Chet had nothing but the alabaster figurine with which to defend himself, and if their unexpected guest was the woman from earlier, she was armed. He needed the element of surprise.

Creeping away from the stairs, he moved silently along the hallway, barely daring to breathe as he made for the flagstoned room where they'd signed the guestbook. The smell of wood-smoke grew stronger, and moments later he was looking into the room. Even in the darkness he could see that the main door was shut, but there was something on the ground, perhaps two metres in front of the entrance. Still brandishing the cherub, Chet stepped towards it.

He was only a metre away when it started to dawn upon him what it was; bending down, he touched the fur of the cocker spaniel, its body

188

totally lifeless.

He spun round and touched the stone floor. Wetness. Footprints. He hadn't noticed them before.

He turned back, and followed them back to the hallway. He could just see that instead of turning towards the stairs they had headed left along the hall. He followed. There was a door at the right—slightly ajar—and one at the end. Chet put his back to the wall next to the open door and slowly kicked it further open.

No sound.

He looked inside. A double bed stood against the far wall and he remembered the old lady saying that she avoided climbing the stairs. He stepped into the room, returning the door to its original position and scanning the shadows using his peripheral vision. Nothing. He approached the bed. The old lady was lying there, face up; next to her, her husband. Chet put his palm an inch above her face. No breath. He bent over and pressed two fingers against her jugular. No pulse. She was already going cold.

Movement. Just a shadow in the corner of his field of view, passing the slightly open door. He turned and exited the room in time to see a figure disappear up the stairs at the end of the hallway, then limped after it.

And it was then that the screaming started.

It came from upstairs, and it was Suze: desperate and panicked. Chet ran to the stairs, ignoring the stabbing pains in his leg, and started to limp up. The screams stopped when he hit the fourth tread; by the time he was on the landing, the thick silence of the guest house had returned.

Light was spilling out of the room where he'd left

Suze. Chet burst through the open door to see the black-clad figure of the woman. She had her back to him; her hair was wet and so were her clothes. Suze was just in front of her, and she was being throttled from behind.

Chet strode into the room, raised the figurine and brought it crashing down on the side of the woman's head. She fell against the wall, releasing her grip on Suze, who gasped horribly as she inhaled. Chet bore down on the woman, fully expecting her to have been knocked senseless by the blow. But she hadn't. Like a cat, she regained her footing, and she turned to face him, pulling a handgun as she did so. In a fraction of a second he took in the bloodied welt on her face, and her expression, filled with a mad fury. Suze was on her knees by the window, her hands at her throat as she continued to gasp for air. The intruder's weapon— Chet instantly recognised it as a Beretta Model 70 semi-automatic—was in the woman's fist and she was raising her arm.

Beretta Model 70. *Harah!* Something clicked in his brain.

Chet lunged towards her. It almost felt like slow motion. Maybe that was because he knew, beyond question, that he was about to take a bullet.

The crack of the Beretta firing was deafeningly loud at this range. Chet managed to knock the woman's hand as she discharged the round. He felt the bullet nick the flesh on the top of his right arm. No pain yet—the adrenaline was masking it—but he knew he couldn't stop. Despite his flesh wound, he got one big hand around her neck.

In a grip like that, most people would panic and wriggle. Not her. With her back against the wall,

190

she raised her right leg and kicked sharply into Chet's groin. He doubled over and released her as his prosthetic leg wobbled beneath him.

Ignore the pain, he told himself. *You must ignore the pain . . .*

He hurled himself at her once more, both bodies thumping against the wall. The Beretta went off again, but the round thumped harmlessly into the mattress. Suze screamed as Chet lifted the woman off her feet and threw her out of the door and on to the landing.

She fell skilfully, still gripping her Beretta, and if the fall caused her any pain, she didn't show it. Her eyes flashing, she scrambled to her feet, and as she saw Chet's bulky frame staggering through the doorway on to the landing, her demeanour remained calm.

Again she took aim, but Chet managed to launch himself across the metre between them and knock the gun from her hand with one swipe of his left arm. As he did so, the pain from his flesh wound kicked in and for a moment his knees buckled. It gave the woman the time she needed to reach over to where the Beretta had dropped, stoop down and pick it up. But by the time she was standing, Chet was there again, his face twisted with both anger and agony. He grabbed the woman by her upper arms, lifted her off the floor and, with all the strength his damaged body could summon, he threw her down the stairs and on to the stone flags below. There was a dreadful clattering as she tumbled, along with the noise of an accidental discharge from the Beretta.

And then silence.

Chet didn't wait. He hurried back to the

bedroom, where Suze had shrunk into one corner, her pale face terrified. 'Is she . . . ?'

'I don't know.'

He opened the window. Heavy rain, falling at an angle on account of the chill wind, splashed into the room. He looked out. They were just above the front porch, its roof only a couple of metres below the window. Impossible for him to climb out with his leg, but Suze could.

He pulled his wallet from his trouser pocket and pressed it into her hands.

'There's money there,' he said. 'Go.'

She froze. 'What about you?'

Chet looked over his shoulder. He could feel his strength sapping away.

'Just go. Get out of here now. You need to head cross-country, and keep going.'

'How will you find me?'

'There's a cairn on the top of a hill about a mile due north of here.' He took a moment to get his bearings, then pointed just to the left of the window. 'That way. I'll meet you there before sunrise. If I'm not there by then, hide. And don't stop hiding.'

'But I . . .'

A sound from downstairs. Movement.

Chet turned back to Suze. 'She's Mossad,' he said.

'*What?* How do you know?'

'Beretta Model 70 semi-automatic. It's their signature weapon. Last time we met I heard her speak. I'm pretty sure it was Hebrew. She's a *kidon*—an assassin. The best in the world . . .'

'Why?'

'I don't know. But believe me—if Mossad have

192

us in their sights, that's as bad as it gets . . .'

Footsteps, coming up the stairs.

'*Go!*' Chet hissed. 'If you ever need any help, track down Luke Mercer, 22 SAS, tell him what you know. But only if you *have* to, Suze. If you don't, stay anonymous. Remember what I told you before. Stay dark.'

'How long for?'

'Just stay dark.'

He pushed her towards the window. 'Go. Don't stop running. Find the cairn . . .'

She made to kiss him, but he pushed her away.

'*Go!*'

She nodded, and started to climb inexpertly out of the window. Just before she disappeared, she turned round to face him.

'*Go!*'

Chet heard footsteps on the landing. His mouth was dry, his heart pounding. He headed towards the door. Towards the fight. If he didn't dig deep, it could be his last.

*   *   *

She had two weapons in her hands: the Beretta in her right, and in her left a brass poker that she had found beside the fireplace downstairs. It wasn't heavy.

But heavy enough.

Her face hurt. Whatever this man had hit her with had been sturdy. She'd felt the cheekbone crack on impact, and now the pain was blinding. It wasn't going to stop her from finishing the job, though. It only made her more determined to see this through.

There was silence on the landing now. The light from the bedroom spilled out. No shadow, which meant neither of them was in the line of the doorway. She needed to be prepared for an attack from elsewhere.

She looked into the room. The window was open, rain splattering in, and the latch knocked against the frame. An unpalatable thought came to her. Had they escaped her again?

Carefully, she stepped inside.

He came at her from behind the door, the figurine in his hand and a look of brutal concentration on his face. She was ready for him. One swipe of the poker at the leg he limped on was all it took. Metal met metal with a dull thud, and he crumpled immediately to the ground.

She set about him with the poker, striking him first on the gunshot wound to disable him further. He gasped in pain as the blood started to flow more freely, not only from the wound, but from new cuts that were opening up on his face and neck; but he still attempted to grab her ankles and unbalance her footing. She was nimble enough to avoid that; nimble enough to stamp down on his hands before she whacked him again hard on his wound.

Another gasp, and his body started to shake.

It would have been so easy to shoot him, so easy to put a bullet in his head and be done with it, but she was clear-headed and professional enough, even in the middle of this struggle, to take the more sensible option. For the third blow of the poker, she raised her hand a little higher in the air. When she brought it down on the side of his head, there was a thump and his body immediately went limp.

Silence in the room. Silence throughout the

house.

She looked at the figure at her feet. The scarred, ugly face was still contorted with pain; there was a puddle of blood oozing around his head, dark and sticky, and the right leg below his knee was jutting out at an angle. He barely moved—just the gentle rise and fall of his chest as he continued to breathe—and the life blood was draining from him.

The woman walked to the window. Nothing except the rain and the darkness. No sight of Suze McArthur, and she felt anger at the thought that she'd escaped.

'*Kalbah,*' she muttered. '*Bitch.*'

Silently she made her way down to the ground floor. She walked across the reception room, silent and dark, and propped open the door of the greasy old gas oven with a coal scuttle. She turned the oven dial on to full. It would be quicker, of course, to turn all the dials, but that would look less accidental. A hiss, and the smell of gas hit her nose. She took a box of matches from the worktop, removed a few pages from a newspaper and stepped over to the front door—edging round the dead dog—and waited.

The smell of gas grew stronger.

Stronger.

It made her a little light-headed, but that was OK. She could step outside before it really harmed her.

She gave it five minutes before opening the door and stepping outside. Standing in the porch with her back to the garden, she twisted the newspaper to make a torch and lit it. She waited for the flame to catch properly, then opened the door again, casually tossed the blazing paper inside and hurried away from the porch.

The explosion was almost silent, but the heat was intense. She felt it against her back as she ran towards her car, and saw the reflection of the detonation in the vehicle's windscreen, her own body silhouetted against it. And as she opened the car door, she saw flames licking from the windows: already fierce, despite the rain. She'd set enough fires to know that the house would be an inescapable inferno within seconds.

Why, then, didn't she feel pleased?

She looked around. Darkness, rain and wind. The bitch could be anywhere out there. It was impossible to find her. A harsh look crossed the woman's face as she got behind the steering wheel and started the car. It didn't matter, she told herself. She *would* finish the job. Somehow. Somewhere. It was only a matter of time before Suze McArthur showed up. And when she did . . .

And so, as the woman drove away and glanced in the rear-view mirror, she even allowed herself a smile. The flames had already engulfed the building now; they had spread to the first floor; they were quickly turning this old Brecon farmhouse into an enormous funeral pyre.

*　　　*　　　*

Suze scrambled.

Her clothes were soaked, and her matted hair was stuck to her tear-stained face. Her body trembled. She was 200 metres from the B&B, up a slight incline, crouching down, still clutching the wallet Chet had given her.

A sudden explosion behind her. She stopped and

turned, and over the next sixty seconds she stared at the orange flames emerging from the windows of the ground floor.

She was cold, but the effect of the wind and the rain against her skin was nothing compared to the chill she felt inside. She knew she should run, but her muscles wouldn't obey her brain and she stood there in the elements, barely able to move. Barely able to turn her head away. The woman *couldn't* have overcome Chet, she told herself. Any minute she would see him silhouetted against the flames, running towards her.

She stared as the flames rose higher.

'What have I done?'

Listen to me carefully. Your mother's dead.

A sob escaped her throat, barely audible above the sound of the weather, and she shook her head as a corkscrew of terror and grief twisted in her heart. What kind of nightmare had she brought upon herself?

The rain fell harder, but it had no effect on the flames. Within ten minutes the whole house was engulfed. When the roof collapsed, she heard the crashing sound even from this distance and over the noise of the wind. She found herself sobbing again, her tears making the conflagration bleary and indistinct. She wiped them away and continued to stare at the fire, desperately seeking the sight she longed for.

It never came. Tears blurred her vision again, and with another sob she turned and stumbled into the darkness.

The terrain started to descend and she found herself in a dip from which, if she looked back, she couldn't see the flames, only the glow as they lit up the sky. But as she hurried desperately in the direction she hoped was north, the gradient increased again and the farmhouse came back into view. It was completely engulfed.

She continued to climb. He would meet her, she told herself. He *would* meet her, like he said he would. Her lungs burned with exhaustion but she kept on climbing, and after twenty minutes she found herself at the brow of a hill. She looked around. About thirty metres to her right, she could see the vague silhouette of a small pile of stones.

As she stood there, suddenly, unexpectedly, the moon appeared. Without knowing where the instinct came from, she threw herself to the ground to avoid being lit up against the horizon, then crawled on all fours towards the cairn.

Suze didn't look back towards the house. All feeling had left her, except the dread that seeped through every cell in her body. She tried to fight it. He would come. He *would* come. The moon disappeared again. The rain continued to fall. She heard sirens in the distance. Soaked and freezing, she hugged the stones, waiting for a figure to arrive. Waiting to hear his voice.

But the only thing that arrived was the dawn.

She lay there, shivering, crying, knowing she should run, but not knowing where to run to. Chet's face and words were all she could hear.

Don't stop hiding . . .

Stay anonymous . . .

Stay dark . . .

She could have managed it with him alongside her. He knew what to do. How to protect them. But he couldn't protect them any more.

The cold penetrated her bones. The rain fell on

her hunched-up body. But only one thought filled her mind: how could she stay hidden—how on *earth* could she stay hidden—now that the one man who could look after her was dead?

FOURTEEN

London, the following day.

It was cold in Hyde Park. Early-morning joggers pounded the pathways, their breath steaming in the air. There were cyclists too, their white and red lamps glowing in the half light, and their luminous-yellow waistcoats gleaming. None of them paid any attention to the two figures walking north to south from Lancaster Gate, along the still, gloomy waters of the Serpentine. A man and a woman: he with a shiny, balding head and wearing thick-rimmed glasses, a thick, shapeless black overcoat and woollen mittens; she a good head taller, with wavy black hair, an altogether more stylish coat, a fashionable black beret and an ugly red wound on one side of her lovely face.

'You've done well, Maya,' said the man quietly in Hebrew as they walked. The language sounded out of place here, so far from the streets of Tel Aviv.

Maya Bloom kept looking forward. Her cheek throbbed, but she ignored the pain, just as she had been taught.

'Not *so* well,' she said, and she pulled her coat a little more tightly around her. Her eyes flickered right, towards her handler. Ephraim Cohen was not a man given to paying compliments. He had a soft spot for Maya, though, and she knew it; but she also knew to take him very seriously. Cohen had a reputation as one of the Institute's most demanding case officers, and plenty of young recruits had had a promising career cut short by a disapproving report from this unassuming-looking man. Which was why Maya couldn't help but feel surprised that he was congratulating her, and not the opposite. 'The woman got away,' she reminded him. Once more, she felt a rush of anger at her failure to eliminate both her targets.

'We'll find her,' Cohen replied with no trace of a smile. 'The word is out. She can't hide for long.'

Maya inclined her head. 'When she pops up,' she said, '*I* should be the one.'

For a moment Cohen didn't reply. When he did, his voice was even softer. 'There is a whisper in Tel Aviv,' he said, 'that the *kidon* Maya Bloom takes too personal an interest in her work. This is a whisper, Maya, that I can safely ignore, isn't it?'

Maya sniffed disdainfully. 'I serve Israel,' she said, 'and the Institute.'

'Your allegiance to the Institute is noted,' Cohen said lightly.

They walked on for twenty metres in silence, ignoring the strident bell of a cyclist, who was forced to swerve off the path and on to the grass to pass them.

'You understand the importance of what you did last night?' Cohen asked once the cyclist was gone.

'I just do what I'm told.'

'Of course. But I want you to know why, Maya. It will help you in the future. You think the Institute has any real interest in a former British soldier with one leg, or in his girlfriend?'

'It depends what they've been up to, I suppose.'

200

'Indeed it does, Maya. Indeed it does. Would you like some coffee?'

They had reached a road running through the greenery, where a small white catering van had parked up. Cohen politely requested two cups of black coffee from the overweight woman behind the serving hatch. He handed one to Maya, took a sip of his own and they carried on walking.

'The truth is,' Cohen continued, 'that I don't know what they've been up to. All I know is this: it was Prime Minister Stratton himself who ordered their removal.'

Maya stopped and looked at him. 'Are we servants for the British now?' The thought angered her.

Cohen smiled. 'Hardly that, Maya. Hardly that.' He looked around the park. 'A green and pleasant land,' he murmured. 'But every land has its secrets. Britain is not alone in that.'

'But why us? Britain has its own . . . resources.'

'True, it does. But the British intelligence services are reluctant to have their people do what you do on home soil. They feel the scope for errors is too great. It is dangerous for their director to claim innocence in matters of political assassinations if its own people are carrying out such actions. You never know.' He smiled again. 'We are lucky, Maya. The Institute makes no real secrecy of its actions. Our own assassinations are personally signed off by our prime minister. It makes life a lot easier.'

'I still don't understand why my orders come from London and not Tel Aviv.'

'Your orders come from me,' Cohen said, with a hint of sharpness in his voice.

'And where do *your* orders come from?'

Cohen didn't like that. She could sense it. It took a few seconds for him to reply, and he sounded like he was choosing his words with even greater care than usual. 'We operate on British soil with the sanction of the British Government,' he said. 'When we need to do something here, they turn a blind eye—provided we are discreet, of course. In return, if the British have a problem of a sensitive nature on their own soil, they sometimes come to us. These occasional favours we perform for them are of great benefit to us, Maya. They are of great benefit to Israel.' He took a sip from his coffee and looked straight ahead.

'Is that all I am?' Maya asked. 'Someone who does favours?'

'Your allegiance to the Institute, Maya,' Cohen echoed his earlier statement, 'is noted.' She immediately understood that that part of their conversation was over. But it didn't make her like it any the more.

Up ahead, two mounted policemen were trotting towards them. They stepped aside and let them pass. 'The police presence is high,' Maya observed.

'As is the terror threat,' Cohen replied. 'London is not quite so dangerous as Jerusalem, but it's not far off. Everybody knows what is coming.'

'This war . . .' Maya murmured. 'It makes no sense.'

'What do you mean?'

Maya stopped and looked around. 'Find me one British person in this park who thinks Britain should invade Iraq. In Tel Aviv or Jerusalem it's different. The Arabs would crush us tomorrow if they had the chance. But Britain?' She made a contemptuous sound from behind her teeth. 'Why should they care? Why is Stratton so keen to take them into a war that nobody wants?'

'I don't know. To be frank with you, Maya, I don't care. A coalition invasion of Iraq is good for Israel.'

'I wish *I* was involved in that,' Maya said.

'You are, in your way.'

'Not like Amit.'

It was the name of Maya's brother that caused Cohen to stop once more. He gave Maya a serious look, then glanced round until he spotted an empty bench. 'Let's sit over there,' he said. 'I have something to tell you.'

'What is it?'

'Please, Maya. Let's sit down.'

'I don't want to sit down. Something's happened. What is it, Ephraim?'

Cohen's brow furrowed. 'It's Amit,' he said quietly.

'What? *What?*'

'He's dead, Maya. I'm sorry.'

She blinked at him as a dreadful sensation coursed through her body. She saw her brother in her mind: the short, stocky frame and rumpled dark hair. The only person in the world that she cared about. The only person in the world that she loved.

'You're lying,' she said.

But she could tell from the way that Cohen shook his head that he wasn't.

Everything fell away: the pain in her cheek, the anger, the cold.

'You should sit down, Maya. You don't look well.'

'How did it happen?' She turned on him and they

were standing so close that he was forced to look up at her.

'How did it happen?'

Cohen bowed his head. 'He was behind enemy lines. Iraq. There was a firefight and Amit took a bullet. It killed him instantly. He died bravely, Maya. Serving his country. You should be proud of that.'

His words were like a torch to paper: Maya felt herself burning up. 'Proud?' she demanded incredulously. *'Proud?* The fucking Arabs killed my parents, Ephraim.'

'I know your history, Maya,' Cohen said mildly.

'No! All you know is what you read in a file. I was seven years old, Amit was eight. We saw our mother lying in the street in Tel Aviv without her arms. *Without her fucking arms, Ephraim!* And my father—there wasn't even anything left of him. And now you tell me I should be proud that these Arab dogs have killed Amit . . .'

'Perhaps I chose my words poorly . . .'

'Perhaps you did.' Maya's face was contorted with terrible pain. If she had been the type of person to shed tears, she would have wept. But her cheeks remained dry even though her insides were burning up with anger and grief. Her body shook, and she stormed away from Ephraim, towards the bench he had pointed out. Sitting down, she put her head in her hands and remained that way for a minute, maybe longer. Gradually she became aware that Cohen was sitting next to her.

'You have my condolences,' he murmured.

'I don't want your fucking pity.'

'I didn't offer you my pity. I offered you my condolences. I shan't do it again. Sit up, Maya.'

She ignored him.

There was a pause of about ten seconds. When Cohen spoke again, his voice was quieter, but a good deal firmer. 'If you ignore an instruction of mine once more, Maya, I shall assume that the Institute no longer has need of your services.'

Maya felt herself sneer behind her palms, but she recognised the severity in her handler's voice, and she knew he was not the type to make threats idly. Slowly she removed her hands from her face and sat up again, though she refused to look directly at him.

'War is around the corner,' Cohen murmured, staring out across the park. 'The Arabs will pay for what they did to Amit. They will pay for what they continue to do to Israel. Saddam Hussein has his missiles pointed at our homeland, Maya. We both know he would fire them if he could. The British and Americans are not going to war to make our lives safer. But that is what they will do, and we must play a part. *You* must play a part, Maya. For Amit, and for Israel.'

Maya was still trying to quell the rage inside her. 'What do you want me to do?' she whispered, looking straight ahead.

Cohen nodded with satisfaction. Then, slowly, he removed a small photograph from his shapeless overcoat. It was a colour portrait of a man in his sixties, perhaps older, with a thin grey beard and glasses. 'Who is he?' Maya asked.

'A British weapons inspector. Well respected, by all accounts. Unfortunately he has taken it upon himself to become a thorn in the British Government's side. He's of the opinion that the Iraqis are not in possession of weapons of mass

205

destruction, and certain interested parties are worried that he might go public.' Cohen removed his glasses and held them out in front of his head, as though checking the lenses for dust. 'That can't be allowed to happen, of course.' He replaced his glasses and turned to look at Maya, who was still avoiding his gaze. 'MI5 can't touch him—it would raise too many suspicions. That's why the job is yours. It needs to look like an accident, Maya. Or, for preference, a suicide. It can be made known that the pressure of work got to him, that he . . .'

'I'm not doing it.'

Silence.

'I don't believe, Maya,' Ephraim said in a dangerously low voice, 'that I offered you a choice.'

She handed him back the photograph. 'Someone else can go after this guy. It won't be difficult. I want direct action against the Arabs. They have killed all my family. All of them, Ephraim. I want to hit back.'

Cohen shook his head. 'You know we can't put you into the Arabic-speaking world. You're a woman. You'd be too conspicuous.'

She treated that comment with the contempt it deserved. 'I'm the best *kidon* the Institute has,' she snarled. 'Do you really think I can't take care of myself?'

'No, Maya. I don't think that. But it still isn't going to happen and you'd better get used to it. The Institute doesn't exist so that you can take revenge. Anyway, this is an important operation. We . . .'

Maya stood up mid-sentence. She couldn't listen to any more. 'Forget it, Ephraim. I'm not interested.'

They locked gazes. Maya could read Ephraim's

206

face like a book. He was sizing her up. Working out whether she was serious. Planning his next move. Fine. He could plan all he wanted. Their talk was over.

'You're making a mistake, Maya,' Cohen said. 'I fight your corner at the Institute. Walk away now and I won't be able to do that any more.'

She continued to stare at him, but in her mind all she saw was her brother's face, and the pain of Amit's death twisted inside her once again. She slowly shook her head. 'You won't need to,' she said.

'Don't make the wrong decision, Maya.'

'The Institute is weak. If *it* won't do what needs to be done, *I* will.'

And then she turned her back on her handler and walked away from the bench. She didn't look round, because she knew that a man like Ephraim Cohen would take that as a sign of weakness.

*   *   *

Cohen watched her leave. He saw her slim, black-clad figure stride along the banks of the Serpentine, then turn and disappear from view. He didn't move from the bench.

A second pair of mounted policemen trotted by, the clip-clopping of their horses uncommonly loud. Cohen barely noticed them. His mind was turning over. Replaying their conversation. Deciding what to do next.

He remembered the first time he had met Maya Bloom. It had been five years ago, and he had been aroused by the sight of this beautiful creature—by the curve of her breasts and her hips, by the way her full, glossy lips parted slightly even when she wasn't speaking. Every member of the Institute knew what a powerful weapon sex was, but that didn't mean any of them were immune to it, and Cohen could remember the daydreams he had entertained that he and his new agent might become lovers. The thought of her warm skin against his, and the dangerous games they would play.

These, he now realised, were the pathetic fantasies of an ageing man.

So far as he knew—and he had done everything in his considerable power to find out—Maya had no lovers. The sex she exuded was shared with nobody. The body that he lusted after would never be anybody's. Maya Bloom had only one thought, and that was for her work. This she carried out with an efficiency that sometimes surprised even the more hardened officers back in Tel Aviv.

He had lied to her, of course, about the cause of her brother's death, but that was a necessity. The information that had come through was sketchy, filtered unreliably through British intelligence. But if it was indeed true that Amit Bloom had perished in a suicide bomb, there was no knowing how Maya would react. It had been important to him—to the Institute—that Maya's loyalty remained unquestioned. But that wasn't how things had played out, and he was experienced enough to know that it changed everything.

A *kidon* was a weapon. The very name meant 'bayonet'. They were a tool of the state of Israel, just as surely as the missiles housed in silos in the Negev desert. If one of those missiles was faulty, the course of action would be clear: it would be dismantled and taken out of service. And what

208

was true for a missile in the Negev was true for a *kidon*—especially one as volatile and dangerous as Maya Bloom.

As Cohen pulled his mobile phone from the pocket of his shabby coat, he wondered whether she might have prevented what he was about to do had she shared herself with him at some point over the course of their professional relationship. He was honest enough with himself, as he called a number, to realise that it would probably have made no difference. In their world, loyalties were not forged between the bedclothes. It was more complicated than that.

Yes. A great deal more complicated.

A voice answered the phone. 'Who's this?'

'It's me. Cohen.'

A silence.

'What do you want?'

'A favour,' he said. 'Or rather, the repayment of a favour. I have a little problem, and I need you to take care of it for me . . .'

*   *   *

As Maya Bloom walked along the Serpentine she could feel Ephraim Cohen's eyes burning into her. Even once she was out of his line of sight, she could sense his watchfulness, as though he was some invisible spirit gazing over her. She understood the way he looked at her. She recognised the lust. She saw it in almost every man she met. There were exceptions, of course. She thought about the guy she'd killed last night. Even through the mask of his scarred face, she had seen his determination. He had looked at her not with the eyes of a suitor, but

209

with the eyes of a killer. It was an expression she knew well. She saw it in the mirror every day.

Maya knew, however, that Ephraim Cohen was not the kind of man you walked away from without there being some kind of consequence. What she had just done had implications.

She left the park and hailed a taxi. Ten minutes later she was letting herself into an unmarked door in Lexington Street in Soho, and climbing up the tacky carpet of the stairs that led into the operational apartment she had inhabited for these past five years. Central enough to be useful, anonymous enough to be an effective safe house, it was a spartan place. Thick net curtains covered the only windows on to the street below, blocking out much of the daylight, but also stopping anyone from looking in. There was almost no sound from the busy streets, though occasionally, through the thin walls, she could hear the hookers next door servicing their clients.

The flat had three rooms: a living space with a small kitchenette; a bedroom with a large double bed, a dressing table, an armchair and a standard lamp; and a tiny bathroom. There were no personal possessions here, nothing that would ever give a clue as to who occupied it and certainly nothing to suggest that it was a woman. No soft furnishings or items of comfort. Just what was necessary. Even the drawer full of make-up in her dressing table was a tool, and once she was inside, Maya headed straight for the bedroom and opened it.

Lipstick. Mascara. Perfume. Sometimes these weapons were as formidable as any gun, and she needed to apply them with care.

First, however, she showered, washing away the

dirt of last night's job with a tub of Swarfega she kept for that purpose. She noticed a spattering of blood on the inside of her wrist, and remembered bludgeoning the wound of her victim the previous night. It was difficult to scrub off, but soon her flesh was clean. She stepped out of the shower, quickly dried her skin and her hair, then returned to the bedroom. She sat naked at the dressing table, where she powdered her aching cheek so that the swelling was less visible, before fixing her make-up and applying a squirt of perfume to the top of her pale breasts.

The clothes she chose from her wardrobe left little to the imagination. Black hold-ups. Lace underwear. No bra, but a short white dressing gown with two pockets. Once she had done it up, she returned to her dressing table and opened an empty drawer. It had a false bottom, which she removed to reveal her small stash of weaponry. Rounds for her Beretta, a 9mm snubnose and a small knife. She took the snubnose and the knife, and placed one in each pocket of her dressing gown. Having replaced the bottom of the drawer, she took a seat in her bedroom armchair.

And here she waited.

As she waited, she thought. Of Amit, of her parents and of the past. And when those thoughts became too much for her to bear, she thought of the future. All her adult life had been devoted to the Institute, from the day she had been admitted into the training academy until today. Now, of course, was when it ended. She had her own battles to fight. If Mossad wouldn't help her wage war on the Arabs, she would have to do it herself.

Time passed. The day slipped away and darkness

211

crept into Maya's flat. She switched on the standard lamp by her armchair and continued to wait. She knew Ephraim Cohen's methods well. She had carried out his instructions often enough, after all. He would send someone today. If a job needed to be done, it needed to be done quickly. And if she refused to leave this flat, *they* would have to come to *her*. That meant she was in control, no matter what anybody else thought.

She heard the first noise a little before ten o'clock. It was very quiet, barely louder than the beating of her heart: the sound of the lock on the street door being picked. She loosened the dressing gown around her cleavage, then slipped her right hand into the pocket containing the snubnose and pointed it through the flimsy material of her gown, towards the door of her bedroom. Perhaps she would need the weapon instantly, but she hoped not. The noise would attract attention.

And besides, Maya Bloom had other plans for her expected, but unknown, guest.

She didn't hear footsteps coming up the stairs, but then she wouldn't have expected to. Any hitman worth the name should be able to tread quietly. The first she saw of him was his weapon, a suppressed handgun peeking round the corner of the door as it slowly opened to reveal a shadowy figure silhouetted in the frame.

Silence.

Her finger slowly caressed the trigger of her weapon.

'Who are you?' she whispered, injecting a note of fear into her voice. 'How did you get into my . . . ?'

'Shut up.'

The figure stepped into the room. Maya saw

a young man, perhaps in his mid-twenties, with black hair and stubble on his face. His voice had a cockney twang. She examined his weapon. A matt-black Glock, safe-action trigger.

'Please,' Maya whispered. 'Don't hurt me. I'll do what you want . . .'

The young man took another couple of steps towards her.

'*Please*,' she said. 'I'll do anything . . .' She kept the hidden gun pointing directly at him, ready to shoot at the slightest hint that he was going to use his.

He eyed her up and down. Maya understood the look. She understood that he was already hers.

Feigning timidity, she stood up. Her dressing gown was tied sufficiently loosely for her breasts to be exposed, and she saw the newcomer appreciating the sight. She understood assassins, understood their love of danger and of risk-taking, and that they were devoid of principle. And she understood men too. She knew what was going through this one's head: that he was going to kill her anyway, so he might as well have her beforehand. It didn't matter how good they were, they always thought with their dick first and their head second. It was one of the first things she'd learned during her training, and she'd used that knowledge more times than she could remember.

'Get over to the bed,' he instructed. 'Lie down. Maybe I'll let you live.' *The arrogance*, she thought. This was why women made better killers than men.

Maya released the grip on her snubnose—she wouldn't be needing it now. She was safe as long as this man's sexual energy remained unspent. She did as she was told, positioning herself so that her

213

knees were bent at the end of the mattress, her feet on the ground and legs slightly open. The man towered above her, lasciviously taking in the sight, then bent down and roughly yanked her knees apart. She felt the cold butt of his weapon being pressed into her right thigh at the same time as she felt herself being exposed by two rough fingers pulling her underwear to one side. And when she felt his tongue inside her, she gasped—feigning the arousal she never felt.

She let him continue for about ten seconds before slowly moving her left hand down to the pocket containing her knife. She moaned as she removed it, just to keep him interested.

'You like that, huh?' she heard him say, like some boorish stud in a porno flick.

'Yeah,' Maya replied in kind. She'd studied the movies, and she knew what guys liked to hear. But as she spoke, she raised her arm above her head. 'Yeah, I like that . . .'

It was a single movement. She used the strength in her stomach muscles to sit up at the same time as she brought the knife arm down with all the force she had. The thin blade slammed into the back of the man's neck with absolute ease, and with a second sudden movement, she pushed his head with her free hand so that he rolled on to his back. As she stood up, she saw his limbs twitching violently; his tongue, which just seconds before had been so busy, was still peeking out from his lips, surrounded by blood. It looked to Maya as though he had involuntarily bitten into it.

It took him about a minute to die. A minute during which a thick pool of blood seeped from the back of his neck and the twitching of his limbs

214

receded into nothingness. Maya watched it happen, standing above her victim semi-clad and with a flat, dispassionate look in her eyes.

His death, she decided, once the corpse was still, was not enough. Her usual habit was to make things look like an accident, but tonight she had a different intention. She tightened her dressing-gown cord, then bent down and hauled his body on to the bed, ignoring the blood that smeared her hands, her feet and her gown. She rolled him on to his front, pulled out the knife and rolled him back again, before going about the awkward business of undressing him. In the end she found herself cutting strips of material away with the knife. Occasionally she scored the skin, but that hardly mattered now. Her victim was about to look a whole sight worse.

Once he was fully naked, she stepped back and examined him. One cut would do it, from the throat, down his abdomen, to the area just above his groin. The knife pierced the skin easily. With the precision of a butcher she sliced his body open in a single movement. Blood seeped from the incision, though not a great deal because his heart was no longer beating. Maya discarded the knife—it had done its work—and then slipped her fingertips into the incision in the belly and ripped the skin apart.

There was a sucking sound as the warm internal organs loosened and spilled out, bringing with them a terrible, rancid smell. The end result was monstrous and Maya, even though her stomach was turned only by the stink and not by the sight, recognised this. She went back to the bathroom for her second shower of the day, leaving bloodied footprints in the carpet as she went.

This time the blood took longer to clean from her skin. The shower ran cold, but she stayed there until the water spiralling around the plughole was no longer pink. When she stepped out, she was covered in goosebumps, so she dried quickly and put on a clean set of clothes, barely glancing at the mutilated corpse on her bed.

It was time to leave. There was nothing she wanted to take with her, except the snubnose, the Beretta and the extra rounds. She would never be returning to this place. She allowed herself one final look at her handiwork. Did it say what she wanted it to say? Did it warn Ephraim Cohen, and the others at the Institute, what would happen to anybody they sent after her?

'*Ken behekhlet*,' she muttered to herself. 'Damn right it did.'

Maya Bloom walked out of the bedroom, descended the stairs and stepped out into the cold night air, closing the front door quietly behind her.

PART THREE

Ten years later, 2013.

FIFTEEN

5 December.

Reg Parker, the driver of the soon-to-depart 16.55 train from Bristol Parkway to London Paddington, was deeply engrossed in his *Daily Express*. He had a thing for Kate Middleton and was glad to be alone in the driver's compartment to lech over the double-page spread plastered with paparazzi shots of her on a beach in Antigua. No sign in the pictures of that chinless wonder Wills, thank God. Just Kate, the sea, the sand and, in his imagination, Reg himself—rubbing factor eight into her back. He looked up in irritation when he heard a tap on the platform-side window.

Some bloody foreigner was standing there, grinning like an idiot. He wore a baseball cap and dark glasses, so Reg couldn't tell what nationality he might be. Chink, perhaps? He had a camera round his neck, so Reg reckoned he was a trainspotter. Bloody weirdos, the lot of them. He shook his head with irritation, pointed back towards the passenger carriages and went back to his paper.

But the trainspotter didn't give up. He tapped louder. Reg, irritated now, threw Kate and her sun-kissed skin to one side, and lowered the window.

'Look, mate, you need to step back from the . . .' he said.

He drew breath rapidly. The trainspotter wasn't smiling any more. And he obviously wasn't a trainspotter either. As soon as Reg had dropped the window he'd stuck his right hand through the opening. He was holding a gun.

'You've got five seconds to open up.' The gunman's accent was heavy and unknown to Reg, who started to tremble.

'Three seconds.'

Reg fumbled desperately as he opened the driver's door. The gunman stepped in immediately, pulled the door shut and slid down, with his back against the lower section of the door so he couldn't be seen from outside.

'Raise the alarm,' he said, 'and I'll kill you. Do anything except drive off on time and I'll kill you.'

Reg swallowed hard. He didn't reply. He couldn't do anything but stare, petrified, at the weapon in the foreigner's fist. His own fist scrunched Kate Middleton's midriff. He was weak with fear and not altogether sure that he wasn't about to piss himself.

* * *

It had puzzled Hussam Hayek, in the weeks leading up to this moment, that trains were not more common targets. Yes, to bring down an aircraft was dramatic. But trains were easy to board and had none of the security restrictions that came with air travel. Unless you were unfortunate enough to encounter a sniffer dog, you'd be practically untraceable on any railway station in the world. And once the train was in motion and between stations, there was little anybody could do to stop you.

The 16.55 to Paddington was in motion and between stations now. One of Hussam's accomplices, if everything had gone according to plan, had the driver under his control. Surely there was no way anybody could prevent this from happening now.

The train's five carriages held about thirty passengers each. Men in grey suits and cheap shoes making the journey up to town sat alongside pensioners, mums and a few schoolkids. One blind man had his guide dog sitting in the aisle by his side, his white stick lying at an angle on the table in front of him. The guard had announced just a minute after the train had left the station that no refreshments would be served on this journey, before warning the passengers to be on the lookout for unattended bags or suspicious packages. Hardly anybody listened. They were too wrapped up in their own activities: doing sudokus, texting, listening to iPods.

In addition to the young man who had the driver at gunpoint, there were four accomplices, all male, all nervous, all sweating. Their clean-shaven skin was dark and their eyes brown, but it would be difficult for anyone to tell that they were lifelong residents not of Bristol, nor of London, but of Gaza, that long, thin strip of land sandwiched between Israel, Egypt and the deep blue of the Mediterranean. War-torn. Blood-spattered. Bomb-shattered. Hell by the sea.

Of these four men, Hussam and one other stood at the end of the front carriage, next to the toilets; the other two stood in the same position at the opposite end of the train. All four had known tragedy. Two were orphans before they reached the age of ten, their parents killed by Israeli bombs launched into Gaza from screaming F-16s on the pretext of self-defence. A third had more physical scars: the side of his body bore the lurid traces of a

221

mess of inexpert stitching where a piece of shrapnel had entered. It had been removed, and the wound repaired, without the luxury of anaesthetic or painkillers. He still carried pain with him every waking second, and it was even worse when he tried to piss.

Hussam Hayek was a little older than the other three and they looked to him as a leader on account of this. Two years ago he had become a father, but he only remained so for three days. His wife and baby son had died within an hour of each other—she for want of antibiotics, he for reasons overworked doctors couldn't fathom. The child's death was not a surprise to anyone. It was just the way things were in Gaza, its borders blockaded, the importation of medicines strictly controlled. Some entered the country via a smugglers' route—the subterranean tunnels that ran under the border with Egypt—but these were a precious commodity and never found their way into the hands of poor men like Hussam Hayek.

Small wonder, then, that these four, like many before them, were radicalised beyond the point of return. That hatred was in their DNA. They had nothing to live for.

But they had everything to die for.

Hussam was wearing a Red Hot Chili Peppers baseball cap he'd bought just the day before because he thought it made him look more Western. The rest of their clothes were loose-fitting, but this wasn't a fashion statement. Beneath their T-shirts and M&S raincoats, each man wore a vest packed with acetone peroxide, or TATP. It was a relatively simple explosive to make—all you needed was drain cleaner, bleach

222

and acetone—but the end result was extremely volatile. In Gaza, you could always recognise the TATP engineers. They were the men with missing fingers.

Some people called this crystalline white powder Mother of Satan: a good name, because it was indeed capable of giving birth to the diabolical. Hussam Hayek smiled to himself. It wouldn't be long before the whole world took notice of Gaza.

As fields and woodland sped past, Hussam fiddled somewhat absent-mindedly with the small switch attached to a wire peeking out from below his left sleeve. All four men wore the same set-up. It was already dark outside, and he could see his anxious reflection in the glass of the side door. He felt weak with nerves. He hadn't expected to. In the days leading up to today there had been a sense of anticipation. Of excitement almost. He'd hoped to feel that excitement now. He was, after all, to be reunited with his loved ones in just a few minutes. But his skin was soaked in sweat and his hand trembled. What if it went wrong? What if somebody stopped them before the critical moment?

He leaned as nonchalantly as he could against a small poster warning that CCTV was operating on this train and looked at his watch. 17.11 hrs. Six minutes until they started.

Six minutes until paradise.

It was crucial to wait. Their controller had been most emphatic about that when handing out their weapons and ammunition and explaining the details of their evening's mission. At 17.17 precisely the train would be equidistant from the two stations furthest apart on their route. That was the prime spot—far away from any possibility of interference.

And there were other reasons for waiting until that exact moment, too. This was just one of a series of coordinated events, all planned to take place at the same time. Hussam Hayek and his team didn't know the details—it was better that way—but they knew they were part of something big.

Like, 9/11 big.

17.13. Hussam glanced at his partner. The kid was sweating too as the movement of the train jolted his thin body rhythmically up and down.

Up and down.

Up and down.

Time check. 17.14. One of the passengers—a pregnant woman who was clearly almost at term—waddled along the aisle and into the toilet. Hussam felt another trickle of sweat down the nape of his neck.

The train jolted.

Up and down.

Up and down.

It brought back a game his father had played with him as a toddler, bouncing him up and down on his knee. His companion glanced at his watch. Hussam did the same. 17.16. One minute to go.

The two men removed the rucksacks from their backs. Hussam fished inside his with his right hand. He felt very comfortable with the weapon that his fingers touched. They'd already spent a long time firing them, as well as practising how to change the magazine swiftly. 'AKS-74U,' they'd been told. Hussam knew a little about guns. He knew that these were shortened variants of the standard 74, somewhere between a submachine gun and an assault rifle. Ideal for close-quarters combat, and for keeping concealed. They had probably

224

been made in the old Soviet Union. How they had made the journey from there to the rucksacks of Hussam's team was anybody's guess, but it wasn't important now: they were coming to the end of their lives.

'You'll be firing 7.62 shorts. Hard-hitting rounds, thirty-round magazines. You get nine to ten bursts per magazine. Count them. When you pack your weapon, be sure you do it barrel downwards. You don't want to be rummaging around when the time comes.'

They had nodded, but not said anything, as they followed the advice.

Once they were ready they had prayed together, beseeching Allah to look with favour on their enterprise, and asking Him to grant them entry to His kingdom when their earthly life was done.

Which would be in a couple of minutes' time.

Hussam's watch clicked to 17.17. The two men nodded and pulled their weapons from their rucksacks, just as the cubicle door opened and the pregnant woman appeared to the sound of the toilet's violent flush.

She stopped, her face aghast, her eyes glued to the sight of the machinery in the men's fists.

Hussam looked at her. He saw her swollen belly and remembered his own wife when she was in the same state. For a split second he wondered if he was doing the right thing. What would she say if she could see him here now?

But then he remembered her lifeless body, still and cold. And their baby, not much bigger than the palm of his hand. This woman in front of him, she had a ruddy glow about her. Her cheeks were full, not like the thin, gaunt features his wife had displayed during her pregnancy through lack of nutrition. This woman had never given the plight of the Palestinian people a second thought. Like everybody in the West, she had sat complacently by while their people suffered and their children died. Why should *she* be allowed to live a life of comfort and safety when his own family were no longer of this world?

He raised his 74 just as the woman opened her mouth to scream.

But no scream came.

It was a short burst, and the sound was almost entirely masked by the sudden and unexpected noise of a train passing in the other direction. The rounds entered the woman's chest, flinging her back through the open door of the toilet as an explosion of blood spattered all around the cubicle. Hussam momentarily lost control of his weapon and the rounds flew up to her face, then back down to her swollen belly. For a split second he thought he saw a flash of the unborn child's body, but perhaps that was just his imagination. He released his finger from the trigger, concerned that he had wasted too many rounds on one kill, then stepped towards the first carriage and made his way into it.

There was no turning back now. It had begun. The nervousness had left his body just as surely as the rounds had left the barrel of his weapon; they had been absorbed by his first kill and now he was ready to see this through to the end.

Hussam worked methodically, starting on his left with a man and a woman, both asleep, she resting her head on his shoulder. Two quick bursts and their sleep became permanent. A stray round shattered the window next to them and it was this, more than the sharp, mechanical sound of the 74, that alerted the passengers nearby to what was happening. A man in the seats to Hussam's right had seen the couple being slaughtered, and was already half up on his feet by the time the Palestinian gunman had him in his sights. A single burst and he slumped back down in his seat, blood foaming from his mouth.

Hussam stepped forward down the aisle to the next set of seats. He could sense his companion was right behind him, ready to take over once Hussam's rounds had expired. The roar from the shattered window was immense, and the wind ruffled Hussam's loose clothing and his hair. He refused to be distracted by any of this, and the killing continued.

He had fired nine bursts and killed nine people by the time his 74 clicked empty. As soon as the magazine was spent, he turned sideways and let his companion take the lead. Hussam knew he might need a little encouragement to take out his first victim, so he urged him on with a reminder of what they were doing: *'For our people!'* he shouted. *'For Palestine!'* But his words were drowned out. So far the gunman had been too swift for anyone even to cry out. That had changed. People further up the carriage had realised what was happening. Strangely there was very little screaming, although some passengers were frantically ringing numbers on their mobile phones and shouting into them. 'They've got guns! *They've got guns!'*

One man—tall and thickset—burst out into the aisle and started running towards them, grasping a black holdall in front of him to protect himself from the shots. *'Get that man!'* Hussam yelled.

227

His companion's arm shot up and to the right as he fired, ripping a seam across the charging man's face with such ferocity that his features were instantly replaced with flashes of skull and blood. The man crumpled to the floor and the new gunman continued the methodical execution of the passengers. There was chaos in the carriage now— shouting and crying and confusion. Hussam ignored it all as he plunged his hand into his rucksack and pulled out a full magazine for his weapon. He removed the spent mag, dropped it on the floor and quickly replaced it, ready to take over from his companion once the second gunman's rounds were spent.

And so they continued, staggering their slaughter like they were playing some horrific game of leapfrog. Panic ahead; total silence behind. Hussam didn't look back at the scenes of indescribable carnage; his eyes did not linger on the bloodied corpses or the flesh and brain matter painted over the windows and walls. He kept his focus, his eyes straight ahead and his mind on the job. They had planned for this moment for a long time, and he wasn't going to mess things up through a lack of concentration . . .

The shouts of panic reached a peak when they were halfway through the first carriage, then started to ebb away as fewer and fewer people remained to emit any kind of sound. Some passengers— braver than the others, or perhaps just more scared—made a run for it into the next carriage. But that was all right, because Hussam knew that his other two compatriots were already clearing the carriages from the opposite end. They would meet in the middle, sandwiching those who had fled and eliminating them in a final orgy of bloodshed. He stepped over the body of the would-be hero and felt his heel land on one of the man's fingers. It crunched beneath him, making a sound like new snow.

When they reached the interconnecting area between the first two carriages, Hussam saw that one of the windows at the sides had been smashed with a heavy object. A chubby woman was holding her toddler—two or three years old, maybe, and it was difficult at a glance to tell if it was male or female—up to the opening. When she saw Hussam, she posted the child through the broken window and it was gone in an instant. The kid surely could not have survived that, Hussam thought to himself as he thumped a burst of rounds into the weeping mother's back. He looked round and saw that the toilet was locked. He could just discern the sound of another woman inside, sobbing desperately. Hussam raised his gun and aimed directly at the door. The rounds made short work of the metal, ripping holes in it and immediately silencing the occupant.

The train sped on through the countryside. The first passenger they came across in the second carriage was the blind man. His guide dog—an old golden Labrador with a jowly face and slight lightening of the whiskers—was sitting anxiously by its owner's feet. When it saw Hussam it started to growl; but Hussam's weapon made mincemeat of the animal. The blind man cried out, as if he knew what he could not see; but any pain he felt at the demise of his guide dog was short-lived as Hussam delivered a burst of rounds to his head, before allowing his companion to leapfrog him once more so he could reload.

There was more blood than he had pictured in his mental rehearsals. More blood, and less screaming. And he was surprised at how quickly he became numb to the sight of death. It held no more horrors for him. No more mystery. When it was his turn once more, he started finishing off the remaining ten passengers in this second carriage with something approaching carelessness, spraying the rounds with less precision—though no less fatality—so that some thudded into the rough material of the seats, and another window shattered, bringing with it the roar of motion and a blast of wind.

They entered the middle carriage and could just see the other two gunmen now. They continued their work, each pair mowing down the passengers as they edged towards the centre of the train. By the time there was ten metres between them, Hussam could see the others clearly. Their eyes were bright and their clothes and faces splashed with the blood of their victims. Hussam briefly wondered if he looked the same. He glanced down at himself and saw red streaks down his garments; with his free hand he touched his face, to find it was sticky. No matter. There were still four more passengers to deal with. They were standing in the aisle, having run here from one end of the train or another, and were now huddled together: two women, a man and a boy of about sixteen. They all looked like they wanted to scream but couldn't.

They could weep, though. And they did.

Hussam didn't shoot them from a distance because he didn't want to risk hitting his accomplices who were on the other side of these final passengers. Instead he strode towards them until he was just a metre away. Their screams grew louder and merged with the sound of the wind rushing through the broken window. The air was thick with their terror.

Hussam downed them with a single burst. The screaming stopped as the rounds ripped into the meat of the passengers' bodies, mashing the teenage boy's face and bursting the jugular vein of one of the women. The group fell as a single unit, and their dead bodies propped each other up like martyrs at a stake.

Only now did Hussam look back. Only now did he pause to contemplate their handiwork: the blood and the gore and the gruesome look of absolute terror on the faces of those victims where the bullets had entered below the neck. It neither pleased him nor appalled him. It was what it was. It was what it had to be.

The four men faced each other, two on either side of the propped-up corpses. Hussam felt a trickle run down his forehead and over his thick, black eyebrows. He blinked hard as a mixture of sweat and blood stung his eyes. He nodded at the others, and they placed their 74s on the ground. Those weapons were finished with. It was time now for the Mother of Satan to do its work.

'*Allahu Akbar!*' He announced the Takbir in a loud voice so that it could be heard over the noise of the train and the wind from the broken window.

The others opened their mouths to return the incantation, but they were interrupted for a few seconds as another train hurtled past them in the opposite direction.

Hussam's eyes glowed. '*Allahu Akbar!*' he

repeated, and this time his prayer was met with a response.

'*Allahu Akbar!*'

The eyes of his compatriots were also burning, their bloodied bodies trembling. All four of them held their left hands aloft, ready to flick the switches that would transport them to paradise. Hussam closed his eyes. For a brief moment he saw his wife and child as they should be.

Smiling at him.

Waiting.

He opened them again, and nodded.

That nod was the sign. All four men flicked their switches, and detonated.

SIXTEEN

19.28 hrs.

It had taken two hours for the images to circle the earth.

The gnarled wreckage of the train, its two middle carriages blown skywards, the front and two rear carriages lying at an angle to the rails and crumpled into the sidings, lay still. Great floodlights had been erected in the field adjacent to the crash site, illuminating the scene of devastation as brightly as a night-time football match, and supplemented by the spots from two choppers circling overhead. There was a constant hum from aircraft and the electricity generators on the ground, and a flash of neon-blue emergency lights from vehicles approaching off-road. Three air ambulances were on standby. As the paramedics combed through the debris, it became increasingly clear that the ambulances would not be required to evacuate the casualties; they would be required to transport the dead.

Fifty metres from the blast site, a luminous-orange cordon had been erected, guarded by uniformed police officers to keep the small crowd of journalists at bay. They were a hard-bitten lot. Like the doctors and policemen, they were used to scenes of trauma. Such sights were their bread and butter, but even they, tonight, were sickened. They remembered 9/11—some of them had been there—and the uneasy sensation everyone had that day that the world was about to change. They had that sensation again now, and these usually pushy professionals were restrained. Their cameras did not deviate from the crash site, where a plume of smoke still rose into the air, disturbed occasionally by a gust of wind but otherwise eerily straight.

One of these journalists was younger than the others. His name was Andy Carrington and he was just twenty-three. So far in his life he had seen three dead bodies. One was a tramp who'd died of exposure when Andy was on the night shift of his local paper back home in Norfolk. One was a car crash victim who'd been hit by a drunk-driver just after chucking-out time, and Andy had been surprised by how little blood there had been. The third had been his grandfather, lying on a bier in the funeral home, as cold as ice but immaculately presented, his skin shiny and his thin hair neatly combed.

None of these corpses had prepared him for the sight of the bodies being taken to the air ambulances that evening.

He'd run over to the point, about thirty metres from the throng of other journalists, where two policemen were holding up the cordon to allow a stretcher carried by two paramedics to pass. As he ran in that direction he was vaguely aware that none of his colleagues was doing the same. He put that down to his own hunger—his determination to show his mettle as a journalist. The previous night he'd been reporting on a film premiere from Leicester Square, and now he wanted to show his quality at reporting serious news rather than tittle-tattle about Angelina Jolie to be printed alongside a shiny picture of her, all lips and tits.

'Stay away, son,' one of the coppers called when they saw him approaching. It didn't sound so much like an instruction as a piece of advice, and it was advice this young man was quick to ignore. The stretcher had passed the cordon now and the policemen had lowered it again.

'Honest, mate, it's not something you want to . . .'

Andy stopped.

He was about two metres from the stretcher when he saw the corpse in its entirety. It was a woman. He could tell that from the remnants of her clothes rather than her features, and this was because she no longer *had* any features. Her face was no longer a face. It was just a canvas of bloodied pap and shattered bone. There were two indentations where the eyes had once been, and a vague protrusion for the nose. Her left jawbone had been shattered and was now hanging from the right-hand side of her face, as though attached by the flimsiest of hinges. Her neck and chest were darkly stained, as if she had vomited blood.

But it was none of this that chilled Andy's soul and made him want to retch. It was what he saw further down the woman's body. She had obviously been pregnant. Her abdomen had spilled open and he could quite clearly see—bloodied and contorted but quite distinct—the figure of her unborn child.

It took a split second for Andy to take all this in. A split second to yank his gaze away as a terrible nausea suddenly overcame him, accompanied by a curious sense of shame, as though he had looked at something that should never be looked at. He realised why none of the older hands from the press corps had joined him.

'If you're going to chuck up,' the same policeman who had warned him away from the stretcher called to him, 'don't do it near us, eh?'

Andy took a deep breath and tried to settle himself. 'They, er . . . they found any survivors?' he asked, more to keep his mind off the sickness than anything else.

The two policemen glanced at each other. 'They'll brief you when there's anything to know,' the copper replied, before looking back over the cordon. 'You might want to move along now. There's another stretcher coming.'

Andy looked over towards it. Two more paramedics, one more body. He could see its outline, but he couldn't bear to look any closer. He nodded at the policemen and started staggering back towards the press pack. The image of that woman and her unborn baby was burned into his mind. He knew it would haunt him for the rest of his life.

As he approached the others, his cameraman came running up to him. 'TX in two, Andy. Jesus, mate . . . you all right?'

Andy didn't answer. He had to get his head together. Formulate the words of his upcoming broadcast in his mind. Settle himself.

Easier said than done.

He was still pale and nauseous as he stood between the cameraman and the cordon, a radio mike clipped to his lapel. The words he had cobbled together tumbled from his wind-bitten lips.

'At approximately twenty past five this afternoon, an explosion is thought to have taken place here on the Bristol to London line.'

The image of the baby flashed in front of his mind, and he stumbled. The cameraman made a rolling gesture with his right arm to encourage him to keep talking. Andy took a deep breath.

'Although the authorities have yet to make a statement regarding the source of the explosion, there seems little doubt that it is linked to almost identical events that occurred at the same time on the outskirts of Washington DC, Paris and Delhi.'

He paused, so that live feeds showing scenes of similar devastation across the globe could be transmitted into the living rooms of the country: daytime in Washington, still night everywhere else, but chaos and calamity and weeping no matter what the hour. In Paris, the camera cut to the sight of a screaming young child being restrained by her tear-sodden mother, clearly howling for a loved one—perhaps her father—on the wrecked train. The journalist could only hear the sounds through his earpiece, and not see the images. He was thankful for that.

'Paramedics have been combing through the wreckage for a little more than an hour,' the young journalist continued, his voice wavering a little. 'So far, the only passengers I have seen have been . . . have been dead.'

He paused.

'As we stand here,' he continued, his voice a little quieter than before, 'relatives of the passengers on the 16.55 are beginning to gather in a neighbouring field, anxious for news of their . . .'

He felt his voice cracking.

He turned, and looked back towards the train. The floodlights. The neon blue. The smoke.

The woman.

The child.

He tried again. 'Anxious for news of their loved . . .'

But his voice failed him once more, and to his horror he realised he was breaking down live on camera. He shook his head. 'I'm sorry,' he said, before putting one hand to his forehead. *'I'm very sorry . . .'*

With these words Andy Carrington walked out of shot, pulling his mike from his lapel. The camera didn't follow him. Instead it kept itself firmly focused on the train. The cameraman could see that Andy was not in a state to talk to the nation, and some sights, after all, need no words to accompany them.

*　　　*　　　*

20.00 hrs.

Albany Manor was a grand estate in rural Buckinghamshire, surrounded by acres of woodland and boasting its own chapel, paddocks and enough outbuildings to house a small village. The phone calls had started a minute after the blast and were still continuing. Alistair Stratton had declined to take any of them.

Stratton's PA, Christopher Wheatly, was an eager young man who hoped one day to go into politics himself. This was why he was willing, despite his trust fund and his lofty sense of entitlement, to suck up to the one-time British PM turned Middle East peace envoy. The outside world saw in Alistair Stratton a man of charm, a man whose conviction was obvious even to those who disagreed with him. Wheatly knew a different person: a person of quick temper and obstinacy, small-minded in many ways and a difficult man to like. When the White House came on the line at 20.10 hrs UK time, Wheatly knocked on the door of his boss's office.

'Come.'

Stratton was standing in front of a painting to which an entire wall of the office was devoted. Wheatly knew nothing about art—it wasn't his thing—but he did know that this particular painting, a hellish scene of burning buildings and dead bodies, was by Hieronymus Bosch and had been acquired anonymously at a Berlin auction for the sum of twelve million euros.

Stratton gave the young PA a crushing look when he announced that Washington wanted to speak to him. 'I said no calls. You do understand what "no calls" means?'

Wheatly felt himself blushing. 'I just thought you . . . you might want to speak to the White House . . . they're jolly keen to . . .'

But Stratton just walked over to his desk, took a seat and picked up a folder. Wheatly caught sight of an ornate, monogrammed 'G' on the front of the folder as he stood there awkwardly. After a few seconds, Stratton looked up, seemingly surprised that he was still there. 'No calls,' he said.

Wheatly was learning fast. Not only that the private personas of the powerful were very different to their public images, but also that the powerful were not always the first people to get their hands on the choicest information. He was astonished when, just after nine o'clock, the TV coverage had been interrupted for breaking news, delivered by a breathless reporter standing at the crash site.

'The BBC has learned that a small militant Palestinian group, the Union for Free Palestine, has claimed responsibility for the attacks. The UFP is loyal to the Palestinian administration, Hamas. So far Hamas have declined comment.'

How had the press had this information before Stratton, the Middle East peace envoy?

As the evening wore on, Wheatly grew increasingly ragged—not on account of the TV footage of the train attacks—but from the long hours of refusing phone calls from the most powerful people in the world. He was no shrinking violet, but the aides in Washington, London and Tel Aviv gave such withering responses to his inability to put his boss on the line that it was starting to get him down. That and Stratton's steadfast silence. With the exception of the short statement he dictated for Wheatly to release to the press wires when the news about the UFP came through, it almost felt as if Stratton was cocooning himself away from the outside world.

At 11.30 a communiqué from London informed Wheatly that an American amphibious warfare vessel, Wasp class—currently on anti-piracy duty in the Gulf of Aden—was heading north into the Red Sea. A 'precautionary measure in the light of the day's events', Washington was telling the media, glossing over the fact that the ship carried a full complement of marines, a squadron of Harrier II ground-attack aircraft and an air group of personnel helicopters. Stratton seemed barely to register the information when his PA announced it. 'Sir, you know what this means . . . the Americans are mobilising . . .' he had started to say. 'The British won't be far behind . . . the Foreign Office need to speak to you . . .' But his boss shooed him away with a flick of his left hand.

Wheatly turned in at about half past midnight. His quarters were away from the main residence in a converted barn, and that meant a 100-metre walk across the grounds. It always made him nervous doing this at night, because he knew that there were never fewer than five armed guards doing the rounds, recruited from some American company, and he saw in them the lazy arrogance that he believed was peculiar to the Yanks. He didn't *think* any of them would mistake him for an intruder, but they weren't all the sharpest pencils in the box, and he was never quite sure.

He fell asleep without even getting undressed, and was groggy and sweaty when his radio alarm clock woke him at six o'clock. As the pips disappeared and the *Today* programme started, he sat up bleary-eyed, feeling decidedly unenthusiastic about the day ahead. The news was full of the train bombings, of course. Frankly he was sick to death of hearing about them. He changed out of yesterday's clothes only half listening to the barrage of repeated information and supposition; but he did stop to pay attention when the recorded voice of the Israeli Prime Minister came over the airways. In the background Wheatly could hear the constant clicking of cameras, and he could sense the nervous tension in whatever room in Tel Aviv the Israeli leader was speaking from.

'*Israel*,' he announced, his deep, gruff voice strangely emotionless, '*deplores these acts of terror.*'

A pause, and the clicking of cameras swelled somewhat.

'*For many years, the Israeli people have suffered at the hands of these terrorists. It brings me no satisfaction to see that their acts of cowardice have now spread into the wider world. I call upon Hamas to denounce these actions. And if they will not, I call upon all right-thinking nations to stand up to this terror, and to destroy it.*'

Wheatly blinked. He knew fighting talk when he heard it, and he knew what it meant—for him, at least. Even more so than last night, the world and his wife would be wanting to speak to the man whose job it was to broker peace between these ancient enemies. If Stratton was in the same mood as he was last night, that meant his PA was in for a very long day. As if in response to that very thought, his mobile phone rang. Number withheld. Wheatly ignored it and went in search of his boss.

Stratton was not in his bedroom, nor was he in the study where Wheatly had left him the previous night. But the study looked out over an immaculate lawn on the opposite side of which, 200 metres from the house itself, was a handsome thirteenth-century stone building: Stratton's private chapel. Wheatly had noticed that his boss had spent more and more time there of late, and at odd hours of the day. He saw him walking out now, dressed as he had been last night. Even from this distance he could see that Stratton looked crumpled and tired, as though he hadn't been to bed. Had he spent more of the night in his office, or in the chapel? Wheatly wouldn't have been surprised to learn that it was the latter, and he groaned inwardly. Most people, he thought to himself, walked out of church full of the milk of human kindness—at least for a little while. Not Stratton. He always emerged from that place even more oblivious to the sensitivities of anyone around him than before.

Wheatly sighed heavily. This really *was* going to be a long day.

He caught up with his boss halfway across the lawn. Stratton didn't smell too fresh, but Wheatly supposed the same was true of himself, having slept all night in his clothes. Stratton didn't appear to notice him until he was standing about a metre away. When he did, the usual look of irritation crossed his face.

'Where've you been?'

'Sleeping, sir.'

Stratton looked around, as though surprised to see that the night had passed, but he made no comment on it and started striding quickly towards the house, his PA trotting alongside.

'We've calls to make,' said Stratton.

Wheatly agreed. 'I've been trying to tell you since . . .'

'The people *will* expect a retaliation,' Stratton interrupted, his voice slightly distant as though he was thinking out loud. 'We've been here before.'

'But retaliation,' Wheatly said. 'That will only

242

lead to . . .'

Stratton stopped and looked at him. For the first time in he didn't know how long, Wheatly felt he was actually being listened to.

'To what?' Stratton asked, his voice almost a whisper.

There was a pause as the two men looked at each other.

'To war, sir.'

Stratton didn't take his eyes off Wheatly, but he nodded slowly, neither smiling nor frowning. It was impossible to tell what he was thinking. And then, with a sudden movement, he turned and continued walking towards the house, leaving his PA standing in the middle of the lawn and wondering if, really, this was the job for him after all.

SEVENTEEN

6 December.

The distance between Albany Manor and the Crown and Sceptre, a pub tucked away in the no-man's-land between the Yorkshire Moors and the Lake District, was about 400 klicks as the crow flew. But in other ways these two places were a million miles apart.

An imposing slate-roofed building sited where two main roads met, the Crown and Sceptre was unwelcoming from the outside and dingy on the inside. No money had been spent on it for years. The windows were frosted over; the walls and ceiling were still nicotine yellow years after the smoking ban; the bar and tables were covered with a sticky patina that no amount of cleaning would remove—not that anyone had tried.

The woman behind the bar was used to this place, and to places like it. They were her natural habitat, and she sought them out in the same way that an insect seeks out the underside of a stone. She had worked in so many down-at-heel pubs she'd almost lost count of them. She never stayed long, moving from one to the next every few months before the punters got too familiar with her.

Because familiarity was the thing Suze McArthur wanted to avoid.

Her 'interview' for this job had followed the same pattern as all the other ones. She'd walked into the pub at a quarter past eleven on a Monday two weeks ago, a holdall containing her few belongings in one hand, a ten-year-old boy tightly clutching the other.

Her little boy. The only reason she'd kept going this long.

'No kids.'

Suze had ignored the bored edict from the barman and walked straight up to him. He was well into his sixties, with bloodshot eyes and body odour that she could smell from a couple of metres away. 'I'm . . . I'm looking for work,' she said.

He had eyed her up and down, his gaze lingering around the cleavage she was displaying for the benefit of men like him.

'Oh aye? You local?'

She'd shaken her head.

'Pikey? 'Cos if you're a fuckin' pikey you can . . .'

'I'm not a pikey.'

'Too many of them round these parts.'

'I'm just looking for a bit of casual . . .'

244

'Where you staying then? You can't stay here, you know.' He paused and his eyes flickered to her breasts for a second time. 'Not unless I ask you.'

'I've got somewhere to stay,' Suze lied hastily. 'I just need a job, all right?' And then, because she'd realised she was hardly going the right way about it, she'd added a bit feebly: 'I've, um . . . I've got experience.'

'Aye, I'll bet you have, love,' the barman leered. 'What about the nipper, eh?'

Suze had pulled the little boy protectively towards her. 'He'll be no trouble, will you, Harry?' she said, her voice suddenly a little hoarse. Harry, bless him, had remained mute—he seldom spoke— but had shaken his head at his mum. 'He'll sit quietly. I promise.'

She could see him doing the maths: a lone woman with a young child, clearly desperate. Perhaps she was on the run from an abusive husband, or a pimp, or the bailiffs. Either way, it meant cheap labour, and if she was really down on her luck, something else.

'Three pound an hour, cash in hand,' he'd said. Suze had started to protest, but he raised a palm to silence her. 'Take it or leave it, love. What's your name, anyhow?'

'Linda.' The name changed every time.

'Oh aye, Linda Lovelace, eh? Well, I won't ask why the boy's not in school, Linda Lovelace. Mum's the word, eh? But he stays out the back and he doesn't bother the punters.'

And so the deal had been struck. It wasn't like she was in a strong negotiating position.

Suze had lived this way for so long she'd almost forgotten how strange her life had become. Almost,

245

but not quite. Fear was her constant companion. She woke up with it, and it lulled her to sleep at night. There were times when, exhausted or depressed, she daydreamed about giving up. Because surely enough time had passed now for her to have been forgotten about?

But then there was the website. She had only stumbled on it by accident one day when she was working in a pub near Bournemouth. There were no customers; Harry, just a baby at the time, was asleep; and so she did what she had often done—hit the internet, trying to find a picture of her attacker. She was a murderer, after all. Perhaps she'd been brought to justice. Perhaps she was safely behind bars . . . It was this line of enquiry that had led her to the website of the Metropolitan Police, and the page listing the force's most wanted individuals.

Suze's photograph wasn't the first on that list. She was nestled between a rapist and a man wanted for possession of an offensive weapon. Her supposed crime: arson. She'd felt all the strength drain from her body when she saw that, and had quickly shut down the computer, grabbed Harry and walked out of her workplace, never to return— as if the computer would grass her up. Now and then, over the years, she had checked the page. The rapists came and went, but her photo was always there. Always staring out at her, looking younger and younger as the years wore on.

She knew she wouldn't be staying in this new job for long, but while she was here, she worked hard: twelve hours a day, six days a week. For the first few nights she booked into a Travelodge on the outskirts of town—luxury compared to what they were used to—but that ate up her daily wage completely, leaving nothing for food. She managed to sneak a curled-at-the-edges ham sandwich into Harry's hungry little hands at lunchtime, but she knew she had to find somewhere else to stay. Somewhere that didn't require ID, and was free. So on the third day she and her son had left the hotel early and started walking the streets.

Suze had known what she was looking for: a derelict building, but still sound. The clue would be a closed curtain in front of a broken window. But over the years she'd developed an instinctive ability to recognise a squat when she saw one. Now she found a red-brick building on the edge of town with large, high windows with small panes, many of them smashed. It looked like some old Victorian factory and it was definitely disused. As she passed it, however, she noticed several black bin liners full of rubbish, and that told her somebody was living inside.

She and her son had become two of their number. Part of the faceless community of junkies and losers that always found their way to these places.

Their nights were spent in the squat, their days in Suze's new workplace. The squat was anonymous; so too, in its own way, was the Crown and Sceptre. The customers were never there for a convivial atmosphere or cosy surroundings. They were there to drink. All the pubs Suze had ever worked in had regulars, who would arrive at opening time and drink their way very slowly but steadily through the day, staring at the blinking lights of the fruit machine or the flickering images of the wall-mounted TV. And though they spoke to Suze—or whatever name she had chosen to give them—several times a day, it was only to order drinks and they never looked at her with anything approaching recognition. They were too far gone for that.

The regulars were in now, about six of them, all old men, dotted around the pub, nobody speaking to anybody else. Harry was in the back room, good as gold. He had black rings under his eyes, and his face was even paler than usual. Both he and his mother had very short hair, inexpertly and crookedly cut by Suze. The short hair was easier to keep clean—important when most of your sanitary activities took place in the washrooms of the nearest McDonald's, just about the only place you could use the facilities without some spotty jobsworth telling you to buy something or get out— and it changed Suze's features quite considerably. Even now, whenever she caught sight of herself in a mirror, she was slightly startled by the way she looked. Which was a good thing, because if *she* was startled, it meant she looked very different to the young woman who had gone into hiding.

As for Harry, he was used to spending his days alone; used to falling asleep just as the pub got busy in the evening, and being woken by a weary Suze after eleven so they could walk back to wherever they were staying. Suze knew what people thought when they saw him, and that was one of the reasons she moved from town to town so often. It would only take a single bleeding heart to report them to social services and all of a sudden they would become a matter of public record.

And that was something she definitely could not risk. The very thought sent ice down her spine. She would hear a deep, masculine voice in her head.

Hide, it said. *Don't stop hiding.* In her mind she would see a blazing farmhouse and a dark-haired woman with cold eyes. And she would hug her child, conceived the very night everything changed in her life, and vow to keep him safe.

The TV was on as usual today, but Suze was the only one watching it. The rolling news about yesterday's train attacks might have been sickening, but the alkies in the Crown and Sceptre only appeared concerned with their own misery. They were oblivious to the scenes, even when Suze pointed the sticky remote control at the TV and turned up the volume. As one of the punters, a skinny middle-aged guy with thinning hair tied in a ponytail, came up and demanded his second pint of the day, she caught fragments of commentary.

'*International condemnation . . . no word from the Palestinian administration.*'

The guy coughed as he handed over the money for his drink.

'*Troop mobilisation across the Middle East . . . precautionary measure . . . tensions running high . . .*'

Suze put his change into his sweaty hand and went back to watching the screen, vaguely aware that, rather than returning to his table, he was loitering around the bar. For the third time that morning she watched the footage of a young reporter unable to cope with the horrific scenes the previous night.

'*As we stand here, relatives of the passengers on the 16.55 are beginning to gather in a neighbouring field, anxious for news of their . . .*'

'Them fuckin' Muslims,' the punter snarled. Suze ignored him.

Suddenly the screen changed, taking Suze

249

away from the repeated footage of the atrocity and back to the studio. An immaculately dressed female reporter with an earnest look on her face was speaking hesitantly, as if she'd just been fed information she wasn't quite sure about.

'*News just in . . .*' she announced, before pausing. '*In the last few minutes, police have released a photograph that they believe shows two of the UK bombers moments before they boarded the fateful 16.55 train from Bristol Parkway.*'

A grainy black and white image filled the TV screen.

Suze stared up at it. And then, as if someone had suddenly flicked a switch, she gasped.

The picture showed a crowd of people—maybe fifteen in all—with two men's faces circled in red. They both wore rucksacks, and it was difficult to make out their features with any certainty.

'Pakis,' the guy with the ponytail muttered. 'All look the fucking same to me.' He scanned around vaguely, as if he was searching for someone to agree with him.

But Suze had barely heard what he'd said. She was staring at the screen as a familiar sensation of dread crept over her body, draining away all her strength.

'What's the matter, sweetheart? Time of the month, is it?' The punter chuckled at his own joke.

Suze couldn't answer. She just stared and stared.

It wasn't the men circled in red that had caught her attention. It was someone else, standing just behind them, with features almost as clear as if she had appeared in the Crown and Sceptre itself. A woman with dark hair, flat eyes. Older than when Suze had seen her last, but without question the

250

same person.

Her fingertips moved involuntarily to her neck as she remembered how the woman had tried to throttle her, and the force with which Chet had pulled her off. And her insides seemed to twist as she remembered watching her from the burning house in which the man who had saved her, and who had fathered the quiet, strange little boy she loved with all her heart, had perished.

'Oh my God,' she muttered.

'What's up, sweetheart?' the punter asked. But he didn't get a reply.

Suze wasn't supposed to leave the bar for long, but she had to. She turned and ran into the back room, where Harry was sitting on a battered sofa, surrounded by crates of brown ale and Schweppes tonic, carefully colouring in a Dora the Explorer picture book. Harry couldn't read, but he would happily colour in childish pictures from morning till night. He stopped when he saw his mum, and looked up at her with big, wide eyes that were full of questions as she paced the room nervously, digging her fingernails into her palms and chewing her bottom lip.

From in here, the sound of the TV was just a distant hum. Suze continued pacing in silence, as though movement would dispel the fear in her gut. It didn't.

'What is it, Mummy?' Harry asked after thirty seconds. His voice was very soft, but it was unusual enough for him to say anything without being asked that Suze immediately stopped pacing and went to sit next to him. She held out his arms and he snuggled up to her. Harry was always ready for a hug. She felt some of her anxiety fall away.

251

Some. But not all.

She started to shake.

'Are you crying?' the little boy asked. His voice was quite matter-of-fact. And when Suze didn't reply: 'You always tell *me* not to cry.' It wasn't an accusation. Harry spoke with such concern that she wanted to cry twice as hard. But she forced herself to get control and, drawing away from her son, she cupped his precious face in her hands.

The look he returned was serious. Not the look of a ten-year-old, but the look of an adult. It made sense in a way. Little Harry had never spent any real time with children his own age, but it caught her off guard sometimes, how much he looked like his father. It was almost as if Chet was staring out at him from behind his son's eyes. '*Why* are you crying, Mum?'

What could she say? How could she explain such things to someone so young? How could she share her fear with someone so innocent? She closed her eyes.

'Mummy's just . . . just a bit sad,' she whispered.

'Why?'

'Because . . . because sometimes . . . sometimes there are people who do bad things.' She opened her eyes again to see Harry's concerned little face still looking up at her.

'But *we* don't do bad things, do we?' he asked.

Suze blinked. *Do we?* she wondered. She thought of the occasional shoplifting he knew nothing about; the secrecy; the deception. She'd never told Harry about his father. She'd never told anyone what happened that night. She didn't have anyone to tell, and even if she did, fear would have held her tongue.

Stay anonymous. Stay dark.

Whenever she thought of going to the police, Chet's words had echoed in her head. She remembered leaving London with him, and the two police officers in the service station bearing down on them. If she made herself known to the police, she could throw her anonymity out of the window. If it had been just her, maybe she'd have done that before now. Maybe she'd have given up. But it wasn't just about her any more. It was about her son, and nothing in the world was going to make her put *his* life at risk . . .

'Well, if *we* don't do bad things, then that's all right, isn't it?' Harry interrupted her thoughts.

She looked at him. He was so earnest. So *right*.

Countless people were dead and Suze was in possession of important information. She had to tell someone.

Not the police. But *someone*.

She took Harry's right hand in hers and squeezed it tenderly. He smiled at her—such a reassuring smile that she almost felt calm again. Like she could think her way through this.

If she couldn't tell the police, who *could* she tell? Her mind flitted back once more to the night of Chet's death. *If you ever need any help, track down Luke Mercer, 22 SAS, tell him what you know. But only if you* have *to, Suze.*

Luke Mercer. The name was etched in her memory. She had no idea who he was, or where he was. From time to time she'd thought about approaching the SAS directly, but she'd never gone through with it. After all, if the police were compromised, why couldn't the army be? She had tried to locate him other ways—not because she wanted to get in touch, but because she knew the day might come when she did. It had all come to nothing. Luke Mercer, whoever he was, had no listing in the telephone directory, nor any mention on the electoral register. He hadn't been married; he hadn't died. The internet had no mention of him whatsoever. It was like he didn't exist.

But he did exist. He had to. Chet wouldn't have mentioned him otherwise. Suze only had one remaining idea of how to contact him, but after everything Chet had said, and after everything that had happened, the thought of doing it made her feel nauseous.

It was too dangerous. It would put Harry at risk.

Suze stood up and, with a sad smile at her son, returned to her position behind the bar. Nothing had changed. The locals were still there, in their usual places, sipping slowly at their pints and ignoring everything all around them. The TV was still on. The rolling news was still rolling.

She stared once more at the images. The scenes of devastation. For the umpteenth time she saw the young journalist breaking down on camera, unable to keep his composure in the face of such horror. And then the picture again: the two Palestinian men circled in red, and Chet's killer, easily distinguishable in the background.

She suppressed a shudder, but remembered what Harry had just said. *If we don't do bad things, then that's all right . . .*

The decision was a sudden one. She grabbed her coat from where she'd stashed it under the bar and went to the back room to get Harry. The little boy looked surprised as she took him by the hand and dragged him towards the front door of the pub—

254

just in time for them to bump into the landlord waddling back in. 'Aye up, Linda Lovelace, where the hell do you think . . . ?'

'Fuck you!' Suze spat at him, and hurried with her boy out into the street.

Half an hour later she was in a local supermarket, spending money she couldn't afford on a pay-as-you-go mobile, choosing the cheapest one that had a camera. Suze hadn't touched a phone all the time she'd been in hiding, and she felt uncomfortable with it as she walked out of the supermarket and continued up the bustling high street. Five minutes later she and Harry arrived at Argos, where a bank of twenty-five display TVs were showing the same channel; and after another five minutes, the picture of the bombers, with her attacker clearly in the background, was repeated on each screen.

Suze held up her camera phone to one of the TVs. It made a click and, as she examined the tiny screen, she was surprised by how well the image was reproduced. The woman's face was perfectly clear. She switched off the phone and put it back in her pocket.

'Can I help you?'

Suze spun round to see a suspicious female shop assistant standing there. She shook her head, grabbed Harry's hand and hurried out. She checked her watch. Nearly half past twelve. She would wait until tonight, when Harry was asleep. Then she would play the only card she had. She just wished it wasn't so fucking dangerous.

Mother and son started wandering back to the squat in silence. And as they went, Suze thought about Luke Mercer. Would he really be able to

255

help her? she wondered. What kind of man was he? And where in the world might he be now?

EIGHTEEN

Luke Mercer was in the back of a Pinzgauer 6 x 6. The canopy was closed against the rain, and his face was bathed in the monochrome light from a VDU about the size of a laptop screen.

The olive-drab vehicle had seen better days, but the modifications it had undergone were state-of-the-art. Mounted on the cab was a high-velocity missile launcher. Known as THOR, it was a four-missile variant of the Starstreak HVM, a high-velocity surface-to-air munition that had not yet seen combat. Top-speed Mach 3.5—three and a half times the speed of sound—laser-guided and each missile containing three armour-piercing darts. These darts were each packed with a pound of explosive. The weapon's sights—regular, thermal-imaging and night-sight—could pick up and track targets at a range of more than seven klicks, even fast-moving UAVs behind cloud cover. All in all, a pretty formidable bit of kit. Not the sort of thing you wanted to entrust to some wet-behind-the-ears crap-hat not long out of nappies.

Some of the younger guys in camp had a habit of taking the piss out of Luke these days. To them, he was the old boy, with a flash of grey round his temples and a body scarred by a long career in the Regiment. Top brass had given him the opportunity to slow down a bit on any number of occasions. Take a training role. Move over to L Detachment

256

as a PSI. Luke had resisted, preferring to mix it with the kids. To keep active. Plenty of the younger troopers thought he was nuts. Why wouldn't you take the same pay for less aggro? Why wouldn't you grab the chance not to have some extremist fuck using your arse for target practice?

Luke had his own reasons. Reasons he kept to himself, and which he probably couldn't have wholly explained even if he'd wanted to. A sense he owed something. Whenever that thought crossed his mind, he would see Chet's face. Scarred. Stony. The knowledge that his best friend was dead, killed in a tragic accident from which he couldn't escape on account of an injury that should have been Luke's. How often had he relived that night in Serbia so long ago? How often had he seen the fragmentation grenade rolling towards him, only to be kicked out of the way by Chet in one moment of selfless bravery?

And what right did Luke have to give up fighting, when the man who had saved his life would never fight again?

To keep fighting meant ensuring his Blade skills were sharper than sharp, his body in peak condition. So when the others were in the Hereford boozers drinking for England, Luke was gymning it or pounding the streets. And when his younger colleagues gave him the sarky comments, they did so knowingly. There wasn't a man in Hereford who didn't think Luke Mercer was the equal of anyone in the Regiment.

With the aid of a joystick, Luke was practising manoeuvring the sight mounted above the truck. Its accuracy and range were remarkable. On the screen in front of him, he could make out individual trees miles away in the distance. The THOR was intended to take out low-flying aircraft, but it also had ground-to-ground capability, and it was this that they were testing today.

'Extra points,' a voice behind him said, 'if you can take out one of those fucking ramblers.'

Luke looked over his shoulder and grinned at Nigel Foster. Fozzie was a good lad. Luke had even forgiven him for getting his team compromised all those years ago in Iraq, when he and Finn had been forced to make a break for the Jordanian border. At least they'd all got out in one piece, which was more than he could say for the Mossad agent they'd picked up on the way. SIS had been quick to bury that one. Thanks, lads, for your help, now be terribly good boys, would you, and don't mention Amit's little personal firework display to another soul. Six months after he and Finn had made it over the border back into Jordan, Luke had made a half-hearted and unsuccessful attempt to locate Amit's sister like he said he would. He'd drawn a blank, though, and there was no way he was going to use his contacts to dig a little deeper. That would have had the Firm sniffing round him like dogs round a bitch's arse.

Luke had sometimes wondered what had happened to Abu Famir, the pain in the neck of an Iraqi do-gooder the coalition had been so eager to get their hands on, and for whose safety Amit had sacrificed himself. He had never seen or heard of the guy again, and sometimes he wondered what the point of the whole fucking escapade had been. Still, it wasn't the first time the Regiment had been sent out to risk their lives on the whim of some bright spark in Whitehall. Wouldn't be the last either.

Luke moved the joystick and the sights panned left. The image on the screen—gridded, and with a set of cross hairs at the centre—was amazingly clear given its distance: 7.3 klicks, at a bearing of 183 degrees. The Pinzgauer stood on a piece of high ground, so the line of sight over the Beacons was uninterrupted.

'You finished admiring the scenery yet, mucker?' Fozzie asked.

Luke didn't reply. He panned slowly east, and just a few seconds later something caught his eye. He adjusted the instruments on the weapon's control panel and the scene came more clearly into view. It was an old house. At least, it had been once. Now it was just a burned-out shell. A memory. And to Luke's eyes, a tomb.

He stared at it for a few seconds, before sensing his mate looking over his shoulder. 'We should lock on to the target, mucker,' Fozzie said quietly.

Luke nodded. 'Roger that.' His voice was emotionless. He panned further east and adjusted the range of the weapon. Within thirty seconds he was locked on to a very different scene. Luke knew the ranges on the Beacons well. Everyone in the Regiment did. They'd all spent more time than they cared to remember in these places on exercises— general weapons training, point of contact, even calling in air assets to drop ordnance. The ranges could be anything from a couple of hundred metres in length to the entire side of a hill. The one they were focusing on today had been decked out with a set of rails and a pulley system which could be used to drag vehicles along to simulate a moving target. The guys had set up an old Land Rover, and Luke

259

had got it in the cross hairs.

As soon as the range came into view, the radio burst into life. 'OK, fellas. We're ready for you. Send.'

It was Fozzie who replied. 'We have eyes on. Repeat, we have eyes on.'

A pause. On the screen they saw the Land Rover start moving.

'Fire at will,' came the voice on the radio.

Luke didn't need to follow the target manually. The weapon system, once it was locked on, followed the Land Rover automatically. In a battle situation, the target—whether an aircraft, a vehicle or even a human—would be moving faster, but that didn't matter. The THOR system could track just about anything. And once it was tracked . . .

Luke pressed a single button to fire. There was a whooshing sound from above the Pinzgauer and then, almost immediately, a loud crack from in front of them. The rocket's main propulsion didn't kick in until it was 400 metres from the firing point, in order to protect the user; then, at Mach 3.5, it would take only seconds to reach the target. The weapon sights kept track of its trajectory, and Luke just had time to see the three lethal darts shoot from the main body of the missile, staying in a circular formation to increase the likelihood of one of them hitting the target, before the Land Rover exploded. The sudden combustion was visible on the screen. There was a two-second delay, then a harsh, metallic sound reached their ears as the sound waves from the explosion crashed past them, echoing across the hills.

'Efficient,' Fozzie noted without much feeling.

Luke didn't have a chance to reply before the

radio came to life again: 'Bullseye, fellas. Time to pack your bags. We're heading back to base.'

Luke and Fozzie exchanged a look.

'We've got three more of these bad boys to discharge,' Fozzie said.

'Going to have to wait. O'Donoghue's called us in. Let's get moving.'

'Roger that,' Fozzie replied. And then, to Luke: 'Sounds like someone's getting twitchy.'

It took just over an hour to get back to base, and another hour before the whole squadron had congregated. Four troops, sixteen guys per troop: there should have been sixty-four men, but as always the squadron was undermanned and in reality there were barely fifty. At 14.00 hrs they congregated in a lecture room in the heart of the Kremlin. It was a large room, big enough to seat them all. Up at the front was an OHP with a laptop attached, and next to it five plastic chairs. Three men in suits were sitting there, along with the Regiment's ops officer, Major James O'Donoghue, and Major Julian Dawson, OC B Squadron. O'Donoghue came from a family that owned half of Wiltshire. Sandhurst, Guards, Regiment—classic headshed career path. He was an ugly fucker and well known for being as tight as a camel's arse in a sandstorm. When it came to military planning, however, everyone knew the Regiment was lucky to have him. As for Julian Dawson, he had the respect of every man in the squadron. Two years previously he'd taken a Taliban round in Helmand, just south of Musa Qala, and he'd been on the ground again within three weeks. In his first twenty-four hours back in action, he'd nailed three Taliban digging in IEDs. Not a man to fuck with, and everyone in the room knew it.

There was a low murmur among the men. Tension. An op was imminent, and you could get addicted to it. The moment O'Donoghue stood up, it was as if someone had hit the mute switch. Everyone went silent, and all eyes were directed towards the ops officer. There were no formalities. No hellos and thank you for comings. Just a businesslike nod towards the three men in suits.

'Edward Duncan, Foreign Office,' O'Donoghue announced in his clipped voice. 'Our two other guests are here from SIS.' No names. It wasn't that the Firm always kept their employees' identities a secret, but if they didn't have to say who they were, they wouldn't. The three suits nodded in the general direction of the men, but the guys of B Squadron weren't interested in them. It was O'Donoghue who would give them their brief.

'All right then,' he said. 'Unless you've been living in a hole—which, looking at the state of some of you, wouldn't surprise me—you'll know what's been happening. Coordinated terror attacks, London, Paris, Washington, Mumbai. Latest estimate, 486 dead.' If the statistic appalled him, he didn't show it, but you could have heard a pin drop in the room. 'It seems the agencies have suspected a major hit like this for some time, but they've had their eyes firmly set towards AQ. Turns out they were looking the wrong way. Our combustible friends were Palestinian. Members of a militant group from the Gaza Strip called the UFP—the Union for Free Palestine. There are any number of these Mickey Mouse outfits along the Gaza Strip. Two or three disaffected Palestinian kids get together with a balaclava and a Kalashnikov and suddenly they think they're a movement. The UFP is a little bigger than most.'

A voice from the back of the room. 'Don't these cunts normally just blow themselves up outside cafés in Jerusalem, boss?'

O'Donoghue nodded. 'Normally. That or Tel Aviv. These attacks are out of character. More to the point, the terrorists were well equipped and well organised. SIS are trying to establish if anyone else is involved, but at the moment that's secondary to the political instability in the region.'

The ops officer pressed a button on the laptop and a map of the Middle East appeared on the wall.

'The political leadership in the Gaza Strip is Hamas. A former terrorist organisation and not internationally recognised, but popular in the Gaza Strip because they stand up to Israel. The UFP claim loyalty to them. The international community have called on Hamas to denounce the bombings. So far they've failed to do so.'

Luke raised a hand.

'What is it, Luke?'

'You said the bombers were well equipped, boss. Do we think Hamas actually supplied them, or were they working on their own?'

O'Donoghue looked over towards the SIS guys. One of them leaned forward slightly in his chair. 'At the moment,' he said, 'it's hard to say. We found the remains of a weapon in the wreckage of the UK train, an'—he consulted some notes on his lap—'an AKS-74U. We checked its serial number and it seems consistent with a consignment of weapons handed in as part of an amnesty at the end of the Balkan conflict. The company given the contract to collect and destroy the weapons is a subsidiary of an American multinational, the Grosvenor Group. Looks like they fulfilled one half of the contract and not the other. We've passed this information on to the CIA. But it seems unlikely that the Grosvenor Group would have direct dealings with Hamas, so our working theory is that the bombers were acting independently.' The spook settled back in his chair and looked back towards the ops officer.

'It's not yet public knowledge,' O'Donoghue continued, 'but the decision has been made to commit four British Army battalions to the region. The Yanks are going in heavy, and the government wants to be seen to be supporting them.'

'Sounds familiar,' someone murmured.

O'Donoghue's eyes flickered towards the Foreign Office representative, and although he said nothing, it was clear Duncan felt as negative about tagging along with the Americans as everyone else in the room. They'd done that once before, and everyone there had mates who'd died in Iraq.

The FO man clearly realised that the mood in the room had changed, so he stood up and inclined his head towards the ops officer, as if to ask if he might say a few words. O'Donoghue nodded, and the suit cleared his throat. 'Gentlemen,' he said in a reedy voice, 'let us not mince our words. If it transpires that Hamas are indeed behind the needless slaughter of innocent British citizens, it will be the obligation of this government to strike back. I can assure you that our allies in America and elsewhere feel the same. It is likely, of course, that a strike against Gaza will be viewed as an act of aggression by other Muslim nations in the region—I'm thinking principally of Iran, who have voiced support for Hamas before now—and

264

I don't believe you need to be instructed in the implications of that.'

He looked around the room, scanning each man in turn. The members of B Squadron stared at him stony-faced.

'So,' he continued briskly, 'if any of you feel at all uncomfortable about operating in that part of the world, I would advise you to start getting used to it. History tells us that events such as this follow a critical path. Unless something is done to bring about a swift resolution, we could be on the brink.'

He turned back to O'Donoghue, nodded and retook his seat.

The ops officer looked slightly taken aback by the FO man's interruption, but he continued in the same matter-of-fact voice as before.

'Alistair Stratton,' he announced, 'is to travel to Gaza in his capacity as Middle East peace envoy.'

Muttering around the room. Stratton had been popular once, even among those members of the squadron who didn't give a shit about politics. But you don't need to see many dead soldiers on the battlefield of an illegal war before you learn to detest its architects.

'All right,' O'Donoghue warned, 'all right. Obviously now's a high-risk time for anyone to be venturing into the Gaza Strip. The Jewish festival of Hanukkah starts on the tenth. That's three days from now.'

A voice from the back. 'What the fuck's Hanukkah, boss?'

'Festival of Lights. Their version of Christmas. One of the most provocative times for the Palestinians to make a statement. Stratton needs close protection, and the Israelis aren't prepared to

265

send anyone into the strip, so we've got the gig.'

'Oh right,' said the same voice. ''Cos Hamas fucking love the Brits, yeah?'

'Shut up. Stratton might be a peace envoy, but he's controversial among the Arabs for obvious reasons. In addition to the CAT team, Whitehall wants a QRF on standby in Israeli territory while the talks are in progress.'

O'Donoghue looked over towards Dawson and nodded. The OC got to his feet and took over the briefing. 'We'll be stationed at an Israeli military base about twenty miles from the strip. I've selected a four-man team to accompany Stratton.' He looked around the room. 'Finn Jacobs, Nigel Foster, Russ Barker, Luke Mercer. Luke, you'll lead the unit. We'll brief you separately and take you through the imagery.'

Luke looked over his shoulder at the others. Finn, Fozzie and Russ. As units went, it was one of the most experienced. No Flash Harrys, just good professionals. Each man looked serious as O'Donoghue took the floor. 'You've got forty-eight hours till departure,' he continued. 'Buses leave here for Brize Norton 14.00 hrs Wednesday. Everyone to remain in camp in the interim. Squadron weapons checked, kit squared away. Each man report to your troop sergeant now. There'll be further briefings over the next couple of days. Let's get moving, gentlemen. Holiday's over.'

There was a scraping of chairs and a sudden hum of noises, like a classroom at bell time. 'Luke,' the ops officer called, 'get your guys together. Briefing in ten, my office.'

Ten minutes later there were six of them crowded into O'Donoghue's office. Spread out

266

on the table was a large satellite map. 'The FO have requested up-to-date imagery from GCHQ,' O'Donoghue explained, 'and we'll have detailed mapping for you to study in the next twenty-four hours. But this'll give you the lie of the land.' Luke examined the map. A long western coastline met the azure blue of the Mediterranean, and where land met sea was a strip of golden beach. From this distance, it looked look like a holiday brochure, but Luke knew that a closer look at this tiny piece of land would reveal a war-torn territory of brutal destruction. Ordnance had been hurled into the Gaza Strip for decades, destroying buildings and infrastructure beyond all hope of repair.

'Hamas are refusing to cooperate,' O'Donoghue told them. Now that he wasn't addressing the whole squadron he seemed a bit more relaxed. 'They've stated that they'll fire on any aircraft violating their airspace, and that includes Stratton. You'll have to take him in by road, but they'll only allow a single vehicle on to their territory.' He pointed at a spot on the Israeli border. 'This is the Karni crossing. It's the checkpoint closest to Gaza City, so you'll cross over there. Tension is high on the streets. The Firm have eyes inside the city reporting that militants are out in the open, and that since the train bombings, half the young men of fighting age have joined them. There's already been some mortar fire over the border into Israel, so these kids are armed with more than just rifles. Stratton's visit won't be a secret. They'll know you're on your way. But don't expect anyone to welcome you with open arms.'

'Last time someone welcomed Luke with open arms,' Finn murmured, 'she was charging by the hour.'

'I like to keep your mum in business, buddy.' But Luke's was a half-hearted response and no one laughed. They were all absorbing everything O'Donoghue was saying. It sounded like they were going to be driving into a war zone.

The ops officer continued: 'The RV between Stratton and the Hamas representatives is to take place in an administrative building in the centre of Gaza City. We'll forewarn them of your route and hopefully they'll do what they can to keep it clear.' He looked up at the four men in the unit. 'But what Hamas say and what they do aren't always the same thing. You'll need to go in heavy, lads. Very heavy. Stratton might be a cunt, but if anything happens to him, the fucking mushroom cloud goes up.'

'Don't worry about it, boss,' Fozzie said quietly. 'He'll be safe as houses.'

Yeah, Luke thought to himself. Safe as houses. Only houses weren't that safe on the Gaza Strip.

He continued to examine the map as his unit stood around him in silence, doing the same.

*   *   *

Now that the whole squadron was in camp, there was a new bustle around Credenhill. There was plenty to do in advance of the op. Each man needed to test-fire and zero his personal weapons, while the SQMS checked that all the squadron assets were available and ready to go, in advance of the hardware being bagged up for transit. There were further squadron briefings in one lecture room or another, and in between times the men went about the business of selecting their own personal gear, suitable for the operation and the theatre in which they might find themselves. Luke and the unit rejected their digital camo in favour of civvies: once they hit Gaza, they didn't want to look military, as there was nothing like the sight of a foreign soldier to provoke unrest. But he'd be wearing his body armour underneath—he'd definitely want that if things went noisy.

Later in the afternoon the squadron OC and sergeant major left camp, part of an advance party heading out to meet with Israeli liaison officers on the ground, while Luke and his men continued to study the imagery of their route in and out of Gaza City. They'd have GPS on the ground, and the ops room would have a handle on their location at all times, but all that wasn't a substitute for a working knowledge of the terrain.

The rest of the day passed quickly. At 19.30 Luke got some scran with Finn just as O'Donoghue walked into the sergeants' mess to tell them that there would be a further briefing the following morning at 07.00. 'Royal Protection Squad,' he said curtly. 'Stratton's usual team when they're in the UK. Do me a kindness, fellas: shake their hands and smile sweetly.' They all understood what he was saying. The Royal Protection boys were trained up by the SAS in the first place. There wasn't much they could tell Luke and his unit about the ins and outs of acting as a counter-attack team. But the unit would press the flesh with Stratton's usual point men.

Once O'Donoghue had left, the men started wolfing down their plates of thick stew and heavy dumplings. 'If you ask me,' Finn muttered, 'Stratton would look a whole lot better with a Palestinian round in his cerebral cortex. Fucker's got a cheek asking for a Regiment guard in the Middle East after everything he's done.'

'Get used to it, buddy,' said Luke. 'Did no one ever tell you we're not here to play politics—just to help the dickheads who do?'

Finn grunted. He hadn't changed much over the years. He was still a shoot first, ask questions later kind of operator. What *had* changed was his relationship with Luke. Their first op together in Iraq had been tense, and Finn hadn't liked following Luke's lead. They were closer now. They'd fought alongside each other for years. It had created a bond.

Tomorrow promised to be another long day, so when he'd finished eating, Luke headed off to the single-bunk room where he kept all his gear and slept when he was staying in base. He was beat and looking forward to getting his head down, so he shut the door behind him, laid down on his bunk and—despite the sound in the corridor outside of his more boisterous colleagues—he was asleep within minutes.

And as Luke slept, he dreamed.

His dreams were vivid. He dreamed of flashing blue lights and the gnarled wreckage of a train. He dreamed of Alistair Stratton, a man he had never met but whose thin face was very familiar. A voice spoke in his head. *Stratton's all right.*

Suddenly Luke saw himself sitting in a scummy bar in the arse end of Serbia. He knew just how to reply. He was reliving a conversation that had already happened, after all. *Stratton is a politician. Therefore Stratton is a wanker. End of.* He turned his head to look at his companion, fully expecting to

270

see Chet as he was back then.

But he saw nothing of the sort. The figure sitting at the table next to him was unrecognisable. His hair had burned away; the skin of his face was charred and suppurating; his clothes were rags, sticking to him in places and non-existent in others.

He didn't know what it was that woke him. The horror of that vision, or the sound of his mobile phone. Luke sat bolt upright in his bed, his skin damp with sweat, and for a moment he wondered where he was. It was the smell that told him he was in camp: the antiseptic, institutional aroma tinged with a hint of cordite. The noises from outside had stopped and the only light in the room came from the phone glowing through the pocket of the trousers that he'd dumped on the floor by the bunk. He squinted at his chunky watch, its hands and face still vaguely luminous. Quarter to twelve. Who the fuck was calling him at this time of night?

Luke hauled his arse out of bed and fumbled in the darkness, pulling his phone from his pocket and shielding his eyes slightly from the brightness of its screen. The phone continued to vibrate in his hand as he looked down to check the caller's number.

His brow furrowed. 'What the fuck . . . ?' he muttered.

He shook his head. His eyes were playing tricks on him. They had to be. Either that or he was still dreaming.

Luke took another look at the phone.

He wasn't dreaming.

He wasn't mistaken.

But what he was seeing was impossible, because the caller was dead. Burned to a cinder in a house fire years ago. Luke had been to the memorial service in a little Hereford church; he'd offered his condolences to the parents of the deceased; he'd shed his own private tears at the passing of a good friend.

More than a good friend. The man he owed his life to.

No wonder, then, that he felt he was staring into the eyes of a ghost. Because how was it possible—how in the *hell* was it possible—that the phone in his hand should be displaying the words 'FREEMAN, CHET'?

NINETEEN

Little Harry was fast asleep. He looked angelic with his eyes closed, his chest rising and falling softly. Suze couldn't imagine, though, as she sat on an upturned milk crate gazing at him, what kind of angel would find itself in a place like this.

The disused factory they called home was as cavernous as a cathedral and as cold. Most of the windows—high up in the brick walls—were broken, and nobody had bothered to sweep up the shards of glass on the concrete floor. During the daytime the windows let in a watery grey light. But at night it was black. There was no electricity here.

The squat never slept. There were always people awake, no matter what the time of night. It was cold out, and most of the other squatters gathered round a brazier in the middle of the building, burning rubbish that they'd gathered during the day, and sharing spliffs. The air smelt of damp, smoke and skunk, but both Suze and Harry were used to that

272

by now.

They kept themselves to themselves. Suze had found them a little corner of the factory that had perhaps once been a manager's office. It no longer had a door, and the walls were in a poor state, but it afforded them some privacy. There had been squats in the past where they'd had a room to themselves, with a window and a bed. Not here. Harry lay on a mattress of old clothes, covered by a thin blanket. But he never seemed to feel the cold.

'Fancy a toke, gorgeous?'

Suze looked round to see a figure standing in the doorway, the glowing dot of a joint between his fingers. She couldn't make out his features, but she knew well enough who he was. He said he was called Danny, but Suze knew that nobody gave their real names in places like this. His black hair was braided into tight dreadlocks, his lower face was covered in a wispy beard and his body reeked of dope and dirt. Get him when he was stoned— and that was every night—and he'd tell you he was an eco-warrior, or an anarchist, or a trustafarian. In truth, Suze knew, he was just a waster, pissing his life up the wall like everyone else she'd met in squats.

Like her.

'No thanks, Danny,' she said. It paid to stay on good terms with your housemates—they could be volatile, and you didn't want them against you— but all Suze really wanted was to be left alone. Especially tonight.

Danny didn't move.

'I'm going to get some kip now, Danny,' she said with a hint of steel in her voice.

'Suit yourself, love,' Danny muttered. He

disappeared back into the factory.

Suze gave it a couple of moments before checking nobody was nearby. She peered round the doorway of their makeshift bedroom to see nine or ten silhouettes congregated around the brazier. There was nobody in her immediate vicinity, so she hurried back to where Harry was lying.

Her worldly goods were stowed in a single bag. A change of clothes for herself and her son; some antibiotics she'd cadged from a mobile drop-in centre intended for junkies, just in case either of them needed some—registering with a doctor was out of the question, after all; a story book, written for children younger than Harry, from which she had intended to start teaching him to read. But there was never time for that. There was only time for the business of survival.

And at the bottom of the bag, hidden away where nobody could find it, a wallet.

It was in a bad state. The leather was cracked and worn, and some of the stitching inside had come loose. There were credit cards, but they had long since expired and Suze could never have used them anyway. On the back of each card, fading now, was a scrawled signature. Sometimes, in her lowest moments—and there were plenty of those—Suze stared at that signature and remembered the hand that had written it. She remembered the way the calloused fingers had felt on her skin. She remembered the urgent look its owner had given her when he pressed the wallet into her hands.

Stay anonymous. Stay dark.

She'd done what Chet had told her and she'd stayed alive. It wasn't much of a life, but it was perhaps better than none at all.

And now she was going to do the one thing that she *knew* he'd tell her not to. Tucked inside the wallet, difficult to find if you didn't know it was there, was a SIM card. Suze had never done anything with it. She'd barely even dared remove it from its hiding place, as if just by looking at it she might endanger herself. She'd certainly never risked fitting it inside the handset of a mobile phone.

She placed the card in the palm of her hand and stared at it for a moment.

Suze didn't even know if it would work. Removing her own pay-as-you-go mobile from her pocket, she slid the back off and took out the card, before replacing it with Chet's old one. She found herself holding her breath, her hands trembling a little, as she switched the phone on. Would this SIM card work? If Chet had been on a contract, it would have been deactivated long ago. But if it was pay-as-you-go, maybe . . .

It took a few seconds to crank up. A glowing screen, but blank. No information. Suze closed her eyes in disappointment.

'Thought you were hitting the sack, gorgeous.'

She spun round to see Danny. He wasn't in the door frame this time, but had stepped inside the room. His voice was different. A little more high-pitched. A little slower. Stoned.

'For God's sake, Danny,' she snapped. 'Leave me alone.'

Danny was silent for a moment. But then he took a couple of steps towards her. 'No need to talk like that, darling,' he said in a strange, sing-song kind of voice. She could hear him breathing deeply.

Suze stood up, and as she did so she felt his

fingertips reach out and brush her cheek.

She didn't hesitate. The years had taught her that if she didn't take care of herself, nobody else would. She grabbed his wrist and yanked it away from her, then quickly pulled a flick knife from inside her jacket. The light from the screen of her phone glinted against the blade and Danny staggered back when he saw it. 'Fuckin' hell, love. Take it easy, hey?'

'*Get out!*'

Suze listened to Danny's echoing footsteps as he hurried back to the brazier. She tried to calm herself with several deep breaths and sat back down on the crate.

Her heart stopped.

The screen on the phone was still glowing in the dark, but it was no longer blank. A single word: Vodafone. And above it, four bars of service. Suze swallowed hard and reached for the handset. Her fingers still trembling, she accessed the SIM's contacts. Slowly, she scrolled through.

The names were all unfamiliar, but then why should she recognise them? She'd only known Chet for a matter of hours. The As and Bs went quickly; there were no Cs or Ds. By the time she'd reached L her stomach was churning. She continued to scroll.

And then she stopped.

'MERCER, LUKE.'

She bit her lip.

You can trust him. Chet's voice rang in her ears. *You can trust him.*

Suze looked over at Harry. Was she doing the right thing? Was she keeping him safe? The little boy turned in his sleep, and in that instant she saw

Chet's features in his face. It caught her heart.

She pressed the call button quickly, because if she waited she might never do it.

A few seconds' pause, then a ringing tone.

She was holding her breath again. Her mind was a blank. What was she going to say? What would this man think of her, calling out of the blue? Would he believe her, or just think she was some nutter?

It continued to ring.

And then it went silent.

A pause. And then: 'This is Luke, leave a message.'

She gasped and quickly ended the call. Her courage had deserted her.

Suze was sweating, despite the cold. The man's voice had sounded curt and unfriendly. For a moment she wondered what the hell she was doing. How could she be so stupid as to use the phone? Didn't she remember what happened that night? Didn't she remember her mother?

But then she saw in her mind the image from the TV. The woman. She remembered her face, and the scenes of devastation around the world. She remembered the feel of her hands around her neck.

And then she jumped.

The phone was vibrating in her hand. Its screen was lit up. The caller ID read: 'MERCER, LUKE'.

*   *   *

Luke sat in the darkness of his room, his mobile pressed to his ear, listening to the ringtone. It stopped, and a voice answered. Timid. Unsure of itself. Female. 'Hel . . . Hello?'

277

He didn't answer for a moment. He'd never expected to hear Chet's voice, of course, but there was still a corner of his mind that thought maybe . . .

'Is that . . . is that Luke Mercer?'

'Who the hell are you?' he demanded finally.

'I can't talk for long. I was with Chet Freeman the night he died.'

A pause. Luke said nothing.

'The night . . . the night he was murdered.' There was a tremor in the caller's voice.

'What are you talking about? Chet died in a fire . . .'

The woman ignored him. 'He said that if I ever needed help that I should come to you. That you're the only person I could trust. Well . . .' Her voice broke down again, and she sounded terribly weak. 'Well, I need help. It's important. I wouldn't have risked calling you otherwise. I know things. Things I haven't told anyone since Chet died . . . about the bombings . . .'

Luke still had no idea who this woman was, but he knew one thing: she sounded sincere. She also sounded scared.

'Where are you?' he asked, ignoring the voice in his head that told him this was a very bad idea.

'I can't say.' Her voice was half desperation, and half relief that he hadn't dismissed her as a fantasist.

'Then this could be a pretty short conversation, honey. How about we cut the crap and you tell me what the fuck this is all about?'

He could hear her breathing heavily. He could almost hear the cogs turning in her brain.

And then the line went dead.

'Hello?' he said. '*Are you there? Hello?*'

Nothing. He stared at the phone. 'For *fuck's* sake . . .'

The handset vibrated and the phone beeped. 'ONE MESSAGE RECEIVED.'

Luke narrowed his eyes in the darkness as he opened the message. It was short and to the point: 'TOMORROW. 5 P.M. STEPS OF ST PAUL'S CATHEDRAL. I WON'T WAIT.'

He quickly called the number to speak to the woman. No dice. The line was dead.

TWENTY

7 December.

It was early morning in the eastern Mediterranean. The sun was just rising. Ephraim Cohen sat in a comfortable chair, but he didn't feel comfortable at all.

He was in the XO's office of the Mossad training academy in Herzlia, just north of Tel Aviv. It was a small, functional room from which he helped coordinate the training of new recruits to the Institute. He'd been in the job for nearly eight years now, and he missed his days running agents. This new position was not exactly a demotion, but put it this way: it wasn't a promotion either.

His desk, as usual, was clear. Cohen was an organised man. A telephone, a laptop that he seldom used and a rather expensive Mont Blanc fountain pen that he had bought many years ago in London. And in the centre, a photograph. Black and white. Grainy. It had appeared on TV screens

279

the world over and purported to show two of the UK train bombers minutes before they boarded.

But Ephraim Cohen wasn't looking at them. He was looking at the woman behind them. And the person on the opposite side of the desk was looking at him.

'Ring any bells, Ephraim?'

Cohen glanced up over the thick black rims of his glasses. Just for a second, so he could judge the way in which his guest was looking at him.

'It's possible, Ehud, yes,' he replied noncommittally. 'Of course, it's not a very good picture.'

That was a lie, and they both knew it.

'If you'd like me to have it enhanced . . .'

'No, no. That won't be necessary.' He sat back in his chair, removed his spectacles and started cleaning them on his plain navy tie. 'Would you like some coffee, Ehud?'

'What I'd like, Ephraim, is some answers.'

Ehud Blumenthal was a man with a reputation. In Ephraim Cohen's experience, most reputations were carefully managed. Blumenthal's wasn't one of those. He was, without question, just what everybody thought he was: a grade-A, bona fide, dyed-in-the-wool bastard. Blumenthal was the Israeli Prime Minister's Rottweiler, nasty policeman to the PM's nice. Everybody loathed him, but Cohen suspected he didn't mind that, because he loathed everyone back. So when Blumenthal had woken Cohen in the small hours of the morning and demanded a meeting at six a.m., Cohen knew he was in for a shitty day.

'How have you enjoyed your time at the academy, Ephraim?' Blumenthal asked.

Cohen shrugged. 'I serve the Institute in whatever way they wish.'

Blumenthal's face lit up. 'Well, that is excellent, Ephraim. Truly, that is excellent. Because the word on the street is that the Director is looking for an enthusiastic candidate to establish a new station in Sierra Leone. Does that sound like your kind of job, Ephraim? Because I'd be more than happy to put in a good . . .'

'You know who she is, Ehud. Why are you coming to me?'

A satisfied look crossed Blumenthal's face, but he didn't respond immediately. He rather nonchalantly brushed down the lapels of his jacket with his right hand, before standing up and pacing for a few moments around the tiny room.

When it came—the explosion of fury—it was so violent that even the normally unflappable Cohen jumped. Blumenthal strode towards the desk with a vigour that belied his age and slammed his fist down with such force that the Mont Blanc pen jumped a few millimetres in the air. 'I have been in government,' he yelled, 'for more than forty years. I've served three prime ministers and spat out sneakier little Mossad shits than you before breakfast! So if you don't want your bollocks hanging from the top of the Western fucking Wall in time for Hanukkah, you'd better tell me what in the name of all that is holy your former *kidon* is doing standing shoulder to shoulder with two murdering Palestinian shitheads . . .'

'I would have thought, Ehud,' Cohen interrupted, standing up as he did so, his eyes blazing, 'that a Palestinian attack on non-Israeli soil would be rather to your liking.'

281

'Are you as stupid as you look, Cohen? Don't you think the CIA will have every analyst in Langley examining this picture? SIS? People will believe anything of us, you know that. They'd be delighted to believe that one of our people set this whole thing up . . .'

Cohen blinked. It was true, he hadn't really thought of it in those terms. He sat down again, removed his glasses for a second time and rubbed his eyes wearily. 'I don't know what you want me to say, Ehud.'

'Where can we find her?'

'I don't know.' That, at least, he could say with some certainty.

'You're going to have to do a lot better than that, Ephraim.' Blumenthal was sitting down again. A little tear of sweat was dripping down his forehead. 'A lot better.'

Cohen had always known that Maya Bloom would come back to haunt him. As the years had passed, he'd managed to put her from his mind from time to time. But he always knew . . .

'I don't know where she is, Ehud,' he said, a little meeker now.

Blumenthal stared at him for a full thirty seconds before talking again. His voice was quieter, almost conversational, as if his previous outburst had never happened. 'You'd better give me something to go on, Ephraim.'

Cohen nodded. 'Maya Bloom was the best *kidon* I ever knew,' he said. 'Too good, almost. Her parents were killed in a suicide bomb in Tel Aviv, and both she and her brother were identified to join Mossad quite young. The brother—I forget his name—died on operations in Iraq. I think that pushed her over the edge.'

'That means she was close to the edge in the first place,' Blumenthal observed.

Cohen inclined his head. 'Perhaps,' he conceded.

'And you didn't spot this? You didn't think to report it to your superiors?'

Cohen stared into the middle distance. He thought back to those days, and remembered the foolish sexual fantasies he'd entertained about his *kidon*. 'We all make mistakes,' he said, 'from time to time.'

'I think you might find,' Blumenthal said, 'that some mistakes are more costly than others.'

The comment made Cohen snap. 'The moment I realised she was a threat, I sent someone to take care of her. She killed him. It's all in the file. I've heard nothing about her ever since. But I can tell you something for sure, Ehud.'

'Then you better had.'

'This . . .' He tapped the picture that was still lying on his desk. 'This doesn't make sense. Maya Bloom was many things. Skilled. Dangerous. Unhinged. But she was loyal to Israel, Ehud. She was *always* loyal to Israel. Maya Bloom in league with Palestinian terrorists? I would sooner believe it of you yourself than of her. I can only assume she's part of some crackpot plot to turn the West against the Palestinians.'

'You'd better hope we find this woman, Ephraim, otherwise you might find yourself answering to less sympathetic members of the administration than myself.' He stood up, brushed his lapels again and turned towards the exit. 'I'll let myself out,' he said.

Blumenthal was just opening the door when

Cohen spoke again.

'Ehud,' he said very quietly.

The politician turned. 'What?'

'You won't find her, you know. I can absolutely promise you that you won't find Maya Bloom. And if you do . . .'

He went silent.

'What?'

Cohen remembered the brutalised body of the agent he'd sent to kill her. The guts spilled out all over the bed. The blood and the stink. The message she'd sent him, and which he had heeded. He wanted to say, 'She'll kill you,' but he thought better of it.

'*What?*' Blumenthal demanded again.

Cohen shook his head and sighed deeply. 'Nothing, Ehud,' he said. 'Nothing at all.' And he watched with an expressionless face as the Rottweiler stormed out of the room, slamming the door noisily behind him.

TWENTY-ONE

Leaving Hereford had been far from straightforward. First there had been the meet and greet with the Royal Protection Squad at 07.00 hrs. Luke hardly heard anything the RPS boys said. He was just replaying last night's conversation over and over again. Trying to make sense of it. Trying to work out what it meant.

I was with Chet Freeman the night he died . . . the night he was murdered.

Part of him thought the caller must have been a

284

nutter, winding him up or playing some sick joke. But his phone was supplied by work. That meant it was encrypted. Impossible to trace and impossible to find the number if you didn't know it already. Luke knew that he had to get out of camp and down to London.

They were scheduled to leave for Israel the following morning. Going AWOL wasn't an option, so he approached O'Donoghue at midday and spun him a crock of shit about having a few personal loose ends to tie up before heading out on the op. The ops officer hadn't been happy. 'Fucking hell, Luke, we leave in twenty-four hours. It's not the time for you to start sorting out your woman trouble.' But he cut his man some slack and agreed to stand him down for a few hours. And so, by early afternoon, Luke had changed out of his camouflage gear and into a pair of jeans and an old hooded top that he normally wore for jogging in the winter. Today he selected it because the hood would disguise his face a little. Before long he was screaming down the M4 to London.

He hit the western outskirts at 14.45 hrs. As a London boy born and bred, it felt like coming home. But it was an uneasy homecoming. By 15.45 he was parking up just off Fleet Street. He was in good time for the RV and that suited him well. He didn't know what this woman looked like; he didn't know if this was some elaborate game; so he wanted to get eyes on the location early.

The light was just failing as he walked up Fleet Street with the illuminated dome of St Paul's rising above him. Luke turned up the collar of his leather jacket against the cold, pulled up his hood and stood fifty metres from the steps, in the shadow of the maroon awning of an Indian restaurant. The smell of curry reminded him how hungry he was, but he put that to the back of his mind and surveyed the scene.

The entrance to the cathedral was lit up, and people were wandering in and out of the huge wooden doors, only just visible behind the temple-like column of the façade. Many of them were tourists—there was a large party of Japanese students with backpacks and cameras—but he saw too a good number of ordinary Londoners, suited and booted. Perhaps, he thought to himself, the events of a couple of days ago had made people more religious. Luke didn't know. It was all bullshit to him. When you're dead you're dead. No pearly gates or swooning angels. Just a hole in the ground, if you're lucky.

The minutes ticked away. Luke stayed in the shadows, watching the steps. Waiting. People came and went. Was the woman he was here to meet one of the crowd sitting on the steps? Impossible to tell.

He continued to watch. It grew cold. He ignored it.

'You hungry, boss?'

He looked round sharply. An Indian man in a grey suit had appeared at the door of the curry restaurant. 'I have very good food.'

Luke shook his head and went back to watching.

Time check: 16.57. Three minutes to RV.

Luke scanned the steps, directing his vision in concentric circles so he covered the whole area. Nobody stood out. He looked at his phone. No calls. He scanned the façade of the cathedral; he checked along its wings for anything suspicious; he searched for loiterers in the general vicinity.

Nothing. It looked like just another London evening.

16.59.

Something caught his eye.

Two people had emerged from the entrance of the cathedral. A woman and, holding on to her hand, a young child. Luke wouldn't have given them a second glance, were the woman not looking around anxiously, as if she too was searching for someone. The child stood calmly by the woman's side. He showed none of the woman's anxiety, but then why should he? He was just a kid.

Luke stayed where he was. A nearby church bell rang the hour and the woman's anxiety appeared to increase. He continued to check for anything suspicious: unmarked cars parked nearby; anyone else observing the steps.

Still nothing.

At 17.03 he stepped out from the shadows. He didn't walk directly up to the steps, but followed a circular route and approached from the side. As he drew nearer to the entrance of the cathedral, the woman's features became clearer. She was thin, with short red hair and bags under her eyes. There was nothing particularly remarkable about her face, but the same couldn't be said of the child who held her hand. He was thin too, with serious eyes and dishevelled brown hair. But there *was* something familiar about him. So familiar, in fact, that just to look at him sent a prickle of recognition down Luke's spine.

He stopped at the bottom of the steps and looked up. The woman was chewing on her lower lip. She glanced at her watch and muttered something to herself, then bent down and spoke to

287

the child. And it was as she was speaking that she caught sight of Luke staring at her.

She stared back and slowly stood up to her full height again. Her expression was questioning. Luke hurried up the steps, but he didn't head straight for her. Instead he bypassed the pair of them and passed through the main doors of the cathedral.

He'd never been inside before. Last time Luke had been in a church was to say goodbye to a member of A Squadron who'd had his bollocks blown off during a raid on a Taliban facility in the badlands between Afghanistan and Pakistan. They'd repatriated those bits of his body they could find, but the guys who'd shouldered his coffin said afterwards that it felt empty. Whatever. The family had something to plant, that was the main thing.

He quickly took in his surroundings: the narrow aisle with its chequerboard floor and row upon row of wooden pews, the massive dome, the highly decorated altar and imposing organ, the huge arches along either side of the aisle leading to the unseen wings of the cathedral—very pretty, Luke supposed, but he wasn't here to marvel at the fucking architecture. At the far end of the cathedral, just in front of the altar, a large choir of maybe a hundred people was rehearsing—a fifty-fifty mixture of schoolboys in blue and grey uniform and men and women of retirement age. Their conductor, clearly unhappy with something, was shouting at them, and his voice echoed meaninglessly around the huge space. Weird, what some people got themselves worked up about. Aside from the choir, there were probably another hundred people in here that he could see, some of them sitting on the pews with their heads

288

bowed, others wandering aimlessly, looking at the architecture, or just talking.

The conductor's shouting stopped and, almost imperceptibly, the choir started singing. It was quiet, but the voices sounded like they came from every corner of the cathedral.

'Monteverdi,' a voice said from behind him.

Luke spun round. A young priest with neatly brushed but thinning blond hair, black robes and a dog collar was standing no more than a metre from him. 'The *Vespers*,' he said with a serene smile. 'So powerful . . . Are you here for contemplation?'

Luke looked over the priest's shoulder towards the main doors. No sign of his date.

'Something like that.'

The man inclined his head. 'Well, I hope you find what you're looking for . . .'

Me too, Luke thought. He moved away, walking ten metres to the right, into the shadow of the first side arch. From here he could keep an eye on the entrance and he didn't have to wait long before he saw her walking into the cathedral. She was clutching the boy's left hand with both of hers and her eyes darted around. When the priest who had approached Luke walked up and spoke to her, she was visibly distressed and scurried towards the aisle without saying a word, pulling the kid along with her. She looked fucking terrified, Luke thought, as the woman walked past the arch where he was standing. Fine by him. He didn't like these cloak and dagger games and if she felt uncomfortable, that made two of them.

He left the shadows of the arch and moved quickly down the aisle. Within seconds he was a metre behind the woman and the boy, but they were quite unaware of his presence.

Luke kept his voice low. 'Walk.'

The woman looked round nervously. He pointed down the aisle towards the altar. 'That way.'

She swallowed hard and, the little boy still clutching her hand, did as she was told. Luke walked just behind her. Less than a metre. Close enough that they could talk as they went.

'First things first. What's your name?'

'I can't tell you,' the woman said quietly. He could only just hear her over the choir. The *Vespers*, whatever the fuck they were, were getting louder.

'Well, here's the problem, honey. I'm not a patient man. Fuck around with me any more and I might just decide to stick your arm behind your back and march you down to the nearest Old Bill. I'll let *you* explain what you're doing with a dead man's phone. Could be an interesting conversation.'

'Oh, God . . .' the woman murmured. She pulled the little boy closer towards her.

'So let's try again. What's your name?'

A pause. And then, with resignation: 'Suze . . . Suze McArthur. And this is Harry.' She stopped and turned round to look at Luke again. They were standing underneath the dome now, and the acoustics had changed. The choir sounded more ethereal, as though a hundred voices were floating around in the air, searching for someone to listen to them.

'Chet's boy,' she said, her voice barely more than a whisper.

Luke blinked.

'What?'

He looked down at the kid. Harry stared up at him. He didn't look scared, not like Suze, and Luke

290

felt the recognition again. He knew she wasn't lying.

'I'm scared someone might find us,' said Suze. 'I don't feel safe.'

'What are you talking about? Who else knows we're here?'

Suze looked back towards the entrance of the cathedral, and her right hand instinctively gripped the boy's shoulder. 'I don't know,' she said. 'I can't tell . . .'

'Either you've told someone or you haven't.'

She shook her head. 'It's not as simple as that.'

Jesus, this woman oozed paranoia. But whatever was going through her head, she clearly believed it. Luke looked around. Up ahead, to the right of the altar, through one of the ornate arches and at the end of the right-hand wing of the church, there was a small, separate altar with three rows of shorter pews in front of it. 'Over there,' he said. 'If anyone's watching us, we'll see them.'

'And what then?'

Luke gave her a flat stare. 'I'll deal with it.'

Together, the three of them hurried between the front of the main pews and the choir, towards the smaller altar. The light was a little lower here, the smell of incense stronger. A cast-iron barrier stopped the public from approaching the altar, which was about two metres wide and on which sat a plain bronze cross, about half a metre high. Behind this little altar was a painting: some Bible scene, all stormy skies and men in robes. The altar cloth was inlaid with gold thread and there were three pews facing it for the faithful to pray in. They were all empty. Luke stood with his back to the altar. To his right there was a clear path to the area

291

under the dome and the choir. Straight ahead he could see back along the side length of the church. It was gloomy, but his eyesight was sharp. A few tourists were milling about, perhaps twenty metres away, but they paid this nervous trio no attention. Between them and the tourists was the top of a stairwell, next to which was a sign with an arrow pointing downwards and the words 'TO THE CRYPT' in big black letters. But the stairwell was cordoned off with a piece of thick rope.

Suze encouraged the boy to sit in one of the pews, which he did without argument. Then she came to stand next to Luke.

'Me and Chet were pretty close,' Luke said. His voice was hushed, but not out of reverence. 'He never mentioned anyone called Suze.'

'We didn't know each other long.'

Luke glanced at the boy. 'Long enough,' he said.

'Yes,' Suze replied without a trace of embarrassment. She sighed deeply. 'Long enough for him to save my life. And lose his.'

'Go on.'

Suze closed her eyes. Her face was drawn, as though the effort of talking was too much for her. But when she opened her eyes and started to speak again, the words were like a flood.

She talked. Luke listened. For all her nervousness, the story Suze told was vivid, as if she had relived the events she was recounting every day of her life since. He could almost picture the rooftop above Whitehall and Suze's little flat. He didn't have to imagine the B&B in the Brecon Beacons because he knew it.

And she started talking about Alistair Stratton. About the Grosvenor Group and a conversation

292

she and Chet had overheard. The words tumbled from her mouth, like they'd been locked up and were now escaping. She didn't seem to notice that the look Luke gave her was disbelieving.

By the time Suze had finished, the choristers were in full song, forcing Luke to speak up.

'So where's this tape now?' he asked.

She shook her head. 'Burned,' she told him. 'In the fire.'

Luke nodded. 'Convenient,' he murmured.

A pause. A dissonant chord echoed round the cathedral.

'You think I'm *lying*?' She said it as if the possibility had never occurred to her. 'Why would I *lie* about something like this?'

'I've never met you, honey. I don't know *what* you'd lie about.' Luke glanced over at the kid. He certainly *looked* like Chet, but that didn't mean the rest of this bullshit was true. And then, like the sun coming up, something clicked in his head. He pulled out his wallet. There was always money in there, never less than a couple of hundred. He removed a thin sheaf of notes. 'How much do you need?' he asked.

'*What?*'

'Chet was a good mate. I owe him. If you need help you don't have to make this crap up.'

'You think I want your *money*? You think I'd wait all these years to tap you up for . . . ?' She looked around desperately, like she wanted to escape but didn't know where to run to. 'You think I'd risk *this* for a few quid?' She was whispering now, and on the verge of tears. She pushed Luke's hand away, sat down next to her boy and put her head in her hands. The little boy didn't seem

293

surprised at his mother's sudden emotion. He just looked calmly up at Luke. Fucking kid. For some reason he gave him the spooks. Luke swore under his breath and took a seat next to Suze again.

They sat there for a full minute, not speaking. The choir grew quieter too.

It was Suze who broke their silence. She sat up straight and stared at the bronze cross on the altar. 'You knew Chet,' she said. 'Do you really think he died in a simple house fire?'

'He was badly wounded,' Luke replied. Even as he said it, though, he doubted himself. Chet *was* wounded, but had that ever stopped him getting around? Like hell it had. Chet Freeman took some killing. Luke knew that better than anyone.

He closed his eyes briefly.

'Why are you telling me all this now? Why didn't you come to me immediately?'

'Haven't you listened to *anything* I said?' she snapped. 'I was scared, all right? I still am. Chet told me to hide and that's what I did. I've been hiding ever since that night.'

'Where?'

'Anywhere,' she said, suddenly full of hopelessness. '*Every*where. I move around. I *know* they're still after me. I *know* that if they find me, they'll . . . they'll do to me what they did to Chet. And there's Harry . . .' She paused to inhale deeply. 'But something's happened. Something important. These bombings. You know about them?'

'You could say that.'

Suze pulled her mobile phone from her pocket. Luke noticed that her hands were shaking as she pressed a couple of buttons and handed it to Luke, nodding at the screen.

The image that it displayed was slightly blurred, but he could make out a black and white CCTV still, and the edge of the TV screen from which the photo had been taken. Two men, their heads circled. It looked familiar. 'I've seen this?'

'The bombers,' Suze whispered, her face earnest. 'They released it yesterday.'

'What's it got to do with you?'

Suze tapped the screen, pointing not at the circled men but at a dark-haired woman behind them.

'What?'

She looked up at him. 'It's her,' she said. 'The woman who came for us. The woman who . . . who killed Chet.'

Luke stared at the picture.

'How can you be sure?'

Suze took a deep breath. Her hands were still shaking. 'Has anyone ever tried to kill *you*?'

'Once or twice, as it goes.'

She quickly recovered. 'Do you remember *their* faces?'

Of course he did. Some things you never forget.

'Chet said she works for Mossad. I don't know how he knew . . . something about her gun?'

'*Mossad?* That doesn't make any sense.'

Suze shrugged. 'All I know is that someone wanted us out of the way because of what we knew. I don't care who she was working for . . . but Alistair Stratton had something to do with it.'

Luke shook his head. 'Listen to me. If Chet was right about her, about a Mossad connection, she could be working for anybody.' Because official allegiances change, he thought to himself. One day you fight for one man, the next day you fight for another. Hadn't the Regiment trained up the Mujahideen before they were public enemy number one?

Suze stood up and walked towards the small altar. For a moment she didn't move, gazing up at the bronze cross, before suddenly turning towards him again. 'Alistair Stratton's a warmonger. He always has been. Don't you see? Doesn't *anybody* see? First the Balkans, then Iraq, now this. Don't you see what he's . . . ?'

Her words stopped abruptly. Her expression changed.

She wasn't looking at Luke, but beyond him. And though she whispered something, it was drowned out by the choir as the piece they were rehearsing entered a crescendo. The colour had drained from her face and her expression changed. Luke recognised it: the look of absolute dread.

He shot to his feet. 'What is it? What the hell?'

He turned and looked back down along the side of the cathedral. And that was when he saw her.

The woman who approached them was thirty metres away, but walking quickly along the shadowy, vaulted wing of the cathedral. The few people who were in her path drew away at a single look. She was dressed all in black—the same colour as her hair—and she walked with purpose, her head slightly bowed but her eyes fixed on Luke, Suze and Harry.

'*Go!*' Luke barked. '*Now!*' He pointed back towards the dome and the milling crowds.

Suze moved like a dart, grabbing Harry, who, for the first time since they'd entered the cathedral, looked suddenly worried as he jumped to his feet. Mother and son ran awkwardly, hand in hand, towards the choir, who were now singing louder than ever.

Luke stayed with his back to the bronze cross, facing the newcomer. His mind was racing. He had no weapon. His Sig was safely locked up in the armoury back at base and even though it was just a woman moving towards him, her right hand was buried inside her jacket. And he knew what that meant.

She was twenty metres away and closing in. She had started to remove her hand from her jacket.

Decision time.

'Choose your fucking battles, Luke,' he whispered to himself. He turned, whipped the bronze cross from the altar—it was fucking heavy—before turning and running after Suze and the kid.

The two of them were about five metres from the conductor and just turning to head back down the aisle when Harry tripped. He fell heavily on to the hard stone floor. By the time he'd scrambled to his feet, all arms and legs, Luke was there with them. If he could get them out of range . . .

'Get down!' he urged them, the choir ringing in his ears. As he spoke, he saw someone else approaching them up the aisle. It was the cleric who had greeted them, only this time his face was a lot less serene as his cassock flowed behind him.

'Please,' he said above the singing once he was just a couple of metres away. 'This is a place of worship. I must ask that you keep silent . . .'

'GET DOWN!' Luke barked at Suze and Harry. *'GET DOWN!'* The priest drew himself up to confront Luke and was rewarded by the force of the Regiment man's forearm against his chest, pushing him to the side of the aisle and towards the pews.

'*FUCKING GET . . .*'

The gunshots were inaudible, clearly fired from a suppressed weapon. Their consequences, however, were there for everybody to see.

The boy was the first to go. The round hit him in the side of the head, just in front of the left ear. There was a spray of blood over the stone floor of the cathedral, but he didn't fall fully to the ground because he was still being pulled along by his mother, who looked over her shoulder in annoyance that he appeared to be slouching.

One glance, however, and she realised what had happened.

By now Harry had crumpled to the floor and slid slightly along the stone, smearing the spatter of his own blood as he went. Luke saw Suze silently mouth her son's name, her face melt into an expression of the purest horror and anguish. Then he heard her voice. 'Harry! *HARRY!*' Behind him the choir, still oblivious to what had happened, soared towards another mighty climax.

'*Hit the ground!*' Luke bellowed at Suze. '*HIT THE GROUND!*'

The shooter was standing in the shadows of the third arch along, and had her suppressed handgun pointed, ready to take another shot. Suddenly she was knocked sideways. An old lady appeared where the woman had stood, wearing a grey woollen overcoat and brandishing a heavy, old-fashioned handbag that she'd just swiped at the assassin. The have-a-go-heroine was clearly furious, but in an instant the barrel of the assassin's gun was touching her head. There was a flash of blood and skull as the old lady's body absorbed the cartridge and the propellant.

298

The shooter had turned again. Suze was kneeling in the aisle, cradling the body of her son. A dreadful, desolate moan escaped her lips. Luke had dropped the bronze cross with a clatter. As he ran towards her he sensed the vicar chasing him. He could see that the top three inches of Suze's head were visible to the shooter above the pews.

The third shot, like the previous two, made barely any noise, but there was a sickening thud as it slammed into the top of Suze's skull, ripping out a chunk of her head and throwing her about a metre backwards so that she clattered into the pews behind her. When her body came to rest, she was spread-eagled, her arms stretched out to either side, her back leaning against the edge of the pews and her face a bloody and unrecognisable pulp.

Luke dived to the ground, falling hard on his shoulder and turning on to his back to take in the situation. A few members of the choir had realised now what was going on. The music began to falter and suddenly there was a scream from one of the schoolboys in uniform—a little kid who couldn't have been more than nine. The priest, who had been chasing Luke, was standing among the dead. His face had turned grey with horror and now he was looking directly at the assassin.

Luke hurled himself forward, diving over the child's body to wrestle the vicar to the floor. But he was too late. The fourth round caught the man on the side of his skull just before Luke's shoulder made contact with his legs. As Luke barged him to the floor, his blood sprayed an arch over the flagstones.

There was chaos now in the ranks of the choir. Panic echoed around the cathedral. Screaming.

299

Kids and pensioners alike were running from their position in front of the main altar, seeking cover from the sniper in the shadows, while some of them looked around desperately for somewhere to hide. Others were frozen by fear. Why shouldn't they be? They hadn't been trained to keep calm under fire. Luke's head rang with the shouts of terror rebounding off the stone walls and around the dome. He did what he could to ignore them.

Still on all fours in the aisle, and under the cover of the pews, he scrambled back to where he had dropped the bronze cross—his only weapon. Looking forward, he saw three old men who had formed a ring around five frightened kids. He grabbed the cross and scrambled along one of the pews to his right. He had to try to get his hands on the shooter, but that meant keeping out of sight until he was almost upon her.

It took him ten seconds to crawl the length of the pew. He emerged seven or eight metres in front of the small altar where he'd been talking to Suze. He kept low and peered round to his right, his eyes sharp for the woman in the shadow of the arch, ready to take cover again at the first sign of being in her line of fire.

He saw her, but it was fleeting: just the shadow of a black figure stepping over the cordon of the stairwell fifteen metres away and leading down into the crypt. Was that a dead end? She had made her first mistake. Luke jumped up from his hiding position between the pews and sprinted towards the stairwell, where he stopped.

The stairs were about two metres wide. He could count twelve steps but there were more out of sight. A dim light was flooding upwards.

300

Was she expecting him to follow? Was it a trap? Was she waiting, weapon at the ready?

Luke gave himself a few seconds to form a sitrep in his head. He was in an impossible tactical situation. If he walked down those stairs he'd be lit up, an easy target, dead before he got to the bottom. If he'd been tooled up, with men at his disposal, with weapons and body armour, they could have just chucked down a flashbang or a frag, laid down fire and gone in noisy. But he had none of that. Just a stupid fucking cross.

He hesitated. Fom beyond the walls of the cathedral, he heard the sound of sirens.

Police.

He looked around. The main body of the cathedral was empty, its occupants crushing round the main entrance to get out. Luke himself had spatters of blood over him from his proximity to the carnage. Was this a situation he wanted to explain to the Old Bill? To his OC?

Like fuck it was.

With a sudden burst of anger he hurled the bronze cross down the stairs and heard it clattering on the hard floor below. His only option was to disappear. Now.

Luke pulled his hood a little further over his brow and put his head down. Nobody, he calculated, would notice another frightened member of the public rushing to escape the carnage, and he was right. A crowd of choristers, visitors and clerics were huddled around the doors of the cathedral, pressing against each other, shouting, desperate to escape.

Luke joined them quietly. Just as it was his turn to leave, he glanced back over his shoulder, ignoring the way the last few stragglers were jostling to get away. He could just see them, the three bodies in the aisle, alone in the massive space of the cathedral. Nobody was anywhere in the vicinity. Nobody was paying them any attention. No churchman was ministering to them. They just lay there, gruesome in death, and alone.

He remembered the face of the little boy. Chet's boy. Now dead, like his father. The thought was a needle in Luke's soul as he pushed out into the open air. The sound of sirens was louder, the chaos intense. Luke hurried down the stone steps and disappeared into the night.

TWENTY-TWO

8 December.
The Manhattan offices of the Grosvenor Group occupied the top three floors of a skyscraper on East 43rd Street. From the penthouse the towers of the city were visible all around: the Chrysler Building, the UN, the Empire State. The two men talking there remembered the days when the Twin Towers loomed over everything. They'd been in this very building when the planes hit. Along with the rest of Manhattan they'd rushed from the city in panic; unlike the rest of Manhattan, the events of 9/11 had brought an upward trajectory in their fortunes. War was always good for business.

Through the floor-to-ceiling windows, the East River was sparkling blue and the bridges and buildings glittered in the low winter sun. The airspace above the city was buzzing with

302

helicopters. Some were giving tourists a bird's-eye view of the island; some were ferrying wealthy businessmen to work or play. Some, of course, were there for security. These two men knew there was never a moment when a gunship wasn't hovering above New York City. It was one of their subsidiaries who supplied it to the DOD, after all.

A bald-headed man with a shiny scalp and tanned skin sat in a comfortable executive chair with his back to the East River and his feet parked on the solid wooden desk in front of him. He listened calmly to the ranting of his colleague: a fat man, who sweated even when he wasn't stressed out and whose voice had a strong South African accent. 'The guy's got us over a fucking barrel,' he complained, waving his arms in the air to reveal dark patches of perspiration in the pits of his shirt. 'He's acting like some fucking Transvaal mercenary. I'm telling you, man, we shouldn't be involved in this shit.'

The bald man smiled blandly. 'You should learn to relax, Pieter. You ever get yourself a massage? I know this girl, comes from Stockholm, got a rack like a fucking balcony. I'm telling you—you could do Shakespeare off it.'

The suggestion only made Pieter more angry. 'God *damn* it, Nathan. I'm not interested in your fucking hookers. You know what this could do to our company?'

Nathan swung his feet back down off the table, stood up and looked out over the East River. His bald-headed reflection smiled back at him. He knew his silence would infuriate someone of Pieter de Lange's temperament. The pudgy South African CFO had a brain for numbers but a tendency to see

303

shadows that weren't there, or at least to see larger shadows than really existed.

'I said,' Pieter repeated, 'do you know what this could do to our company?'

Nathan turned. 'Sure I know,' he said. 'Double its market capitalisation value? Triple it, maybe?'

'Ah, man,' Pieter replied. 'How much of that money do you think you'll be able to spend in a Federal jail, eh? The only hookers you'll find in there will be kaffirs with twelve-inch dicks.'

Nathan laughed. Pieter was a crude motherfucker when he wanted to be and the Grosvenor Group's CEO quite enjoyed that. It made a change from the usual po-faced Brits he spent so many of his days with. But it wasn't so much the guy's choice of words that tickled him. It was the suggestion that either of them would face any kind of negative consequences for . . . well, for *anything*, really.

'Tell me, Pieter, how long have you been with us now?'

'Five years.'

'Five years. And in those five years, how many former presidents of the United States have you dined with?'

Pieter shrugged. 'Two,' he said.

'And members of the Senate? I bet you can't even remember.' Nathan could tell he was right, because Pieter didn't reply. 'How many share options in the Grosvenor Group have you drawn up for prime movers in Washington, Pieter? How many millions in dividends did we pay out to sitting members of Congress in the last financial year?'

'Plenty,' Pieter mumbled.

'Yeah, plenty. You know how the world works,

304

Pieter. You think any of those guys are going to let us go down when they know they could come down with us? Huh?'

Pieter shrugged.

'I've been at this a long time. And I've juggled more slippery skittles than Alistair Stratton, believe me. He's just a greedy little man who wants to fill his boots. You really think he's going to go public about our arrangement with him? He'd be up in front of The Hague quicker than you can say "war crime".'

'Then why are you supplying him? Why are you giving him access to our intelligence networks?'

Nathan gave him a flat look. 'Think of it as a speculative investment, Pieter. You accountants understand things like that, don't you?'

'Don't patronise me, man. I just don't see what's in this for Stratton.'

'Pieter, Pieter,' Nathan smiled blandly. 'You must trust me to handle Stratton.'

'Ah, I don't know, man. I don't like it. I don't like *him*.'

'Come on, Pieter. Look what we made from Iraq while everyone else was worrying about oil. Stratton's like war—good for business.'

He walked round to where the South African was standing and slapped his palm in a comradely fashion against the back of his sweaty shirt. 'I'm going to get you that chick's number,' he said. 'You look like you could use a good time. All work and no play makes Pieter a dull boy, and we really wouldn't want that now, would we?'

*   *   *

305

RAF Brize Norton. 15.00 hrs.

A dull-grey C-17 Globemaster III sat on the tarmac. None of its four jets was yet in motion, but the aft door was open, revealing the massive belly of this packhorse of an aircraft.

Parked no more than twenty metres away were four white minibuses. They'd exited the barriers of Credenhill three hours ago. They were entirely nondescript. See them drive past and you might have thought they contained a local football team, or labourers on their way to a site. And a peek at the men inside wouldn't have given you much else to go on, all of them dressed in civvies. And although they all wore sturdy boots, there wasn't a speck of olive drab or DPM in sight.

At the back of the lead minibus, one man had stared out of the window as they left Hereford. There were bags under his eyes as he gazed into the middle distance, seeing but not registering the dingy suburbs as they headed towards the motorway. He should sleep, he knew that. But sleep wasn't possible. Not with the events of the previous night spinning in his head. Luke Mercer was no longer shocked by death, though he didn't doubt that the sight of Chet's lad sliding in a pool of his own blood would stay with him for the rest of his days.

'If that's not a professional job,' he had heard his neighbour saying when they were no more than a minute from base, 'I'm a fucking Chinaman. Headshots, at that range, no sign of the shooter. You ask me, that's agency work.' Luke had turned to see Finn with a copy of the *Sun* open in front of him. He'd already seen the headline that morning—'MURDER IN THE CATHEDRAL'—and a

306

grainy telephoto shot of the scene that was so sharp in his memory. He hadn't had the stomach to read any further.

'Not sure about the kid, though,' Finn mused. 'Doubt he was spilling state secrets. Or the coffin-dodger. And it sounds like the priest just got clipped in the crossfire. Don't reckon he'll be rising on the third day.' He carried on reading, his voice becoming slightly distant. 'I'm telling you—train bombs, snipers—there's something in the fucking water this winter.' He looked up from his paper at Luke. 'Christ on a bike, mate, you look bloody terrible.'

Luke had wondered for a moment whether he should share with Finn what had gone on last night. They went back a long way, after all. They'd seen some things together, and there was no doubt it would do him good to talk about it. But what would he say? He couldn't even fit the pieces of Suze's bizarre story together in his own head, let alone explain it to someone else. And to admit that he'd been in St Paul's last night? That would be plain stupid. Finn was a good lad, but he'd be almost obliged to tell someone.

'Thanks, buddy,' he'd muttered. 'You look like a pissing toad yourself.'

He'd turned away and spent the rest of the journey in silence, ignoring the banter that came from the other B Squadron men. As they travelled, scenes from the previous night kept flashing through Luke's mind. He kept hearing fragments of the strange woman's conversation.

You knew Chet. Do you really think he died in a simple house fire?

... she works for Mossad ... Don't you see?

Doesn't anybody *see? First the Balkans, then Iraq, now this* . . .

They sounded like the ravings of a paranoid fantasist, a conspiracy theorist. Luke wanted to believe that was what they were. But in the light of what had happened just minutes after she'd spilled her heart out, he couldn't help thinking they had the ring of truth—whatever that truth might be.

Now it was time to debus. It didn't take more than a few minutes for them to carry the crates which held the squadron's weapons and ammunition up into the C-17 and secure them inside the webbing. The ops sergeant took a headcount and, once he was satisfied everyone had boarded, he gave the word to the loadie. The aft door closed up and the engines started to rumble.

It stank in the aircraft. Aviation gas wasn't the worst of it. Luke could detect a vague whiff of rotten meat. The C-17 was a versatile beast. It wasn't just suited to the wholesale movement of troops and equipment. As it could operate on short runways, and even had capability on those that were unpaved, it was suitable for use close to the battlefield. That meant it was a good choice for casevac, and for its evil twin: the repatriation of the dead. Impossible to say how many corpses this machine had ferried since it had been in service. Impossible, too, to say whether the stench inside the plane was related, but there was something sobering about being strapped into an aircraft which doubled as a hearse—two lines of men, facing each other, silent not only because the increasing noise of the engine made talking difficult.

Flight time to Ben Gurion International Airport,

fifteen klicks south-east of Tel Aviv: four hours. Four more hours for Luke to try to make sense of things. But in the end, he tried to put it from his mind by running over the details of this morning's briefing. The next twenty-four hours were going to be full-on and he needed a clear head.

It was a relief when he sensed the C-17 losing height, the wheels finally hitting the ground. The aircraft taxied for a full ten minutes after touchdown as the pilot manoeuvred it to a secluded part of the airfield. The aft door opened to reveal night-time and allow a blast of cool but humid air into the aircraft. A Mediterranean rainstorm was on its way.

A small convoy of unmarked black transit vehicles, covered with a thick layer of sandy dust, were waiting immediately behind the plane, and standing outside them were a handful of people. Luke immediately recognised the OC, Julian Dawson, and Sergeant Major Bill Thomas, who'd gone out as an advance party. The others were also in civvies but making no attempt to hide the assault rifles strapped round their bodies. They were clearly members of some branch of the Israeli Defence Forces, ostensibly there to help the squadron load up and escort them to their operational base, but nobody was under any illusion that they were there to control more than to assist.

Luke had never been to Ben Gurion before. His operations in the region had always taken him further east, into Jordan, Iraq and the Stan. He knew, though, that the Israelis had good reason to be paranoid. Their principal airport had long been a target for terror attacks, dating back to the early seventies when Black September—the same

Palestinian terrorist group that later orchestrated the massacre of Israeli athletes at the Munich Olympics—landed a hijacked 707 on the runway. The Israeli Government had called in their elite special forces, Sayeret Matkal, more commonly known as the Unit. The Unit was based on the SAS, even down to sharing the same regimental motto, 'Who Dares Wins'. They had stormed the 707, taking control in less than ten minutes and nailing two of the four hijackers as well as one passenger. Since that day, Ben Gurion had been one of the most highly defended airports in the world, with both uniformed and covert police and the IDF operating round the clock.

Luke eyed up the Israeli soldiers as he unstrapped himself from his seat in the C-17. To a man they had shaved heads and tanned skin. Some of them were so dark as to look Arabic. Were these guys members of the Unit? Maybe. No way they'd tell him and he wasn't going to ask. One of them shouted something in Hebrew as a passenger jet thundered overhead, and the others opened up the back of the transits while the Regiment men unloaded their gear from the aircraft and packed it into the waiting vehicles. Ten minutes later they were speeding across the airfield. At the perimeter they passed a checkpoint that made Heathrow look like a Center Parc. It was guarded not only by armed personnel, but by three open-topped technicals with .50-cal machine guns mounted on the top, each one manned by a cold-eyed Israeli soldier. A regular level of security, or laid on in response to the volatile international situation? Luke didn't know.

'Hope no one's over their booze allowance,'

Fozzie announced as the plainclothes IDF lads negotiated their way out of the airport. A couple of minutes later they were speeding away from the airport towards a wide, well-maintained main road.

They travelled for forty-five minutes before pulling off the main road. Five minutes after that they slowed down some more, coming to a halt at the edge of a high fence with rolls of barbed wire perched on top. There was a huge yellow sign—'Hebrew for "Fuck off",' Fozzie suggested— and at a break in the fence was a barrier, manned by two armed soldiers in olive drab. They were clearly expecting the convoy: one look and they opened the barrier and waved them on.

It was pitch-black outside. At first Luke couldn't see much of the immediate surroundings. In the distance, though, he caught sight of the red lights of control and communications towers, and they were not far inside the perimeter when a chopper flew overhead. He had the impression of an immense military installation, and that impression was confirmed a couple of minutes later when the central hub of the base came into view.

It was a sprawling mess of low, single-storey buildings, aircraft hangars and equipment warehouses. Each building looked like it had been stuck there without much thought, as if the whole place had grown up randomly over a long period of time. Even though it was late, there was plenty going on. Military trucks were swarming round. As they drove past a hangar, Luke caught sight of an F-16, brightly lit and surrounded by engineers. There was even a missile of some description, mounted on the back of a mobile launcher and being moved from one side of the base to another, where there was a small forest of signalling gear—masts, satellites, the works. Men in olive drab were everywhere, illuminated by bright floodlights that wouldn't have looked out of place at Old Trafford. No one seemed to pay any attention to the convoy. Hardly surprising, Luke thought to himself. The whole base had the air of being in readiness for war, so a couple of busloads of extra soldiers was hardly enough to get tongues wagging.

The convoy trundled through the base for another couple of minutes until it came to a small group of buildings set apart from the main body of the base. They were low and functional, constructed from bare breeze-blocks, and unlike the rest of the camp, there were no military personnel milling about here, nor any military vehicles. B Squadron debussed outside these buildings and filed into the largest of them.

An ops room had been set up here. Nothing fancy. Didn't need to be. A few tables and chairs, with laptops and comms equipment dotted around. One wall was plastered with mapping of the region—both satellite and topographical—and the windows had all been covered up from the inside using simple black bin liners. The Regiment might be on friendly territory, their presence might not be a secret to the Israeli authorities, but what happened inside these buildings was covert, and nobody would welcome prying eyes.

Once they were all inside, the OC called them to attention. He pointed to a door at the far end of the ops room. 'Briefing room through there. Bunks in the adjacent building, weapons store beyond that. There's a cookhouse in the main base—you can get some scoff after you've unloaded the gear.'

312

'I could murder a bacon sarnie, boss,' Fozzie called out from the back.

Dawson smiled. 'You might be in for a bit of wait. All right, fellas. Get moving.' He picked out Luke and the other three members of the four-man unit carrying out the op into Gaza. 'You four, get some kip, and no bashing the bishop. You need to be out of here by 06.00 hrs, and it would be a crying fucking shame to keep Hamas waiting, right?'

Truth was, Luke wasn't even thinking about Hamas. He was thinking about Chet's boy.

'Right, Luke?' the OC repeated himself.

'Right, boss,' Luke replied. '06.00.'

He picked up his Bergen and left the ops room. Tomorrow was going to be a long day. Fuck knows what it would bring, but he needed to be ready.

TWENTY-THREE

9 December.

05.00 hrs.

Luke was the first of the unit into the briefing room, but O'Donoghue was already there. His tired eyes were bloodshot and he reeked of sweat. Luke could tell at a glance he'd been up all night. He was sitting staring intently at a laptop. When he saw that Luke had entered, he nodded. 'Seen this?' he asked.

Luke went over to his desk. The screen, which refreshed every five seconds, displayed an outline of the eastern Mediterranean. He could make out the shape of Israel, with the Gaza Strip on its western edge. To the north, Lebanon; south, Egypt;

east, Jordan. A hundred and fifty klicks into the Med he saw the island of Cyprus, where he'd been on decompression more times than he could count. But there was more than just the geography to look at. Fifty clicks south-east of Cyprus were two flashing red dots, and in the flat terrain north-west of Jerusalem, three triangles.

O'Donoghue poked the dots with a thick, calloused finger. 'Yanks,' he said. 'Marines. Ground attack aircraft.' His finger moved to the triangles. 'British Army, IDF, Canadians and Ozzies in from Germany. Five thousand men mobilised already and they're still coming. We've got half the fucking RAF sitting on the tarmac in Cyprus.' He sniffed. 'I'm telling you, if Stratton doesn't get the right noises out of Hamas, they're going to do a Dresden on the Gaza Strip. And I wouldn't put it past Israel to send a few over into Lebanon and the West Bank either. Every raghead east of Bradford's going to be signing up. The Yanks have sent over satellite imagery. There's troop movement along Iran's western border and we're getting reports of Yemeni activity in the Gulf of Aden. Even the fucking Iraqis are making the wrong noises.'

The two men continued to watch the screen in silence until, a minute later, the rest of the unit walked in, accompanied by the squadron ops sergeant carrying a computer printout. 'Foreign Office report just in, lads,' he announced. 'Anti-Western demonstration in Gaza City last evening. Unrest overnight and unconfirmed accounts of small-arms fire across the border. We're changing your route to avoid the trouble spots. Orders are to get Stratton to Hamas, but if things get hairy, turn around. Stratton won't like it, but those are your instructions. Nobody wants any casualties. Especially not him, especially not today. Got it?'

Luke gave a curt nod.

'Call sign Tango 17. You've got an hour.'

The unit made their way to the weapons store. The SQM was already there, ready to check out the gear they'd need. Plate hangers first. Luke made sure his body armour was strapped up tightly, then pulled on his ops waistcoat. Each man was issued with an HK53—a good weapon for close-protection jobs, especially in urban areas because of its shorter barrel. The 5.56 NATO rounds came in thirty-round magazines, which they stashed in their waistcoats along with two fragmentation grenades each, before drawing their Sig 9mm handguns from the store. To their arms they fitted satellite markers which would transmit their location back to the ops centre, then attached their patrol comms to their chests—MBITR radios with earpieces and boom mikes, plus Iridium sat phones for comms with base.

The vehicle waiting for them was a black Land Cruiser. A plush interior—leather seats and all the trimmings. From the exterior it looked just like any other 4 x 4 of its type, but Luke knew the tinted windows were 40mm bullet-resistant polycarbonate; the bodywork was of hardened ballistic steel; the hinges, shock absorbers and springs were reinforced; and the tyres had special inserts to allow them to run when flat. There weren't many small-arms rounds that could penetrate a vehicle like this. Short of driving a tank into hostile territory, it was the closest they'd get to maximum protection.

The ops sergeant was waiting for them by the Land Cruiser. He handed detailed maps to Russ covering Tel Aviv, the route from the capital to the border crossing with Gaza and substantial imagery of Gaza itself. Russ accepted them quietly. He did *everything* quietly. He was the tallest of the four of them, with a close-shaved head, a Barry Manilow nose and the navigation skills of a homing pigeon.

Fozzie took the wheel. As a member of mobility troop he was the best qualified to drive if things went noisy; Russ was in the passenger seat, GPS and mapping at the ready; Luke and Finn sat at the back. A nod from the OC and they hit the road.

They drove in near silence, the only words being spoken by Russ as he navigated Fozzie away from the military base and towards Tel Aviv proper. Luke was glad of the silence. He was about to come face to face with Alistair Stratton. If that poor woman who had been slaughtered in St Paul's was right, he was up to something. But what could he do? Nothing. All he could do was go with it. Stick close to the bastard.

It was early enough for the streets of Tel Aviv to be almost deserted. As they headed towards the centre, Luke had the impression of a modern, thriving city, a far cry from some of the shitholes he'd seen in the Middle East. The sun had not yet risen, but a clear moon glinted off shining tower blocks and street lamps lit up stylish shops and pavement cafés. They headed west through the city, and soon the Mediterranean coast came into view. Easy to forget, Luke thought, as the tower of the Sheraton Hotel came into view, that Israel bordered the fucked-up wasteland of Lebanon, with Hamas knocking on its gate and the network

316

of Arabic allegiances just a missile's flight away. Iraq, Iran, Syria, Egypt—countries like these didn't always see eye to eye, but they were united in one thing: a hatred of Israel. There was no doubt that the shining towers of Tel Aviv, the restaurants and nightspots, didn't tell the whole story. Not by a long way.

It was 06.30 hrs by the time they pulled up outside the Sheraton. Quite why Stratton wasn't staying at the British Embassy was anyone's guess. Certainly if Luke had been in charge of his security, he wouldn't be staying somewhere that any Tom, Dick or Harry could walk straight into. The Sheraton was situated right on the beachfront, and the sun was now lighting up the sky. Luke didn't have to examine the concourse in front of the hotel for more than a few seconds before he clocked the two plainclothes Israeli operators standing on either side of the revolving doors, their shoulders a little too broad for their dark suits and open-neck shirts. These two men had clearly clocked the Land Cruiser too. One of them put his sleeve to his mouth and spoke into a concealed mike.

Part of the concourse was covered by a solid canopy with the name 'Sheraton' in solid red letters. There was only one other vehicle parked there—a black Mercedes. Its rear door was being held open by a chauffeur. A suited businessman climbed in and the Merc slid away. Fozzie manoeuvred the 4 x 4 into its place.

'OK, fellas,' Luke muttered, 'me and Finn'll go and make contact with the Cardinal.'

'Roger that,' Fozzie replied. 'Mind your p's and q's, boys. Very important man, that Alistair Stratton. Doesn't want to be bothered by a couple of plebs like you.'

The security men gave them only the most cursory of nods as they entered the hotel. They weren't leaving their posts for anyone. Inside, the foyer was deeply carpeted and there were plush leather sofas and armchairs dotted around, but Luke was more interested in the four security cameras he spotted hanging from the ceiling. Two of them were pointing at him and Finn. A handful of guests were milling around—no more than six—and the three receptionists behind the faux-mahogany counter were chatting idly. Their day had not yet begun in earnest. As Luke scanned the foyer, he was aware of one of them—a heavily made-up woman in a blue uniform—tugging on her male colleague's sleeve and pointing in Luke's direction. Luke ignored them and continued to scan. He was looking for their point man and he picked him out five seconds later. The guy was sitting in a comfortable armchair in the far left-hand corner of the foyer, a *Washington Post* that he wasn't reading spread out in front of him. He put one hand to his ear, then looked directly at Luke and Finn. Someone had just alerted him to their arrival. He stood up and walked in their direction.

'Gentlemen,' he greeted them in a thick Israeli accent. Luke immediately noticed the covert earpiece in his right ear, and a tiny microphone clipped to the lapel of his suit.

Luke and Finn nodded at him.

'I'll need you to surrender your weapons while you're in the building, gentlemen.'

They'd left their 53s in the Land Cruiser, but were still carrying their Sigs, and as far as Luke was

318

concerned, it was going to stay that way. 'Sorry, buddy,' he told him. 'No can do.' He gave the Israeli intelligence officer a flat stare and there were a few seconds of impasse. The officer turned and walked about ten metres away from them, and Luke could see him talking quietly into his mike. A minute later he returned, an unfriendly look on his face.

'All right,' he told them. 'Follow me.'

He led them behind the reception counter where two lifts were already waiting at the ground floor. The three men stepped inside the left-hand one, the Israeli pressed the button for the twenty-third floor and the doors hissed shut.

'He's a handful, your man,' he commented as the lift lurched upwards.

'Not *my* man, buddy,' Luke replied.

'Are you taking him into Gaza?'

Luke said nothing.

'Rather you than me.'

But Luke wasn't in the mood for small talk. The lift came to a halt, the doors opened and the men filed out.

It was clear which suite was Stratton's: it was at the far end of the corridor, manned by another two guards in pale khaki uniforms. A lot of muscle for a peace envoy, Luke thought to himself as they approached. A nod from the Israeli intelligence man and one of the guards knocked on the door.

'Come,' a voice called from inside. The guard opened the door. Luke and Finn exchanged a look, then the three men walked inside.

As he entered the room, Luke squinted. The far wall was a floor-to-ceiling window, looking out over the Mediterranean, where the early morning sun was by now blindingly bright. A figure was standing with his back to the window, silhouetted by the sun, so it was impossible to see his face or even the full shape of his body. But Luke knew who it had to be and his skin prickled.

The door shut behind them.

Silence.

It was only when the figure walked to the left, out of the glare of the sunlight, that Luke made out his features. Stratton looked thinner than he did on TV. Smaller. Gaunt. He was wearing a grey business suit with a red tie and he looked unusually relaxed, given what the day ahead held.

He stepped towards Luke and Finn.

'SAS?' he asked. His voice was very soft.

Luke and Finn nodded.

'Are we ready to go?'

'Ready, sir. Israeli secret service officers will take you as far as the border. We'll follow as a counter-attack-team escort. Once we cross over into Gaza, you'll be with us.'

Stratton nodded, then turned his back on them to look out over the sea.

'We'll be making a diversion,' he said.

The three men looked at each other.

'With respect, sir,' Luke replied carefully, 'diversions aren't a good idea. Our route has been carefully planned.'

A pause, and then Stratton turned round again. He walked straight up to Luke—who was almost a head taller than him—and looked the SAS man up and down. 'With respect, sir,' he said, 'you're here to escort me. Not advise me.'

The two men stared at each other, while Finn and the Israeli looked on.

'Where are we diverting to?' Luke asked finally. *'Sir.'*

'Jerusalem.'

Luke recalled the mapping he'd examined. Jerusalem was about twenty-five klicks south-east of Tel Aviv. It would only take them an hour to get there, but it knocked the whole fucking op out of shape. He heard Finn swear under his breath.

'Can I ask,' Luke said, his teeth gritted, 'whereabouts in Jerusalem?'

'Of course,' Stratton replied mildly. He smiled a dazzling smile. 'The Garden of Gethsemane, at the foot of the Mount of Olives.' He paused. 'The name means nothing to you?'

Luke shook his head. 'Should it?'

'It certainly should, if you'd listened to the scriptures at school.' He inclined his head. 'Perhaps you weren't the type.'

'Perhaps I wasn't.'

'The Garden of Gethsemane is where Our Lord prayed on the night he was betrayed.' He turned to look out of the window again. 'The world,' he said, 'is on the brink of war. If my negotiations go well, perhaps it can be avoided. I shall go there for a few moments of quiet reflection before we enter the lion's den.' Suddenly the smile was gone and he started walking towards the exit of the room. 'We leave now.'

Luke, Finn and the Israeli officer gave each other a look. But Stratton had already left the room and they had no option but to follow him.

* * *

07.15 hrs.

321

'Zero, this is Tango 17.'

'Tango 17, this is Zero. Send.'

'The Cardinal's demanded a diversion. Requesting permission to travel via East Jerusalem, Garden of Gethsemane.'

A pause. 'What the fuck . . . ?'

Luke scowled at Stratton, who was striding on ahead through the hotel foyer. 'Tell me about it,' he muttered. He and Finn followed him through the doors of the hotel and out to where the Land Cruiser was waiting, along with a black Mercedes and two police outriders. 'You'd better come back with that permission sharpish, buddy,' he said. 'Or even better than that, refusal. He looks pretty eager to move.'

'Roger that,' said the radio operator, and the connection to the ops room fell silent.

* * *

07.18 hrs.

Julian Dawson, OC B Squadron, looked at his radio operator in disbelief. *'Diversion?* Half the fucking IDF are mobilised to get this wanker into Gaza. What's he playing at?'

The radio operator could only shrug.

'Get me London,' Dawson ordered. 'Now.'

* * *

07.30 hrs.

It was not by chance that the Director Special Forces and the Director General SIS were sitting in the same office in the SIS building when the call came through. Today was a major operation for both services. High-profile. If either of them had their way, the Middle East peace envoy would be safely tucked up at home. But they didn't have their way—it was the politicians who made the decisions, leaving others to live with the consequences. Today it was crucial that their lines of communication stayed open. Both men knew that if it all went to shit today, their actions would be scrutinised minutely. The two men didn't always see eye to eye, but today they had a common purpose.

And a shared sense of foreboding once they heard what the Regiment representative had to say.

Neither of them had any love for Alistair Stratton. But they knew what was riding on him. They knew how he was the darling of the Israeli administration, and the Americans too.

They knew that what he said went.

They barely needed to discuss it. Within less than a minute the DG had picked up his phone. 'I need the PM,' he instructed. 'And after that the Israeli Defence Minister. *Quickly.*'

*   *   *

08.16 hrs.

'I can't *believe* we're screwing around like this so some bastard can go *pray* . . .'

It was the third time Fozzie had said it. The rest of the guys just sat there with scowls on their faces, none of them quite able to accept that the plans they'd been briefed on so carefully were being altered on a whim.

'Pray, my arse,' Finn muttered. 'He's probably got a bit of skirt hidden away. Wants her to wring him dry before he goes to meet the ragheads.'

Fozzie snorted. 'He's not the fucking type.'

They drove in convoy: two police outriders, a black Merc with tinted windows carrying Stratton, and the Land Cruiser at the back. They'd left Tel Aviv forty-five minutes ago and the outskirts of Jerusalem were just coming into view. The moment Luke had returned to the vehicle from the hotel, the unit's conversation had been a string of expletives. And it was even worse when word came through that Stratton's demand had been indulged. Even now, local law enforcement were vacating the Garden of Gethsemane area of tourists. Someone somewhere clearly thought enough of Stratton to give him the full VIP. Luke had other ideas. 'Something's not right,' he muttered in the back of the Land Cruiser, his hand resting gently on his 53.

'What's that, mucker?' Fozzie asked, both eyes firmly on the traffic ahead.

'You not suspicious?'

'Suspicious of what?'

Luke looked out of the window. 'I don't know. I just don't think this guy's as holier-than-fucking-thou as he pretends.'

Silence.

'I just can't believe,' said Fozzie, 'that we're screwing around like this so some bastard can go and *pray* . . .'

08.30 hrs. It was the height of Jerusalem's rush hour and the convoy moved slowly as they headed east through the network of bland white-grey modern blocks, green open spaces and wide boulevards. There were well-heeled areas and those that were run-down, noisy, fume-filled. It could have been any other sprawling Mediterranean town, if you ignored the unusually high police

324

presence. There seemed to be a blue and white patrol car on every street corner, and Luke noticed a fair sprinkling of uniformed soldiers and khaki military vehicles. He remembered being in London in the days after 9/11, not long before he'd been deployed to Afghanistan for the first time. Jerusalem had the same atmosphere. The same tension. It was a city waiting for something to happen.

08.45 hrs. The imposing walls of the Old City loomed into view, and beyond the walls, golden in the morning sun, the Dome of the Rock. Luke fixed his attention more firmly on the convoy ahead and the surrounding traffic, picking out potential firing points or suspicious activity, clocking the military presence, which was increasing the closer they came to the Old City.

Russ had been almost silent since they left the base. Now he suddenly spoke. 'Holy city for ragheads, Yids and Bible-bashers,' he murmured. 'You ask me, they're as bad as each other.'

The convoy didn't head straight for the ancient walls of the Old Town, but skirted round to the north instead. Twenty minutes later they found themselves heading back south, down a road that ran between the elevated eastern wall of the Old Town and a gently sloping hill, covered with squat olive trees. It was quieter in this part of the city. Less traffic, fewer people. East Jerusalem, bordering on the West Bank: where Israel met the Arab world. Fifty metres ahead, he saw three Israeli police cars, their blue lights flashing. They had congregated beside a stone wall about three metres high. On either side of the road, Luke saw that the access panels at the bottom of each of the street lamps had been taped over to prevent anyone secreting anything there, and a couple of waste bins had been sealed too. The Jerusalem authorities had clearly responded very quickly to Stratton's change in plan.

As the convoy approached the police cars, Luke saw a low rectangular gateway. Two armed Israeli soldiers stood outside. On the other side of the road a small crowd of locals had gathered. Why had the area been cordoned off? they wanted to know, and who was about to arrive?

Luke and the guys were the first to exit their vehicle. They brought their 53s with them, and as they approached, the soldiers and the Israeli police officers gave them the kind of look that you soon got used to in situations like this. Not friendly, certainly; but grudgingly respectful. They knew they were being approached by military personnel of a different tier.

'Who's in charge?' Luke asked no one in particular, but one of the Israeli soldiers stepped forward. 'Is the area secured?

'My men are performing a final sweep.'

Luke gave a curt nod, then checked out the entrance. Above the gate was an inlaid stone with the words 'Hortus Gethsemani', and beneath it a small blue arrow indicating the entrance. Luke walked inside to see a walled garden, well tended, although the ground was dusty. There were olive trees dotted around, many gnarled and ancient. He could tell at a glance that the police and IDF had done their job. It was entirely deserted. Adjacent to the garden, and just visible through the trees, was an old church—more like a highly decorated temple. Famous, probably.

326

He walked back to Stratton's Merc and opened the back door to see their man sitting serenely, face forward. 'OK, sir. Let's go.'

Stratton got out of the car and walked towards the gate, with Luke shadowing him just a metre behind. As they approached, the guards stepped back to allow the peace envoy through. Luke stuck close, sensing Finn just behind him. The three of them walked through the gate and several metres into the garden before Stratton stopped.

He took a deep breath and appeared to be soaking in the atmosphere of the place.

'Leave me,' he said.

Luke and Finn glanced at each other.

'Our instructions,' Luke replied in a level voice, 'are to provide close protection. The close bit is important.'

Stratton turned to them, and his eyes shone.

'At the other end of this garden,' he said, 'is the Church of St Mary Magdalene. If you think I am going to allow you into such a sacred place carrying weapons . . .'

Luke saw red. 'If *you* think I'm going to try and defend you armed with a fucking prayer book . . .'

Stratton's lips thinned. 'You forget yourself, soldier.'

The two men stood their ground for several seconds. Finally Luke turned to Finn. 'Check the church,' he instructed. 'We'll guard the entrance while he'—he glanced at the peace envoy—'while he does whatever he has to do.'

Finn didn't look too happy. 'Luke, mate, we . . .'

'Just do it.'

Finn nodded, strode across the garden towards the church and disappeared inside, leaving

Luke and Stratton to stand awkwardly together, surrounded by the distant noise of the East Jerusalem traffic and the cheeping of the birds in the olive trees.

Five minutes later Finn returned. 'It's clear.'

Luke nodded at Stratton. 'All yours.'

Stratton surveyed Luke with a mistrustful glare before marching up to the church with the two Regiment men following behind. The façade of the building was highly ornate, with three large arches forming its entrance. He disappeared into the gloom, while Luke and Finn took up their positions outside.

'I don't know why you're winding the fucker up,' Finn said. He sounded almost as pissed off with Luke as Stratton did.

'I'm just a bit fed up with the holy-man act,' Luke replied.

Finn shrugged.

Luke glanced into the temple. 'No one diverts from a meeting as important as the RV with Hamas just to kneel before a fucking altar. Holy man or no holy man.' He turned back to his mate. 'Wait here,' he said. 'I'm going in.'

He made to enter the temple, but Finn grabbed him by the arm. 'Mate, what's going on?'

For a moment Luke thought of telling him. But where the hell would he begin? No. Now wasn't the time or the place. He pulled away from his friend. 'I don't want a bollocking from the Ruperts for leaving him alone. He doesn't have to know I've got eyes on.' Without another word, he slipped into the church.

It was musty, thick with incense, all gold and marble. The ceiling was vaulted and the air colder than outside. Stratton stood about twenty metres ahead at the altar, his head bowed. He looked very small in the large chamber of the church, and he stood very still. Luke crept to the left-hand side of the building, much as he had done in St Paul's two nights previously, only this time he had his 53 in his fist and his Sig strapped to his body. Stratton did not notice his presence as he crept silently up the church, before stopping behind a metre-thick pillar, out of the peace envoy's view.

Luke had heard a noise.

Footsteps.

He barely breathed. His back was pressed against the pillar, so he was looking towards the front entrance of the church. On the ground to his left, the stained-glass window behind the altar had cast a colourful arrangement of reds and blues and greens on the marble floor. Luke looked down at it. A dark shadow there would give him a split-second warning of anyone approaching; and it was difficult, in the echoing acoustic of the church, to work out from which direction the footsteps were coming, or where they were headed.

They stopped after a few seconds and for a moment there was silence.

Someone spoke. A woman. She had a husky voice and a pronounced Israeli accent.

'This had better be important,' she said, speaking only just loud enough for Luke to hear. 'You know Jerusalem isn't safe for me.'

'You don't need to worry,' Stratton replied. 'The church is empty. So is the garden. I've seen to it.'

'Obviously. But if *I* know about the tunnel to the crypt, other people will know about it too.'

'Right now this is the most secure place in

Jerusalem. We can talk freely here.'

'I don't like it.'

'I didn't ask you to like it.' Stratton's voice was sharp now, like he was reprimanding an employee. 'That little bit of housekeeping in London. Ostentatious, wouldn't you say?'

There was a pause. Luke could feel his blood pumping in his veins.

'I thought you'd be pleased,' she said, though her voice didn't indicate that she cared either way. 'And you should know I don't like loose ends.'

'Was the kid really necessary? The old woman? And the priest, for heaven's sake?'

The woman made a sound almost as if she was spitting. 'Don't give me that,' she said, her voice full of derision. 'What difference do they make?'

'Four bodies attract more attention than one,' Stratton retorted.

'It would be better,' the woman said, 'if *I* worried about what *I'm* good at.'

'Are you sure nobody saw you?' Stratton persisted.

A pause.

'Don't try my patience, old man.'

'*Are you sure nobody saw you?*'

'Have I come all the way to Jerusalem to hear you complain?'

'You've come to Jerusalem because I told you to.' Stratton had raised his voice slightly. 'Don't forget who you are working for.'

'*Quiet!*' The woman's voice was little more than a whisper.

A brief silence. 'For crying out loud, woman. Put that weapon away.'

The woman didn't reply. Suddenly Luke heard

her footsteps again. They were coming in his direction.

He moved his left arm very slowly, so as not to make a noise, and felt for the safety catch on his 53. His fingers pinched the switch and turned it very gently.

The footsteps grew nearer, perhaps five metres. Luke saw a shadow on the colourful pattern of the stained glass. He could determine the outline of a person, with a weapon in their outstretched hand. He prepared himself for it to go noisy.

'*Maya!*' Stratton sounded almost schoolmasterly. 'There's nobody in this church. It's been checked. Now get back here. We haven't got much time.'

Silence.

The shadow receded, but one word echoed in Luke's head just as surely as it echoed softly around the church.

Maya.

For a moment he was no longer in Jerusalem. He was many miles further east, by the side of the road in Iraq, at night. A gravely wounded Mossad operative was shaking in the car. He was close to death, and knew it.

You must find her. You must tell her what I did.

Luke shook his head as the memory came flooding back. What did it mean?

And then Stratton was speaking again. 'Do you know where we are?'

'Of course I know where we are,' the woman replied.

'But do you *really* know? Here, at the foot of the Mount of Olives. Do you *really* know where you are, Maya?'

'What are you talking about?'

Footsteps again. But not towards Luke this time. Away from him. He pictured Stratton hurrying up to the altar. 'The Book of Daniel,' he announced loudly. 'It tells us it is here that the End Times will start. It's quite clear about that, Maya. Quite clear.'

'Keep your voice down,' the Israeli hissed.

'There are two bone-headed men with guns obeying my orders to guard the entrance,' Stratton replied. 'Nobody will come.'

'You don't know the risk I take being here.'

When Stratton spoke again, there was a quiet fervour in his voice. 'Tell me, Maya. Do you want to be part of history?'

Footsteps again—quick and deliberate, but this time most definitely heading away from Luke.

'*Move!*' Maya Bloom said. 'There's a room at the back. If you trust your two guards, you're an idiot.'

There was a shuffling sound.

And then silence. A thick, impenetrable silence that seemed to suffuse the whole place. Luke realised he was sweating profusely. He returned his 53 to the safe position. Then, very slowly, he peered round the corner of the pillar. Stratton was nowhere to be seen. Nor was Maya Bloom.

Luke wanted to follow them, but something held him back. Stalking Stratton was one thing; stalking a Mossad agent was quite another. Maya Bloom must have heard or seen something just now. If he pushed his luck, they'd be on to him. Given what he'd just heard, that wasn't an option.

But something was happening. Luke didn't know what, but it involved Alistair Stratton and it involved Maya Bloom. With Suze McArthur dead, he was the only one on to them.

Luke looked back towards the entrance to the

church. He should get out of there—he'd pushed his luck already and if those two caught him there'd be fireworks. But something held him back. He had to know more. It was ten metres from here to the altar, to the left of which he saw a wooden door. He moved quietly towards it; seconds later he had his body pressed against the front wall of the church and was listening intently.

Maya Bloom was silent, but Luke could hear Stratton's voice. He was talking quietly and the sound was muffled. Luke tried hard, but he couldn't make anything out. Silence. Bloom spoke. Her voice was slightly clearer. 'Where?' she said.

It was about five seconds before Stratton replied, and because his response was just two words, clearly spoken, Luke reckoned he caught it: 'Here. Jerusalem.'

Another silence, longer than the last.

'When?'

The reply was indistinct again. If he hadn't heard the word spoken at the briefing back in Hereford he'd probably have missed it.

'Hanukkah.'

Another pause.

Stratton's voice again: 'The first day of the celebrations. One hour before midday.'

And then footsteps.

Luke sprinted lightly back to the column where he'd been hiding, then gave himself five seconds to listen. Nothing. And so, keeping in the shadows along the side of the church, he hurried silently back to the entrance.

A noise from the altar end. He froze. Stay fucking still, he told himself. If he moved, even slightly, he'd be clocked.

They were re-entering the main body of the church: Bloom first, Stratton second. Bloom was moving swiftly and even from this distance Luke could see that her face was severe. She turned to look at Stratton. He was strangely expressionless and for a few seconds an unanswered question seemed to hang in the air.

And then she turned. Without saying a word, she disappeared into the shadows beyond the altar. Stratton watched her go. For a dread-filled moment, he thought Stratton would see him. But he didn't. Instead he faced the altar and bowed his head in quiet reverence.

Luke took his chance. He slipped towards the exit and seconds later he was outside, in the bright sunlight.

Finn looked narked. He raised an eyebrow, clearly waiting for some sort of explanation of what his mate had just seen. But at that very moment Stratton stormed out of the church. He walked straight past them both without acknowledging their presence, and headed towards the exit of the Garden of Gethsemane.

'Wanker,' Finn muttered.

'Wanker doesn't come close.' Together they followed their principal through the gnarled olive groves. As they went, Luke activated his comms. 'Zero, this is Tango 17,' he spoke into his radio mike. 'The Cardinal's leaving the garden now. We're on our way.'

A brief pause and his earpiece crackled again.

'Tango 17, this is Zero. Understood.' A pause and then: 'Get a fucking move on, Tango 17. This little detour's already cost us two hours.'

Ten metres ahead, Stratton was walking through

334

the gate and out into the street.

'Roger that,' Luke said. He gripped his 53 a little firmer. A voice in his head told him he might be needing it very soon.

TWENTY-FOUR

The young Palestinian crouched deep underground. He was sweating. Not because he was hot—there was no warmth down here—but because he was scared.

He could hear the scratching of rodents both behind him and up ahead, and occasionally he would see a scrawny rat scurrying in the beam of the battery-operated torch he was using to light his way. He didn't like rats. The thought of their long, sinewy tails brushing against his skin made him shudder and he knew the stench that reeked in his nostrils was their droppings.

But it was not rats, or rat shit, that scared him.

The tunnels were, by rights, illegal, even though everyone knew they existed. From time to time the authorities cracked down. Not because they had any real objection to the existence of the tunnels, or their purpose; but because to arrest someone was a good way of extorting money from them. Fail to pay—and this young man did not have the means to do that—and you could be sure of ending up in a Gazan prison.

But it was not the threat of discovery that scared him either.

It was the threat of a sudden and stifling death.

The tunnel was about two metres high and one

metre wide, though because it had not been dug by experts, the height was not uniform and there were places—like the spot where he was now—where the ceiling was too low to stand. It was held up by a series of wooden joists, each one spaced a couple of metres apart and supported by timber poles that sagged in the middle. He had good reason to be fearful down here. These tunnels had a limited life. It was not a question of *if* they collapsed, but *when*. It always seemed to happen when there was somebody down there. Perhaps it was the vibrations they caused as they moved gingerly along the tunnel. Perhaps it happened when they knocked against one of the timber poles. There are many ways to die, and he had contemplated most of them, but being crushed by the weight of so much earth was not the method the young man would choose for his own martyrdom. Now he whispered a fervent and continuous prayer to himself as, torch in hand, he crawled over the loose dirt and rodent shit and moved further along the tunnel.

He had started out in a small house a hundred metres from the Egypt–Gaza Strip Barrier—a buffer zone between the two states with a steel and concrete wall that was even more impenetrable than the high wire fence that segregated Israel and Gaza. The basement of this house was the starting point of one of the many tunnels that crossed from the Strip into Egypt and Israel. Gaza's neighbours had done everything they could to destroy these tunnels. The Israelis had bombed any house suspected of secreting an entrance—regardless of how many innocent men, women or children were inside. Egypt had gone so far as to start work on an underground wall to block these subterranean access points. But they couldn't block tunnels they were unable to see, and many remained.

How far had he come? It was so difficult to say in the darkness. A hundred metres, perhaps? That would put him almost exactly underneath the border. It would mean the Gaza Strip lay behind him and Egypt ahead. With any luck, he would soon see . . .

He stopped. Lights up ahead. He couldn't make out the distance yet. Thirty metres, maybe more? The young man's heart beat a little faster. He was pleased to make contact with somebody else; but he was apprehensive about the package he was to take delivery of. It was really not the sort of thing you wanted to have with you down here. Ordinarily, these tunnels were used for smuggling essential goods under the border from Egypt to Gaza. The Israeli blockade of this tiny state's eastern and northern borders meant that food and medicine were increasingly scarce. The Israelis allowed a certain quantity of these commodities over the border, but nothing like enough for the whole population. So it was that in Gaza, thanks to these tunnels, the black market in antibiotics was almost as buoyant as the black market in Western cigarettes.

Of course, it was not just food and medicine that found their way through these secret passages. Gaza may not have been officially at war, but there were enough angry men in that tiny strip for it to feel like a state perpetually on the edge of military conflict. Militants need weapons. They need ammunition. These tunnels had transported countless Kalashnikovs and rockets, and untold boxes of rounds and explosives. And they had transported armies, too. Not large armies, like those that the bigger nations could muster. Gaza was small, and had to make do with its meagre resources. Her forces consisted of handfuls of martyrs, armed with vests packed with explosives, tiny electrical detonators and a willingness—an eagerness—to die for their cause.

The lights ahead grew closer and the young man could hear voices. He cursed under his breath. Why couldn't they keep the noise down? Didn't they know what could happen if they spoke too loudly? He felt the sweat dripping down his face, and continued to pray and crawl.

They met about twenty metres further on. There were two of them, Egyptians in their mid-twenties—a good five years older than him. They didn't look nearly so scared. It was possible to stand up in this part of the tunnel and the three men stood close together, eyeing each other mistrustfully. He could smell the coffee on their breath. One of them was taller than the other—it was difficult to make out his features without shining a torch directly in his face—and he was carrying something. The young man directed his torch beam at it.

It was a box, about fifty centimetres square and thirty deep. It was made of something resembling balsa wood—the kind of thing that might be used to carry fresh fruit, but sealed at the top. On the side of the box facing the young man was a curved mark. He was not a great reader, especially of non-Arabic lettering, so to him the ornate red 'G' was a meaningless symbol.

The Egyptian man thrust the box towards him.

'Be *careful* with that,' said the young man. 'Don't

338

you know what it is?'

He took it from the Egyptian, gripping it with both hands.

The shorter of the two men made a hissing sound between his teeth. 'Fucking Gazans,' he said. 'Maybe it's soap for you to wash your mother's filthy arse.'

The young man stood perfectly still. 'My mother,' he said, his quiet voice disguising a world of emotion, 'is dead.'

The smaller Egyptian shone his torch directly in the face of the young man, who wanted to look away from the bright light but refused to. 'Good,' said the Egyptian. 'One less for me to waste my spit on.' And he spat a mouthful of saliva on to the young man's left cheek.

The two Egyptians laughed; but they fell silent when they heard an ominous creaking sound. For a few seconds, all three men froze.

More creaking. Impossible to say where it came from. It sounded like the whole tunnel was groaning.

The young man held the box a bit tighter to his body. 'If you knew what was in here,' he said, his voice trembling slightly, 'you wouldn't stick around.'

He raised his torch to light up their faces.

All of a sudden they looked a little less sure of themselves. As they glanced at each other, they shot the young man a hateful look. Then they turned and hurried back down the tunnel. They were careful to be quiet now. He had the impression that they wanted to get away quickly.

Wise decision, he thought to himself.

The journey back along the tunnel was even more scary than before. In those places where he could stand, the young man held the wooden box tightly. When he had to crawl, he placed it on the floor and pushed it ahead of him. He had been told that the contents were not especially volatile, that they needed a special kind of detonator. He didn't find that especially reassuring. It would only take a small mishap for him to be not only crushed, but burned.

Fifty metres to go. The tunnel creaked again. Again he froze, not knowing whether to keep moving so as to get out of there quickly, or to stay still and avoid disturbing the structures down here. But he knew he couldn't remain immobile forever, so he started crawling once more, pushing the box along and muttering his constant prayers.

Minutes passed like hours. With, he estimated, twenty-five metres to go, he realised he was heading uphill. The end of the tunnel was close and he wanted to speed up, to get out as quickly as possible. But he tried to stay calm. To stay slow. Whatever was in the box would not become any less dangerous just because he was nearly on home soil.

He could hear voices now. And suddenly, perhaps fifteen metres ahead, he could see a light. He whispered a few words of profound thanks and finally allowed himself a little more speed. A minute later he was standing underneath a trapdoor in the cellar of the house, carefully passing the box up into an outstretched pair of hands. Once the box was dealt with, he allowed himself to be pulled up into the cellar.

It was tiny and cramped, with a low ceiling and barely enough room for the three others who were waiting for him.

'How did it go?' one of them asked.

The young man shrugged. 'Fine. No problem.'

'Any trouble with the Egyptians?'

'Only when I told them their mothers were stinking whores.'

The others laughed.

'You've done well. That little box . . .' He pointed to where it was lying on the ground. 'That little box has a big job to do.'

The young man looked at it. Down in the tunnel it had seemed huge and ungainly. Up here, it appeared much smaller. He had questions. He reached out and brushed his thumb over the 'G' on the box. 'Where do we get this from?' he asked. 'Normally we have to make do with Mother of Satan. Who's sending us this stuff?'

'Ah,' his comrade waved one hand in the air. 'Who cares, so long as we have it. Come on. Shut the trapdoor. We have to get it out of here. There isn't much time.'

The young man did as he was told. The trapdoor echoed slightly as it shut. He followed his friends as they left the cellar, then the house, and stashed the box of C4 plastic explosive among some blankets in the boot of a very old, very rusty car. They drove away from the separation barrier with Egypt and further north, into the young man's tiny, war-torn homeland.

*   *   *

The convoy containing Stratton's Merc, the police outriders and the Regiment's Land Cruiser came to a halt.

Jerusalem was three hours behind them. Its urban bustle and ancient beauty felt a million miles

341

away. So, too, did the Garden of Gethsemane. They found themselves in a flat, desolate wasteland. A sturdy wire fence, about four metres high, ran north to south for as far as Luke could see. On this side of the fence was Israel; on the other side, Gaza. The Israeli side was littered with enormous bulldozers and military vehicles—tanks, Jeeps, the works. The Gazan side was empty for several hundred metres, but in the far distance Luke could see the telltale signs of a city above the horizon. The summer sun had baked the ground on either side of the fence hard, and the winter rains had failed to soften it much. Here and there, Luke could see craters of varying width and depth. He'd been in enough theatres of war to recognise the pockmarks of artillery fire on the skin of the land.

The convoy had stopped at the front of a large cargo checkpoint. From photographs shown in briefing Luke recognised it as the Karni crossing. It was a vast jumble of steel and concrete buildings, barriers and warehouses. It had the air of a place which, when it was operational, would be very busy. But there was no civilian activity here today. No goods vehicles crossing to or from Gaza. The only presence was military. Five IDF vehicles waited for them, and Luke counted eleven Israeli soldiers positioned at various points around the crossing, armed with assault rifles and wearing Kevlar helmets and body armour. He knew there were probably more they couldn't see. All of the soldiers were facing towards Gaza, their hands resting on their guns, clearly on high alert.

They had good reason to be. The Karni crossing had been closed by the Israelis since a network of tunnels had been discovered directly underneath it two years previously. There hadn't been much doubt that the purpose of these tunnels was to pack them full of explosives and bring the crossing down. The Palestinians had also smuggled a number of suicide bombers through the Karni crossing, while the Israelis had used it to move tanks, personnel and artillery into Gaza. Look carefully on the ground and you could still see the markings of the tank tracks embedded in the earth.

'Fucking lovely,' Fozzie announced as he drew the Land Cruiser up alongside Stratton's Merc. He filled his lungs with air. 'Reckon I'll come here for my holidays again next year.'

Luke peered out of his side window. Up above, he could see a chopper. It was hovering low— maybe a hundred feet—with its nose slightly dipped, but staying resolutely on the Israeli side of the fence. It looked like it had eyes on, but on what?

Luke exited the Land Cruiser and opened up the back. This was where all their additional equipment was stashed. He removed a small hand-held scope and used it to scan beyond the border fence. The buffer zone between the two states was about 500 metres wide, and there, making no attempt to stay hidden, was an open-topped technical. A Palestinian man stood on the back in desert fatigues and a black and white keffiyeh. On his shoulder he was carrying what looked to Luke like an old Blowpipe anti-aircraft rocket launcher. The Blowpipe was a pile of shit, almost impossible to fire accurately—the British Army had covertly offloaded all theirs to the Mujahideen in Afghanistan back in the 1980s when the Javelin came into service. Next to the THOR launcher that Luke had been training with on the Brecon Beacons it was prehistoric.

He lowered the scope, returned to the 4 x 4 and reported his finding.

'Nothing like a warm welcome,' Finn muttered as they disembarked from the vehicle, 53s slung round their necks.

'I'd rather have a potato gun than a Blowpipe,' said Fozzie.

Luke wasn't so sure. The Blowpipe might be old, but because it was neither heat-seeking nor laser-guided, it wasn't susceptible to modern countermeasures. The chances of the raghead on the other side of the fence bringing down the heli if it infringed Hamas airspace were small. But he might get lucky and no doubt there were plenty more of his type waiting to do the mopping up should the first line of Palestinian defence fail. He remembered someone telling him once that the Muj in Afghanistan had taken to using them not as anti-aircraft weapons, but anti-vehicle. It wasn't lost on him that they'd soon be driving within its range.

The chopper was the only thing that made a noise out here. Otherwise this crossing was silent. Like the personnel on both sides of the border were holding their breath. Luke opened the back door of the Merc and leaned in to look at Stratton. 'We'll transfer you to the Land Cruiser now, sir,' he said.

Stratton didn't answer for a moment. He was staring out of the other window, lost in thought. Suddenly he snapped out of it.

'What?'

'Get out. It's time to cross.'

Stratton nodded and shuffled awkwardly along the back seat of the Merc. Once he was out of the car, he looked around, but Luke immediately grabbed him by the right arm and manoeuvred him towards the armoured vehicle. Stratton looked like he was going to protest, but a harsh glance from Luke ensured he kept quiet.

As Luke was leading Stratton into the back of the Land Cruiser, one of the Israeli military guys approached. He had a shaved head, tanned skin and deep, dark bags under his eyes. 'You ready?' he asked.

Luke nodded.

The man pointed to the chopper. 'The pilot's reported some kind of presence on the other side of the buffer zone. Three vehicles. Armed. Be careful over there.'

Luke looked over at the anti-aircraft gunner on the other side. 'Seems pretty tense,' he said.

The soldier shrugged. 'Half the citizens of Gaza would be happy to live side by side with us. Same goes for the Israelis. But it's not the moderate ones you have to worry about. It's the extremists, and there's plenty of those. And those Hamas *mamzer*. Wouldn't surprise me if they tried to pick you off the moment you get over there.'

'They're welcome to try,' Luke said.

The soldier inclined his head. 'Rather you than me, my friend. I'll instruct my men to open our barrier. Once you go through that, you're on your own.'

He turned on his heel and headed back towards the terminal buildings. Luke climbed into the back of the Land Cruiser with the rest of the unit. Stratton was sitting in the middle, eyeing the Regiment men's weapons nervously. 'I hope those things are safe,' he said.

345

Luke scowled at the stupid question. 'Depends which end's pointing at you,' he muttered. He caught sight of Fozzie in the rear-view mirror. 'They're opening up the barrier,' he said, before activating his sat phone. 'Zero, this is Tango 17.'

'*Go ahead, Tango 17. Send.*'

'We have the Cardinal on board. Crossing the border in figures two.'

'*Roger that, Tango 17. We have your position marked.*' A crackly pause. '*It's hotting up in the capital, Luke. Reports coming in of militants taking to the streets. Don't come home in a box, yeah?*'

Luke took a big breath and his eyes flickered towards Stratton.

'Roger that, Zero.' He disconnected the sat phone and nodded at Fozzie. 'Let's go,' he said.

Fozzie drove the Land Cruiser slowly. The barrier, when they came to it, was a sheet of solid steel. It took two armed IDF men to slide it to one side before waving the Regiment unit through. Russ, Finn and Luke adjusted the position of their weapons so they were facing towards the window. They couldn't fire them from this position, of course—not through the bullet-resistant glass of their vehicle—but it meant that if the worst came to the worst, they could kick open the doors and their guns would be ready. With a bit of luck it wouldn't get to that. Even the stupidest Palestinian squaddie would know that a high-value target like Stratton would only venture on to Gazan soil at a time like this with a special forces team. And a special forces team meant special force.

Beyond the barrier there was the buffer zone, a bare patch of no-man's-land extending from the wire border fence to another, lower fence on the

346

Gazan side. The zone was even more scarred by artillery fire than the Israeli territory they had just left, and the ground was littered with twisted pieces of shrapnel. The road across the buffer zone, such as it was, ended with another steel barrier. The Land Cruiser trundled towards it and, when it was about ten metres away, the barrier opened seemingly of its own accord, a gateway into Gazan territory.

The terrain beyond the barrier was as featureless as the Israeli side, the grey December sky and the dusty ground a mirror of each other. But the Land Cruiser was still five metres from Gazan soil. Luke saw that a very different welcome awaited them. A second technical, mounted with what looked like an old Russian DShK machine gun, stood directly in their path, the weapon pointing straight towards Stratton and the unit. Flanking it on either side were two Land Rovers, their doors open to protect a team of keffiyeh-wearing soldiers armed with assault rifles.

Fozzie ground the Land Cruiser to a halt and the vehicles faced each other.

For thirty seconds, nothing moved. It was silent in the Land Cruiser too, until Stratton spoke quietly. 'They won't fire,' he said. 'Not with me on board.'

'Shut up,' Luke told him. He saw Fozzie look at him in the rear-view mirror. 'Sir,' he added under his breath.

Stratton looked like he was going to respond, but at that very moment the technical started to reverse. It steered round the back of the left-hand Land Rover, leaving the road ahead clear.

'Guess that means a green light,' Fozzie said. He

347

knocked the Land Cruiser into first gear and moved slowly through the barrier.

It hardly mattered that the vehicle was armoured. A burst from the DShK and a barrage of rounds from the assault rifle would be enough to make things difficult: a pitched battle on what was effectively enemy territory was exactly what they needed to avoid. So, as they approached their hostile receiving line, the tension among the men was palpable. They passed a jumble of corrugated-iron storage buildings and concrete watchtowers, many of them little more than piles of rubble, others plastered with graffiti. The Arabic lettering was meaningless to Luke, but he did notice a five-pointed star of David with a crude image of an assault rifle stamped on it. A picture telling a thousand words. On one side of the road was the burned-out shell of an old VW van, and beyond that a cargo lorry from which the wheels had been removed and whose chassis was rusting away.

They drove on in silence. As they passed the Land Rovers, they felt the eyes of the Palestinian gunmen. Once they'd cleared them, Stratton let out a huge breath.

'Don't start relaxing,' Luke said, looking over his shoulder. He saw that the DShK on top of the technical had rotated like an anti-aircraft gunner and still had them in their sights. But Fozzie accelerated, and within two minutes the welcoming committee had faded into the distance.

The Gaza Strip was a tiny territory. It was about twelve klicks from the crossing to the centre of Gaza City, where they were headed. Difficult to say how long it would take, because it depended what they met up ahead. Anything between twenty minutes and an hour, Luke estimated. The road was about ten metres wide and had clearly once been in good condition. Now, though, the tarmac was crumbling and the way ahead was littered with potholes, forcing Fozzie to keep his speed down to about 30mph and to swerve now and then to avoid the dips in the road. The terrain on either side was flat and bland: fields of patchy grass and bare earth, the shell of an occasional building long since deserted. The whole place was like a fucking ghost town.

'Where *is* everyone?' Russ asked after they'd been driving for another minute or so. It was a good question. The road was strangely deserted for a main thoroughfare—the shortest route from the border to Gaza City, the outskirts of which were only a couple of miles away. Luke looked out of his window. On the side of the road, about ten metres from the edge, he saw the rotten carcass of an animal. A horse? Difficult to say. Its ribs were exposed, its skin was dried and shrivelled and its insides had at some point been plundered by a hungry scavenger.

A hundred metres further on they passed a little group of what were once buildings. They'd been destroyed by artillery fire, long enough ago for the rubble to be covered with hardy weeds. And as that ruined scene retreated, the view up ahead began to change as the bleak nothingness of their surroundings morphed into a rising sea of concrete buildings in the distance.

'Gaza City,' Russ said.

Nobody replied.

Fozzie had started to slow down. Fifty metres ahead there was a crossroad, and as they drew near it became clear why the road from the Karni crossing had been deserted. There were six military Jeeps here, and twice as many armed soldiers. Luke knew a roadblock when he saw one. Sometimes, in zones like this, they were unofficial, having been erected by enterprising locals attempting to make a buck. That didn't appear to be the case here. One of the Jeeps had a green flag flying from its bonnet, with white Arabic writing; the vehicles themselves had green lettering on their sides; and two of the soldiers were standing by a radio set up on the bonnet of the other Jeep.

'Hamas,' Fozzie murmured when they were thirty metres distant. 'Looks like they've been waiting for us.'

'Is that good or bad?' Finn asked.

'I guess we're going to find out.'

'Stop the vehicle,' said Luke. Fozzie hit the brakes fifteen metres between them and the roadblock. Luke activated his sat phone. 'Zero, this is Tango 17.'

'Tango 17, this is Zero. Send.'

'We've got ourselves a roadblock. Looks official. Can you sort it?'

'Wilco, Tango 17.'

The comms went dead.

Silence in the Land Cruiser as it sat motionless in the middle of the road. The soldiers up ahead looked at it warily. When a few of them exchanged words, they did so without taking their eyes off the Regiment's vehicle. And while no one had their weapons pointing directly at them, the soldiers all had both hands on their assault rifles and looked like they knew what they were doing.

A minute passed.

Two minutes.

Suddenly Stratton, seemingly unable to restrain himself, snapped. 'Just talk to them,' he instructed. 'It's obvious they've been waiting for us. Just roll down the bloody window and talk to them.'

'Nobody's rolling down the windows,' Luke said calmly. 'They're there for a reason.'

'Don't be ridiculous,' Stratton snorted. 'Nobody's going to attack *me* . . .'

He cut himself off short as each of the four SAS men turned to look at him with cool expressions on their faces.

'Nobody's rolling down the windows,' Luke repeated, and silence fell once more inside the 4 x 4.

They had to wait another three minutes for anything to happen. One of the radio operators up ahead started talking into his handset; moments later they saw him bark some kind of instruction to the others. A couple of them jumped up behind the wheels of two of the Jeeps and reversed them out of the way. The remainder continued to stare at the Land Cruiser. They made no indication that the Regiment unit was permitted to cross, but Fozzie didn't wait for that. He moved the vehicle forward and through the roadblock. Luke could sense Stratton fuming. The guy clearly didn't like being told what to do. Fine. As long as Luke was in charge of the safety of the men in this vehicle, Stratton could like it or fucking lump it.

Luke had seen his share of battlegrounds. He'd walked the deserted streets of Musa Qala and dodged sniper fire in Sangin. He'd been involved in pitched battles in Basra and seen the brutal effects of many wars in central and eastern Africa. Gaza

City, he knew, wasn't a war zone like Afghanistan. It wasn't Darfur or Somalia. Every conflict, however, was different in its own way. Despite everything, Gaza still functioned as a state. But it was a state on the edge. Its people were poor. Many desperate. Even more were angry. As the Land Cruiser approached the capital, Luke felt he could taste the tension in the air.

The outskirts of Gaza City were a mishmash of tall apartment blocks, single-storey warehouses, the occasional mosque. Almost everything appeared to be built from concrete, or rendered in bland grey or yellow plaster that was cracking and falling away. Suddenly there were more vehicles too. Not many of them looked roadworthy, at least by British standards, and there were fewer than might have been expected for a city the size of Gaza. Even if the inhabitants could afford a car, petrol was hard to come by. There were rather more pedestrians— thin, ragged and with weather-beaten faces—than there were drivers.

The black Land Cruiser, with its tinted glass and shining chrome, attracted attention and Luke didn't like that. A CAT team would normally take one of two options. They would either follow the principal in an unmarked vehicle—an old baker's van or a utility truck, something that would merge into the background—if they didn't want to be seen. If the situation required a more overt, threatening presence, the unmarked van would be replaced with a Jeep mounted with a .50-cal or a Gimpy—something to make people think twice about engaging them. But Hamas's insistence that only a single vehicle could cross had chucked the SOPs out of the window. The Land Cruiser was an unsatisfactory halfway house and Luke felt that every Palestinian citizen they passed—most of them dressed in shabby Western-style clothing, though a few wore more traditional robes and headdresses—was staring at them with ill will.

Fozzie followed Russ's directions and they continued to head north-west through this run-down suburb. They were now no more than four klicks from the Karni crossing and already they could see the effects of years of Israeli bombardment of the territory. More than half the buildings they passed bore scars of some sort—perhaps just a boarded-up window or a spray of bullet marks across the façade. Plenty, though, were reduced to a shell, or even to a pile of rubble and steel. One thing was clear: these crumbling structures on the outskirts were not administrative buildings or military targets; they were apartment blocks and people's houses. As the Land Cruiser passed one of these demolished buildings, Luke saw a small makeshift tent, constructed from bleached canvas and metal poles bound together with string. The front side of the tent, about a metre wide and two metres high, was open to the road and it had been erected to house not people, but a large photograph of a man. Garlands of flowers were strewn around the photograph, but they were withered and dried out. It was plainly a shrine of some sort, there to commemorate a life lost when the building that had stood there was destroyed.

'Two o'clock,' Finn said suddenly, his voice tense. 'Someone's got eyes on.' Luke looked in the direction his mate was indicating.

'Got him.'

The man Finn had pointed out was on a street

corner, standing by the grubby awning of a meat shop that had the carcasses of a few animals hanging in the window. His head was wrapped in a keffiyeh, and he made no attempt to hide the AK-47 that was slung across his front. He had a mobile phone pressed to his ear and he was clearly watching the Land Cruiser as it passed. An official pair of eyes, or something else? Impossible to say. The unit passed him in silence.

A couple of hundred metres on they drove by a building site where attempts had been made to reconstruct one of the bombed-out edifices. A single storey of grey breeze-blocks was completed, but it was clear from the faded Arabic lettering graffitied over the blocks, and from the broken pallets littered around the site, that no work had been done here for many months. A thin man sat on the pavement outside it. Spread out in front of him were a few pairs of shoes and a couple of handbags. He had a rather hopeless demeanour, and behind him two kids were crouched, hugging their knees with their hands. It didn't seem likely that this man would be selling much today. His eyes followed the Land Cruiser as it passed, just like everyone else's.

The Regiment men's faces were grim as they ventured deeper into the city. 'What happens to the poor bastards who get bombed out of their homes?' Fozzie asked out loud.

It was Stratton who answered. 'There are a number of refugee camps dotted around the Strip,' he said. 'Two in Gaza City itself.' He sounded matter-of-fact about it.

'Nice,' Fozzie muttered.

Stratton's jaw was set.

'If things go to shit today,' Luke said quietly, 'they might need a few more of those IDP camps.'

'Absolutely,' Stratton replied, a bit too quickly and with very little emotion.

'Absolutely,' he repeated, a little quieter this time.

'You don't sound very concerned?'

'I'm *very* concerned,' Stratton replied, still looking straight ahead. 'I can assure you of that.'

It was a sudden thing. For a split second Luke was back in St Paul's, listening to urgent warnings. A wild conspiracy theory that he would never have believed if it hadn't been confirmed by the dull thud of four fatal rounds just a couple of minutes later. Now he was in Gaza City, war-torn and fucked up . . .

I'm very concerned. I can assure you of that.

The mist in Luke's mind was starting to burn away.

Back in Jerusalem, Stratton had asked Maya Bloom if she wanted to be part of history. Quite what that meant, Luke couldn't imagine. But Stratton was planning something. And whatever he was planning, one thing was suddenly clear to Luke.

This was part of it.

Don't you see? Doesn't anybody *see? First the Balkans, then Iraq, now this . . .* Stratton and the woman were planning some sort of terrorist atrocity in Jerusalem on Hanukkah. Sticking close to him wasn't enough. *Luke had to prevent him from reaching Hamas. He had to abort the mission.*

Somehow.

He fingers felt for his radio as he started formulating a communication in his head.

He felt Stratton's eyes. Somehow he knew the

355

bastard was on to him.

They had to turn back. Luke opened his mouth to give the command.

But too late.

On Russ's instruction, Fozzie had taken a sharp right-hand turn at a crossroad and started heading north-east up a busy commercial street. With no warning, he hit the brakes and the Land Cruiser came to a screaming halt.

'Er, Houston,' he said. 'We have a problem.'

Luke leaned over and stared out of the front windscreen.

Then he looked out the rear.

Fozzie was right. They had a problem. Big time.

TWENTY-FIVE

It took Luke just a few seconds to size up the situation.

It was a busy street. The concrete buildings along either side were mostly four storeys high. One of them, fifty metres ahead, had a flagpole sticking out at an angle, with the bright green flag of Hamas hanging limply from it. Many had balconies on the upper floors, and although some of these were dilapidated and clearly not suitable for anybody to stand on, others were occupied.

At ground level there was a smattering of parked cars on either side of the road. The street was lined with shops, most with metal grilles closed over them, and the grilles themselves were covered in graffiti. Behind the Land Cruiser and to the right, twenty-five metres from their position, was

356

a particularly run-down building. There was no glass in the windows, and the concrete façade was streaked with black marks which suggested a fire had raged through it at some point in the past.

But it was something else that told the unit things were turning to shit.

About 150 metres ahead, the road was blocked—not by vehicles this time, but by a mob of people, maybe a hundred of them. They were advancing chaotically, but even at this distance and through the bullet-resistant glass of the Land Cruiser, the voices of the crowd were audible. They were shouting some slogan—a dull, rhythmic sound, like the beating of drums—and at least twenty of them were waving rifles in the air.

Behind the vehicle the same story—a crowd had appeared from nowhere and closed off the access to the street. The mob to their rear was perhaps half the size of the one in front, but it was closer—100 metres maybe. Luke looked left and right, searching for side streets from which they could exit the position. Nothing.

He was aware of Finn raising his weapon to his closed window. 'Let's not go the way of those Signallers in the Province,' his mate said. Luke knew what he was talking about. During the Troubles two green army boys were driving round Northern Ireland when they came across a Republican funeral, heavy with IRA marshals. The Provos mistook them first for a Protestant hit team. A crowd developed round the car and some of them dragged the Signallers out and examined their ID. One of the soldiers had been stationed in Herford, Germany. The IRA misread that as Hereford and the moment they thought their

357

captives were SAS, their fate was sealed: they were stripped naked, dragged over some wrought-iron fencing, where one of them had his calf ripped off, and then they were executed with their own pistols.

If the Signallers really had been Regiment, it might have been different. The SOP would have been quite clear—start shooting before the mob managed to drag you out of the car. Finn was preparing to do just that.

Fozzie put the Land Cruiser into reverse. He hit the accelerator and the tyres screeched as he sped backwards, moving faster and faster towards the smaller crowd.

'What's going on?' Stratton demanded.

'You tell me,' Luke retorted. Through the rear windscreen he saw a few members of the crowd run to either side of the road as the Land Cruiser approached, but the bulk of them—about thirty men—stayed where they were, chanting and thrusting their fists in the air.

'Hamas?' Finn demanded.

'They wouldn't dare,' spat Stratton.

Luke was still looking through the rear windscreen. *'Incoming!'* he shouted. He had picked out the shooters when they were about seventy-five metres from the crowd: two men in jeans and T-shirts and carrying old AKs. The age of the weapons made no difference: they pumped several bursts of 7.62s at the Land Cruiser.

Moving instantly, Luke pushed the back of Stratton's head violently down so that he was bending at the waist and out of view of the rear window. As he did this there was a sudden drilling sound at the back of the vehicle. Although 7.62s, especially from that range, weren't nearly enough to penetrate the armoured Land Cruiser, they still made an ear-splitting noise as they hammered into the black metal. Several rounds had hit the rear windscreen. They had failed to shatter it, but three sudden spider webs with bullet-hole centres splintered their way across the toughened polycarbonate.

'*Stay down!*' Luke roared at Stratton, who was wriggling under his fierce grip like a petulant child. '*Fozzie, fucking get out of here . . .*'

Fozzie spun the steering wheel as the rhythmic shouting of the advancing mob grew more frenzied. He swerved the vehicle round 180 degrees so they were facing the smaller crowd, which had fired on them, then shoved the gear lever into first and revved the engine to screaming point. When he let his foot off the clutch, the 4 x 4 lurched forward violently, jolting all the passengers as it shot towards the crowd like a stone from a catapult. Fozzie accelerated, his face set. It would have been obvious to anyone who saw him that he had no intention of stopping for anything—or anyone—in his way.

He did stop, though. He had no choice.

It was Russ who noticed it first. '*RPG!*' he yelled when they had gone barely thirty metres.

'What the *fuck*?' said Luke. This was a street mob, not an insurgency. How the hell did they get themselves a piece of kit like that? But then he too caught sight of a thin Palestinian man at the front of the smaller crowd with a rocket launcher on his shoulder. The crowd had parted behind him to avoid the back blast, and as soon as Luke clapped eyes on him the grenade left the tube.

If Fozzie had waited half a second more to

yank his left hand down on the steering wheel, they'd have been mincemeat. As it was, the Land Cruiser swerved to the side of the road as the RPG thumped into the tarmac. The impact and explosion sent a shockwave right through them, and the blast caused the right-hand rear wheel of the vehicle to raise what felt like a good metre into the air. When it hit the ground again—to the accompaniment of shrapnel from the RPG showering down on the roof—there was an ominous crunching sound from the undercarriage.

Fozzie tried to reverse again, but as his foot left the clutch there was a terrible grinding noise and a smell of burning.

'Fucking axle's twisted!' he shouted. He looked over his shoulder at Luke. 'We're not going anywhere in this piece of crap, mate.'

Luke removed his hand from the back of Stratton's neck and recced the situation. It looked bleak. The two groups were closing in on them, the smaller one twenty metres away, the larger about fifty. There was a crater in the road where the RPG had hit, and although the shooter had disappeared along with the immediate threat of a second grenade, Luke knew it only took a couple of seconds to reload a launcher. The shouting from the approaching crowds was growing louder.

They had to make a decision. And fast.

'Finn, you and me are going to lay down warning fire. We need to disperse these crowds. And no stiffs. We start nailing people, we're going to be in the middle of a riot . . .'

'We are already,' Finn shot back. 'A few rounds in the air won't do fuck all . . .'

'What the hell's going on?' Stratton butted in.

360

His face was moist with sweat.

'You,' Luke frowned at him, 'shut up. Warning fire, Finn. I fucking mean it.'

His mate looked uncomfortable with the order, but nodded his agreement.

'Exit in three, two, one, *go!*'

The two men opened the rear doors of the Land Cruiser and kicked them wide with their feet. In the same movement, Luke raised his 53 so that it was aimed well above the heads of the larger crowd and fired two quick bursts. He heard Finn doing the same and the harsh, mechanical noise of the discharged rounds ripped through the air. Stratton shouted in alarm, but Luke ignored him and, semi-protected like Finn by his half-open rear passenger door, kept his weapon aimed firmly towards the mob.

At first the sound of the rounds had the desired effect. About half the crowd hit the ground, their hands covering their heads. The thought crossed Luke's mind that these were people used to the sights and sounds of combat. Perhaps that was a good thing. Perhaps it meant they would take a burst of counter-fire seriously. From the edges of the larger crowd he saw perhaps ten people run to the side of the road and take cover in doorways or behind parked cars. There was still a hard core, though, some thirty or forty who weren't deterred by the warning fire. Most of them were wearing black and white keffiyehs and waving their assault rifles in the air. It crossed Luke's mind that the threat of death didn't seem to worry some of them. He'd encountered enemy like that before, in the Stan. It was a dangerous man who wasn't scared of dying.

Rounds from the crowd. Two of them thudded into the window where Russ was still sitting next to Fozzie in the front.

Finn's voice. Urgent. 'The fuckers are still advancing.'

'Go again!' Luke shouted, and fired a third burst over the heads of the crowd.

It was as the sounds of these shots died away, and the advancing mob failed to disperse any further, that Stratton spoke again. His voice was shrill. 'Shoot them down,' he urged. 'These people will only disperse if . . .'

'Shut the fuck up!' Luke roared. But he had to admit to himself that their options were diminishing. He didn't want any casualties—not because he was squeamish, but because he knew that in an urban combat situation like this, to slot the bastards would make things ten times worse, not to mention the wider implications of a British unit mowing down Gazan citizens—but if they kept coming, he wouldn't have much choice.

'Shoot them!' Stratton repeated. 'That's an order!'

'Fozzie.' Luke's voice was as bleak as his mood. 'If he speaks again, grease him.'

'Roger that,' Fozzie replied. Luke didn't look over his shoulder to see what Stratton's reaction was. He lowered his weapon so that now he was pointing directly at the crowd and not above their heads. They were about thirty metres distant now. If he fired, things were going to get messy.

He tried to keep a clear head, to work out what the hell was going down. Had these people been sent here directly by the Hamas administration? On the face of it, it seemed unlikely. They were a cobbled-together bunch with little organisation and a mixed bag of weapons. There were no vehicles. No fire support.

But only Hamas had known the route they were taking through the city. As Luke kept his aim on the crowd, a thought jumped into his head. Surely not even Hamas would be so foolish as to make an overt hit on Stratton? But they could leak details of his movements down to the militants in their state who had no such concern for the balance of international relations.

'We need to nail them, Luke!' Finn shouted.

Nail them. Finn's default setting. Luke remembered being in Iraq, and how Finn had wanted to waste Amit from the first instant.

'Luke!'

Finn's warning snapped Luke back to the present. He closed his left eye and with his right looked through the sight mounted on the body of the HK53. Members of the crowd ahead came into sharp focus, the cross hairs juddering over their heads and bodies as they jumbled forwards.

His forefinger, resting on the trigger, twitched.

They'd been forced into a corner. Their choices were limited. In fact, they were non-existent.

'Fire in three...' Luke shouted over the pounding noise of the mob's chanting.

He could sense Russ and Fozzie unlatching their doors.

'Two...'

Through the sight of the 53, Luke saw a commotion at the front of the crowd. There were four men in their twenties, wearing jeans and black and white keffiyehs round their necks. They had surrounded someone and were pushing him

363

forward. Luke directed his sight into the middle of this little group, every instinct telling him that this was where he needed to direct his weapon.

'*HOLD YOUR FIRE!*'

He roared the instruction at the top of his voice the moment the scene unfolded with more clarity.

The group of men had parted to reveal a kid. Thirteen, fourteen maybe. He was a skinny little runt with sunken eyes, and the 53's sights clearly picked out the unshaven hairs on his upper lip. They picked out, too, the expression of absolute terror on the boy's face.

As Luke shouted, the noise of the mob suddenly fell quiet. His voice echoed briefly off the concrete walls of the street.

The kid stood motionless a couple of metres in front of the mob. In fact the crowd were shrinking back from him. Luke kept the child in his sights. He could see now that he was trembling. The boy took a step forward. And another. He appeared to be unarmed, so why were the mob retreating?

Fozzie's voice. 'What the hell's happening?'

Luke paused a couple of seconds before answering. His sights had scanned the kid's body. He was wearing a coat that came down to his knees. A raincoat, but it wasn't raining.

'We've got ourselves a suicide bomber,' he stated.

He could almost feel the kid's anxiety, even from this distance. It wasn't just the way he trembled. It was his faltering steps, the nervous darting of his eyes left and right, the way he clenched and unclenched his palms as he grew closer and closer to the Land Cruiser.

The mob was running now in the opposite

direction, taking cover behind parked cars and putting a good thirty metres between themselves and the boy. Luke flicked the safety catch on his 53 to semi-automatic and kept his cross hairs directly on the kid's face. A single head shot was what he needed to put him down safely.

But something stopped him. And it wasn't just that downing this kid would push the crowd over the edge.

He was back in St Paul's. A shadowy figure had just discharged her first round into the head of a child not much younger than the kid Luke had in his sights.

Chet's kid.

His face flared with anger at the memory of it.

Now he was about to do the same.

The boy was still advancing. Still trembling. Luke could see beads of sweat dripping down on to his unshaven top lip and chin. He could see the fists closing and opening, faster now than before.

'*Shoot him!*'

Stratton's voice was hoarse.

'He's a terrorist. *Shoot!*'

Luke blocked it out. If he was going to fire, it would be his decision, not Stratton's.

'Luke, mate . . .' Fozzie's voice was quiet and tense. '*Now* would be a good time to take the fucker out . . .'

But Luke didn't move. Something wasn't right. He knew he had to nail the kid if he got much further, but *something* wasn't right.

The kid stopped. He closed his eyes. Opened them again. And continued walking.

Fozzie's voice again. 'Russ, take him out.'

'*Hold your fire!*' Luke barked.

The fists. Clenching and unclenching. There should be a detonation switch in one hand or the other. A cord peeking from one of his sleeves. But there was nothing.

Remote detonation. He'd seen it in the Stan— kids forced into martyrdom against their will, their generals in charge of the moment of bliss in case they bottled it. Was there was someone watching, ready to blast this child to paradise when he'd cause the most destruction?

'This is madness,' Stratton hissed. 'Will someone just *do it*?'

'How many more kids are going to die, Stratton?' said Luke. He focused in on the bomber's eyes.

'This is *insanity* . . .'

Luke almost missed it. The kid's eyes flickered upwards and to the right, before returning to the road ahead. It was the smallest of movements. Hardly anything at all. But it was enough.

He redirected his weapon so that it was pointing not at the boy, but across the street. The street was deserted at ground level, but the kid had looked upwards, so Luke raised his sights, scanning the buildings opposite. He moved his field of vision left and right, picking out the cracks in the wall and the railings at the front of balconies.

'*What the fuck are you doing, Luke?*' Fozzie didn't just sound on edge, he sounded angry. Luke knew he didn't have much time before the unit started ignoring his instructions and opening up of their own accord.

He scanned the buildings. Left to right. Up. Right to left.

When Luke saw him, it was only momentary. He had to pan back quickly to get him in his sights

366

again. The figure was alone on a fourth-storey balcony, about twenty-five metres up and thirty-five metres from Luke's position. He was looking down at the street below, concentration all over his swarthy face. Luke picked out his short black beard and flat brown eyes; and panning down half a metre, he saw something in the man's hands. It was the same size and shape as an old-fashioned mobile phone, but it had an antenna, about five inches long, sprouting from the top.

Luke moved the cross hairs back to the man's head.

'*Jesus, Luke . . .*'

'Hold tight, fellas,' he said, just as the man in his sights turned his head to notice that Luke had eyes on and was staring directly into his sights.

Luke knew he had only a millisecond. The range was fine, but he had just the one chance. With the cross hairs directly over the man's forehead, he squeezed the trigger. The 53's butt jerked sharply into his shoulder, and the sound of the discharge cracked loudly, echoing from one side of the street to another. The recoil of the shot had nudged the target out of Luke's sight, and he was forced to realign his weapon to see what the result was.

A direct hit.

The man was slumped precariously over the balcony's railings. On the wall behind him blood was spattered; more was dripping from the head wound down to the pavement below. Luke redirected his aim towards the kid in the road. He was looking frantically left and right and didn't appear to know what was happening.

His ignorance didn't last for long.

Luke sensed movement on the balcony and

looked over just in time to see his target topple over the railings. He seemed to fall through the air for an eternity, before hitting the ground with a crunch that was audible from the Land Cruiser on the other side of the road.

The kid stopped in his tracks.

He stared at the fallen man.

He turned round to look at the silent, retreating crowd, the nearest members of which had retreated to a distance of thirty-five metres.

And then he ran after them. His arms and legs were flailing and ungainly, but he bolted like a hare, just as the crowd realised what was happening. They parted to let him through, but their silence ebbed away, to be replaced by a low muttering, which quickly grew to something more sinister as they started to advance again.

'*Shit!*' Luke cried. First blood had been drawn. Some of the crowd had seen the dead man. It would be only seconds before the rest of them understood what had happened. And then the unit's only option was to fight.

He turned to the guys in the vehicle and pointed through the front windscreen towards the dilapidated building with the scorch marks on the frontage, which was now fifteen metres from their position. 'We need to head in there!' he shouted. 'It's a defensible position.'

Fozzie nodded.

'Finn, Russ, cover me. I'll get Stratton inside first.'

The two men didn't hesitate. Russ kicked the passenger door open and started firing towards the crowd, his weapon resonating in unison with Finn's. Again they aimed above the heads of the mob, now advancing once more. They slowed down, but how long for, and how long until they returned fire, it was impossible to say.

Luke grabbed Stratton and pulled him forcibly from the 4 x 4. His clothes were soaked in sweat. As Russ and Finn laid down another burst of rounds, Luke yanked him towards the building. The doorway was wooden and looked solid, although its yellow paint was peeling. Luke kicked it with his right foot but it didn't budge, so he took a couple of steps back and aimed his 53 at the lock. A quick burst and the wood splintered and cracked. Another kick and it was open.

Not before time. The mob was now just twenty metres from the vehicle. Russ and Finn, who were still next to their respective passenger doors while Fozzie remained in the front, continued to fire warning bursts, but these were no longer sufficient to hold them back. If they grew any closer, the unit would have to start killing people. Then it could only go one of two ways: a retreat, or a massacre . . .

Luke thrust himself into the building, his weapon pointing up then down as he checked if it was occupied. No sign of anyone. He exited again. '*Get in!*' he bellowed at Stratton, who was staring wide-eyed at the stand-off. When he didn't move, Luke grabbed hold of him again and sent him flying through the door with such force that he fell heavily to the ground the moment he was inside.

But Luke wasn't much concerned with Stratton. All of a sudden his attention was elsewhere.

It was Finn who made the first kill. A round from one of the Palestinian AKs had just ricocheted off the Land Cruiser's armoured chassis. Finn lowered his weapon so that, instead of pointing above the

369

heads of the mob, it was aimed directly at them. As he fired, he panned from left to right; and although the burst from his 53 didn't last much more than a second, it was brutally effective. The front line of the crowd crumpled like toy soldiers knocked over by a child. There was a heavy groan from the mob, with one man offering up a horrific counterpoint: he had clearly taken a round that had failed to kill him, and was screaming uncontrollably.

Luke ignored the shrieking. He ignored the sudden line of dead, torn bodies. He had noticed something else and he had almost no time at all to deal with it.

'*Get away from the vehicle!*' he screamed at his mates as he raised his weapon. '*GET AWAY FROM THE FUCKING VEHICLE!*' But he saw Fozzie was still behind the wheel and the others were pinned down . . .

Twenty metres away was the guy with the RPG launcher. He had reappeared at the front of the smaller mob, the simple tube of his weapon raised up on his right-hand shoulder and with the curved and pointed shape of a fresh grenade clearly visible at the end of the spout.

Luke stood in the doorway of the building, pressed the butt of the 53 into his shoulder and searched his sights for the shooter. His senses seemed to slow everything down.

The crowd, whose noise had waned, grew louder.

The air was suddenly filled with the renewed chugging of Finn's 53 as he slaughtered a fresh wave of Palestinians. He had ignored Luke's warning to get the hell away from the Land Cruiser—perhaps he hadn't heard it—but hadn't clocked the RPG either.

370

It was up to Luke to lock on to the target. The cross hairs hovered over the shooter's chest.

Both men fired at the same time.

The single shot from Luke's weapon cracked in the air at precisely the same time as the RPG fizzed towards the unit's vehicle. The shooter went down, but it was too late.

The projectile hurtled with absolute accuracy towards his companions. The Land Cruiser was tough, but it wasn't tough enough to withstand that. The grenade crashed through the windscreen. It was inside the vehicle when it detonated.

The explosion was brief, but it was powerful. It sent a shock wave emanating from the 4 x 4 that threw Luke a metre backwards into the building. He fell heavily on his left shoulder, but was able to look back out through the doorway just in time to see the carnage.

Fozzie couldn't have known what hit him. There was no doubt that the blood and gore that spattered the remaining windows as the RPG's shrapnel peppered them from inside was his. Russ and Finn were less lucky. As they were both standing at the open rear passenger doors, the shrapnel that emerged from the openings darted into the backs of their bodies in the fraction of a second before they were thrown forward, away from the vehicle. Luke saw Russ's body flying though the air on the other side of the Land Cruiser; Finn landed on his front no more than three metres from where Luke was lying. Blood was pissing from the back of his neck; his clothes were scorched and burned away; and although there was insufficient life left in him to scream, his body twitched and shuddered like someone was passing an electric current through him. It didn't take a genius to tell he was fucked.

That all three of them were fucked.

A huge roar erupted from the crowd, and several celebratory AK rounds were fired, both up into the air and towards the vehicle. Luke knew there was nothing he could do for the rest of his unit now. He gave himself a couple of seconds to regroup. It was just him and Stratton now. Him, Stratton and the mob. They were surrounding the Land Cruiser, stripping the dead men of their weapons. Luke reckoned it was thirty seconds before the braver ones among them would follow him and Stratton into the structure where they had taken cover. It was as dilapidated inside as out, pungent with the soot-soaked smell of a previous fire. The bare brick walls were crumbling, but from the right-hand side of a hallway a narrow wooden staircase led all the way up the building and it still seemed to be sound. Stratton had shrunk into the shadows just beyond the staircase. His face was pale and he looked rather small, almost childlike. Luke grabbed his arm.

'*Up*,' he barked, and when Stratton hesitated, he just pushed him so that he stumbled up the stairs. He looked back through the door. No sign of the mob, but he could hear them. They were getting louder.

'*UP!*'

Stratton started scrambling up the stairs. It was very dark here and precarious too because the banisters had mostly been burned away and there was a sheer drop to the ground floor. Every ten steps or so, Stratton stumbled; but each time he fell, Luke was there to pick him up by the scruff of his neck and urge him on.

372

They were three storeys high before he heard the sound of voices echoing up the stairwell. Sharp voices, barking instructions. Stratton stopped and looked behind him, to be rewarded with another push from Luke. As the older man scrambled further up the stairs, Luke aimed his weapon down the stairwell and fired a short burst. The sound echoed all over the building and for a moment the voices ceased. It wouldn't be for long, Luke knew. The crowd had a taste for blood.

They were coming.

On the fourth-storey landing there was an opening where a door had once been, but only the rusted hinges now remained. It looked out on to a set of rusted metal steps that clearly gave access to the roof. 'Get up there,' Luke barked. Stratton looked anxiously towards the steps, but he didn't need any more encouragement. He climbed them, swiftly followed by Luke, and they stepped on to the rooftop.

Both men were black with soot and drenched with sweat. Luke looked around. They were on a flat roof, about thirty metres square. The metal staircase had emerged through a small open skylight approximately five metres from the back wall; on the street side of the roof, also five metres from the edge, was a grey breeze-block shed, about two metres high and four wide, which looked like it housed the building's electrical supply. There was no barrier around the roof. The front looked straight out on to the street below, the rear on to a concrete courtyard and there was a gap of about six metres—too far to jump—between the adjacent roofs. The sound of the mob below drifted upwards. It was getting angrier.

Luke glanced down the skylight. Nothing yet. He looked over his shoulder to see Stratton cowering by the blockwork shed—a truly wretched picture, but at least he'd had the presence of mind to stay out of sight of both the street below and the windows of the buildings opposite. Three good men had just lost their lives protecting this tosser, thought Luke.

He turned his back on Stratton and activated his sat phone. 'Zero!' he shouted into the mouthpiece. 'This is Tango 17!'

'Tango 17 this is Zero. What the hell's happening th . . . ?'

'I've got three men down. The Cardinal is safe for now but I've got limited ammo. I'm on a rooftop—do you have my position marked?'

'Roger that, Tango 17.'

'I need a fucking chopper, buddy.'

'Tango 17, your location is a no-fly zone. Attempt return by vehicle or foot . . .'

'Fuck the no-fly zone! I can hold these bastards for five minutes. Ten minutes tops. Leave it any longer, you'll be scraping what's left of Stratton off the fucking rooftop.' And me, for that matter, he thought, but he didn't say it.

Luke disconnected the sat phone. The ops room had all the intel they needed. They'd either infringe the no-fly zone or they wouldn't. His priority was to go about defending their position.

But there was something he wanted to do first.

He checked the skylight again, then strode towards Stratton. As he grew nearer, he realised that his man wasn't cowering at all. He was on his knees with his head bowed, his hands clenched together, and his lips moving silently. For some reason the sight just infuriated Luke even more. He grabbed a clump of Stratton's hair and pulled him shouting to his feet before throwing him down on to the ground again. Towering over him, Luke aimed his 53 directly at Stratton's head.

'All right, you piece of shit,' he growled. 'Let's talk.'

Stratton's face was a mixture of outrage and defiance. He appeared to be quite unconcerned by the sight of the weapon as he pushed himself up on to his elbows. 'I think,' he whispered, 'that the time for conversation is running out.'

As if to confirm Stratton's observation, Luke sensed movement over by the skylight. He turned in time to see a black-haired head poking out. '*Get down!*' he shouted as he raised his 53 and discharged a single round into the new arrival's skull. There was a cracking sound, followed by a tiny fountain of blood, before the head disappeared as its owner tumbled back down the stairs. With luck that would discourage anyone else. For a bit, at least.

Luke turned back to Stratton. Far from looking to protect himself, the idiot was back on his knees.

Again Luke sensed movement. Again he turned to fire a single round in the direction of the skylight, and to down the enemy that was bravely—or stupidly—coming for them. And again he returned to Stratton, and this time swiped his weapon down on the side of his face, knocking him from his kneeling position so that his body slammed against the shed and a large welt appeared immediately on the side of his face. Luke bent down, grabbed him by the collar and pulled him back up to his feet, before pressing him against the wall.

'What are you planning with Maya Bloom?' he demanded.

Stratton's eyes widened. 'Maya Bloom. She has even more enthusiasm for killing people than *you* do . . .'

'*What are you planning?*'

But Stratton just smiled.

Movement from the skylight. Luke turned and discharged a third single round as the top of a head appeared. They weren't giving up. But neither was Luke. He returned his attention to Stratton, who still had his back to the wall of the shed. He looked a mess—his clothes ripped and his face dirty and bruised—and yet that strange smile was still on his face. Luke felt an overwhelming urge to get rid of it.

'Do you know how easy it would be for me,' he said, 'to shoot you now and tell everyone you caught an enemy round?'

No reply. Luke pressed his weapon against Stratton's forehead.

'You think I won't do it? Ten years ago, you ordered that woman to take out a friend of mine. I should kill you now just for that . . .'

No reply.

'I know you've got something to do with the train bombings. You and Maya Bloom . . .'

Stratton's eyes shone, but still he gave no reply.

'*Why?*' Luke yelled, suddenly losing control of any restraint he had. '*Money? The Grosvenor Group?*'

When Stratton finally spoke, it was barely more than a whisper, and at first Luke thought he'd misheard.

'*He* told me to do it.'

376

Luke blinked. 'What?'

'I pity you,' Stratton said, 'if you have no faith.' He stared at Luke with such arrogance that the Regiment man yanked him by the collar once more and hurled him to the ground so that he was lying on his front with the left side of his face pressed against the roof. Kneeling down, Luke dug his right knee sharply into the man's back, knocking the wind from him, and pressed the 53 hard into the fleshy area under his ear.

'You think I'm not serious, Stratton? You think I won't waste you right now? I'm going to give you one more chance—*who told you to do it?*'

Luke could hear shouting from below the skylight, but all his attention was fixed on Stratton, who had started to whisper again. 'I told you you should have paid more attention to the scriptures.'

Luke twisted the butt of the 53 harder into Stratton's flesh.

'The troops of the prince who is to come shall destroy the city and the sanctuary . . .' Stratton went on.

'What the fuck are you on about?'

'Its end shall come with a flood . . .'

More noise from below the skylight.

'And to the end there shall be war . . .'

Luke raised his 53 again. He'd had enough of this bullshit. He struck the side of Stratton's face once more and this time the cunt gasped with the pain. But he continued whispering, repeating himself. 'The troops of the prince who is to come shall destroy the city and the sanctuary . . .'

'What city?' said Luke. 'What are you talking about?' And then, almost without hesitation as he remembered the conversation he'd overheard with

Maya Bloom, 'Jerusalem?'

Stratton smiled again. A chilling smile, devoid of mirth. 'Hanukkah is almost here. When the wall falls, no one will be able to stop the war that is coming . . .'

'When *what* wall falls?' He hit the side of Stratton's face again. 'What the *fuck* are you planning?'

He didn't have time to listen for an answer. Two things had caught his attention. The first was the noise of an aircraft in the distance. But at the same time he saw another figure emerging from the skylight, forcing him to turn his 53 in that direction to nail him. Luke aimed and squeezed the trigger, only to feel and hear a loose click. He swore. The mag was empty. He had another in his ops waistcoat, but to reload would take about fifteen seconds. The enemy was almost out—Luke could see his shoulders.

Luke got to his feet and yanked Stratton up from the ground, dragging him behind the shed, where he threw him down again. 'Don't fucking move,' he said as he removed the empty mag and inserted a fresh one. He'd been at it long enough, though, for the guy he'd just seen to be on the roof, and maybe more of them.

A round pinged past the shed, a couple of feet from Luke's position—close enough for him to feel the air displacement. Sweat poured off him and as he tried to work out his next move, he was aware of Stratton's voice. The man had fallen to his knees again. 'I know that my rewards will be in heaven,' he said. 'Yours, no doubt, will be in a different place.'

Luke delved once more into his ops waistcoat

and brought out a fragmentation grenade as the sound of the approaching air support grew louder. He squeezed the detonation lever, pulled out the pin and hurled the grenade over the shed.

One second passed.

Two seconds.

Three.

The frag exploded with a sudden sharp crack, which was followed by the sound of screaming. Luke pressed his back against the corner of the shed, pointed his weapon around the corner and fired a random burst, before peering round to take stock of the situation.

The frag had done its work well. Three militants were on their backs. Two of them were motionless; the third had blood pumping from his leg and was rolling about so frantically he was painting the area around him red. Luke aimed the 53 in the wounded man's direction and with a quick double tap put him out of his misery.

And then he looked up.

Two helis, both coming in sharp and from a great height. One looked like a Puma; the other, smaller and hovering just above and behind in a chaperone position, was clearly an Apache. Luke pulled his second and final fragmentation grenade from his waistcoat, yanked away the pin and lobbed it into the opening of the skylight. The muffled crack of its explosion was followed by more screaming. Luke blocked that from his senses, and pulled Stratton round to the front of the shed. He waved at the descending chopper, but the pilot clearly already had a trace on his position and was coming in to land, while the attack helicopter stayed about thirty metres clear, hovering at an angle so that its formidable arsenal was pointing directly at the roof. The roar of the two sets of rotary blades was immense; as the Puma touched down it was like a force-nine wind had blown over the building. The side door opened and Luke recognised B Squadron's Sergeant Major Bill Thomas shouting at them to run on board.

'*Go!*' Luke roared at Stratton over the deafening noise. He kept his 53 aimed towards the skylight.

Stratton didn't move. He was looking from the chopper to Luke as if he couldn't decide what best to do.

'*GO!*' Luke pushed Stratton in the direction of the aircraft door. The crew member grabbed Stratton by the arm and pulled him into the helicopter. Luke followed, throwing himself into the hard, metallic interior of the chopper. The instant he was on board, the Puma lifted off the roof with a lurch. Luke looked back out of the opening to see the bloodied bodies he'd nailed on the roof below; as they grew higher, he could see the remnants of the mob still rioting in the street; and for a brief moment he saw the Land Cruiser.

The image of Fozzie's blood spattering over the inside of the vehicle replayed itself in Luke's mind; he remembered the way Finn's body had twitched and jolted, and the sickening thud of AK rounds slamming into Russ. It went against every one of Luke's Regiment instincts to leave the bodies of his mates down there on enemy territory, but he knew he'd had no other option.

And so far as he could tell, all this had happened because of one man.

He turned and saw Stratton huddled on the floor of the Puma, a dark frown on his face. Luke felt as

380

if some other force was controlling his body. He threw himself at the older man and whacked him with a heavy fist. Stratton was like a rag doll. He didn't even try to resist as Luke laid into him; and by the time two of the aircrew had pulled him away, he'd managed to thump his fist three times against the former PM's face, hearing the nose joint crack each time and seeing blood smear over the lower part of the guy's face.

Luke didn't struggle as he was restrained. He knew there was no point. His squadron comrades were holding him and shouting something at him, but he didn't even register what it was. Just white noise. Interference in his head. He slumped on to the floor of the Puma, suddenly exhausted, his mind ablaze.

His stomach churned.

It wasn't the bloodshed that made him feel nauseous.

It wasn't even the brutal and sudden death of his mates.

It was Stratton.

It wasn't over yet. Alistair Stratton. Maya Bloom. The Grosvenor Group. Together they'd caused death on an unimaginable scale. And from what Stratton had said, there was more to come . . .

He felt the man's eyes on him and he looked across the body of the Puma to see a battered face staring at him, blood streaming from his badly broken nose.

To the end there shall be war.

Stratton's voice rang in Luke's head as the fields and rooftops of Gaza slipped away underneath him and the aircraft sped out of Hamas territory, back over the border into Israel.

TWENTY-SIX

15.00 hrs.

There was a queue outside the security gates leading to the Western Wall, but not as long as usual. Ordinarily there would be swarms of tourists in this part of Jerusalem, waiting patiently to gain access to the ancient site. Not today. Even if the governments of the West hadn't issued travel warnings, the mobilisation of troops in the area would have put people off. Not to mention the increased activity in Israeli airspace, and the military presence that was high, even for Jerusalem. There were some visitors to the city, with their cameras and baseball caps and rucksacks, but nothing like the usual number.

A young man who had just joined the queue to clear security before approaching the wall counted twenty people ahead of him, all men as the women were obliged to use an adjacent entrance. Eight of these men were dressed in traditional clothes: black suits, white shirts and wide-brimmed black hats. The remainder had their heads covered with skullcaps or ordinary hats. They were not tourists; they were here to pray at their holy site and they knew the regulations. The young man knew the regulations too. He had been coming here every day for the past two weeks, though before that he wouldn't have been seen dead in such a place. His skin was perhaps slightly darker than the others', but not so dark that he looked out of place in a traditional Hassidic suit. As the queue moved, he shuffled patiently along. And by the time he reached the security gate he had already recognised one of the guards from his regular visits. He nodded in greeting at the soldier, dressed in his olive uniform and with an M16 slung across his front. The guard nodded back and handed him a small tray.

The young man put his hand into his pocket and pulled out a bunch of keys and a handful of coins—a mixture of one-, two- and five-shekel pieces. He dumped these metallic objects in the tray, before passing through the airport-style metal detector. It made no sound. With another nod to the guard, he recouped his keys and his loose change, returned them to his pocket and continued on his way.

A flight of stone steps led down to the Western Wall plaza—a large, flagstoned square about seventy-five metres square, populated this morning by about a hundred people, twenty or thirty of whom were close to the wall, facing it and praying. The young man ignored all these people, as he always did, and headed straight for the far corner of the plaza, which adjoined the left-hand side of the wall. There he passed through a small archway to find himself in a room that gave access to Jerusalem's ancient tunnels. There were more men in here, praying against the covered section of the Western Wall, which continued along to his right. Beyond them, a passageway led straight on. They paid him no attention as he continued in this direction.

The Western Wall tunnel, he knew, extended about 400 metres—well into the Muslim Quarter of the city. He wouldn't go that far. He shuffled along, with the ancient stones of the wall to his right atmospherically lit by yellow lamps embedded in the floor, past the occasional visitor looking up at the wall and at the information plaques that explained its history. But he wasn't interested in history. His mind was firmly on the future.

After about a hundred metres, he arrived at his destination. In the wall to the left there was a metal grille, about a metre square, its bars creating gaps roughly ten centimetres by fifteen. Beyond the grille it was dark, and the air around it was slightly colder. It was impossible to see how far back or down the space extended, but he knew it was enough for his purposes. The young man looked around to check nobody was watching. The immediate vicinity was deserted.

From the inside pocket of his jacket he pulled a resealable transparent plastic freezer bag with a thirty-centimetre length of fishing line attached to it. He removed the coins from his pocket and placed them in the bag, which he sealed and— checking once more that nobody was watching— pushed through one of the lowest row of holes in the grille. He kept hold of the fishing line as the bag dropped below floor level, before tying the other end securely round one of the vertical bars.

He knew that anyone looking very closely would see that there were eleven other bits of fishing line attached to the bottom of the grille. Further investigation would reveal that each line suspended a similar bag of coins. But as he stood up, he felt quite sure that nobody would notice this little cache. The coins were safe. They could wait there until they were needed.

Which wouldn't be long, he thought to himself, as he shuffled out of the tunnel, back into the plaza and away from the Western Wall. Five minutes later he was walking around the Old Town, back towards East Jerusalem, his job complete.

For now.

*　　　*　　　*

The Regiment ops room back at the Israeli military base had been emptied, the entire squadron confined to quarters.

The Puma had touched down three and a half hours ago, but that meant nothing to Luke. He was suffering from a kind of numbness. As he'd been escorted off the Puma by the flight crew, he'd been only half aware of the Foreign Office reps who had crowded round Alistair Stratton. Luke had barely registered the looks of incredulity that the Ruperts had given him when the flight crew explained how he'd laid into Stratton on the chopper, breaking his nose; and he'd been entirely submissive as he was escorted to a holding area on the edge of the Regiment's operations base.

It was a small room with nothing but a wooden chair in it. Luke hadn't bothered opening the door to check whether it was guarded. Of *course* it was fucking guarded. He'd collapsed into a corner and closed his eyes. He could just hear Stratton's voice; just imagine what bullshit he was saying about what had occurred on the ground.

Time slowed down. Luke felt like he'd relived a thousand times the moment the RPG hit the Land Cruiser. But, sickening though the memory was, it was not nearly so sickening as the thought of Stratton's rantings. In his head he replayed the desperate conversation on the Gazan rooftop.

He remembered someone telling him once that psychopaths were often to be found in the corridors of power, but it was more than that. He'd been quoting the fucking Bible at Luke, at least that was what it had sounded like—the sort of shit you'd expect from some nutter with a sandwich board walking down Oxford Street predicting the end of the world.

To the end there shall be war.

The memory of Stratton's words chilled him, but he couldn't get the bastard out of his head.

The Book of Daniel. It tells us it is here that the End Times will start.

Was he really saying that? Was he really saying that the end of the world was coming and that he had something to do with it? Had he really tipped over the edge into genuine insanity?

But then Luke recalled the few moments he'd spent that morning looking at his ops officer's laptop. The US naval fleet advancing across the Med; the coalition forces grouping in the plains of northern Israel; troop movement along the Iranian border; even Yemen was mobilising. When it came to orchestrating wars, Stratton had form. Just look at Iraq. And so far as Luke could tell, he was orchestrating this one like a fucking maestro, with Maya Bloom—ruthless and without pity—as his accomplice. If Stratton wanted the world to burn, all it needed was a spark. And if everything Luke had heard was right, that spark would be lit in Jerusalem.

Hanukkah. The first day of the celebrations. One hour before midday.

He thought back to the briefing they'd had at Hereford. The ops officer had mentioned

Hanukkah. What had he said? *Three days from now.*
Luke did the maths. The first day of Hanukkah was
tomorrow. And at 11.00 hrs something big would be
going down . . .

Nobody would believe him, of course. Not
once Stratton had filled everyone's ears with shit.
Nobody would believe a simple Regiment sergeant
over the former Prime Minister. Which narrowed
his options. He had to get to Jerusalem. Catch up
with Stratton. Catch up with Maya Bloom. Stop
them, somehow . . .

17.00 hrs. The guards who burst into the holding
area and took him to the ops room were less than
gentle. There were just two people in there: B
Squadron's ops officer, O'Donoghue, and the
OC, Dawson. They were standing in front of
O'Donoghue's laptop as Luke entered.

'You—' the ops officer indicated the guards
'—out. You—' he pointed at Luke '– here.'

The guards left quickly and Luke approached
the computer. The three men were silent while
a piece of black and white camera footage played
on the screen. There was no sound. At the bottom
right-hand corner was a time code, and the footage
had clearly been taken by the camera of the Apache
that had chaperoned the Puma towards Luke and
Stratton's position on the rooftop in Gaza City.
Although the helicopter was moving quickly,
its height gave the impression that the city was
slipping away slowly underneath. After a minute
or so, however, it started to descend. The rooftops
became sharper and twenty seconds later the
camera was focusing in from a distance on one in
particular.

At first it was difficult to make out what was

happening, but it took only a few more seconds to become clear. A man was face down on the roof. A second figure had his knee pressed into the man's back, and a weapon pointing directly at his head.

O'Donoghue turned to Luke, his face a mixture of fury and astonishment. 'What in the name of ... ?' He was so angry he couldn't even finish the question. 'Jesus!' he spat finally, shaking his head. 'We'd better hope this never gets into the wrong hands. It would be the fucking money shot for Wikileaks.'

'It's not what it looks like,' Luke muttered.

'Really? So what were you *doing* there? Offering to clean the fucking wax out of his ears with an HK53? Christ, Luke, Stratton's on the warpath.'

'You can say that again.'

The ops officer ignored the comment. 'He says you lost it on the ground. Says you opened up on a crowd of locals and that's why I've got three dead men on my hands and God knows how many Palestinians. Have you got any *fucking* idea what a shit storm this is going to cause? Stratton says . . .'

'I don't give a *toss* what Stratton says.' Luke's outburst silenced the ops officer immediately. 'He was going nuts out there.'

'What do you mean?'

'*Totally* nuts. He was spouting scripture at me . . .'

'I'm not fucking surprised, Luke. He was in the middle of a riot and you were sticking a weapon to his head. He probably *was* praying . . .'

'How long have you known me, boss? Do you really think I lost it down there? Do you really think I put the lives of my unit at risk? Do you *really* think that?'

'What I *really* want you to do, Luke, is explain why I've just been looking at footage that shows you . . .'

Suddenly the door burst open. A short, tanned man around sixty, with thick white hair, an expensive but crumpled suit and bags under his eyes, stormed in.

'Who the fuck is he?' O'Donoghue demanded of Julian Dawson.

'I,' the man said, 'am the British ambassador to Tel Aviv. *You*'—he waved his right hand at the three men in general—'are in ten tons of shit.' He looked from one to the other before his eyes settled on Luke. 'Is this the man? I want him transferred to Tel Aviv. There's a high-security unit there with an SIS presence. We need to make sure nobody can look back on our decisions and say we . . .'

'He's not going anywhere.' The ops officer's voice was firm.

A pause.

'I hardly need to remind you,' the ambassador said, dangerously quietly, 'that I am the representative of Her Majesty's . . .'

'He's under my command. He's not going anywhere.'

'Don't be a bloody idiot . . .'

O'Donoghue had turned away from the ambassador in mid-sentence. He walked up to Luke and stared at him for a full thirty seconds. He looked like he was deciding on the best course of action.

At last he spoke. And if Luke had been encouraged by the way he'd stood up for him in front of the ambassador, now was the time to change his mind. O'Donoghue sounded fucking livid. 'I don't know what the *hell* you were thinking of, Luke,' he said. 'Frankly, there hasn't been a fuck-up like this since Libya. I'm putting you in solitary.'

'Boss, you've got to . . .'

'Forget it, Luke. I haven't got a choice. Wait here.'

The ops officer marched out of the room, leaving Luke alone with the OC and the ambassador. 'This isn't the end of it,' the ambassador announced. 'I won't be steamrollered like this.'

Dawson ignored him. All his attention was on Luke and the look he gave him was bitter. The look of an officer who'd just lost men and was taking it hard. 'Hope you didn't have anything planned for the next ten years, Mercer,' he muttered. 'You're doing time for this.'

Luke didn't reply. There was no point, not with the footage from the Apache.

He eyed the door. His 53 had been taken off him while he was in the Puma, but his Sig was still strapped to his ankle. That at least was something.

At that moment O'Donoghue returned, along with four members of B Squadron that Luke recognised but didn't know well. It only took one glance at them to realise word had spread that Luke had lost it—that everyone in that room thought they had a madman in their midst.

'On your feet, Mercer,' Dawson instructed, before turning to the four Regiment men. 'Get him out of my sight.'

One of the guys—a short man who had shaved his head to hide his encroaching baldness—stepped forward. 'I'll need your weapon,' he said.

Luke cursed inwardly. He looked towards

390

Dawson. 'Boss, I . . .'

'*Do it,*' the OC told him, like a stern schoolmaster with an unruly kid.

A pause. 'Right, boss,' Luke said quietly.

He bent down to loosen the disco gun in its ankle holster. And as he did so, he checked out each of the other men in the room. Only the four new arrivals were armed, but their rifles were slung casually across their fronts—clearly no one expected to be using them. Two guys were standing by the door; the other two were about five metres from Luke's position. Closest to him were Dawson and O'Donoghue—who were behind a desk—and the ambassador, who stood just a couple of metres from Luke, surveying the situation with a bleak expression.

'Get a move on, Mercer,' Dawson said impatiently.

'Yes, boss,' he murmured. He removed the gun.

Luke knew he had to move hard and fast. The ambassador might have been a soft target, but the other men in the room were as highly trained as he was and just as strong. What they didn't have, though, was the element of surprise.

He did it all in a single movement: pulling the gun from the holster, stepping towards the ambassador, hooking his left arm around the man's neck and pressing the handgun against the side of his head. The ambassador breathed in sharply and Luke could feel his body suddenly shaking.

'Get away from the door,' Luke instructed.

No movement.

'*Get away from the fucking door!*'

The two Regiment men on either side of the door looked towards Dawson, who nodded. They

391

stepped aside.

'Hands on heads and get to the back of the room, all of you,' Luke ordered.

'Do it,' O'Donoghue said. And then, as the men moved: 'Put the gun down, Luke. Your career's already over. Don't make it even worse.'

'Where's Stratton?'

'You know I can't tell you that . . .'

'You think I've lost it? You think I'm mad? I'll fucking show you when I nail this piece of shit. *Where's Stratton?*'

It was the ambassador who replied, his words tumbling over themselves. 'Airlifted to Ben Gurion. He's taking a UN flight back to London tonight.'

'Put the fucking gun down, Luke,' O'Donoghue warned.

But Luke was doing nothing of the sort. The ambassador was still trembling, and wheezing now on account of the firm neck lock he was in. Luke pictured the area outside the ops centre. It was open ground, at least 100 metres before he could get to any cover in the main part of the camp. As soon as he stepped out of that door, he'd be a sitting duck. Unless . . .

He looked over at O'Donoghue. 'Where's the key to that door?'

The ops officer remained stony-faced, so Luke tightened his arm lock on the ambassador, who started to whimper like a kid.

'*Where's the fucking key?*'

O'Donoghue moved slowly, clearly worried that his actions would be misinterpreted. He pulled a bunch of keys from his pocket, selected one and then held it up.

'I want to know it's the right one. Lock the door.'

O'Donoghue's face hardened. He examined the keys again, selected a different one and moved over the door. He inserted it into the lock and twisted it back and forth. Luke heard the lock click shut and open again.

'Leave it there and get back to where you were.' O'Donoghue did as he was told. Luke forced the ambassador towards the exit. 'I'm taking him outside. If I see the door open, I'll kill him.' He released the man, then grabbed the keys, opened the door and pushed him through it. Two seconds later he had locked his Regiment mates in the ops room.

It was twilight now. The floodlights were already lit, bathing the camp—which was as busy as ever—in their fluorescent glow. Luke immediately saw three choppers coming in to land. An open-topped truck with at least thirty IDF troops in the back was trundling past the Regiment buildings.

'This is an outrage,' the ambassador spat.

Luke didn't reply. He just raised his Sig and brought it crashing down on the ambassador's neck. The man fell, unconscious, to the ground.

And then Luke ran.

He didn't have more than a minute, he estimated, before O'Donoghue and the others broke their way out of the ops office; and they'd be on the blower, raising the alarm right now. He ran into the crowded central area of the base and tried to get the geography of the whole place straight in his head. To get to the exit meant going through the main centre of operations, back past the F-16 hangar and then north. It was a couple of klicks, though, across open ground, and from memory there were two armed Israeli soldiers at the barrier.

If he was going to stand a chance of getting out of the base before the whole place was locked down, he needed a vehicle. But first he needed something to keep all the soldiers crawling around the base occupied, otherwise O'Donoghue and Dawson would have every last fucker looking for him.

The canteen was twenty-five metres to his right, a low prefab building with wide double doors that were currently shut. There was nobody immediately outside—it was too early to scran up yet—and Luke sprinted over to it and tried the door. It was unlocked, so he disappeared inside.

The dining area of the canteen was about twenty metres by twenty, with rows of long tables and benches. Although Luke could smell cooking, the dining area was empty. At the far end was a serving hatch about four metres wide, and to its right was a closed door. Luke headed towards the door, which turned out to be locked and couldn't be opened from this side without a key. But the serving hatch had a metal roller blind in front of it and this had been left partly open. He climbed through the hatch into the kitchen before pulling the blind down behind him and checking the door. From the inside, it opened fine.

The kitchen was about half the size of the dining area. Along the far wall there was a bank of catering ovens with huge stainless steel pots of food bubbling away; on either side of the room there were long metal worktops with hot-water urns, racks of knives and large toasters; and in the middle of the room there was a large food preparation island. In the far left-hand corner was an open door. There was nobody else in the kitchen, but Luke could hear voices from outside.

He grabbed a seven-inch boning knife—sharp and flexible—from the worktop and headed for the door. There were two men standing out the back, five metres from the door, dressed in food-stained white overalls, each of them smoking a cigarette as they chatted quietly. They didn't see Luke approach until he was pulling the door shut. One of them shouted out, but by then the Yale-type door lock had fastened shut. Luke rammed the tip of the boning knife into the lock, then yanked the handle down at a ninety-degree angle. The tempered-steel blade snapped, leaving the tip in the lock. Nobody would be opening that door in a hurry.

He ran back to the ovens and extinguished the hobs before looking around. He knew what he wanted to achieve. All he needed was the tools to do it. A gas pipe entered in the middle of the back wall at a height of about 1.5 metres and ran down the wall to the rear of the ovens. Good. Looking back to the central island, he saw a heavy cleaver. He grabbed it, then scanned the kitchen for a final piece of equipment.

He saw a copy of the *Jerusalem Post* sitting on a metal trolley. He picked it up before taking the meat cleaver and slamming it into the gas pipe.

The pipe dented, but didn't break. Luke whacked it again and the dent grew bigger. It was the third strike that split it, and a sudden rush of gas hissed loudly into the kitchen.

Back at the central island he helped himself to another long chef's knife before moving over to one of the large toasters along the side worktop. He loosened a couple of pages from the newspaper, stuffed them into the toaster and pushed down the lever.

Thirty seconds before they caught fire, he reckoned. Thirty seconds to get the fuck out of there.

Luke hurried towards the door that led into the dining area. He quickly let himself out, shut the door behind him and disabled it with the knife. And then he ran.

In the end it took just over thirty seconds for the gas to ignite. Luke was about ten metres from the canteen when a massive explosion erupted behind him. He felt the heat against his back as the twilight glowed suddenly orange while he walked calmly away. Over to his left, seventy-five metres away, he could see men congregating outside the Regiment buildings. But all around him panic was breaking out. Men running and shouting. Nobody knew it was an exploding gas main—no doubt they'd all assume it was a Palestinian missile got lucky. Immediately Luke found himself among a chaotic crowd of soldiers, some of them sprinting towards the source of the explosion, some sprinting away. But all of them camouflaging him just the way he wanted.

Twenty metres ahead he clocked a WMIK. The driver had stopped and climbed out of the vehicle. As Luke approached he saw him running in the direction of the canteen, leaving the driver's door open and—he realised ten seconds later once he was alongside—the engine running. He looked over his shoulder. Great clouds of smoke were billowing up from the canteen, three military vehicles had screeched up in front of it and everyone's attention was on the burning building.

Which meant nobody gave Luke a second glance as he slipped into the driver's seat of the WMIK, turned the vehicle round 180 degrees and drove away.

If he floored the WMIK, he could be at the exit barrier in three minutes. But to speed through the built-up area would just draw attention to himself. It took all his self-restraint to accelerate slowly, his Sig on the dashboard where he could reach it easily and his hand resting gently on the gear stick in case he suddenly needed to shift. In the passenger seat was a Bergen. It looked like it was full of gear, but Luke had no time to check it.

Thirty seconds. A hundred metres. More soldiers were running towards the canteen. Another fifty metres along, he passed the hangar containing the F-16. On the night they'd arrived, it had been surrounded by mechanics. There was nobody in the hangar tonight. The aircraft was ready to fly.

Rain started to spot the windscreen. Luke turned on the wipers and the glass became immediately smeared with dust. It took a few seconds to clear, by which time he was driving past an equipment warehouse.

Suddenly he remembered the satellite marker strapped to his left arm. It was still attached from the op and it meant the ops centre could track him to within a couple of metres. He struggled to remove it from his arm while steering with one hand, then wound down the window, ready to ditch it. But just then he saw something better. A logistics truck was approaching, its driver clearly unaware of the chaos ahead and its open-topped back piled with full bin bags. As it trundled past the WMIK, Luke chucked the marker up on to the top of the bags and watched in the rear-view mirror as the truck headed in the opposite direction. If the

397

marker had remained still, anyone tracking would have realised he'd just dumped it; if it was moving, maybe he'd buy himself a bit of extra time.

He continued to drive steadily towards the exit of the base.

A minute passed. Five hundred metres of ground. He'd cleared the main part of the camp so he accelerated up to 70 kph, but kept looking in the rear-view mirror expecting to see vehicles speeding towards him; or maybe a chopper would land effortlessly on the road in front of him. Neither event happened, but his mouth was still dry when, a couple of minutes later, he saw the main entrance 300 metres ahead: a high wire fence with barbed wire rolled across the top, a sentry point with two guards and a lowered barrier.

Luke slowed down, reached for his Sig and rested it on his lap. Regiment SOP would be to nail the two sentries before they had a chance to raise the alarm . . .

He drove towards the barrier.

It was sixty metres away.

Fifty.

Lights in the rear-view mirror. Headlamps. Three sets. They were moving quickly.

Luke accelerated. It was his only option: pick up enough speed and the barrier couldn't stop him.

The rain was falling more heavily. The figures of the two guards were indistinct, but he could see them standing by the barrier, assault rifles slung across their fronts. It didn't look like they'd clocked him yet. If he burst through, it would shag the front of the WMIK and they'd certainly fire on him. Assault rifles could take out his tyres, shatter the rear window—but at least he'd be out of the camp.

He accelerated some more.

Thirty metres to go.

Twenty.

The headlamps behind him were getting closer.

Suddenly, and to Luke's astonishment, the barrier rose. Had word not reached the sentries? Were the headlamps behind just regular army vehicles? He wasn't going to stop and find out. Seconds later he was speeding through the barrier. He caught sight of one of the guards, who looked surprised that the Land Rover had zoomed through at such a rate. But the day was drawing to a close, and it was raining hard. By the time Luke looked in the mirror again, the barrier had closed behind him and the sentry was taking shelter.

He kept his foot down and his eyes firmly on the road ahead. He'd been lucky, and experience told him that such luck seldom lasted. He tried to get his head straight. Stratton was at Ben Gurion—if he hadn't already flown. The security there was fucking ridiculous. On his own, Luke would never get close to him.

He had only one choice. To get to Jerusalem. Because if he didn't pull something out of the bag by eleven o'clock tomorrow, Stratton and Maya Bloom's plans would come to fruition.

Which meant that right now his only friend was speed.

*　　　*　　　*

The air at Ben Gurion was thick with rain. It poured on to the chassis of a UN cargo TriStar as it refuelled, and on to the military presence—heavy, even for Ben Gurion—that surrounded it. An armoured Jeep was cutting through the darkness across the airfield from a nearby helicopter pad. The vehicle stopped just a couple of metres from the steps that had been placed at the rear of the TriStar. Two armed personnel climbed out of the front of the Jeep, and one of them opened the rear door to allow a thin man to exit.

Alistair Stratton looked a far cry from the smart, statesmanlike politician the world knew. His skin was smeared with dirt, blood and sweat; his nose was clearly broken; his clothes, in places, were torn. But although this usually unruffled figure looked like he'd been plucked from a war zone, it was not this that was most noticeable about it him. The Middle East peace envoy looked like peace was the last thing on his mind.

Soaked by the rain, he swiftly entered the body of the TriStar. He stood in its cavernous body, surrounded by crates of equipment and even a number of vehicles marked with white UN lettering, the scrapes and shouts of equipment being loaded echoing all around him. A second man approached, wearing camouflage gear and a UN armband. When he spoke, however, his clipped tones identified him as a British soldier, and an officer at that.

'We should be off the ground in half an hour, sir.'

'Why so long?' Stratton's voice was hoarse.

'We've just received a communication from B Squadron SAS.'

The former PM looked at him sharply. 'What?'

'One of their men has gone AWOL. Nothing for you to worry about, sir, but a Regiment unit is on its way by helicopter.'

400

The politician's bleak face grew bleaker. 'I want men stationed at every entrance to this aircraft. Is that understood?'

The officer looked mildly surprised.

'We're quite secure, sir . . .'

He cut himself short. Stratton's face had turned dangerous. 'Is that understood?'

'Yes, sir.' The officer turned to march off and attend to Stratton's instruction, but not before asking, 'Do you . . . do you need some medical attention, sir?'

Stratton didn't reply. As the officer disappeared, he stood alone in the belly of the TriStar, staring into the middle distance for almost a minute with the air of a man whose thoughts were far away. The loadie approached and spoke with a scrupulously polite Midwestern American accent. 'I need to ask you to take a seat, please, sir.'

A pause.

'Mr Stratton, sir?'

Stratton blinked, then nodded. Thirty seconds later he was clicking himself into a window seat up at the front of the plane. He gazed out at the tarmac, where, through the heavy rain, he could see a fuel lorry pulling away from the aircraft.

He continued to stare out on to Israeli soil.

Hallowed ground.

He didn't need to ask who the SAS man was, but he was insignificant. There was no way he could prevent what was going to happen. No way he could stop the great events that were about to unfold . . .

Stratton was still staring from the window, lost in thought, when the aircraft's engines started up; still staring as it taxied to the runway, accelerated and took to the skies. The TriStar juddered with turbulence through the rain and the cloud cover. When it finally broke through, he saw the waxing moon hanging bright in the sky and, a couple of minutes later, a different kind of light. There was a gap in the clouds, revealing the sprawling shape of a city below. In its centre, easily visible even from this height, was the Temple Mount.

Jerusalem. Stratton felt a thrill as he gazed down on the sacred place. His pale lips moved faintly. Silently.

A sudden lurch as the aircraft banked to the left and, as quickly as the Holy City had come into view, it disappeared.

It was another fifteen minutes before the cloud cover dispersed again and Stratton caught a glimpse of the ground below. Here it was less populated, with much smaller towns dotted around. But the terrain was flat and, after staring for a minute, something caught Stratton's eye. Two aircraft, at a much lower altitude than the TriStar, were circling above a built-up region, maybe a couple of square kilometres, with two runways very clearly marked out in yellow lights. Stratton knew what he was looking at: a coalition military base. The aircraft were no doubt bringing in troops, equipment or supplies.

It was all coming together.

'Everything all right, sir?'

A figure had appeared in the aisle by his seat. A soldier, in digital camouflage and wearing a distinctive beret with the emblem of a winged dagger.

'I understand one of your men has gone missing,' he said. He lightly touched his painful, broken nose. 'He lost his mind, you know? Quite lost it.

Post-traumatic stress disorder, I suppose. Terrible thing. I'm rather afraid for his own safety.'

'He won't get far, sir,' the Regiment man replied stiffly. 'I promise you that.'

'Good. I'm glad to hear it. For his own sake.'

And without another word, Stratton turned to look out of the window again, to gaze at the sight of his armies gathering on the plains below.

TWENTY-SEVEN

It looked like being a brutal night to follow a brutal day.

Luke knew the Regiment would be after him. Most likely the Israeli Defence Force too. Once they worked out what he'd done, the whole area would be cordoned off and the guys would be out in force. And while Luke had nothing but a 9mm and the dirty clothes on his back, B Squadron would be fully equipped: night sights, thermal-imaging gear, choppers. Luke reviewed his options. He could put himself on hard routine in the surrounding countryside. Maybe he'd evade capture for twenty-four hours, but they'd get him. And the moment the Regiment had their hands on him, Stratton had won.

He had to get to Jerusalem. There he could become anonymous and work out his next move. He estimated that the city was thirty to forty miles away. His deadline was 11.00 hrs the following day, but he had to get there sooner than that if he was to have any chance of stopping whatever Stratton had planned. He had to get there now.

Luke killed his lights. It made no difference to a chopper with thermal imaging or night-sight capability, of course, but such an asset would take time to mobilise. He pushed the vehicle as hard as it would go along the unpopulated road that led from the military base and within a few minutes he'd covered at least five klicks and was in sight of the main road that had brought them from Ben Gurion. He hit the brakes when he was about twenty-five metres from the junction.

He knew he had to ditch the WMIK. It wouldn't take long for the guys back at base to realise what he'd done and the whole fucking Israeli police force would be looking for the vehicle. He wanted to hide it, but his options were limited. There were no buildings by the side of the road behind which to secrete it. Just a ditch on the right-hand side, perhaps a metre deep. Luke swung the vehicle off the road and it jolted and bumped into the ditch. A chopper would still see it, but it would now be a bit more difficult to pick out from ground level.

He allowed himself thirty seconds to rummage in the Bergen that had been left on the passenger seat. Its contents were neatly packed. Luke pulled everything out: a thin base layer that didn't smell too good, an IDF cap, two packets of rations and a wallet containing a military ID card and a small sheaf of used banknotes. Luke didn't bother to count the money. He just shoved the notes in a pocket and returned everything else to the Bergen, along with his Sig and the scope that was still in his waistcoat. He then removed his waistcoat and body armour to leave just a black T-shirt. Hardly much protection, either from a round or from the rain, but nothing would make him stand out like his

404

ops gear. Shouldering the Bergen, he ran from the WMIK through the rain towards the main road.

It was busy in both directions—cars passing each way at a rate of one every ten seconds—and fully dark. The headlamps shining at him through the rain obscured the shape of the cars that passed, and dazzled him. He ran across the road—that had to be the Jerusalem direction, he figured. Within a minute his clothes were drenched from the spray of passing trucks as much as from the rain. He tried to flag one down, all the while keeping an eye over his shoulder in the direction from which he'd come.

Panic rose in his stomach. No one was stopping. He didn't blame them. He looked like a down-and-out, wild-eyed, dirty and drenched. And with the region on the brink of war, everybody was suspicious and on edge. But he *couldn't* stay by the side of the road—might as well have a fucking firefly on his head. He found himself shouting at the passing traffic. 'Stop! *Fucking stop!*'

Nobody did.

He checked over his shoulder and his stomach tightened with dread. Lights. Airborne. A couple of klicks? They were hazy in the rain, but they came from the direction of the military base and they were heading his way. Luke started to run, against the line of the traffic but frantically waving his arms in a desperate attempt to persuade someone to stop.

Still nobody did.

The chopper was approaching. Impossible in these conditions to judge its distance or its speed. Certainly too close for comfort, and Luke reckoned he had no more than thirty seconds. Decision time. Did he go offroad? He couldn't tell in the dark what kind of cover there was. Perhaps he'd risk standing out even more. But to stay here, waving down cars . . . He tried to put himself in the position of a search team. How much time would *he* need to track someone down in his position?

No time at all, he realised. *No fucking time at all.*

He could hear the chopper. It was hovering just beyond the junction with the main road, clearly scanning the area below. It was only seconds before . . .

Suddenly another wave of spray hit him, chill and muddy. Luke cursed—but then he saw that the vehicle which had caused it hadn't driven past but had come to an abrupt halt just five metres up ahead. Luke ran back. The vehicle was a VW minibus, its front half painted yellow, its rear half white and with Hebrew lettering along the side. Underneath, much smaller, was the word '*Sherut*'.

As Luke came alongside, he saw that the side door had slid open to reveal a ramshackle, poorly cared-for interior with banks of worn seats, about half of them occupied. The driver had one arm on the wheel and was leaning over in Luke's direction, calling impatiently to him in Hebrew. As Luke threw himself into the vehicle and slammed the door behind him, the driver grew more irate and Luke felt the eyes of the other passengers on him.

He turned to the driver and blinked stupidly at him. It took a couple of seconds to work out where he was. All the passengers had some kind of luggage next to them or at their feet; the driver himself had stretched out his palm. Luke twigged that he was in a shared taxi. He'd seen vehicles like this—usually in a state of profound disrepair—up and down Africa, but he hadn't realised they

406

were a feature of the Israeli transport system. He plunged his hand into his pocket and pulled out the sheaf of notes he'd taken from the stolen Bergen. He peeled off a couple and thrust them into the fist of the driver, whose instant silence suggested that he'd overpaid. Luke took a seat by the window and silently urged the taxi to slip back into the lane of traffic. But the driver was taking great pains to stow away the money in a leather purse, and it was an agonising twenty seconds before the vehicle moved again.

Luke's wet clothes clung to him and cold rainwater dribbled down his neck. Trying not to alert the other passengers, he kept an eye on the chopper, still hovering over the junction. He pictured the crew staring intently at the violent colours of a thermal-imaging screen as they scanned the surrounding area; and he found himself holding his breath.

The heli's searchlight swung round in the direction of the taxi and momentarily blinded Luke. He became vaguely aware of the passengers muttering to each other, no doubt wondering what the chopper was looking for and perhaps suspecting it was their bedraggled new companion. Luke ignored them. As his vision returned, all his attention was on the helicopter. And on the searchlight, which he could see had lit up an abandoned WMIK in a ditch by the side of the road leading back to the military base . . .

The taxi moved beyond the chopper's position.

Fifty metres.

A hundred.

Looking back, Luke saw that it was still hovering

there. And then suddenly it turned—not in Luke's direction, but the other way.

He sat back in his seat, closed his eyes and tried to control his breathing. He was safe, for now. But as the minibus sped along the main road, the knot in his stomach refused to go. His mind churned over everything that had happened over the past few days. Suze McArthur. Gaza. His men, dead.

But above it all were two faces. Alistair Stratton and Maya Bloom.

He suddenly turned and looked at the passenger behind him—an elderly man with silver hair and a tanned, lined face.

'Do you speak English?' he muttered.

The man looked taken aback. 'Of course,' he said.

'What is the next stop?'

The elderly passenger was looking at him like he was a lunatic.

'Why . . . Jerusalem, of course,' he replied.

Luke blinked.

He checked his watch. 18.35. Less than seventeen hours till Stratton's spectacular came off.

Less than seventeen hours to stop him.

*   *   *

20.15 hrs.

The taxi ride was painfully slow. The road was good, but it was busy and the weather was fucking awful. Every time one of the travellers started talking into a mobile phone, Luke had to fight the paranoia that they were raising the alarm about his presence. It made him want to reach for the Sig that he'd stashed in the Bergen, but he kept his cool.

After nearly two hours the rain eased and Luke could make out the outskirts of a city.

It wasn't much more than twelve hours since he'd been in Jerusalem. Christ, it seemed like a lifetime. He felt like he was returning a different person. Through the rain he saw flashing blue lights. A hundred metres further on, parked by the side of the road, he even caught sight of the slanted turret of a Merkura battle tank and its 120mm MG253 gun. When the taxi got stuck behind a military truck heading towards the centre of the city, Luke felt his fingers twitching for his own weapon again. When the taxi finally stopped, Luke was the first to grab his bag and jump out. He found himself on a wide boulevard, indistinguishable from almost every other street they'd driven down since they'd hit the centre. The pavements were fairly crowded, but the road itself was jammed with vehicles. Those restaurants that were open appeared to be doing a good trade. Despite that, he could sense tension all around. Hardly fucking surprising. Troops were camped out on the Israeli plains. West and East were mobilising and when it came to a head—*if* it came to a head—chances were these streets would be the battleground . . .

A chopper flew overhead, causing Luke to shrink instinctively against a shopfront. He told himself that the city was on high alert for reasons unrelated to *his* presence, but that didn't make him feel any less nervous. Looking round, he saw a small tourist sign shaped like a pointing hand. It had Hebrew lettering on it, but underneath it was translated into English: 'TO THE OLD TOWN'. Luke took that direction, but he hadn't walked more than ten

409

metres before he stopped. Up ahead, perhaps thirty metres away, three Israeli soldiers were walking towards him with rifles slung across their fronts. He changed course, ducking into a dingy little side road at ninety degrees and hurrying down its length.

It was quieter here. More sheltered. He passed two old ladies wrapped in black robes and headscarves and deep in conversation as they walked towards him, but nobody else. Luke was shivering with cold from his earlier soaking and his brain felt like it had shut down. He needed to get something hot inside him to raise his body temperature. When he passed a shop with its grille open and a picture of a steaming cup painted on the window, he checked for security cameras inside. Seeing none, he entered.

It was warm in here, and almost empty. That suited Luke just fine. There were four tables, each with foil ashtrays, and a Formica counter behind which stood a young woman of about twenty with dark hair, dark eyes and a good couple of inches of cleavage on show. She smiled and looked him up and down. She didn't seem at all put off by his dishevelled state. Quite the opposite, in fact. She gave Luke an appealing smile, which he didn't return.

'Coffee,' he said. 'Black.'

She inclined her head. 'English?' she asked in a throaty voice.

Luke nodded and continued to look around the room. There was only one other customer—an incredibly ancient man dressed in an old black suit and with a black hat perched on the table in front of him next to his coffee cup. He looked up at Luke with piercing blue eyes. Just behind him, against

410

the left-hand wall, was a low shelf with an old beige computer and a stool at which to sit. Alongside the screen was a Perspex rack of free postcards and tourist leaflets.

'But not on vacation?' the woman said. 'Who would come to Jerusalem on vacation right now . . . ?'

'Can I use that?' Luke interrupted her, pointing at the computer.

She looked a bit offended by his lack of interest. 'Sure. I'll get your coffee.'

Luke sat down at the terminal, flicked through the tourist brochures and pulled out a map of the city. Then he nudged the mouse. Immediately the screen flickered on, already open on the Google.co.il homepage. His fingers hovered over the keyboard for a moment as he thought over the events of the day. He put himself back on the roof in Gaza and closed his eyes as he recalled Stratton's rant. *The troops of the prince who is to come shall destroy the city and the sanctuary* . . .

He typed the words slowly, his cold, dirty fingers feeling too big for the keys, then pressed enter. A bewildering array of results appeared in front of him. He clicked through to a few at random to find some dense religious texts, in English but so impenetrable that they just seemed to dance in front of his eyes. Bullshit.

A mug of coffee suddenly appeared next to the keyboard. Luke only glanced up when he realised the young woman was standing over him.

'You don't look the type,' she said.

He reached out for his coffee and took a gulp. The hot liquid scorched his throat. 'What do you mean?' he grunted. She wore a musky perfume and

411

it smelled good.

'All that millennialist shit,' she said pointing at the page he had open. '*Ben kalba*, we see it all in this city. All the lunatics and the ...'

'What's a millenni ...?' Luke interrupted her. But the young woman had turned her back on him and was sashaying back to the counter. It crossed Luke's mind that she was moving her hips more than she would had he not been looking. A week ago he'd have been like a dog on heat. Not now. For a brief, irrational moment he considered storming up to her, putting one hand round her pretty little throat and asking her what the hell she was talking about.

'Daniel, chapter nine.'

It was the old man who had spoken. His voice was dry and croaky and his lined old face surveyed Luke without expression.

'What?'

The elderly customer glanced at the screen. '"The troops of the prince who is to come shall destroy the city and the sanctuary. Its end shall come with a flood, and to the end there shall be war ..." You're shaking, young man. You need to put some warmer clothes on.'

But Luke went on staring at the screen, and from the mass of text in front of him picked out the very words the old man had just spoken. 'What does it mean?' he asked. 'What's the sanctuary?'

'The Temple, of course,' the old man said quietly. He gave a sad little smile. 'Some people say that it has already *been* destroyed. That the prophecy of Daniel has already been fulfilled and the Western Wall is all that remains of that holy place.'

Luke blinked as Stratton's voice echoed in his head. *When the wall falls, no one will be able to stop the war that is coming . . .*

'Our poor city has been the scene of much fighting over the ages.' The old man raised his coffee cup with trembling, bony hands, the veins blue and pronounced. He drank slowly, thoughtfully, before putting the cup back down. 'Some, of course, think that the destruction is soon to come.' He smiled. '*That* the tour guides don't tell you.'

The old man looked down at his hands, which were clasped on the table. He looked like he'd lost interest in the conversation.

'*Who* thinks that?' Luke pressed. 'Who are you talking about?'

The old man suddenly pulled a white handkerchief from his sleeve and blew his nose noisily before he turned back to Luke. 'Those who believe,' he replied, 'that a sequence of violent events will announce the Second Coming of the Messiah, and that his reign on earth will last for a thousand years.' He paused. 'You look shocked that people might hanker after such things, young man?'

He took another sip from his coffee.

'Violent events . . .' Luke muttered.

'That's what they say.' He waved his hand dismissively at the computer. 'I'm sure your . . . machine knows all about it. I'm told they know about everything.'

But Luke wasn't looking at the computer. Alistair Stratton was a warmonger. Violent events stuck to him like shit to a shovel.

'You know,' the old man continued, almost as

though he was talking to himself, 'the world makes a mistake when it believes the only fundamentalists belong to Islam. Oh, it's true that there are many who would destroy the Western Wall and return the Temple Mount to the sole control of the Arabs. But there are many Christian men and women who live in expectation of Armageddon, and who believe it will be preceded by a great conflict in the biblical lands . . .' He stopped short. 'Forgive me,' he said. 'I'm boring you.'

He picked his hat up from the table, placed it on his head and started to stand.

'Wait,' Luke said.

The old man inclined his head.

'If the Arabs destroyed the Western Wall, what would happen?'

For a moment he didn't answer. Halfway between sitting and standing, he forced his gnarled body upright.

'Destroyed the Western Wall?'

Luke nodded.

'With the countries of the world on a knife's edge and armies circling the Middle East like vultures around carrion?' The old man glanced towards the computer screen where the webpage Luke had been reading was still up. 'Well then, it will be as the Book of Daniel has foretold,' he said. 'To the end there shall be war.' He smiled, then raised his hat a little. 'Good evening to you,' he rasped, 'and happy Hanukkah.' He headed to the exit and didn't look back before he disappeared into the night.

Luke sat there stunned. He was vaguely aware that the woman behind the counter was still looking at him, that her lips were slightly parted and her dark eyes full of meaning.

414

But his thoughts were elsewhere.

The pieces of the jigsaw were falling into place.

Alistair Stratton had already persuaded Maya Bloom to orchestrate one atrocity in Britain. Now it was just a matter of time before she orchestrated a second here in Jerusalem. And with the world on the brink of war, this was the final act that would push it over the precipice. Stratton hadn't got into bed with the Grosvenor Group for money. His aims were altogether more apocalyptic than that. He was insane, of course, but that didn't mean he wasn't dangerous. Quite the opposite. He was manipulating the Palestinians into bringing about their own destruction. And when that happened . . .

Luke jumped to his feet, startling the young woman behind the counter. Recovering herself, she asked, 'You don't want another coffee? Something to eat?'

But Luke had already put a note on the counter and was heading for the door.

'I get off work soon . . .' the young woman called after him. A great crack of thunder echoed across the skies. Luke was already outside and running— sprinting—towards Jerusalem's Old Town.

TWENTY-EIGHT

A pair of eyes stared out of the open window of a dark attic. They were perfectly still as they looked across the ramshackle rooftops. They were unblinking, when a crack of rainless thunder seemed to shake the very bones of the city.

But it did not shake Maya Bloom.

She stared, and she stared. Two hundred metres away, over the last of the roofs, she could just see the top of the Western Wall. And rising above it, bathed in light, was the cupola of the Dome of the Rock. The place from where, according to Islam, the Prophet Muhammad ascended into heaven.

Her lip curled. People could worship their imaginary gods if they wanted to. Maya Bloom had long since given up any belief in the supernatural. Death was death. She'd learned that at a young age when her parents were taken from her by a cowardly Palestinian; she had learned it when her brother, the only human being for whom she had retained a spark of feeling, had been killed by the Arabs in Iraq. She did not know which angered her more: the golden dome, so honoured by the people she hated with every scrap of her being; or the Western Wall, where men offered up prayers to a God who had failed to protect her family.

The thunder cracked again. Maya Bloom continued to stare as the face of Alistair Stratton rose in her mind.

The Book of Daniel. She heard his voice as clearly as if he was in the tiny room with her. *It tells us it is here that the End Times will start. It's quite clear about that, Maya. Quite clear.*

A cold wind gusted in through the open window. She felt it blowing the hair back from her face.

Do you want to be part of history?

A church bell rang in the air. Maya Bloom counted the chimes. Ten. When the last one had faded away, she turned and looked into the tiny, anonymous room—the only place in all Israel where she felt sure she could be safe. On the small single bed, laid out neatly, was a small arsenal.

416

A Knights Armaments M110 sniper rifle. Two handguns. Silencers. Match-grade ammunition in ten-round magazines. A twenty-centimetre knife with a black handle and a white blade.

Thunder echoed across the skies. The city shook. Maya Bloom stared implacably through the window as she waited for Hanukkah to arrive.

*   *   *

23.03 hrs.

If he'd been here with the Regiment, Luke would have had all the assets he needed. Every square centimetre of Jerusalem Old Town would have been covered by detailed mapping. The expertise of the Israeli law-enforcement agencies would have been at his disposal. He'd have had unmarked vehicles, sights, scopes and men at his disposal; he'd have had access to the intelligence feeds of all the major agencies. And enough weaponry to start a small war.

But tonight was very different.

His imagery consisted of the tourist map he'd swiped from the café. It told him that the Western Wall was located in the eastern part of the Old Town. It was part of the Temple Mount compound and no more than fifty metres from the Dung Gate, one of the entrances in the high wall that surrounded the Old Town. He had no vehicle. And far from having men and access to intelligence, every time he saw a police officer or a member of the IDF, he put his head down. He was familiar enough with the way things worked to be sure his image had already been circulated and he couldn't risk being recognised. But if Stratton truly was planning an atrocity at the Western Wall, Luke needed to get eyes on the potential strike area as quickly as possible: to work out *how* the place was most likely to be attacked and to spot any suspicious activity in advance of the hit.

The entrance to the Western Wall compound was buzzing with security. In the fifty metres between the entrance and the perimeter wall of the Old Town he counted eight armed soldiers among the hundred or so members of the public that were milling around even at this late hour. There were two security gates, one for men, one for women. Each gate had a metal detector. Luke knew that a small amount of metal—a watch or a bracelet—probably wouldn't set one of these devices off; the Sig in his Bergen, however, definitely would.

He retreated from the entrance and made his way back into the Old Town, down narrow, winding commercial streets with few pedestrians and even fewer cars. Here he soon stumbled across an alleyway where big metal bins and overflowing bin bags were parked against one wall. He slipped into the alleyway and secreted the Bergen underneath a pile of bin bags. He'd be back within an hour to pick it up, he reckoned. It should be safe for that time.

Luke hurried back to the security gates. There were about fifteen people in the male queue and it moved slowly as each visitor passed through the gates and one or two were patted down by the soldiers on guard. Luke drew some strange looks in only his trousers and a T-shirt when the December night air was cold, but he could live with that. It was if anyone recognised his face that he had to worry. He passed through the metal detector with no problem and less than a minute later he was standing alone at the back of a large plaza which extended some seventy-five metres from his position. At the end of the plaza, lit up in the darkness, was a landmark he knew from the TV: the Western Wall.

The section of the wall he could see was about twenty metres high and fifty metres wide. Ancient. Sturdy. There were maybe fifty people standing close to it and praying—half of them at the male section to the left, many wearing traditional black suits and wide-brimmed hats; the other half at the female section to the right. The two sections were separated by a barrier about a metre high. A further hundred or so people were milling around the plaza. At each end the wall was illuminated by a large spotlight which lent the honey-coloured stones a mystical air. Easy to see how people could be impressed, but Luke wasn't here to have his breath taken away. He was here to stake the place out.

If Stratton was planning an atrocity at the wall, how would he do it? You couldn't attack from the air, because the second an unknown aircraft violated Israeli airspace it would be taken down. A ground attack? He'd seen for himself how high the security was at ground level. Smuggling weapons into the Western Wall plaza through the metal detectors was almost impossible.

As he examined the wall from a distance, he became aware of a group of people approaching from his left. No more than ten, their cameras marking them immediately out as tourists, and one of them—a fat man with a jowly face—wearing a T-shirt under his denim jacket with the words

419

'Cincinnati, Ohio'. Fucking idiots, Luke thought, visiting a place like this at a time like this. One of them—a young man—stood apart from the others. He spoke with a slightly raised voice, in English, but with a strong Israeli accent that immediately reminded him of Maya Bloom.

'The Western Wall is constructed on the site of the original Temple,' he announced, sounding like he'd spoken these words a thousand times before. 'Half of it dates from the end of the Second Temple period and was constructed around 19 BC by Herod the Great. The rest of it was added around the seventh century. It has long been an object of conflict. After the 1948 Arab–Israeli War, it came under Jordanian control. Israelis were banned from the site for nineteen years until the Old City was recaptured in 1967. What you can see from here is the exposed section. It continues behind the buildings to our left, and extends as far as the Muslim Quarter of the city . . .'

The tourist group moved on, leaving Luke to continue his examination of the area. From his vantage point he tried to spot any plainclothes operators. These would be men or women pretending to be visitors, but who stuck around for a suspicious amount of time. He saw no one, but that didn't mean they weren't there—any decent security arrangement would involve some kind of rotation; and the guys—or girls—guarding this place would be pros. He counted six armed IDF soldiers, in their olive-green uniforms, circulating around the plaza itself and even approaching the wall. Clearly the security restrictions didn't extend to their assault rifles and he immediately identified that as a security weak spot. Might an Israeli soldier be involved in an atrocity here? Men could be bought, of course, and a couple of guys with M16s could kill a lot of people. But what had Stratton said? *When the wall falls*... It would take more than an assault rifle to cause the sort of damage he'd implied.

Luke needed a closer look at the wall itself. With his head down, he started walking across the plaza, losing himself in a little crowd of tourists who were doing the same thing. They passed a post, about a metre high, bearing a tourist sign written in Hebrew and English: 'ON THE SABBATH AND HOLY DAYS, SMOKING, PHOTOGRAPHY AND CELLPHONE USE ARE STRICTLY FORBIDDEN.'

A voice. Behind him. 'Excuse me. *Excuse me!*' It was urgent. Luke felt his fist clenching as he turned to look. A thin man with a wispy beard and square spectacles was running towards him, suspicion on his face. 'You, sir. Stop.'

Thirty metres to the exit. If he wanted to get out of here, he needed to do it now.

'You cannot approach the wall bare-headed,' the man said.

'What?'

The guy held out a thin cardboard skullcap. Luke felt his muscles relaxing.

'Right,' he muttered. 'Thanks.' He put on the cap and continued his approach. On his left, he passed a low, sand-coloured building with a series of arches built into the foundations. Most of his attention, however, was on the wall itself.

The lowest seven courses of the wall were made from blocks about a metre wide and half a metre high; above that, they were a quarter the size. The blocks were sturdy, certainly, but also crumbling

421

away in places and with weeds and plants growing out of the mortar here and there. It struck him that a Regiment demolitions expert could bring the wall down in minutes. He observed a couple of tourists squeezing hand-written notes into the cracks. It occurred to him that the cracks in the wall could easily be filled with explosives, but he discarded that idea as soon as it came to him. The wall was surely guarded 24/7—stick anything except a prayer note in it and you'd be flat on your face with an M16 in the back of your head.

Think like the enemy, he told himself. Anticipate their movements.

Prepping for a combat situation, he would learn in advance what he could about the enemy's SOPs. In Iraq they'd been alert to the dangers of roadside bombs. In the Stan, IEDs. He understood the psychology of war. He understood that if a method of combat worked well once, chances were it would work well again. The Micks had never stopped using car bombs or letter bombs just because Special Branch were cute to it. Even the Yanks and the British were addicted to their drones and guided missiles. In battle, you do whatever gets the job done best.

What were Stratton's SOPs? How was he going to strike?

To his left, as he faced the wall, there was a low arch leading into the building adjoining the plaza, about two metres at its highest point, and a single glance told him that the wall itself continued just as the tour guide had said, forming a kind of tunnel. Luke approached it. If the wall was not just the exposed section at the plaza, he needed to examine the rest of it. To put himself in the mindset of a terrorist and work out where the weak points of this target were.

He was in a dimly lit room with a vaulted ceiling. Beyond it the tunnel continued. There were thirteen people in here, all dressed in traditional black garb, sitting on seats. The atmosphere was quiet, prayer-like. One of the men looked over his shoulder and, seeing Luke—casually dressed and dirty—gave a look of disapproval. But then he went back to his praying and Luke passed through the room and along the tunnel.

He moved quickly, but as he went he took in the geography. The tunnel followed the wall, along which there were more men seated and praying. After another hundred metres or so, he arrived in a second, wider room that was more populated than the first one—thirty people, maybe more. Against the wall there was a Perspex plaque with white writing—in Hebrew at the top, and underneath in English: 'OPPOSITE THE FOUNDATION STONE AND THE SITE OF THE HOLY OF HOLIES'. Luke edged through the little crowd, and continued his recce.

As he continued north, the tunnel became less well lit, the walls more roughly hewn. He passed a metal grille on his left, and anterooms off the main tunnel. Further on, the tunnel was held up by a series of wooden joists and columns. There were fewer people here, and he passed what looked like ancient water pits. A sign told him they were cisterns from long ago. Checking to see he was unobserved, he worked a small piece of loose mortar away from the opposite wall and dropped it into the cistern. It took a second or so before he heard the mortar hit the ground. Three or four metres deep, he reckoned. Possible to cache something there? Unlikely—to remove it would risk drawing attention to yourself. He continued down the tunnel. When he had walked about 400 metres in all, the tunnel ended abruptly. Perhaps there had once been an exit, but now it was blocked.

Luke hurried back along the tunnel. Past the cisterns. Past the joists and columns. Past the grille.

He suddenly halted and looked back.

The grille was ten metres behind him. Retracing his steps, he bent down to look at it. Where did this thing lead? Could it be removed? Could you stow anything behind it?

Then something caught his eye.

It was difficult to see in the dim light of the tunnel, but Luke's eyes were sharp. Tied round the lowermost metal bars of the grille were lengths of fishing line. Worming his fingers in through the grate, he pulled at one of the lines. Weight at the end. He pulled the line up, and what he found puzzled him. A clear plastic bag, filled with coins. Tugging on each of the other lines, he found the same thing. What the fuck was this? Some weird ritual, like chucking loose change into a fountain? Or was it something more suspicious?

A few bags of shekels weren't going to bring down the Western Wall. But something nagged at him as he returned to the plaza and checked his watch.

23.30 hrs. Fuck, the clock was ticking.

Think, Luke told himself. Think SOPs. *Think.*

How had Stratton and Maya Bloom struck last?

He remembered the images he'd seen of the train bombings. The pictures of the Palestinian men who'd blown themselves up. He remembered the kid in Gaza, his body strapped with fuck knows

424

what kind of explosive.

The Palestinians used suicide bombs. They were well known for it.

And Stratton? Stratton used the Palestinians.

Luke narrowed his eyes as a scenario formed in his mind. To bring down the Western Wall you had to get close. To get close, you had to remain unobserved. Suicide bombers would do that. And even if one was discovered, there'd be others to back him up. There were no countermeasures—you either spotted the bomber or you didn't. And even if you did, you had to take him out before he knew you had eyes on.

But what about the security? How could you get past security—the metal detectors? Luke ran through the make-up of a suicide vest. Explosives—they'd get through the gates easily enough. It was the rest of it that would be problematic. A detonator—anything that could send a surge of voltage into the explosives. And most vests were packed with shrapnel to cause maximum collateral damage . . .

Shrapnel.

The bags of coins. Small, hard lumps of metal. Get one of those in the skull and you'd know about it. They'd cause just as much carnage as the usual nuts and bolts that got stuck into suicide vests . . .

'Fuck,' Luke breathed. The mist was clearing. What if the bombers had been bringing in the makeshift constituent parts of their equipment in piece by piece?

He was already moving back towards the tunnel when something else caught his eye. Two of the soldiers who had been patrolling the plaza were standing next to each other, almost exactly at the

425

midway point between Luke and the Western Wall. They were conferring and looking very obviously in Luke's direction.

He cursed again as several possibilities shot into his mind. Had the Regiment circulated his image to the Israeli authorities? Or were the military and police simply on high alert? Did Luke just look suspicious, standing there staking the place out? Either way, it wasn't a conversation he wanted to have with anybody. He moved immediately, as fast as he could without running, in the direction of the security gates. His skin prickled as he went, but he resisted the temptation to look over his shoulder as he hurried out of the exit. He retraced his steps to the alleyway where he'd cached his weapon.

If he was right, and a suicide bomb attack was planned, he had to consider everything he knew, everything he'd ever learned, about such things. The bombers would be ordinary people without military training, but they'd be organised by someone who knew what they were doing. Was that where Maya Bloom came in? She'd been involved in the train bombings. She was, or had been, a Mossad agent. Somebody with a background similar to his own. If he was organising the bombers, what would *he* tell them to do?

It was rudimentary that they shouldn't walk any further than necessary in a suicide belt. They'd be nervous. Sweating. Conspicuous. And with Jerusalem in a state of high alert, no one in their right mind would risk them being on the streets for any longer than necessary.

What about the bombers themselves? Would he trust them to go ahead with their suicide mission? He thought back to Gaza, to the kid with

426

the remote detonator. Truth was, even the most idealistic nutter could bottle it at the last minute. If Luke was organising this thing, he'd give the bombers as little information as possible, and only issue their final instructions at the very last minute. He'd make sure they got as close to the target site as possible before leaving them to their own explosive devices . . .

His Sig was where he'd left it. Luke shouldered the Bergen and hurried from the alleyway. Slowly, he was working on a plan.

If the squadron was here with him, he'd have eyes on every gate in the city and the Western Wall plaza would be surrounded by snipers. But there was no squadron. No backup. Just Luke. And if he let anybody know where he was, there'd be a team on its way to lift him within minutes. All he could do was watch the gate nearest to the Western Wall.

The tourist map of the Old Town was a photograph in his mind. He headed south between the city's Jewish and Armenian Quarters. When the road forked, he headed south-west and five minutes later he found himself approaching the Zion Gate. It was small—barely the width of a car—and as Luke passed through it he looked back up at the city walls. The area around the stone entrance was pockmarked with bullet holes—a reminder of Jerusalem's violent past.

Luke kept his head down as he skirted east round the city walls. In just a couple of minutes he arrived at another gate. His mental map told him that this was the Dung Gate, the closest access point to the wall. It formed a lower entrance than the Zion Gate—about three metres—but at five metres was a little wider. To its left was an olive

427

tree; to its right, three palms. There were no bullet marks here. But more people were walking in and out. Cars. Pedestrians. It was late, but still busy.

He stood for a moment and stared at the gate. If he was right, any bomber heading for the Western Wall would be likely to pass through here.

If he was right.

From somewhere nearby, the smell of cooking food reached his nose. A couple of old men passed him, speaking loudly and clearly arguing. A kid went by with a pile of postcards that concertinaed out into a long strip.

Just ordinary life and it made him pause. He remembered the way his Regiment colleagues had looked at him back at the base. Like he'd lost it. Luke closed his eyes for a moment. He couldn't be imagining all this, could he? He couldn't be mad? Was he on the wrong track? About Stratton? About the bombers?

But then he remembered Chet and Suze and the troops mobilising around the Middle East. He remembered the ruthlessness of Maya Bloom and the madness in Stratton's eyes.

A church bell rang somewhere in the distance. He counted the chimes. They were sombre. Stately. Twelve of them.

Midnight.

Hanukkah had arrived. In eleven hours, he would know.

In the meantime, he couldn't loiter here. With the military presence so high he'd soon be observed. But he needed to set up surveillance on the Dung Gate, and quickly.

And that meant finding a workable OP.

TWENTY-NINE

10 December.

07.00 hrs.

On the eastern outskirts of Tel Aviv, in a well-to-do suburb where the roads were gated and the houses large, the previous evening's storm was just an unpleasant memory. The sky was clear and crisp, and a white bus was waiting outside the Scheiber Elementary School for Girls, its engine running. The front door of the bus was open and a pretty young woman with dark, curly hair and almond eyes stood just next to it with a clipboard in her hand. On the pavement in front of her was a well-behaved line of little ladies, all aged either seven or eight. They wore home clothes, and little backpacks over their shoulders which contained lunches that would no doubt be eaten before they'd gone a few kilometres.

Today was a holiday, of course. The first day of the Festival of Lights. The teachers were glad to sacrifice one of their precious holiday days to give the girls the chance to travel to Jerusalem, to see the celebrations in that holy place for themselves. A visit to the Western Wall and then back to their families, to light the first of the eight candles of Hanukkah, eat a special meal and sing festive songs. No wonder they'd all looked excited as they said goodbye to their mums before joining their schoolmates in the queue and filing into the bus. There were thirty-five girls in all, with four teachers to look after them. Miss Leibovitz ticked each child's name on her clipboard as they boarded the bus and then, when she was sure everybody was there, she climbed up into the long vehicle herself.

The driver was a man in his forties with a small paunch and an open-necked shirt. He pressed a button and the door closed.

'All ready?' he asked above the children's babble.

'All ready,' the teacher replied with a smile. And as she strapped herself into her seat at the front— her three female colleagues having already installed themselves among the party—the bus moved off.

'How long till we get there, Miss Leibovitz?' a voice asked from behind her.

She looked round to see the face of one of her favourites—an earnest little girl called Natasha, who wore red ribbons in her beautifully plaited pigtails.

'Two hours, Natasha darling. Just two hours. We'll be there before you know it.'

Natasha smiled, then sat back down in her seat and gazed out of the window just as they passed a green sign with a white arrow and a single word in Hebrew.

'ירושלים', it read.

Jerusalem.

*　　　*　　　*

Jerusalem.

A city divided. A Jewish Quarter. A Christian Quarter. An Islamic Quarter. An Armenian Quarter. A place for everyone and no one.

And then there was East Jerusalem. Occupied by the Arabs and governed by the Palestinian Authority. Adjoining the Old Town and the West Bank, a symbol of the city's warlike past and

430

fractured present.

It was in East Jerusalem that four people found themselves now, in the basement of a poor and unassuming house. Three men, one woman. The men were naked apart from their underpants; the woman had covered herself with a long white T-shirt that did little to hide the swelling of her five-month-pregnant belly. Their semi-nakedness didn't embarrass them. They had more important things to think of.

A single, bare bulb hung from a ceiling which bowed under the weight of the building above; and beneath the bulb, a table. They stood in silence, staring at the table's contents.

There was a kitchen rolling pin, a roll of heavy-duty electrical tape and next to it a wooden box, its lid beside it. Inside the box were tightly packed blocks of what looked like brown modelling clay.

One of the men stepped forward. He was just seventeen. But he had been waiting for this moment for as long as he could remember. Certainly since he was a boy, playing war games with decommissioned rifles on the streets of Gaza City. He gingerly removed a block—ten centimetres by ten centimetres by five centimetres—from the box and laid it on the table. He was breathing heavily as he picked up the rolling pin and he closed his eyes when he pushed it down on to the block of C4 plastic explosive. He didn't fear an explosion— none of them did—but they wanted it to occur at the right place and the right time.

As the young man continued to roll out the explosive, it became more malleable, until eventually he had a sheet just a couple of millimetres thick and the size of a piece of A4 paper. He carefully picked it up, then turned and nodded to one of his male companions before pressing the C4 against his torso. His companion took the tape, removed a long piece and stuck the explosive to the young man's skin, repeating this another three times for each edge of the sheet.

Ten minutes later the young man had a second sheet taped to his back, with the two sheets joined by a flat strip of the explosive, and a second strip running down the inside of his right arm. He moved to the other end of the room, where some clothes were hanging. First he put on a white cotton vest which had a pouch sewn into the front. After that, a white shirt, then black trousers, black jacket, a wide-brimmed black hat and black slip-on shoes. His companion then picked up a black electrical wire and pipe detector of the kind that could be bought in any hardware store. He switched it on and carefully brushed it up and down the young man's body to check nothing caused it to beep.

Nothing did.

He put the detector down on the table, nodded at his friend and started to frisk him like an airport security guard. He paid special attention to the torso, back and right arm, but came away clearly satisfied that the sheets of explosive were contoured so closely to the young man's body as to be undetectable.

The young man stepped back. He knew he was wearing enough plastic explosive to take many people with him. Without a detonator to deliver a charge, however, the C4 was inert and useless. There were no detonators in the room and he didn't know how they'd be supplied. Or where. Or

432

when. He'd find out soon enough, though. They all would. In the meantime, the other two men and the pregnant woman needed to undergo the same process. They did so in solemn silence, in the full and certain knowledge that soon they would be four walking weapons. Unrecognisable. Untraceable.

And, *inshallah*, unstoppable.

*   *   *

08.00 hrs.

Luke's OP was far from perfect, but it was his only real option.

He'd been here since just after midnight, staking out the Dung Gate from the top of a three-storey concrete building on the other side of the perimeter road and approximately 100 metres from the gate itself. The building was a detached office block. On approaching it he'd peered into the main entrance—a pair of wide, smoked-glass doors that looked into a bland reception area with a shiny tiled floor and pot plants. A security guy sat at a desk in front of a bank of CCTVs, but he was listening to an iPod and his nose was in a book. Luke hadn't entered the building, but skirted round the back to where there was a parking lot and a line of empty metal bins. More doors, too, all locked. But Luke saw that a metal ladder was fixed to the back of the building and ran all the way up to the roof. It echoed as he climbed up it.

The rooftop, was about twenty metres square, and it suited his purposes well enough. The perimeter of the roof was surrounded by walls a couple of metres high. The roof itself, sealed with pitch, was covered with bird shit, and in the centre there was a glass skylight measuring about two metres each way. On the western side of the roof was a small corrugated-iron hut, similar in size to the one he'd taken cover behind in Gaza City. A quick examination told him that it contained the guts of the building's power supply.

He'd taken up position on the northern edge of the roof. His first move was to wolf down the two MREs in his stolen Bergen—kosher meals of beef and pasta that tasted like shit but at least replaced some calories. The energy and warmth were sapping from his body and he needed all the help he could get to stay alert.

Once he'd eaten he removed the scope and the Sig from his bag and staked out the view in front of him, lying on his front with the handgun by his side. From here he could see right across the rooftops of the Old Town and, beyond, the lights of the rest of Jerusalem. His angle of view allowed him to see over the top of the perimeter wall and further to the entrance gates of the Western Wall plaza; and of course the golden cupola of the Dome of the Rock, glowing in the darkness.

To the left of the gate itself he could see the olive tree; to the right, the three palms and a souvenir stall that had closed down for the night. Even though it was late, there were still people walking in and out of the gate and the perimeter road was reasonably busy.

Also busy was the airspace. He counted four helicopters hovering over Jerusalem with searchlights angled down at the ground. Training his scope on one of them, he could make out the outline of a Minigun. If ever there was a city on high alert, this was it. He knew that if any of these choppers flew over his position and spotted him, he'd be fucked. But they didn't come closer than about 200 metres.

It grew light just after 06.00 hrs. By 07.00 the traffic on the perimeter road was heavy—civilian vehicles, police cars, the occasional tourist bus—and there were more pedestrians. Luke trained his scope on individual faces, committing every minute detail of the scene below to memory. He clocked a military Jeep driving past the gate. Exactly eighteen minutes later it passed again. And eighteen minutes after that. It was clearly doing a circuit and Luke would have bet his bollocks it wasn't the only one. With the troop mobilisation occurring in the north-western part of Israel and the eyes of the world on this troubled city, Luke didn't doubt that every soldier and every policeman was on standby.

As was Luke. He didn't take his eyes off the area between himself and the Old Town. And even though he didn't know exactly what he was looking for, he knew he had to trust his judgement.

Trust his surveillance skills.

Trust that he'd made the right call, and that whatever was about to happen, he'd know it when he saw it.

*   *   *

08.59 hrs.

The queue to pass through security into the Western Wall plaza had been growing steadily since first light. Reuben Sharon, a nineteen-year-old IDF recruit, had been here since 06.00 hrs and if he looked pissed off, it was because he was. Not

435

only was he working on Hanukkah, but he had the shittiest job imaginable: watching the crowds flock through security into the plaza for a full eight-hour shift. Like *this* was what he joined the army to do . . .

So far, most of the visitors had been old-timer Hassidim. Fucking weirdos as far as he was concerned, with their strange clothes and their constant worshipping and lamenting. Some of these guys turned up at the Western Wall twice a day to mutter at the stones. Reuben didn't get it. Any free time *he* had was spent chasing tail in the bars of downtown Jerusalem. Then again, he wondered how much pussy worth having was one of these *misugena* likely to get, dressed like that?

As that thought went through his mind, there was a sudden beeping of the metal detector. The young Hassid stopped and his eyes flickered towards Reuben's M16 as the soldier immediately stepped in his way. He jerked a finger to indicate that the visitor should step to one side.

'Arms outstretched,' he ordered. He didn't really feel much pressure to be polite.

The visitor did as he was told. He looked straight ahead as Reuben brushed a hand-held detector up and down his arms, legs, torso and back. And he stood as still as the stones that made up the Western Wall as the soldier put down the detector and started frisking him with his hands. Fuck, Reuben thought as he padded down the guy's body. He was bonier than a Gazan orphan. Hung like a horse, though, he realised as his hands strayed too far up the inside trouser leg. Shame he wasn't likely to get a shag.

'All right,' he said once he was satisfied the

436

visitor was clear. 'On you go.'

It was another five minutes before the alarm went off again. The guy who triggered it couldn't have been more different to the last. He was also young, younger maybe than Reuben. His features were Arabic, but unlike most of the Muslims normally to be seen around the Temple Mount, this guy didn't look the type to hang around the mosque. His hair was cut short and he had a good couple of days' worth of stubble. He wore baggy jeans and a hooded top with earphones resting round his neck. As he chewed on a piece of gum, he looked arrogantly at Reuben, who was now barring his way.

Reuben didn't let his feelings show, but they were strong. The Western Wall plaza was open to anyone, regardless of their religion—Jewish, Christian, Muslim. And though Reuben was hardly devout, he certainly had his opinions.

He pointed at the long table where he kept the detector.

'Hands on the table,' he instructed.

The youngster gave him a lazy look filled with contempt. For a few seconds he didn't do anything, but then he shrugged, moved over to the table and bent over slightly so that his hands were flat down on it.

'Legs apart,' Reuben told him.

Another pause. Then, making an obvious meal of it, the kid moved each leg in turn a few inches outwards.

Reuben was meticulous with the detector, scanning every square centimetre of the kid's body. It didn't take long for the device to start beeping.

'What have you got in your pocket?' he

demanded.

Very slowly, the kid stood up straight and turned round. He didn't take his eyes off Reuben and as he slowly put his fist underneath his hooded jumper, the soldier moved his own hands to his assault rifle, ready to use it.

'What's going on?' the next person in the queue called. 'There's people waiting here . . .'

Reuben ignored the complaint and watched carefully as the kid removed his hand. He didn't quite know what he expected to see; in the event, the object was a relief. A mobile phone, connected to the kid's earphones.

'Give it here,' Reuben said. He was being awkward and the kid knew it; he rolled his eyes as he pulled out the jack and handed over the phone.

Reuben made a great show of examining the device. It looked brand new, with no scuffs on the shiny black back or the screen. There was, however, something that caught Reuben's sharp eye. Along the left-hand edge of the phone, there was a tiny indentation, as if the device had been forced open with a small screwdriver or tampered with in some other way.

Reuben looked more carefully at the phone, then back at the kid, whose arrogant expression hadn't changed.

'Get a move on!' A few other muttered voices echoed the next visitor's impatience.

With a sigh, Reuben handed the phone back. 'No mobile phone usage on feast days,' he grunted before turning back to the queue and waving the next visitor through. He did see, from the corner of his eye, the kid's sarcastic little nod, but he chose not to respond. It was too early for arguments, the queue was increasing in size, and he had a long day ahead.

* * *

Miss Leibovitz was flustered.

The journey from Tel Aviv to Jerusalem was taking much longer than they had expected. One of the girls in the back of the bus had puked, which had delayed them for half an hour. And then, on the main road between the two cities, they had hit a temporary roadblock. Two armed soldiers had entered the bus and walked up and down the aisle, their weapons on display. It was not the first time any of these children had seen men with guns, of course. But really, the teacher wondered to herself, was it necessary for them to perform this ridiculous charade? It was only a busload of kids on a day out. She had followed them up the aisle, saying so. The soldiers had been stern and silent. They were going to do their job, no matter what.

Already it was ten o'clock and they were only just approaching the outskirts of Jerusalem. Miss Leibovitz leaned forwards in her seat and asked the driver, 'How much longer now, do you think?'

The driver was a lot less jolly now than when they'd set off. 'Depends if any of your girls are going to be sick in the back of my bus again.'

'I'm sure they'll be fine,' Miss Leibovitz replied quietly.

The driver said nothing more. He just kept his eye on the road as they made their way into Jerusalem.

* * *

10.26 hrs.

Luke's muscles ached from his stationary position. He continued to scan the area with his scope. The souvenir stall by the palm trees had opened and there was a line of six people. What was their body language? Were they looking around, checking if they were being followed? Did they look like they *should* be there? He asked himself these questions about everyone he scoped out. Standard surveillance techniques. Was anyone walking with a sense of purpose? Was anyone doing anything out of the ordinary?

The answer was no.

The pedestrians all looked up as one of the choppers circling above the city suddenly appeared, hovering menacingly before heading north again. The military Jeep passed once more. A tourist bus pulled up on the far side of the main road along the Old Town's perimeter wall.

And Luke heard a noise.

It was behind him and he tensed up. He quickly grabbed his Sig, rolled on to his back and pushed himself to his feet as the noise continued: an echoing, metallic sound that he now recognised from when he'd climbed up the ladder leading to the rooftop. Luke sprinted to the cover of the electricity shed. As he did so, some gulls that had settled on the walls surrounding the rooftop flew away in fright. His back was pressed hard against the concrete wall of the shed, his Sig unlocked and ready, when the rattling of the ladder stopped and he could hear footsteps going across the roof.

Luke remained perfectly still.

He listened carefully.

There was a series of clunking metallic sounds. Four of them, about ten seconds apart. Then silence. The gulls settled once more on the wall.

Slowly, silently, Luke peered round the edge of the shed.

The new arrival was lying in exactly the same position Luke had adopted, looking through a scope. But unlike Luke's, this scope was attached to the top of a sniper rifle. The rifle was pressed into the top of the shooter's shoulder, and the shooter's finger rested gently on the trigger.

But the focus of Luke's attention wasn't the gun. It was the person handling it. Dressed in black. Dark hair.

Female.

He couldn't make out her face very clearly, but he didn't need to. Luke knew exactly who he was looking at.

She was armed to the fucking teeth and clearly preparing to kill.

THIRTY

Luke felt a wild surge of relief. Stratton's right hand was here, just ten metres from his position. What was she doing with her sniper rifle at the ready? Preparing to take out a dignitary? Maybe the Israeli Prime Minister was to come to the wall for the first day of the Hanukkah celebrations? Or maybe she was there to cause a diversion while the day's real business got underway? But Maya Bloom wasn't going to kill anyone else today. He fucking had her.

He held his breath and kept the Sig pointing in

441

her direction, one finger lightly on the trigger. Five metres. He fought the temptation to plug her there and then. This was the bitch who'd killed Chet. And his boy.

But he also wanted her to talk.

He was no more than three metres from her position when it all started to go to shit. It was the fault of the fucking gulls. They'd remained undisturbed as he silently approached, but suddenly his movement disturbed them and they flew off the wall together, squawking as they went. Maya Bloom reacted instantly. She spun round on to her back and, in the same movement, pulled a small, suppressed snubnose from a shoulder holster and raised it towards Luke's body.

If he'd acted a nanosecond slower, he'd have been fucked. As it was, he just had time to lurch forward and stamp his left foot on the woman's wrist as she discharged the weapon. The round flew harmlessly to the other side of the roof, while Luke violently ground her wrist against the hard pitch. Full of the urge to hurt her, he allowed his body to fall with its full weight so that his right knee dug with fierce momentum against her chest. He felt the softness of her breasts beneath his shin; more than that he felt her ribcage sink a good couple of inches.

Maya Bloom started to cough and gasp, the air clearly knocked from her lungs. Luke didn't let up. He nudged the ribcage down again to stop her breathing, then smashed the barrel of his handgun hard against her right cheek. Once. Twice. Three times. He felt something crack, and a spray of blood and mucus spattered from her nose.

Only then did he speak.

442

'OK, honey,' he said. 'This is what's going to happen. You're going to tell me exactly what that cunt Stratton's got planned. You've got ten seconds. Fuck me about and the first round will go in your bladder. I'll only finish you off when you beg me.'

The woman's breathing was strained and noisy. She still managed to give him a look of absolute hatred. Luke shunted his weight on to her ribcage again. Maya strained and spluttered once more as he held the gun directly to her forehead.

'Five seconds.'

'*I don't know.*' Her voice was barely there.

'Not good enough, honey.' He hit the weapon against the same side of her face again.

Maya Bloom's sudden movement came as a total surprise. Luke felt a deadening thump in the small of his back as she raised her right knee and dug it viciously into his spine. Now it was his turn to have the wind knocked from him. With unexpected strength, and in the same movement, she sat up and hurled him away. Luke scuttled hard on to his back two metres from where she was now sitting. He felt the flesh on his back scraping, but more worryingly he saw her retrieve the snubnose from the ground where it had fallen from her hand.

Luke made to discharge the Sig almost on autopilot. Nothing. He hurled the handgun in her direction and it hit her wrist just as she fired the snubnose. There was a dull thud, but the round flew harmlessly a couple of feet to Luke's left. He dived towards her, knocking her head back down on to the ground and wrestling the gun from her fist. Jumping back, he aimed the suppressed weapon at its owner.

'Two seconds,' he said.

Maya Bloom was a mess. Her nose gushed blood and the side of her face was bruised and swollen. Neither injury looked like it bothered her a bit. Her eyes flashed.

'*What's he planning?*' Luke pressed as he pushed himself back to his feet.

'You stupid squaddie, you've got it all wrong...'

'Listen to me, you bitch. You think I'm not going to kill you? I *want* to kill you. Does the name Chet Freeman mean anything?'

Her eyes narrowed.

'Friend of mine,' Luke said.

'You're going to fuck everything up...' She painfully, defiantly started to stand.

He lunged forward and, with brutal force, brought his knee up into her stomach. She doubled over and Luke slammed his gun down on the back of her head with all the strength he had.

The woman collapsed. A limp, silent heap on the floor.

Luke stood there for a moment, sweat pouring from his body, breathing heavily. A number of gulls landed back on the perimeter walls.

Bending down, he put two fingers to her jugular. A faint pulse. He knew how hard he'd knocked her. She wasn't waking up any time soon.

Time check: 10.36 hrs. Twenty-four minutes to go. No time to get information out of her. Too dangerous to risk her waking up and becoming active again. He looked her up and down. He bent down and started to remove the laces from her boots. Rolling her on to her front, he yanked her arms behind her back and tied her wrists together, binding one of the laces several times round and finishing it off with a sturdy sledge knot—impossible to untie. With the other lace he bound her legs together. Tied up like that, the only way she was getting off the roof was by jumping.

With Maya Bloom immobilised, Luke turned his attention to her weaponry. The sniper rifle was still lying in its position. To its right was a black rucksack. Luke emptied the contents on to the roof. There were rounds for the snubnose and the sniper rifle; a set of binoculars; and a knife. Its handle was black, its blade white. Luke picked it up. It was light.

Ceramic. Which meant no metal.

He looked over his shoulder at the woman as she lay there out cold. Why would she have a ceramic knife unless she intended to pass through metal detectors with it? Luke felt a brief, grudging measure of professional respect. She knew her trade.

Suddenly he became aware of something from the corner of his eye. He looked over the edge of the rooftop, back towards the Dung Gate. A white van had pulled up on the side of the road nearest the building. Even from this distance Luke could tell it wasn't a tourist bus. Nor did it have the yellow and white paintwork of a shared taxi. He got down on all fours and took Maya Bloom's earlier position at the sniper rifle, closing his left eye and examining the scene through the scope with his right.

The scope was powerful, with fine, calibrated cross hairs. Luke moved the sights so they were focused on the palm trees by the gate. He was looking for movement of the leaves, anything that would tell him which direction the wind was blowing. The rifle might not have been zeroed in for him, but he could increase the accuracy of his shots, if it came to that, by taking account of the conditions.

No movement. The wind was still. He redirected the rifle to the white van.

His heart was thumping. What if he *did* see suspicious individuals? He had no way of making a positive ID. No way of knowing whether he was shooting terrorists or innocents.

A minute passed.

Two.

No movement from the white van. That in itself was suspicious.

A second vehicle approached. A bus. It passed behind the white van before parking up immediately adjacent to it. Luke trained his scope on the side of this second vehicle. He saw Hebrew lettering along the side, and then, underneath, in English, 'SCHEIBER ELEMENTARY SCHOOL'.

'Shit,' he muttered.

There was another thirty-second pause before anything happened.

The side door of the van slid open. Luke concentrated on the interior of the vehicle. He could see movement, but there was insufficient light in there for it to be distinct. On the periphery of his vision, he could see the front passenger door of the school bus opening and was aware of a figure stepping out.

Back to the van. Two men climbed out. They were wearing traditional Hassidic garments and, once they had emerged, they stepped back from the vehicle to allow two more figures to exit. One of these was a man. He was dressed like the other two; the second figure, however, was female. She wore a black headscarf and rather dowdy shawl. But the most noticeable thing about her was her swollen belly. She looked heavily pregnant and waddled awkwardly.

As soon as she was clear of the van, a shadowy figure closed the side door from the inside. The van pulled out into the road and drove away.

Every instinct Luke had told him that these were his people. Every ounce of experience screamed this at him. They'd arrived when Maya Bloom was keeping stag and minutes before the atrocity was planned to kick off. If she was there to cause a diversion, she needed to know they'd arrived. They'd stayed in the vehicle for longer than he'd have expected. Were they receiving a final briefing?

Luke aimed the cross hairs at the head of one of the three men. His finger twitched on the trigger. He didn't have any more time to delay. The decision had to be made.

Now.

He had to go with his gut . . .

'*Fuck . . .*'

His line of sight was blocked. Four little girls had appeared, all plaits and ponytails, holding hands in pairs and walking across the scope's field of view. Behind them was a tall woman with dark, curly hair, and then more kids. The woman turned and appeared to announce something to the girls and they congregated in a group in the precise vicinity of Luke's four targets. Ten seconds later, as one, they all started to cross the road.

He tried to pick out the targets, but they were just part of a crowd now. A crowd that was heading through the Dung Gate and into the Old Town.

Towards the wall.

447

He jumped to his feet. Maya Bloom was still lying motionless. He had to leave her there. But first he clicked the mag release catch between the magazine and the trigger guard and removed the mag from the sniper rifle. The remaining hardware—including her snubnose and his Sig—he stashed in the Bergen. The ceramic knife he kept in his hand. Without hesitating for another second, he ran across the roof, past the skylight and back down the ladder, gripping the knife between his teeth.

At the base of the building, he dumped the rucksack in one of the bins. He took a moment to collect his thoughts. To gather his breath. To steady his nerve.

And then he ran towards the Dung Gate.

*　　　*　　　*

Alistair Stratton's study at Albany Manor was dark.

He had closed the curtains and locked the door. The only source of light was the television against the wall, set to BBC News 24. The sound was down low, but the image showed an aerial view of an American warship ploughing through the waves. The text banner along the bottom of the screen rolled continuously: 'AMERICAN TROOPS CONTINUE TO MOBILISE IN THE MIDDLE EAST . . . PRESIDENT STATES HE WILL STAND "SHOULDER TO SHOULDER WITH OUR ISRAELI ALLIES IN THE FIGHT AGAINST TERROR" . . . MIDDLE EAST PEACE ENVOY ALISTAIR STRATTON'S NEGOTIATIONS WITH HAMAS ADMINISTRATION "INCONCLUSIVE" . . . UNCONFIRMED REPORTS OF ANTI-WESTERN RIOTS IN THE GAZAN CAPITAL . . .'

Stratton sat perfectly still in an armchair. His

448

clothes were still torn and dirty. His face was still bruised and his broken nose had started to bleed again. He ignored the moistness that dripped from his right nostril, over his lips and on to his chin. He hadn't showered, changed or received medical attention since Gaza.

He didn't care.

To his right was an occasional table with a powered-up laptop on it. He had directed the browser to a live webcam image of the Western Wall. It was grainy and juddering, refreshing only every few seconds, but it was sufficient for him to see the exposed section and the crowds around it. Sufficient for him to witness his work, even though he was many miles away.

The picture on the TV changed, to show footage of the current Prime Minister shaking hands with his Israeli counterpart in a conference room in Tel Aviv. The caption read: 'IRAN STATES IT WILL SEE WESTERN AGGRESSION TOWARDS ANY ISLAMIC COUNTRY AS "AN ACT OF WAR" . . . UN OBSERVERS REPORT "SUBSTANTIAL ACTIVITY" ON THE LIBYA–EGYPT BORDER . . .'

Stratton glanced at the time in the top-left corner of the screen. 08.37. Which meant 10.37 in Jerusalem.

Twenty-three minutes to go.

He remained seated. Still. His pale face was bathed in the light of the television and the laptop. His eyes were darting between the two and his lips were moving constantly. But they made no sound.

*　　　*　　　*

Miss Leibovitz felt like she needed eyes in the back

449

of her head. The entrance to the Western Wall plaza was crowded and although there were three other teachers as well as her to look after the girls, it was difficult to keep tabs on them. They were swarming in a rather disorganised way around the security gates, chattering happily, clearly excited and totally oblivious to the stern-faced troops on the other side of the body scanners.

'Girls . . . *girls!*' Even though her voice was raised, it had little effect on her charges. But then she saw something that made her raise her voice even louder. 'Clara . . . excuse me, Clara! *What* do you think you're doing?'

If there was one thing Miss Leibovitz couldn't stand, it was inconsiderate behaviour from her girls. She was looking at such behaviour right now. Little Clara, normally such a well-behaved thing, was so excited that she had barged right in front of a pregnant lady who was just approaching the security gates.

'Clara, *please* be more considerate to the people around you,' the teacher snapped. The child hung her head, shamefaced. And the pregnant woman stopped for a moment. She was wearing a headscarf and a shawl round her shoulders and she looked rather taken aback.

Her eyes flickered towards the armed guards on the other side of the gate.

She looked at Miss Leibovitz, and at Clara.

And then she too cast her eyes to the floor and walked through the body scanner. It made no sound and the guards didn't give her a second look.

'Now then, girls,' Miss Leibovitz called. 'Form an orderly queue, please. I want you to be a good example of your school, and I *really* don't want to have to speak sharply to anybody else, today of all days . . .'

*   *   *

The plaza was filling up.

There was a buzz about the place, a sense of celebration. The Israeli flag flew from a pole at the back of the square. Little groups of friends and family had gathered here and already the crowd of worshippers by the wall itself was three people deep—the men segregated to the left, the women to the right. A military aircraft flew overhead; seconds later an enormous bang resounded across the skies as it broke the speed barrier. Most of those assembled looked up; but the sight and noise of the aircraft did nothing to spoil the atmosphere. It was Hanukkah, after all.

The defiant party spirit extended to every corner of the plaza and even a little way along the Western Wall tunnel. The further north you went along the tunnel, however, the less populated it became. About 200 metres down and on the left was a little anteroom. This was occupied by a small group of people, huddled by the doorway so that they could see if anybody approached.

They were eight in number. Three young men in traditional dress, one woman in a shawl and headscarf, her belly swollen. These four oozed anxiety. The men were sweating; the woman's hands were trembling. One of the four remaining young men by their side had stubble, a black and white skullcap, baggy jeans, earphones round his neck and a mobile in his hand; and three others were similarly dressed, brandishing phones and

451

appearing a lot cooler than their companions.

The stubble-faced man looked around. Then, from the large pockets of his hooded top, he brought out a clear freezer bag, sealed at the top and with a length of fishing line attached to it. The bag was filled with one-, two- and five-shekel coins. Some people used the word shrapnel to describe loose change like this.

They didn't know how accurate they were.

There were eleven more such bags in his top. He divided the whole lot between the three men and one woman—four bags each. The men slipped the bags between the buttons of their shirts and into the pouches they were wearing beneath. For the woman it was different. Her undergarments were not so easy to access, so she merely placed the coins into her shoulder bag. It didn't matter that they were not close to the explosives. She had more taped to her belly than the others. The coins would easily do their work on the crowd, while the plastic explosive took care of her, her unborn child and of course the wall.

When the improvised shrapnel had been dealt with, the four young men removed their synchronised watches and handed them over to the others.

'The detonators?' the woman asked in Arabic when the watches were all fastened.

The man with the stubble nodded and unplugged his phone. He handed it to the woman, then detached the lead from the earphones, unthreaded it from under his top and handed it over. The woman plugged the lead back into the phone and pulled the earbuds from the other end of the lead to reveal two wire probes. These she inserted into a

452

section of the plastic explosive that was just peeping from below her right sleeve. As she did this, the remaining phones were handed over to the three men—each device with a lead ending in two probes that they pushed into their C4 body casings.

The other four men stood back warily. 'You don't need to do anything,' said the guy with the stubble. 'We'll call the numbers at eleven.'

The bombers looked at each other, then back at their point men, who were edging away now.

'*Allahu Akbar*,' the pregnant woman muttered.

The stubble-face man replied in kind, but he did not sound enthusiastic. Ten seconds later he was out of sight of the bombers and so were his companions.

The four of them were on their own now. The pregnant woman nervously checked her watch. 10.40 exactly.

Twenty minutes to go.

Twenty minutes to paradise.

Twenty minutes until they changed the world forever.

The bombers whispered a quiet prayer and, after one last, long look at each other, left the anteroom, split up and walked slowly, unassumingly to their positions.

*   *   *

Luke sprinted across the main road, causing the traffic to brake and swerve as he burned towards the Dung Gate. He passed an armed IDF man at the entrance to the gate. As he ran past, the guy shouted something at him in Hebrew. Luke didn't stop. He could see the security gates to the Western

Wall plaza fifty metres ahead. He crossed that distance in seconds but was brought to a halt by a line of men and a line of women, queuing to go in.

Somewhere nearby a bell tolled. Three strikes. 10.45 hrs. Luke was still brandishing the ceramic knife, the black handle in his right hand, the white blade pressed up against the inside of his arm. Looking behind him, he saw the IDF man making chase. He cursed under his breath and quickly slipped the blade into his trousers, covering the handle of the knife with his T-shirt.

The soldier was covering the ground quickly. Thirty metres between him and Luke. Closing.

Luke sidestepped, then barged along the length of the queue to the front. A father and his young son were the next to go through the body scanner, but Luke pushed in front of them. He heard shouts from behind, harsh instructions in Hebrew, and it didn't take much intuition to realise it was his pursuer. As he stepped through the security gate, he almost winced, expecting the alarm to go off; but it didn't, and a few seconds later he was running down towards the plaza.

He stopped at its edge, his heart sinking. The square was five times as crowded as it had been the night before. Scanning the crowd, he estimated that there had to be a couple of hundred Hassidim here, all dressed in the same way as the bombers; and a similar number of women were crowding round the female section of the wall.

He froze with indecision. Try to find his targets here? It was like looking for a needle in a fucking haystack.

It was noisy. The noise of a crowd. But suddenly, from somewhere near the wall, came the ancient,

454

wavering, piercing sound of a horn being blown. Luke looked in the direction of the sound and could just make out the end of a long, gnarled animal's horn, held up to the lips of an old man with a white beard. The sound continued for a good ten seconds before it was accompanied by another noise.

Shouting. Behind him. Luke looked over his shoulder. The IDF guy was there—only now he had three others with him and they'd spotted him.

He looked into the crowd. Could he lose himself among them in time? He had to. Luke burst forwards and seconds later he was engulfed by people. They were pushing, shoving—jostling to get towards the wall. For a couple of seconds Luke felt himself being taken along with the tide.

And then there was a tap on his shoulder. He spun round. One of the soldiers was there, glaring at him and talking quickly in Hebrew. Luke felt his knuckles clenching as he looked left and right, trying to decide on an escape plan. But then he realised the soldier had switched to English.

'This,' he snapped. 'You dropped it.' He was holding something up in his hand—a black wallet.

Luke shook his head. 'Not mine,' he said in a level voice.

A pause. The soldier looked rather offended that he'd chased after Luke for no reason. He sighed heavily before forcing his way back out of the crowd, barking orders as he went.

Luke checked his watch. 10.48. Sweat poured from his body as he turned and used his bulk to force his way towards the wall.

* * *

On a nearby rooftop, Maya Bloom's eyes shot open.

The first thing she felt was pain. A stinging, burning pain across her face and a dull ache in her abdomen. She could deal with that.

The second thing she felt was anger. That she couldn't deal with. Not one bit.

She sat up suddenly. A wave of giddiness crashed over her. It took her two seconds to realise she was tied and another two to realise she was alone.

A sound drifted through the air. A horn. The shofar, which she had heard ever since she was a young girl. And it was coming from the Western Wall. It meant the people had congregated.

She looked around.

Her assailant had removed her bag. That meant she had no weapons and no blade. She closed her eyes. Breathed deeply.

And then she looked around again.

Her eyes fell upon the skylight and immediately she had a strategy. Lying down lengthwise, she rolled towards the glass before sitting up again with the lower part of her legs stretched out upon it. She inhaled deeply again and, with a sudden, violent strike, raised the heels of her boots as high as possible and brought them slamming down on the glass. There was a splintering sound and a crack webbed out from the point of impact. She raised her heels again and slammed on the glass for a second time.

As it shattered she felt a hot stinging as the sharp edge of the glass remaining round the edge cut into the skin on the back of her legs. She quickly realigned her body so that she was lying on her back diagonally across one corner of the skylight.

456

Fumbling blindly, she manoeuvred her wrists so they were touching a jagged shard, and started to make small movements back and forth.

It was impossible to slice just the bootlaces and not her skin. As she rocked her wrists back and forth, she felt flesh tear and moisten. But she barely noticed the pain. She rubbed away at the laces and in just over a minute she felt the tension around her hands suddenly release. Rolling off the glass, she brought her hands round to the front. They were gashed and bloodied, but that didn't slow her down at all. The knot around her ankles she couldn't untie, so she broke a shard of glass off the remnants of the skylight. It was about the size of her palm and shaped almost like an arrow tip with an evil-looking point, which she used like a saw to hack away at the second bootlace.

Seconds later she was free.

She jumped to her feet just as she heard the shofar ring out a second time. The image of her assailant rose in her mind.

He was going to ruin everything.

She wasn't going to let that happen.

Maya Bloom stashed the piece of glass in a pocket and rethreaded the remnants of her laces into her boots, ignoring the way the blood oozed over her hands and nails.

That done, she ran to the other side of the rooftop and started climbing down the ladder. She was at ground level in thirty seconds, and already sprinting.

THIRTY-ONE

10.49 hrs.

Luke pushed through the crowd. Those waiting patiently to approach the wall shouted at him in Hebrew, but he ignored them. Luke was a head taller than almost everyone else here, and a lot stronger. There was nothing anybody could do to stop him barging through.

Ten metres from the wall he halted. The strange sound of the horn had filled the air again, and for some reason it chilled him.

He scanned around. More men in traditional dress.

Stop, he told himself. *Think.*

He'd seen four people emerge from the van. Four bombers, he reckoned. But they wouldn't be together. That would be a tactical fuck-up, because if one was caught, they'd all be caught. No, Luke's targets would be spread out, along the wall. He looked forward and to the left, where he saw the entrance to the tunnels. There'd be fewer people there. Easier to spot one of his targets.

Luke started shoving his way through the crowds again. Thirty seconds later he was at the entrance to the tunnels. He burst into the room that led into them. There were about twenty-five men in here, talking to each other quietly. Those who paid Luke any attention frowned at his appearance. He scanned their faces, trying to recognise one of the people he'd seen at a distance, or to identify anything suspicious about any of them.

Nothing.

He hurried through the room and took the tunnel leading north.

His field of vision was full of people. Many stared at him as he headed along the tunnel, keeping the covered section of the Western Wall to his right, and he just stared back at them, occasionally wiping away the sweat that ran into his eyes.

Peculiar glances.

Suspicion.

Once or twice one of the celebrants said something to him in Hebrew. He hurried past, every sense heightened.

Luke was fifty metres along the tunnel when he saw him. There were fewer people here now. The tunnel had just opened up slightly and there was a single Hassid facing the wall. His head was bowed, his eyes closed and his lips were moving silently. Luke stopped five metres from the man and didn't have to look at him for more than a couple of seconds to know something was wrong. The guy was shaking. A thin trickle of sweat was dripping down the side of his face—a face whose skin was several shades darker than that of any of the Hassidim he'd seen so far.

And in his right hand there was a mobile phone.

Luke instantly recalled the tourist sign he'd seen yesterday in the plaza: 'ON THE SABBATH AND HOLY DAYS, SMOKING, PHOTOGRAPHY AND CELLPHONE USE ARE STRICTLY FORBIDDEN.' Surely a devout man would know that?

He slid the ceramic knife from behind his belt; just as he did this, the guy opened his eyes and raised his left hand to look at his watch. But then he noticed Luke.

His eyes widened and a look of panic crossed his

face.

He glanced down at the phone in his right hand.

But by then Luke was on him. He hurled himself towards his target, thrusting his left hand up to his neck and slicing the knife across the back of his right hand. There was an eruption of blood; the man cried out in pain and his fingers spread out of their own accord as the blade severed his tendons. The phone hung loosely from the wire that was threaded up his sleeve and the man grabbed at it with his left hand.

Too late. Luke pulled the device loose, then yanked the man's sleeve several inches up his arm. A strip of plastic explosive was taped to the skin. No doubt about it. He had his man.

Luke looked along the corridor. He saw three figures approaching from the direction of the plaza, but they were deep in conversation and after a few seconds they stopped anyway to face the wall. Looking north, nothing.

The bomber was shaking violently now, and the blood was flowing more freely from his hand. Luke pocketed the mobile, yanked the guy's left arm behind his back, just a fraction of an inch from breaking point, and forced him down the corridor, out of sight of the approaching men.

Now they were alongside the ancient cisterns Luke had recced the night before. He tightened the bomber's arm another few millimetres. The man gasped and the shaking became uncontrollable.

'Where are the others?' said Luke.

The man just shook his head.

Luke didn't fuck about. He put his spare hand over the bomber's mouth and yanked the arm upwards. There was a sharp crack as the bones broke and splintered, followed by a muffled, deadened shout of pain.

'Where are the others?'

It was the bomber's eyes that told Luke everything he needed to know. They flickered, almost involuntarily, in the direction of the plaza. Luke sighed. It was time to dispense with the fucker.

He let go of the broken arm, which flopped awkwardly. He moved his left hand from the bomber's mouth so that his palm was under his chin, which he pushed upwards so that his throat was fully exposed. It was the work of less than a second to slice the sharp blade of his knife across the bare flesh to create a gash half an inch deep and three inches wide. The wound vomited blood and the bomber tried to scream. No sound came from his throat, however. His larynx was severed and the life was draining from him. Luke knew how deep the cistern was. It took barely any strength to push the body sufficiently for it to fall into the cavity. The bomber's body fell more heavily on to the ground than the mortar he'd thrown down last night—out of sight. They'd only find him when he started to stink.

Luke's hands and T-shirt were spattered with the man's blood. It didn't matter now. He was already sprinting away.

*   *   *

Maya Bloom's wrists were still stinging and sticky and her hands were clenched against the pain. None of this slowed her down. None of this was going to stop her doing what needed to be done.

461

Her head was down and her eyes forwards as she ran towards the gates leading into the plaza. The female queue snaked a good thirty metres back, but she hurried straight to the front, deaf to the shouts of complaint as she pushed through the body scanners. Moments later she was looking out over the crowded plaza.

She studied the crowd, paying particular attention to the area round the wall. Was there anything untoward there? Anything unusual?

Nothing. Just the faithful gathered on their holy day.

Her eyes caught movement. Three armed IDF soldiers pushing clumsily through the crowd towards the entrance to the tunnels. She turned to the right. A woman, her face lined and her body wrapped in a black robe, was about to walk past her, back towards the exit. Maya Bloom stood in her way.

'What time is it?' her hoarse voice demanded in Hebrew.

The woman looked taken aback. She glanced at Maya's bloody hands, then back up at her face. 'Five to eleven,' she stammered nervously then continued to stare, clearly alarmed by the woman's total lack of expression. The old lady sidestepped, put her head down and continued to walk. 'Happy Hanukkah,' she muttered as she passed.

Maya Bloom said nothing. Her mind was already elsewhere.

*   *   *

Luke stormed back down the tunnel. There was no way he could hide the blood on his clothes and skin, so he didn't even try; and as he approached little groups of the faithful, who were either facing the wall or standing in learned discussion, he was aware of the horrified looks they gave him as they stepped aside to let him pass.

As he approached the opening to the plaza, he saw three Israeli soldiers fifteen metres ahead of him. One of them was giving instructions to the other two, and they immediately split up, one of them heading to his left at right angles to the main tunnel, two of them heading towards Luke.

He quickly backtracked, retracing his steps until he reached the entrance to a small anteroom opposite the wall. He ducked into the shadows, gripping the knife handle firmly, but with the blade hidden. Luke didn't want to take these guys out, but if he had to, he would.

Footsteps approached. He found himself holding his breath. The soldiers were talking quietly to each other. Their voices grew more distinct as they got nearer, though Luke understood nothing of what they said, then they faded away as they walked past his hiding place. He gave it ten seconds, then slipped out again and ran towards the plaza.

The crowds were buzzing and he felt a moment of nausea as he emerged blinking into the light. It was a sea of people. Hundreds of them. How the *hell* was he going to find the remaining bombers among this lot?

Think, he told himself. Fucking *think*! What's the bombers' objective? Where will they *be*?

When the wall falls . . .

The wall was the target. Not the crowd, not the plaza. And to take out the wall you had to get close.

Luke rushed forward, pushing through the

lines of people waiting to approach and pray. He knocked three men from their feet—they toppled back into the crowd and several people started shouting at him, but he hurried on. The wall was towering above him now, all twenty metres of it; and the horn rang through the air for a third time. Luke barely heard it. He barely heard anything. He was behind the front line of worshippers now, pushing himself along the length of the wall and examining the hands of each man he passed. Some were pressed, palm forwards, against the stones. Others had their hands clenched together in devout prayer. One or two were even kneeling down, with their arms stretched up to heaven.

One man, though, was doing none of these.

Luke was about fifteen metres from the tunnel entrance when he saw him. He was dressed just like the other bomber in a black jacket and black hat, and was standing quietly with his head bowed. His shoulders were shaking slightly but there was no sign of prayer. And no sign of his hands, which were secreted in front of him . . .

Luke took up position behind him. Slowly, so as not to alert anybody around him, he drew his knife and held it in his left hand. With lightning speed, he hooked his right hand round the man's waist. His thin body went suddenly rigid, and there was a fumbling of his hands, but by that time Luke had a grip on the mobile phone he was carrying.

'Take it easy, buddy,' he said. His fingers had already located the lead which was plugged into the base of the phone and ran up the man's sleeve. He pulled it from the socket and felt for the telltale consistency of soft plastic explosive. Sure enough, it was taped to the inside of the man's arms.

Positive ID.

The bomber was shaking, just as his mate had done. So far nobody around them had clocked exactly what was happening. Luke didn't know how long that would last. A commotion would alert the remaining two bombers, though, and that was the one thing he couldn't risk. He hooked his knife hand around the man's waist and, with a sharp, brutal tug he rammed it into the soft flesh of the bomber's belly. The bomber exhaled like a punctured balloon and, as Luke slid the blade across his abdomen, he felt the guy go heavy. He removed the phone from his grip and pulled the knife from his body just as the man sank to his knees, head against the stone. For the moment he looked like he was praying.

Luke left him there, disappeared into the crowd and continued along the wall.

*   *   *

10.58 hrs.

All Alistair Stratton's attention was on the laptop by his side. He could see his damaged face reflected in it, but his own injuries barely registered in his mind as he stared in the darkness of his room at the flickering image of the Western Wall.

There was a knock on his office door and his PA stepped inside. '*Get out,*' Stratton whispered without looking up. The kid was sensible enough to disappear.

Stratton's hands were trembling and a bead of sweat dripped down the side of his dirty face. His lips moved silently.

Something caught his eye. Movement at the

465

wall. Not the regular ebb and flow of the visitors, but something else. A number of Hassidim were drawing away from a certain point on the wall, like ripples of water from a stone.

Stratton's muttering stopped. He squinted at the screen. The resolution was poor but he thought he could just make out what they were retreating from: a figure, kneeling at the stones.

Only now he wasn't kneeling. He had tumbled to one side and was lying limp and still.

The Hassidim continued to step back and Stratton thrust his face at the screen.

'Now,' he whispered, as if he could somehow be heard in that square so far away. And then he shouted, his voice hoarse. Desperate.

'DO IT NOW!'

*   *   *

Luke could sense commotion behind him. A shout. The dead bomber kneeling at the wall must have been discovered. How long till the remaining two realised what was happening? Minutes?

Seconds?

Still he scanned the crowds, aware that the mood of celebration was changing to one of panic. He put that from his mind. He had to concentrate ... To focus ...

The third bomber's mistake was to turn around. It was obvious he'd been alerted to the disruption further along the wall. Luke was just two metres from him when the man looked back to see what was happening. It was obvious, too, that he realised Luke was on his case. Alarm creased his face and as Luke plunged the two metres to get him, he raised

466

his right hand in defence, revealing the mobile phone he was holding. Luke clocked the lead trailing up his sleeve. He saw the man fumbling with the device with his left hand.

It was the last thing the bomber ever did.

Luke couldn't be covert. There wasn't time. He raised his knife, its white blade still bloody from its previous work, and slashed it across the bomber's right wrist. It sliced the wire just as effectively as the flesh and for a split second the bomber looked in horror as the blood seeped from the wound. A split second, though, was all he had. Luke thumped him against the wall, jarred his chin violently upwards and whipped the blade across his throat.

He didn't wait to watch the bomber slide down the wall into a heap on the ground, nor even to gather up the phone. He'd already turned by then, to see the crowd backing away from him in horror. He also registered another disturbance about ten metres away. A quick glance told him that at least two Israeli soldiers were pushing through the crowd in his direction. One of them barked an instruction, but Luke was already on the move. Now that his bloodied knife was in full view he didn't have to barge through the bodies—they retreated aghast from him.

In his mind he had a picture: the image he'd seen from the rooftop of the four bombers emerging from the white van. Three men, one woman. He could see the barrier separating the male and female sections of the wall five metres ahead. He hurried towards it and, seconds later, vaulted over.

He stopped to recce. The female section was just as crowded as the male, and though the panic hadn't fully reached here, its ripples were just beginning. Facing the wall itself, and touching its stones, was a crowd of little girls. They seemed oblivious to the disturbance but their teacher, a tall, thin woman with dark, curly hair, was looking around in alarm. Her eyes widened as she saw Luke and the spatter of blood on his face, and she opened her mouth as if to scream. No sound came, but she gathered a few of the girls towards her, hugging them helplessly.

Luke paid no attention to her. The movement of the girls had caused a space to open out in front, occupied by just five terrified kids. He could see six or seven metres along the wall and there, in the middle of the crowd of children, one hand pressed against the stones of the wall and with her head turned in alarm towards Luke, was a pregnant woman dressed in a headscarf and a black robe.

Shouting. Behind him. The soldiers had reached the segregation wall between the male and female sections. They were screaming at him, first in Hebrew, then in English: *'Drop the knife! Drop it or we fire!'*

But Luke had one more job to do.

And all of a sudden he had a much bigger problem on his hands than the Israeli soldiers.

He was just launching his way towards the pregnant woman when he saw Maya Bloom coming towards her from the other side. She was ripping her way through the crowds, pushing the worshippers aside, her head slightly lowered but her eyes burning. She was five metres away now.

Suddenly the kids between Luke and the pregnant woman started screaming. He pushed them to one side, not caring if he scared or hurt them, as he lunged along the wall towards the

468

pregnant woman. Her eyes were wide, her face horrified by the sight of Luke bearing down on her.

Bloom was still a couple of metres away when he hurled himself at the pregnant woman with the full force of his body. They collided with a vicious thump. The pregnant woman fell to the ground beneath him; three little girls were knocked over too, and they were screaming now at the tops of their voices as they saw Luke with his dripping knife at the ready, held above the pregnant woman's throat, ready to strike.

But he didn't.

The woman, who was whimpering and shaking, had raised her arms up above her head and Luke immediately saw that something was wrong. Her headscarf had slipped and her hair was dyed white blonde. There was nothing in her hands. No detonator.

His blood ran cold.

Luke grabbed the front of the woman's robe. When he finally brought his knife down, it was not to cut into her body, but into the material of her clothes. He sliced open her robe with a single swipe, then ripped it apart with both hands. He saw her heavy breasts, encased in a flesh-coloured maternity bra. He saw the naked skin of her swollen belly. But he saw no explosives.

She was the wrong person.

The screaming was deafening now. It included not only the girls and their teacher, but also the pregnant woman, lying uncovered and petrified on the floor.

Luke looked up.

The first person he saw was Maya Bloom. She was standing above him, and from inside her jacket

469

she removed the shard of glass—as sharp as the knife Luke was carrying and just as red from the blood that was oozing from her wrists. He prepared to push himself back up to his feet, but in that instant the soldiers were there. Two of them had their rifles pointing directly at him. The third—bigger than the others—bent down quickly, pulled Luke up to his feet and slammed him hard against the wall.

The knife slipped from his hands.

His head cracked against the stone.

Like a photographic snapshot he saw the crowds teeming with panic; he saw the barrels of the soldiers' rifles; and he saw Maya Bloom, who was standing just two metres from his location, turn quickly away. In the same instant, a helicopter appeared above the Western Wall plaza: a Black Hawk, dark olive green, no doors fitted and no markings; a side gunner was manning a Minigun and panning across the crowd, and a fast-rope arm protruded a metre from the chopper. It had all the features of an SF aircraft. Half the crowd hit the ground and all of them, or it so it seemed, were now screaming.

'There's a suicide bomber,' Luke roared at the three soldiers, but he could barely be heard above the noise of the chopper and the screaming. 'A pregnant woman! *THERE'S A FUCKING SUICIDE BOMBER! CLEAR THE AREA!*'

The troops remained in position, their clothes flapping in the wind from the downdraught of the heli—which was no more than fifteen metres above the crowd—staring dumbly at him. Luke shook his head. This was it. The screaming was growing louder, and across the roofs of Jerusalem a church bell sounded.

Eleven o'clock. *Eleven o'fucking clock . . .* He'd failed. He wouldn't even survive to see the consequences.

From his pocket came a ringing sound as someone, somewhere, tried to remote-detonate one of the bombers he'd neutralised; five seconds later the second phone he had confiscated joined in.

And it was from this position, unable to move, unable to do anything more, that he witnessed it all happening.

*　　　*　　　*

Maya Bloom scanned the wall, blocking out the sound of screaming, ignoring the air currents of the chopper and the chaos and alarm it was causing; ignoring the shouts of the idiot British soldier. It didn't take more than a couple of seconds to locate her. She was approximately six metres further towards the south end of the wall, also dressed in a black robe, with a headscarf and a shawl, her face slightly fattened by pregnancy; and she was the only woman in the vicinity, with the exception of Maya herself, who was not crazed with panic.

Far from it. She appeared calm and resolute.

Not as resolute, however, as Maya Bloom.

She knocked two children out of the way and now there was open ground between her and this second pregnant woman. It took less than a second to cross it. And in that brief window of time, a scene flashed before her eyes. She was a child, standing on the streets of Tel Aviv. Her brother stood beside her and together they looked upon a sight of indescribable carnage. Their mother was there,

471

lying on the ground. The clothes had been burned from her torso; the skin was charred, filling the air with the stink of smoking flesh; both arms had been ripped from her body. The young Maya was screaming and she continued to scream even when Amit put his arms around her and pressed her face against his chest so that she would not have to look upon the aftermath of the Palestinian bomb that had just torn their parents—and their lives—apart.

The pregnant woman had a mobile phone in one hand and as she saw Maya Bloom coming towards her she was gripping it firmly. The Israeli threw herself at the woman. As they tumbled to the ground, she thumped the woman's right wrist against the stones of the Western Wall. Her grip loosened and Maya Bloom tugged the phone from her. The device became disconnected from the lead to which it was attached.

A fraction of a second later it started to ring.

Maya Bloom threw the detonator to the ground and raised the shard of glass up above her head, gripping it hard even though its sharp edges cut into her palms. A second later she brought it slamming down into the exposed neck of the pregnant woman. The point of the glass sank into the flesh like a knife into dough. Once it was a couple of inches in, she rotated it clockwise through ninety degrees. Then back again. She repeated this twisting motion three times and with each turn the river of blood that gushed from the wound grew stronger. A harsh gargling sound escaped the victim's lungs and her limbs started to shake. It took her no more than twenty seconds to die, but even when her body was still, Maya Bloom didn't stop. She raised the shard again and brought it stabbing down on the woman's face. Piercing, puncturing, as all the hate she felt spilled out.

By the time her frenzy had finished she was almost as bloody as the murdered woman. She was on all fours, an animal in the wild, and it was only the feel of cold steel against the back of her head that brought her back to the here and now. She looked over her shoulder to see the appalled face of a soldier who was pressing his rifle against her, and she became aware once more of the screaming of the children and the other women as they fled the horror.

And then the soldier started to shout as well. His voice was hoarse. He needed to scream to be heard over the noise of the chopper hovering above the heads of the crowd.

'Lie on the ground with your hands on your head! Lie on the ground! *Lie on the fucking ground. NOW!'*

THIRTY-TWO

Luke's head was pounding. He didn't understand. Maya Bloom was working for Stratton. What, then, had just happened?

The plaza was chaos. Noise. Children and women screaming and running, the chopper blades thundering overhead. Men, too, shouting on the other side of the barrier. IDF soldiers, one of whom had him at gunpoint, looked like they were on the verge of panic, glancing at each other, clearly wondering what the hell to do.

He felt Maya Bloom's eyes on him, saw the

473

calculating look in her face as she slid her makeshift weapon back into her jacket and glanced from her gruesome handiwork to the hovering chopper to the soldier who was shouting at her to get down on the ground. When she snapped back at him, it was with authority. The soldier didn't lower his gun, but Luke could see that he was suddenly less sure of himself. Bloom continued to speak. Fast. Harsh. It sounded like she was issuing instructions and he could make out one word repeated several times: *Mossad.*

Twenty seconds later Maya Bloom was standing right in front of him. 'If you try to run,' she shouted, 'they'll shoot you.'

'What the fuck have you told them?'

'The truth,' she replied loudly. 'That you're a terrorist.' She nodded at the guards, who pushed Luke away from the wall towards her. She was close now, less than half a metre. 'If you don't do what I tell you,' she said so that only Luke could hear, 'neither of us will get out of the plaza alive. I promise they'll kill you if I give the word.'

Luke believed her.

They moved in convoy—the two soldiers a metre behind Luke, Maya a metre in front, barking instructions at the crowd to let them through. The terrified people parted when they saw that the soldiers had a prisoner. It took less than thirty seconds to cover half the length of the plaza, by which time the chopper had set down ten metres to Luke's right. He saw troops spilling out from either side: their cutaway Kevlar helmets, M4s and chest rigs confirmed that they were SF. He briefly considered getting their attention, but as soon as the thought entered his mind, Maya Bloom was alongside him. 'Don't make a mistake,' she spat. 'One step wrong and I'll tell them to shoot you.' She looked back over her shoulder and barked at the soldiers, who prodded Luke like he was cattle, urging him to move faster.

Forty metres from the wall and suddenly another six soldiers, wild-eyed and confused, were in front of them. Maya Bloom issued more instructions, and immediately they marched ahead, screaming at the crowds to let them through. Luke barely heard the chopper or the crowds. All his attention, all his focus, was on the woman. What was she doing? What was she orchestrating? Why was she setting things up to allow Luke to escape too?

Perhaps she didn't want him to start telling the authorities what he knew about her. Even if he were dead, his corpse would be identified and this might set up a trail that would lead to her.

Luke saw the security gates twenty metres ahead. People crowding to get out. The six new IDF men rushed forwards and started clearing the way; as they did so, Maya Bloom looked back at him. It was a deadly look. He decided she intended to get him out of the way, so she could dispose of him.

The convoy triggered the alarm on the security gates as it went through, which did nothing but add to the general sense of panic. On the other side, the area between the plaza entrance and the Dung Gate was a confusion of people—families and friends looking for each other, kids on their own crying, traditionally dressed Hassidim hurrying away from the danger area. There had to be more than a couple of hundred people, Luke reckoned, and he could lose himself among them in seconds, safe in the knowledge that the soldiers wouldn't open fire on the public.

But he wasn't going to do that. Lose Maya Bloom now and he'd never find her again. She had too many questions to answer.

She was clever. She'd manoeuvred them out of the plaza—a place they'd never otherwise have escaped from. Now he had to second-guess her next move. If *he* could escape into the crowd now, so could she. But if she wanted him dead, she had to do it before she disappeared.

If Luke was right, she was about to make an attempt on his life.

She barked at the soldiers to stop when they were fifteen metres from the security gates. She turned to face them and there was a brief moment of stillness that allowed Luke to take in his position.

Maya Bloom didn't hesitate. She strode up to one of the two soldiers who had Luke at gunpoint and barked at him. He and the other soldier looked at each other nervously. When she shouted again, to Luke's amazement the first soldier lowered his weapon and handed it to her.

She turned, assault rifle in hand. Passers-by, when they saw what was happening, moved quickly from the area and now there was a clearing a good fifteen metres in diameter around them. Maya Bloom continued to speak to the soldiers. All eight of them had her attention now and it was clear from her voice and their movements that she was instructing them to return to the plaza.

The ranking Mossad agent, organising the troops while she arrested the enemy.

Only Maya Bloom wasn't Mossad. Not any more. And her attention wasn't really on the IDF soldiers. It was firmly fixed on Luke.

'Move,' she said. 'Hands on your head.' She nodded in the direction of the Old Town.

Luke was at gunpoint. He had no option. He turned and walked.

Twenty seconds later they were in a long, narrow street and moving against the crowds, who clearly knew something was going down and were rushing to get out of the Old Town. Luke heard people shouting as they saw him being marched down the road at gunpoint, but no one tried to step in. They weren't that stupid. They just wanted to get away.

Luke knew he only had minutes. Maya Bloom wouldn't execute him in front of everyone, but the moment they were alone he was a dead man unless he did something . . .

They passed a side street to their left. It was deserted, and Maya Bloom shouted at him to turn into it. And when a long, narrow alleyway—much like the one where Luke had cached his Sig the night before, and completely deserted—emerged fifty metres down on their right, she again ordered, 'Turn!'

Luke felt himself tense up. As he rounded the corner he suddenly crouched, turned and jutted out his right foot so it connected sharply with the woman's left shin. Gunshot. The noise of the round echoed, but by that time Luke was on her. He hurled himself forward and thudded the heel of his fist directly against her right breast. She gasped and for a fraction of a second she was disabled.

And that was all Luke needed.

He pulled the rifle from her grasp and quickly, brutally, whacked the butt against the side of her head. Maya Bloom staggered. By the time she had her balance again the tables were turned. Luke was in control. She was at gunpoint.

Luke said nothing. He just pointed down the empty side street and she understood. She walked slowly until she couldn't walk any more: a dead end, twenty-five metres further down.

Maya Bloom stopped and turned. She looked up and around, taking in her new surroundings: the cobbled ground; the ramshackle buildings on either side, three storeys high; the metal bins stashed outside the doorways on either side, each one about ten metres apart; the thin dog sniffing around one of these bins, oblivious to everything.

'Get to your knees. Hands behind your head,' Luke said.

She did it slowly. With him standing five metres from her, the rifle aimed at her face, it was clear she had no choice.

There was a moment of silence.

'Who the hell are you?' she demanded. 'Why did you attack me on the roof?'

'Why did *you* take out the last bomber?' Luke retorted. 'I was with Stratton in Gethsemane. I heard you planning this.'

She sneered. 'You're even more of an imbecile than I thought. I would *never* be involved in something like this . . .'

'Bullshit. The train bombings,' Luke replied flatly. 'You were there. I heard you discussing them with Stratton.'

Maya Bloom's face suddenly filled with fury. 'The train bombings,' she spat back, 'were different.'

'Suicide bombs, hundreds dead. Can't see the difference myself.'

'You wouldn't understand.'

'Try me.'

She stared defiantly at him. When she spoke it was in little more than a whisper. 'I was helping Israel's enemies attack her allies. That way the world would turn against them . . .'

Luke stared at her. 'I don't believe you.'

Suddenly, though, she was raging. 'Why would I attack my own people on their most sacred site? What do you think I was doing on the roof in the first place? If you hadn't fucked things up, I could have taken out the bombers before they even got through the gate.' Her eyes were filled with contempt. 'I thought Stratton had the same agenda as me. That's what he told me. To mobilise the West against the Arabs. But in Gethsemane . . .' Luke saw her nostrils flare. 'In Gethsemane it turned out he's out of control. He wants to start a war in Jerusalem. He's a madman . . . a fucking millennialist . . . he thinks he can bring about the Second Coming. I told him I wanted nothing to do with it.'

Luke stared at her. He didn't want to believe Maya Bloom, but so many things were falling into place.

She was breathing heavily now. 'Someone needs to stop him, or he'll try this again. He's insane,' she said. '*We* can stop him. Put the fucking gun down and we can stop him.'

But Luke didn't move. He remembered her ruthlessness in St Paul's. He remembered Chet. He reminded himself that Maya Bloom still wanted him dead.

'This has been a long time coming,' he said.

She scowled. 'What do you mean?'

'You killed my friend. You killed his kid and you

killed the boy's mother. And you did it all for that piece of shit Stratton.'

'I did *nothing* for Stratton. Everything I've done, I've done for my people . . .'

She jutted out her chin, defying Luke to finish her off.

He didn't shoot her in the head, or in the chest, but in the stomach. Killing her wasn't enough. He wanted her to suffer. To bleed. To beg for mercy before he ended it. The retort of the round's discharge echoed around the alleyway and Maya Bloom, shot from little more than four metres, was thrown violently against the dead-end wall, her knees barely able to support her as she clutched her stomach and looked down with horror at the blood that was seeping between her fingers.

Luke was aware of a whining sound from the stray dog somewhere behind him as he bore down on her. And another sound, further away but growing nearer: sirens.

Maya Bloom coughed, a retching sound. When she had finished she gasped for air. Luke watched as her chin dropped to her chest. It felt right that her life was slipping away. And it felt right that he should tell her something else before she died.

'I knew your brother,' he said.

The words were like a shot of adrenaline. Maya Bloom looked up again. Her lips were blue. Her skin grey.

'I don't believe you . . .'

'His name was Amit. I was with him when he died.'

'When the Arabs killed him,' she spat.

Luke shook his head slowly. 'The Arabs didn't kill him,' he whispered. 'Amit took his own life.

480

I saw him do it. Blew himself up and took a checkpoint full of Iraqis with him.'

Maya Bloom started to tremble. Luke leaned over, closer to her. 'Amit sacrificed himself for his cause. *He* was a good man. A soldier. You? You just kill innocent people. That's not war. That's murder. If he knew what you were, he'd fucking despise you.'

'*NO!*'

The woman's shout was hoarse, but so forceful that Luke was momentarily shocked. She raised her right hand from her bleeding stomach and fumbled in her jacket pocket before pulling out the piece of glass. It was almost pitiful, the way she lifted her weapon. She weakly held up the shard, hatred and agony on her face.

Luke didn't even bother to shoot. He just whacked the end of the rifle against the side of her head and watched as she collapsed. She coughed again, and this time blood flowed from her mouth and her body started to shake. Luke kneeled down next to her and put the gun to her right temple. It was time to finish it.

But suddenly there was shouting.

Even before he turned his head he could tell there were at least six men. They wore olive drab, Kevlar helmets and chest rigs; they had M4s pressed into their shoulders and were advancing down the alleyway in a V-shaped formation.

Israeli SF. Twenty metres. He couldn't understand their shouts but he knew what would happen if he didn't put the gun down. Now.

He looked at the dying woman. Her eyes were halfway gone, her breathing like a fucking bellows. But as Luke slowly lowered his weapon, he heard her speak.

It was just a whisper—slow, agonised, barely audible. But the words were clear enough.

'Your friend died like a dog. He died limping like the cripple he was. He was pathetic . . .'

And as she delivered her insult, a defiant smile crossed her death-white face.

A sudden jolt of anger shook Luke, and he squeezed the trigger, pumping a fatal shot into her head.

Two more rounds rang out instantly. One of them missed Luke, passing a couple of inches to the right of his head. The other found its target. It pierced his back just to the right of his spine.

He slammed to the ground.

He tried to breathe, but no air reached his lungs. Two figures loomed over him. He heard them shouting. He tried to move his arms, but he had no strength. Only pain. The shouts of the soldiers dissolved into a blur.

Then there was darkness.

PART FOUR

The following day

THIRTY-THREE

There was a gentle breeze. It came from the east, but it was not so chill as to make the little crowd of fifteen people standing near Alistair Stratton's private chapel hurry inside. They appeared quite happy to remain outside, chatting easily. The former prime minister stood on the edge of the group. He had a series of SteriStrips across his broken nose and his right eye was bruised and shiny. He was immaculately dressed, as ever. As his guests, one by one, approached to shake his hand and enquire after his well-being, he smiled brightly at them.

It had long been Stratton's habit to invite members of the public from the nearby village to join him for the Sunday morning service. The generous benefactor. But they had been the last thing on his mind when he had walked towards the chapel that morning, discreetly flanked by his bodyguards and with Wheatly, his PA, following several metres behind. He had indulged them out of exhaustion. And guests, of course, were always delighted to rub shoulders with a man of such importance. They'd dine out on it, telling their friends of the neatly clipped lawns and topiary and of the serenity of that little chapel.

How different their experience would be if they saw Alistair Stratton's personal office: the flat-screen television hanging loosely from the wall; the laptop computer smashed on the floor; the canvas of the Hieronymus Bosch torn; the furniture upended and one window broken. But they were never going to see that. Wheatly had locked the door and his boss's loss of temper of the previous day had not been mentioned by anybody.

A priest in white robes appeared at the entrance to the chapel. He was a kindly old man whose only vice was an excessive love of model railways. He held his hands out in benediction. 'Shall we, ladies and gentlemen?'

The congregation started to file in, leaving Stratton to stand outside with his PA and his close protection lingering nearby. When he did finally enter the chapel, Wheatly followed but the two close-protection men took up position on either side of the entrance. They rolled their eyes at each other once they knew they were alone. Sunday morning was the bum shift, but at least they didn't have to sit through the service. The Grosvenor Group paid them well, but almost no money was worth having that religious shit inflicted on you every seven days. Besides, it was a pleasant morning. Peaceful. The birds were singing in the trees and it was good to be outside. As soon as they were alone they lit cigarettes, leaned against the church and started soaking up the early morning sun.

* * *

At the Mossad training academy, Ephraim Cohen stared at two images.

They were the stuff of nightmares. Of Cohen's nightmares, at least. Maya Bloom's face was barely recognisable. It was no surprise she'd come to a violent end.

The door opened. Ehud Blumenthal walked in.

There were no niceties. He stared at Cohen for a moment like he was staring at a turd in the road.

Cohen removed his glasses. 'Ehud,' he said mildly. 'I'm surprised to see you here?'

'It's not out of choice, I assure you, Ephraim.'

Blumenthal's face was drawn. Grey. He looked like he'd aged fifteen years. Perhaps it was Cohen's imagination, but a little of the arrogance he'd displayed at their last meeting seemed to have left him.

'What's the situation in Jerusalem?' he asked.

'The Temple Mount is still cordoned off. The streets of the Old Town are deserted. Everyone is waiting for a reaction.'

'And how long will they have to wait?'

Blumenthal's forehead creased. 'There will be no retaliation,' he replied.

Cohen raised an eyebrow and waited for an explanation. Blumenthal tapped the picture of the man that was lying on Cohen's desk. 'Whoever he was, he had two mobile phones in his pocket. They'd been adapted to act as detonators and were called within five seconds of each other at eleven o'clock. We traced the handsets that called them to a location in East Jerusalem. Sayeret Matkal went in.'

'Anyone?'

Blumenthal shook his head. 'But we did find something of interest. A wooden crate. Forensics confirm it had been used to carry C4 plastic explosive.'

Cohen shrugged. 'There's not much we can do with a wooden box,' he said.

'Let me finish,' Blumenthal said. He drew a deep breath. 'The box had a marking. It was supplied by an American company called the Grosvenor Group.'

'I've heard of them?'

'We passed this intelligence on to Washington. I've never seen a government react so fast.'

'What do you mean?'

'Two days ago the Americans were shoulder to shoulder with us. Two hours ago they ordered the withdrawal of their fleet in the Red Sea, and the President has made it clear that if we want to retaliate, we're on our own. They don't want to know.'

Cohen blinked. It didn't make any sense. He looked down at the pictures on his desk.

'How did Maya end up . . . like this?'

'That's classified.'

'My clearance is . . .'

'Not high enough.'

For the first time, Blumenthal looked a little bit pleased with himself, but Cohen ignored it as he tried to fit the jigsaw together himself. Maya Bloom, somehow, had foiled a terrorist attack at the Western Wall. Was her killer in league with the bombers? It seemed the most likely explanation, but somehow it didn't quite add up.

Blumenthal stood. 'I'm instructed to inform you that your *kidon* is to be honoured posthumously,' he said. 'The Medal of Valour—Israel's highest honour. It will reflect well on you, I am sure.' As he said this, his face was sour. It was quite clear that the prospect of Ephraim Cohen's success brought him no pleasure.

And somehow, it brought no pleasure to Cohen either. He just nodded briefly and watched as Blumenthal walked out of the room, leaving him

488

alone with his thoughts.

*   *   *

The priest stood in front of the altar, two candles flickering behind him. He spoke in a strident voice that echoed from the vaulted ceiling of the chapel. 'The Lord is here.'

And the congregation replied: 'His spirit is with us.'

'His spirit is with us.' Alistair Stratton intoned his response a fraction of a second after the others.

The priest glanced briefly at him, then looked away when he saw a sudden fierceness on Stratton's face. He continued with his Eucharistic prayer a little more quickly. There was a strange air in the chapel and he wanted the service to be over.

*   *   *

In London, the Director General SIS stared at his most trusted analyst, a small man with balding ginger hair who'd worked for the service for three decades. He blinked in disbelief. 'Say that again,' he instructed.

The analyst looked nervously from the DG to the Director Special Forces, who was standing by the window. He'd been working through the previous night and was dead on his feet. He coughed slightly. 'We've monitored all the IP addresses connecting to the Western Wall's webcam for the period 10.55 to 11.05 Israeli time this morning, sir. One of these IPs is registered to Albany Manor. Alistair Stratton's residence. We've confirmed he was there at the time.'

489

The DG blinked again. 'Leave us alone,' he told the analyst. The little man appeared glad to leave quickly.

There was a long silence.

'You think there's a link?' the Director Special Forces asked finally.

'Of course there's a bloody link, man.'

The Director didn't rise to the DG's outburst.

'Look at the critical path,' the DG continued. 'An SAS operative thinks he has something on Alistair Stratton. He goes AWOL, then pops up to stop a terrorist plot that Stratton's watching, in real time, hundreds of miles away . . .'

'If you think Alistair Stratton has something to do with this,' the Director said, 'I can have him extracted from his residence within the hour. Give me another hour and I'll have a full confession and no visible signs of coercion.'

The DG appeared to consider the suggestion seriously. But then he shook his head. 'I'd never get the authority.'

The Director Special Forces, who knew a thing or two about the operations sanctioned by SIS in the past, gave him a cynical glare.

'Don't look at me like that, man,' the DG retorted. 'If you were sitting where I'm sitting, you'd make the same decision. But I'll tell you one thing: from now on, Alistair Stratton doesn't even take a shit without me knowing about it . . .'

'But he gets away scot-free,' the Director interrupted, and his expression made it quite clear how he felt about that.

'Yes,' the DG snapped. 'He does. And I don't want any of your people getting funny ideas. If they do, I'll know where it's come from.'

'Of course,' the Director replied with a curt nod.

The conversation was over. With military stiffness the Director Special Forces marched from the room, leaving the DG sitting at his desk, staring into the middle distance, his face—his whole demeanour—quite impossible to read.

*   *   *

In the chapel, the congregation stood in an orderly line down the length of the aisle. Stratton was at its head. The priest stood at the altar, a small silver salver in his hands, and he gave a nod to indicate that Stratton should approach, before taking a Communion wafer between his thumb and forefinger and placing it into the former PM's hands.

'The body of Christ,' he murmured.

As Stratton consumed the wafer, he replaced the salver on the altar and picked up an ornate goblet.

'The blood of Christ.'

He held the goblet forward, but Stratton didn't move. He had a blank look on his face, as though his mind were a million miles away.

'*The blood of Christ*,' the priest repeated, and Stratton blinked. He took the goblet but before he was able to hold it to his lips, it slipped from his hands. Scarlet wine splashed over his shirt and then on to the marble floor of the altar. Stratton stared at it. He barely moved.

'Idiot!' Stratton spat at the celebrant, ignoring the fact that it was he who had dropped the cup, not the priest. '*Idiot!*'

Neither the priest nor any of the congregation knew what to do.

It was not yet light in New York City. The CEO of the Grosvenor Group was pissed off to be out of bed. Even more so at the sight of Pieter de Lange, his aggressive South African chief financial officer, standing by the exquisite early Picasso line drawings that hung on the wall in the lobby of his enormous SoHo townhouse. The moment he saw his CEO, Pieter started to gabble.

'Jesus, Nathan . . . that shit in Jerusalem . . . it was him, wasn't it? It was Stratton. You think they're not going to find out? *You think they're not going to fucking find out?*'

Nathan put a weary hand over his eyes. 'We've had this conversation before, Pieter. We're too well connected. Now come on. You look like you could use a cup of coffee . . .'

'To *hell* with your fucking coffee, man. We've got to do something about Stratton before he . . .'

'Do *what*, Pieter?' Nathan snapped. 'Ask him nicely to keep his mouth shut? Or were you thinking of something more permanent?' He shook his head. 'You really don't get it, do you, Pieter? I've told you before. Stratton, and men like him— they're our bread and butter.'

He turned round and the two men stared at each other in silence.

'Go and get yourself cleaned up, Pieter, for God's sake. You smell like a fucking tramp.'

Pieter inhaled deeply. Shakily. But he didn't say anything. He just turned and headed for the oak-panelled door.

'Oh, and Pieter?'

The CFO turned.

'I'll be very dismayed if anything happens to Alistair Stratton. If anybody decides to take things into their own hands, I *will* know about it. I have people watching him day and night. You understand that, don't you?'

Pieter's face twitched.

'Don't you?'

The CFO looked down at the floor. 'Yes, Nathan,' he said quietly. And he left the room without another word.

*   *   *

The priest appeared shaken, but determined to finish the service. He had picked up the goblet from the floor, but the pool of wine remained. The congregation, their Communion cut short, had retaken their seats, and it was time now for the dismissal. He raised his voice a little and held his right palm forward.

'Go in peace,' he announced, 'to love and serve the Lord.'

The congregation solemnly intoned their reply: 'In the name of Christ. Amen.' There was a moment of awkwardness in the chapel. Of shoe shuffling. The priest looked expectantly at Stratton, who stood up suddenly and looked around the chapel to find all eyes on him. From his front pew, he moved towards the aisle and strode down it, avoiding the gaze of the congregation, his shoes echoing on the flagstones as he went.

Stratton pushed open the heavy oak door of the chapel and squinted as his eyes adjusted from the dimness of the interior to the brightness outside.

The door swung shut behind him and it was only a second later, when his eyes had become used to the daylight, that he saw the state of his close-protection men. They were slumped on either side of the doorway, their backs against the front wall of the chapel, each of them bearing exactly the same injury: a small entry wound on the forehead, and a much larger exit wound at the back of the head. The chapel's wall was spattered with blood and brain matter and the men were quite still.

Stratton's blood chilled. He looked from left to right. From one corpse to another. And then he looked up. He saw nothing. Just his house, straight ahead, 100 metres away across the lawn. And to his left, at a similar distance, the woodland that extended to the perimeter of his land.

He heard the birds singing in the trees.

He considered running. Or should he go back into the chapel?

He looked at the dead bodies again and an overpowering nausea crashed over him. He felt dizzy. His knees grew weak.

And then he sensed a figure walking around the side of the chapel.

As Stratton turned, his eyes widened. The figure wore a heavy hood that covered his eyes and he remained absolutely silent. He just raised his right hand, which carried a pistol, its barrel lengthened by the addition of a suppressor.

Stratton shook his head just as his legs gave way. He fell to his knees and looked up as the gunman lowered his weapon to keep it aligned with his target's skull.

'I know you,' Stratton said.

Silence.

Stratton bowed his head and closed his eyes. He knew what was coming.

The sound of the round that killed him was just a low thud. Like somebody rapping their knuckles sharply on a door. Stratton didn't hear it, of course, and his body hadn't even finished slumping to the floor before the shooter had turned and started moving round to the back of the chapel.

The birds continued to warble in the trees. Their song was only disturbed thirty seconds later when the door of the chapel creaked open again, and a middle-aged lady with neat hair and a tweed skirt screamed at the bloodshed all around her.

*   *   *

The gunman knew he couldn't rely on speed. Only stealth. By the time the scream from the chapel had caused the birds to fly from the trees, he was already in the cover of the woods. And when—ten minutes later—he heard sirens in the distance, he had reached the northern perimeter of the estate. An old dry-stone wall marked the boundary here, but there was a tumbledown section a couple of metres long. Eventually he managed to climb over it and kept on walking.

A solitary figure, making his way across the countryside.

It was approaching midday when the figure arrived at the tiny railway station of Lesser Michelstone. It was not the nearest to Stratton's residence, because he knew by now the area would be crawling with police, but at a distance of five kilometres it was the furthest he could reasonably walk. There was no ticket office here, and no other passengers waiting on the platform. A single security camera, but pointing away from the station bench where he sat, his hood still covering his head. In his right hand—the skin of which was blotched, unnaturally smooth in some places, unnaturally wrinkled in others—the hooded man held a fifty-pence piece. He flicked the coin in the air, watched it spin and caught it in a firm grip.

Flick, catch.

Flick, catch.

When the train arrived at the station three minutes later, he pocketed the coin and limped to the edge of the platform. A set of doors stopped immediately in front of him. He pressed the door-release button and awkwardly climbed inside.

There were only three people in the carriage. An old woman with blue-rinsed hair and a young couple necking three seats along. Hardly surprising, he told himself, that people were edgy about train travel just now. He took a seat at the opposite end of the carriage and stared out of the window as the train slid away.

'Tickets, please . . .'

The voice of the ticket inspector as he entered the carriage snapped him out of his reverie. The gunman removed a wallet from his pocket and opened it up. It was almost empty. There was nothing in there that could identify him: no credit cards, no ID. Just some cash, the return ticket and a cutting from a newspaper. He had read it a hundred times already over the past few days, but as he waited for the ticket inspector to approach, he read it again now.

There were four photographs at the top of the article. Below the pictures was a headline:

496

'SCOTLAND YARD STILL UNABLE TO IDENTIFY TWO OF FOUR CATHEDRAL VICTIMS'. And beneath that, an increasingly breathless, and regurgitated, account of the shootings in St Paul's. He couldn't help staring at the images. One of them was of good quality and showed the smiling face of a young priest; the second was of an old lady. The remaining two were less distinct, clearly stills from a CCTV image. They showed a woman in her late thirties with a hunted expression; and a young boy with tousled hair.

'World's gone mad, if you ask me.'

The gunman looked up and as he did so the hood fell back from over his eyes. He scrambled to cover his head again, but by then it was too late. The ticket inspector's eyes had moved from the clipping to his face and they widened at the sight of him. At the sight of the patches of his head where the hair had burned away and the skin was scorched and withered; at his face, with its vicious scar down the side and the area of damaged flesh that stuck to his skull like cling film; at his neck, the state of which hinted that the burn marks were not limited to his head, but continued down the rest of his body.

The ticket inspector blinked, then coughed with embarrassment as he tried not to stare. 'Ticket, please,' he repeated.

The gunman bowed his head and wordlessly handed his ticket over. The ticket inspector clipped it, returned it to its owner and moved swiftly on to the next carriage.